CONSTANTINOPOLIS

Dear Angie:

I hope you
enjoy this journey
th rough time!

CONSTANTINOPOLIS

JAMES D. SHIPMAN

LAKE UNION
PUBLISHING

Published by Lake Union Publishing, Seattle
www.apub.com

Amazon, the Amazon logo, and Lake Union Publishing are trademarks of Amazon.com, Inc., or its affiliates.

ISBN-13: 9781477827420
ISBN-10: 1477827420

Cover design by David Drummond

Library of Congress Control Number: 2014952405

Printed in the United States of America

I would like to thank Becky and all of our wonderful kids for their help, support, and understanding during this process. I also dedicate this work to everyone at Lake Union Publishing and Amazon for finding me and believing in me.

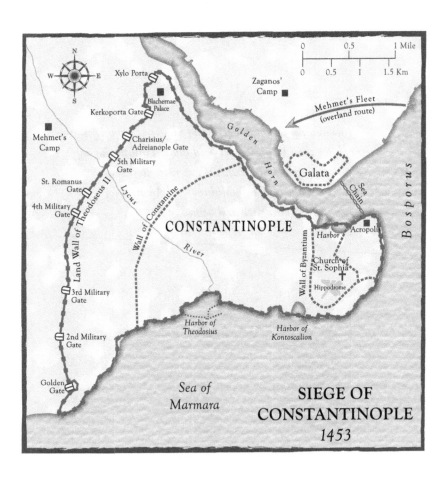

Xylo Porta

Zaganos'
Camp

Mehmet's Fleet
(overland route)

Blachernae
Palace

Kerkoporta Gate

Charisius/
Adreianople Gate

Golden Horn

5th Military
Gate

Galata

Mehmet's
Camp

Sea Chain

St. Romanus
Gate

Lycus

Wall of Constantine

Bosporus

4th Military
Gate

CONSTANTINOPLE

Land Wall of Theodoseus II

Harbor

Acropolis

River

Wall of Byzantium

Church of
St. Sophia

3rd Military
Gate

Hippodrome

Harbor of
Theodosius

Harbor of
Kontoscalion

2nd Military
Gate

Golden
Gate

Sea of
Marmara

**SIEGE OF
CONSTANTINOPLE
1453**

N
W E
S

0   0.5   1 Mile

0   0.5   1   1.5 Km

CHAPTER ONE

SUNDAY, SEPTEMBER 3, 1452

Mehmet held the twisting adolescent tightly while he drove the dagger deeper into the boy's throat. Blood pumped from the wound, but Mehmet was behind the body and most of the hot liquid splashed onto the cobblestones. The boy's muscles convulsed beneath his hands, trying to break free, but Mehmet kept his left arm wrapped tightly around the boy's waist while his right hand gripped the knife. Soon the body went limp, and he let it slide gently to the ground. He knelt down and wiped the dagger clean on the boy's robes, then walked on casually into the darkness.

Mehmet waited a moment in the shadows, listening for voices or footsteps, then continued prowling the midnight streets of Edirne. He was dressed in simple clothing that hung loosely on his frame. He was tall, with dark features, a thin hooked nose, and full, almost feminine lips. He was twenty-one, although he appeared older, particularly his eyes, which held a cautious wisdom.

He enjoyed his walks in the dark. He liked Edirne. The city formerly called Adrianople still contained a large Greek population but also was home to an increasing number of Ottomans. The narrow stone streets ambled through mixed neighborhoods with closely huddled residences, opening periodically to the impressive churches and cathedrals now largely converted to mosques. Edirne had served as the capital of the Ottoman Empire since its capture in 1365, taking the distinction from Bursa, in Anatolia. Bursa continued to serve as the religious center of the empire, and contained the tombs of the Ottoman founding fathers: Osman, for whom the empire and people were named, and his son, Orhan.

As Mehmet walked through the sleeping city, he let his thoughts wander, trying to relax. He loved the night—his quiet time to escape. He could mull over the questions and issues he had experienced during the day without the multiple interruptions and problems he was typically forced to address. He needed peace and quiet. He did not trust people, particularly those closest to him. Out here he could let down his guard. He also liked to eavesdrop, seeking information in the shadows that he would never learn otherwise.

At a crossroad, he came across a street sweeper who growled at him to move aside. As Mehmet turned, the sweeper looked into his face and gasped, falling to the ground in prostration. Mehmet sighed in annoyance and again drew his dagger, plunging it deeply into the sweeper's neck. The man struggled, surprised, blood gurgling from the wound. Mehmet held him to the ground with his knee until he stopped moving, then again wiped his blade clean on his victim's clothes and continued on. Two tonight. More than typical. He hated these interruptions. Why wouldn't people simply leave him alone?

As he walked, he strained his ears to pick up conversations that would sometimes emanate from the thin walls of the closely crowded houses. He was searching for the thoughts of the city. He paused at a number of locations to pick up conversations, but he heard nothing of interest. Then, as he passed the outside courtyard of a wealthy merchant's home, he discovered what he sought.

"Times have changed," stated a deep voice, speaking Turkish. Mehmet could speak Turkish and Greek, as well as Farsi and Arabic.

"What do you mean?" answered another man, with a slightly higher voice. Both spoke the educated Turkish of the middle and upper classes.

"Murad is dead. I think our days of glory are over. At least for now. For a hundred and fifty years our sultans have expanded our empire at the expense of the infidel Christians, but we can hardly expect that to continue."

"Yes, Allah has favored our people."

"Until now. We have conquered Anatolia and driven our way far into Europe. We have defeated the Italians and Hungarians and every crusading army sent by the infidels. But how can we hold these gains? With a young sultan who twice had to give power back to his father? Who could not win control of his own household guard? I am afraid he will be driven from power, and we will return to the bad days of civil war among our people."

"Come now, Ishtek, you are hardly being fair. He was only ten or eleven when he was made sultan the first time. Murad should have kept the sultanate until the boy was ready. I do not agree with you. I think he will do fine. Perhaps he will even be greater than Murad."

"Bah! You are ever the optimist. I will be content at this point to live out my life in Edirne, without being driven back to Bursa or farther by the Hungarians. Can Mehmet stand up to John Hunyadi? Murad hardly could. I would not be surprised if Hunyadi's armies were massing in the north right now, ready to strike against us."

"Truly Hunyadi and the Hungarians are a threat. But we have not lost a major battle against the infidels. I do not think we will start now, even under a weak sultan. We still have Grand Vizier Halil. He practically led our empire during the last few years of Murad's reign, particularly when Murad relinquished power to his son. He will know what to do."

"Ah yes, Halil. Allah bless him. If only he were our sultan. He is wise and holy, and cares for the people. He practically *is* the sultan. We must put our trust in him. He will lead us even if Mehmet cannot."

"Mehmet. How can he come from Murad? We have had such good

fortune. We have had such great leaders. Now we are left with an arrogant boy. We must pray for our salvation."

Mehmet, sultan of the Ottoman Turks, walked away from the home, having heard enough. He continued his walk, pondering the words of the overheard conversation.

He was angry. He had almost burst through the door and killed the men right then and there. How could he, though? They were right, of course. Mehmet had failed terribly when he first became sultan. He had wanted to do too much, too fast, and his father's councilors and viziers had worked against him. They had embarrassed him, let him make foolish mistakes, and then called his father back. Soldiers had appeared one day, and he was surrounded and dragged from the throne while his "councilors" looked on with smiles. He was carted off to a faraway province in the empire and forgotten. His father had not even deigned to see him, to explain why he had given him everything and then taken it away.

His father! Mehmet stewed when he thought of him. His father had never shown him any real affection or spent significant time with him. Mehmet was not, after all, the original heir to the sultanate. He was a second son who became heir only when his older brother died. Mehmet had been forced from then on to endure a frantic and often harsh tutoring process. He was just beginning to grasp his responsibilities at the age of twelve, when his father had retired and named him sultan. He had done the best he could to govern, but in short order Grand Vizier Halil had called his father back to take over the throne. Halil should have helped him, should have supported him. Instead he had watched and reported Mehmet's shortcomings to his father, betraying him and leading to his humiliation.

From then on Mehmet had bided his time. He had learned to keep his thoughts and emotions to himself, to trust no one. He had studied everything: military art, languages, administration, and the arts. He had worked tirelessly so that when he next ruled he would not only equal his father but exceed him. He would be the greatest sultan in the history of his people, Allah willing.

His chance came when Murad finally died only two years before, as Mehmet turned nineteen. Mehmet quickly took power, ordering his baby half brother strangled to assure there would be no succession disputes, and set to organizing his empire. He had learned to be cautious and measured, leaving his father's councilors and even Halil in power to assist him. From there he had slowly built up a group of supporters. They were young and exclusively Christian converts to Islam. These followers, many of whom now held council positions, were not nearly as powerful as the old guard, but they were gaining ground. They were the future, if Halil did not interfere.

Halil. His father's Grand Vizier and now his own. He had always treated Mehmet with condescending politeness. He was powerful, so powerful that Mehmet could not easily remove him. So powerful it was possible he could remove Mehmet in favor of a cousin or other relative. Mehmet hated him above all people in the world, but he could not simply replace him. He needed Halil, at least for now, and Halil knew it.

This dilemma was the primary reason for Mehmet's nighttime wanderings. He needed time away from the palace. Time to think and work out a solution to the problem. How could he free himself from Halil without losing power in the process? He could simply order Halil executed, but would the order be followed or would it be his own head sitting on a pole? The elders and religious leaders all respected and listened to the Grand Vizier. Only the young renegades, the Christian converts who owed their positions to Mehmet, were loyal to the sultan. If Halil was able to form alliances with the other members of the old guard, Mehmet had no doubt that the result would be a life-or-death dispute.

Mehmet needed to find a cause that could rally the people to him. The conversations he heard night after night told him this repeatedly. The people felt that his father, Murad, had been a great leader, and that

Mehmet was not. If he could gain their confidence, then he would not need Halil, and the other elders would follow his lead.

Mehmet knew the solution. He knew exactly what would bring the people to his side, and what would indeed make him the greatest sultan in the history of the Ottoman people.

The solution, however, was a great gamble. His father and his father's fathers had conquered huge tracts of territory in Anatolia and then in Europe, primarily at the expense of the Greeks. Mehmet intended to propose something even more audacious: to conquer the one place that his ancestors had failed to take. If he succeeded, he would win the adoration of his people and would be able to deal with Halil and any others who might oppose him. If he failed . . .

The sultan eventually made his way back near the palace, to the home of his closest friend, Zaganos Pasha. Zaganos, in the prime of his middle age, was the youngest brother of Mehmet's father-in-law. Born a Christian, he had converted to Islam at age thirteen, and was Mehmet's trusted General and friend. Mehmet found Christian converts the best followers. They were new and righteous in their faith to Allah. More important, they were ambitious and had no ties to Halil. Zaganos was the most prominent member of this group.

Zaganos was up, even at this late hour, and embraced his friend, smiling like a proud uncle or father. He showed Mehmet in and ordered apple tea from his servants. Zaganos was shorter and stockier than Mehmet. He had receding dark brown hair. A long scar cut across his forehead and down over his left eye. He looked on Mehmet with smiling eyes extending into crow's-feet.

"How is my midnight vagabond? I trust you didn't depopulate the entire city tonight?"

Mehmet smiled. "I was recognized only twice."

"Good thing, because this habit of yours is thinning the population too quickly. I can't say I entirely approve, and in any case, why kill them?"

Mehmet flushed in irritation. "I don't need to be recognized. That is my time, the only time I have to myself. Is it not too much to ask that I be left alone?"

"Well, it would seem at some point the population would get the message. Just remember, we may need some of those people for our army."

"I heard more talk this evening. More talk of my father."

"Random killings aren't my only problem with your evening wanderings. Listening to this gossip is no good for you. You are the sultan; it doesn't matter what these people think or say about you. You are their ruler by Allah's will. You should kill a few of the people spreading such rumors. And quit listening to them."

"Ah, my friend, but they speak the truth. Why should I punish those who simply speak what everyone is thinking? The people have no love for me. That much is very clear. They only remember my father— my past failures. They think I'm a child. They think I will bring them to ruin. I need to do something that will unite the people. Something extraordinary. I know what that something is."

Zaganos stared at Mehmet for a moment before responding. He breathed heavily, clearly weary of a topic they had discussed too often.

"Constantinople? You make my head ache with this talk. Over and over you go on about taking that city. Constantinople is a curse to Islam. The city has not fallen in eight hundred years, despite our faith's many attempts. Your father and his father tried again and again. How would failing once more before the city's subjects improve your position? You will give Halil all he needs to usurp your position, or replace you."

"That city is a thorn in our side. It sits in the middle of our empire. The Greeks are through. Their territory now consists only of the city. Why should we allow a separate state hundreds of miles within our domains? A state of despicable infidels?" Mehmet could feel himself growing angry, and his hands shook. "We can never be a true empire while Constantinople remains in the Greeks' control. We must take it!

I was born to take it! It is Allah's will. Did not the blessed Prophet, peace be upon him, predict its fall, and that the people who captured the city would be blessed?"

"That is true. But remember that your ancestors have built their empire step by careful step. Osman began in Anatolia with just a few hundred warriors, a leader among many leaders. He carefully built your territory up, as did each sultan, one after the other. Your father shored up the empire's power against Hungary, and in Anatolia. He would have taken Constantinople if he could, but he could not." Zaganos took a step forward and placed his hand on Mehmet's shoulder.

"Your father was powerful, beloved by his people, with the full confidence of all his advisors, and in the prime of his life. Still he could not take the city. You must place yourself in the same position if you wish to try. You are not ready for that task yet, Sultan. You have so many summers ahead of you. I advise you to take your time. Win some small victories against the Serbians or the Bulgarians. Build up your forces. Win the confidence of the people slowly. Then you can try Constantinople. Too many empires and armies have died at those city walls. Do not add yours to the tally."

Mehmet stared hard at his friend. "You have known me all my life, Zaganos. Do you think I am less than my father? Do you think I cannot take Constantinople if I want to? I will not waste my life under Halil's boot. Every day he questions my authority. I see him whispering among the elders. I know he works against me. I will not continue to tolerate this. I must act decisively. I will take the city and then I will end that traitor's life!"

"You'll never get to the city, my Sultan. As you know, these sieges require months of preparation and the full resources of the empire. You cannot simply order the attack. I know that Murad could and did, but if you do, you risk Halil making a move against you now, when you are weakest. He would have far too much time to maneuver against you."

"Then I will call a council and win the full approval of my advisors."

"A council? Nothing could be worse, my friend. They won't approve the plan, and you give Halil power to voice his concerns in public. He can defy you openly while acting as if he simply is trying to give you advice. Please do not do this. Please follow my advice and start with less ambitious projects. You know I will follow you no matter what, my friend. You are my Sultan, I am your servant, but I am afraid you try too much too quickly. Remember the lessons of your youth!"

"I remember them well."

Several days later, Mehmet sat on his divan in the presence of the council. The Ottoman Council, an informal group of the top advisors of the empire, was made up of the sultan, Grand Vizier Halil, the religious leader known as the Grand Mufti, and a number of lesser viziers, generals, and members of the religious and civil community. In all, nearly thirty men assembled to hear the sultan's proposal. Many of the men came from established Ottoman families; just a few were Mehmet's first-generation Christian converts. There was a crackling air of tension in the palace room, with the two factions eyeing each other distrustfully. Zaganos and the younger members stood in a group slightly apart from the senior council, emphasizing the divide.

Mehmet rose to address the room. The murmuring of greetings and small talk fell, and soon it was quiet with all eyes focused on the sultan. "My friends, I speak to you today of Constantinople. Since the Prophet himself, peace be upon him, walked among us, it has been our destiny to capture this ancient city. His standard-bearer was slain before the city walls almost eight hundred years ago. Since then, we have battered the walls. We have fought and died before them. Still the city stands.

"We have had great victories in Europe. We own the land for hundreds of miles in each direction from Constantinople. The Greek Empire is all but a memory. We have brought our blessed faith to hundreds of thousands of converts."

Mehmet paused, looking around the room to gauge the faces of the council. He saw what he expected: His supporters nodded, but many others simply watched impassively. Too many. *I must convince them.*

"This success means nothing. All of our triumphs mean nothing while this city sits in our midst. Constantinople is an infidel mockery of our faith, of our people. If we cannot take the city, we cannot be a true people, a true empire. The Prophet, peace be upon him, predicted that a blessed people would take the city. We are that people. And the time is now. I propose that we make immediate preparations for the siege and capture of Constantinople. We will take the city for Mohammed, for Osman, for Allah!"

There were mixed cheers and murmurs from the council. Zaganos Pasha quickly rose to respond to the sultan.

"My Sultan. You speak with wisdom beyond your years. It was your father's great dream to capture the city. Alas, he could not do so before he left for paradise. But you will fulfill his dream. As a general, I have studied Constantinople. I have studied the histories. We have the forces necessary to capture the city. We need only the will of our leader, our sultan, and we will prevail. Let it be done."

More cheers accompanied Zaganos's response, although Mehmet noticed these came almost exclusively from his Christian-convert faction.

Halil now came forward to speak, first bowing before the sultan.

"My dear Sultan and assembled council, I humbly speak as grand vizier. I appreciate our sultan's enthusiasm for this project, but I must respectfully disagree.

"I certainly agree that capturing the city would do wonders for our empire, for our people, for our faith. However, our sultan tells us these things without addressing the obvious problem: How to accomplish the task?

"I would point out that it was not the will of his ancestors that prevented the capture of the city. Certainly it was not the will of Murad, who desired this above all things. It is the city itself that prevents this, not the will of a sultan, strong *or weak*." Halil's eyes fell on Mehmet as he finished the sentence, a slight smile on his face.

"How is the city to be captured? Is not Constantinople surrounded on three sides by water? We have no fleet to speak of, my Sultan. We have difficulty enough ferrying a few troops back and forth across the narrow waters of the straits without interference from the Greeks. And the Greeks possess their Greek fire, the terrible weapon they use to burn our ships and kill our sailors. The only way the city has ever been taken is by sea, and then only by the Venetians and other Latins, who *did* possess a great fleet."

Mehmet watched carefully as Halil delivered his speech. Predictably, the old guard nodded and bleated out affirmations like sheep. He felt the uncertainty rising inside him. They would never follow him. Not without Halil. How could he force Halil to follow him?

The grand vizier continued. "Could we defeat the city by land? We outnumber the foolish infidel Greeks ten or twenty to one. But they have the walls. As you know, my Sultan, the city is only exposed by land on one side. A triple network with a moat protects the land approach to Constantinople, with two huge walls surmounted by scores of defensive towers. The city can be defended against our hundreds of thousands of men by a tenth of that number. The walls have not been breached in a thousand years."

Halil swept his cloak up in his arms, gesturing grandly, a pointed finger raised toward the window.

"What of the West? Will they sit by and watch, my Sultan? Time and again our attacks on the city have served as oil on a fire for the pope and the kings of Europe to rise against us. We have fought battle after battle to preserve our territory in Europe. When will we prod this hornet's nest too greatly? Our strength is in the petty squabbling of the Christian kingdoms. Can we afford to unite them? We may lose more than Constantinople; we may lose Europe in the bargain. Think of John Hunyadi, my Sultan. He is perhaps the greatest Christian warlord we have faced. We have a truce with him now, but if we attack the city? With our forces diverted to the center, what will stop him from attacking the north? We could lose everything gained in the last hundred years in a single winter.

"My Sultan, I advise caution. Do not repeat the mistakes of your youth. Accept the advice and guidance of this council. In time, you will have the support you seek in these things." Halil bowed again, his eyes resting on Mehmet.

What is he thinking? Is it a challenge? Mehmet wondered. Finally the grand vizier turned and stepped back amid several elders who placed supportive hands on him.

The Grand Mufti, religious leader of the Ottomans, now came forward to speak. Mehmet felt tense. Much would ride on the opinion of the Mufti, who he hoped would support him.

"My Sultan, I agree that it is the will of Allah to capture the city."

Mehmet smiled. With the Mufti's support, he would not fail.

The Mufti hesitated. "However, there is of course the question of timing. With all respect, you are still young in years, my Sultan. We have many enemies, including not only John Hunyadi but also the White Sheep of Anatolia. These enemies but wait for an opportunity of advantage to attack us. I agree with Halil: If we rob our borders of forces to embark on a lengthy siege of the city, then we leave ourselves open to attack.

"Also, think of what a failure would bring. You have not won any great victories as sultan. The West watches you closely, perhaps considering you the most vulnerable sultan in many years. If you fail at Constantinople, you will have lost the faith of your people. We will have expended our treasury, depleted our troops. We will be vulnerable.

I agree with Halil. We could lose everything. That is certainly not what Allah intends. We are his keepers on this earth. We cannot gamble recklessly with our duty. I cannot support this plan, my Sultan. I, too, urge caution."

Halil came forward again. "My Sultan, you have our support and advice for so much. Please do not react recklessly to our response. It is intended only for your own good. We will be here to assist you in all your endeavors. Forget Constantinople for now. I have many suggestions for you that I believe you will find promising and will assist you in your future rule."

Mehmet could feel his blood rising.

"I see no reason to wait. We have waited long enough to take this city. My father should have captured it when he had the opportunity. These Greeks have nothing left to fight with. He had Constantinople in his grasp, and he let it fall through his fingers. I won't make the same mistake."

"Your father was very wise. He didn't make a mistake in not taking the city. It was his choice. If he didn't choose to take the city, then, with all respect, Sultan, you should heed his actions. He had the love of his people, a lifetime of experience, and the trust of his council."

"And I do not have that trust!"

Halil bowed. "Of course I do not claim that. However, the more time you are in power, the easier it will be to accomplish what you wish. You have already had a revolt while you previously ruled. *I certainly* would not wish for that event to be repeated. Let your people see you leading them wisely. Listen to the advice of those who advised your father. In time you will have the people's trust, and when the time is right we can consider attacking Constantinople again, if appropriate."

Mehmet was incensed. How dare Halil speak to him of patience? Of caution? Mehmet was Allah's servant on earth. Who was Halil? His servant? He was no one. Mehmet let the anger burn through him without showing any emotion; he simply stared thoughtfully at the council.

He saw that almost exclusively the old guard backed Halil and the Grand Mufti. Only a few of the younger members surrounded Zaganos and obviously supported him. His hands were tied.

"Very well," he conceded finally. "I will wait for now. But this decision will not be long delayed. It is *my* destiny to take the city! I will take Constantinople! I suggest you all reconcile your position with this and begin working toward a solution. I am the sultan! I will not be denied what I want!"

He was losing control and he hated it. He sounded like a petulant child. He couldn't afford to show weakness before these men. He saw a slight smile on Halil's face, and the grand vizier looked around knowingly, making eye contact with several other council members.

Mehmet had heard enough, and showed too much. He dismissed the council, waving even Zaganos away. As the servants extinguished candles, the room fell into darkness.

Despite his orders, Zaganos held back. He approached his sultan carefully. "I admire your courage and your enthusiasm, but I caution you again to be more patient. We will take the city when it is time. You are not alone, my Sultan." With that Zaganos bowed and left Mehmet to his thoughts.

Mehmet sat in the blackness in impotent rage. Why was he not loved and trusted like his father? Was he not Allah's shadow on earth? Was he not ordained to lead his people in triumph against the infidels? Why did his father place him in charge before his time?

Could he even trust Zaganos? The general seemed to be on his side, but so had Halil before he betrayed him and sent for Murad again. He could trust no one. He must rely only on himself. He could use Zaganos and count him as a supporter. However, he must never completely trust another again. They must all be watched, spied on, checked on.

Mehmet felt his rage boiling up again. They would pay. All of those who had laughed at him, threatened him, who had sat smugly by and done nothing while he lost his throne and was sent away in humiliation. First he must obtain true freedom of action. The key to his freedom was taking the city. He must convince the council to allow him to proceed with his plans.

As for Halil, the grand vizier may have felt he had won and stopped Mehmet's plans. The dog was wrong. But this dog controlled his council of sheep. The council had bleated their fears: the walls, the sea, the West. They did not believe the city could be taken. If the council needed assurances to proceed, then with the help of Allah he would answer these fears, and he would lead his people in his rightful destiny.

He spent the night in the darkness, in prayer, contemplating the solutions to these seemingly impossible obstacles.

With the dawn, he rose and pulled out a number of maps, spreading them out on the floor. One particular map, inherited from his father, was immense. It showed Constantinople and the immediate surrounding area. He paced back and forth over the map, studying the lay of the land, the surrounding seas, and the ever-imposing walls. He would take the city. He just had to decide how to convince the council. He wasn't sure how to accomplish that yet, but he was beginning to formulate some plans.

One thing he knew for sure: He would keep these foolish Greeks busy while he made his decision.

CHAPTER TWO

SUNDAY, NOVEMBER 26, 1452

Constantine wept. He wept quietly, facing away from the city and looking out over the broad blue expanse of the Sea of Marmara to his right and the Bosporus Straight to his left. From the heights of the extreme northeast corner of Constantinople, near the ancient Acropolis, Constantine could survey the waters leading in both directions into the ancient city, meeting at the end of the peninsula and flowing into the natural harbor of the Golden Horn.

Constantine XI Palaiologos, Greek emperor, successor of the Roman emperors, was in his late middle age, having turned forty-eight in the past year. His black hair was peppered with gray now, his beard even more so. He was tall, well built, and still in excellent physical condition, but his face was careworn. The weight of the world had sat on him for too long.

As he looked out over the serene waters of the Bosporus, gateway to the Black Sea beyond, he felt overwhelmed. Overwhelmed by the impossibilities before him. He ruled an empire that had once encompassed all of the Mediterranean and, in ancient times, when the seat of power was Rome itself, had ruled most of Europe as well. Now the empire, if it could be called that, extended barely beyond the walls of the city. Constantine could claim to rule a few scattered islands in the

Mediterranean, the Peloponnesus, and a few villages and fortresses near the city.

Constantinople was a mere shadow of its former self. Built by the Roman Emperor Constantine the Great in AD 330, on top of the ancient Greek city of Byzantium, the city became the capital of the eastern half of the Roman Empire. After the fall of the western half of the empire, Constantinople carried on the legacy of Rome. With a population of more than five hundred thousand, the city was the largest and most opulent in the Christian world for a thousand years.

The city and the empire had fallen into decline gradually, and at the beginning of the thirteenth century Constantinople was captured and sacked by crusaders from Europe who were supposed to be attacking Egypt but were diverted to the city by the doge of Venice. The Latins controlled the city until 1261, when it was recovered. However, Constantinople never truly rose again. It was a ghost town, with fewer than one hundred thousand inhabitants and the vast wealth of the city stripped and carted off to Venice and the West. Constantine wondered what it would have been like to rule during the Golden Age of his empire, with a bursting city and legions of warriors to command.

What would his life have been like if he wasn't constantly having to scrounge and beg for a few resources to battle the impossibly powerful Ottomans? Would he hold his borders or expand? Build up the treasury? Construct great works in the city? He often dreamed of leading the once-great empire of the Romans and the Greeks, not the feeble shadow over which he presided.

How much longer could he hold on to even these remaining scraps? His few territories were surrounded for hundreds of miles in each direction by the infidel enemy. He was forced into the humiliation of serving as a vassal to the Ottoman sultan and paying a tribute each year for the protection of the Turks, a tribute he could not afford. The payments made it impossible for Constantine to invest in food stores or arms, or to hire mercenaries, or even to perform the necessary maintenance to the essential city walls. What hope did he have to change anything? He was doomed. His city was doomed. Rome would finally fade into the oblivion of the past.

Constantine felt a hand on his shoulder, a gentle but firm grasp from slender fingers. He turned and smiled. Zophia was here. He looked into her dark eyes, smiling at her youthful, beautiful face and long black hair. Zophia, his love. A daughter of nobility, she was only twenty-four, but so wise. Wise and beautiful. She smiled too, just for him. Knowing. Understanding. Caring.

"Do not weep, Lord. I know you weep for our city, for our people. God will protect us. You will protect us. You always have. You must have faith. God and the Virgin have always blessed this city. They blessed us with you. You lead us."

Constantine felt her warmth flow over and through him. He closed his eyes as she embraced him. He immediately felt calm. He sensed the warm day, the sound of birds singing nearby, and the rustle of the light wind against the trees. He always noticed the little things when he was with Zophia. All the problems of the world would drain out of him. She could keep all his problems and his fears away, if just for a little while.

She was beautiful. Not tall, yet her powerful presence made her seem taller. She had skin as pale as marble. She was dressed in light blue robes flowing down to delicate sandals on her slender feet.

Her physical beauty was nothing compared to her heart, her inner spirit. He could feel this now, pouring into him through her touch. He felt her strength, her faith. She was so much younger than him, yet her soul was ageless, beyond him. She seemed to live in this world and the next. She was his angel on earth.

How could this young woman have such an effect on him? No person ever had before, woman or man. Constantine prided himself on his control, his ability to keep his emotions in check and to present a strong leadership persona to his people, even to his close friends. He had developed this talent during his exceptionally difficult youth and early adulthood, when he was always at risk of kidnapping and even death—not only from the Ottomans, but also from his own brothers, who constantly conspired for the throne.

Somehow Zophia saw through all this. He couldn't seem to even make the effort to try to present this front to her. He craved the moments when he could be alone with her and let it down, allowing her to cradle his head and tell him it would be all right. He knew this peace could not last forever. He was pushed from every direction to marry, marry quickly, and marry for the greatest possible political advantage. The city needed allies who could provide money and troops to defend against the Ottoman attack that must come at any time— that was threatened and had been constantly attempted for more than a century.

Already Constantine had received marriage overtures from several eastern kingdoms, including Trebizond and Georgia, concerning potential princesses for his consideration. He knew that eventually he would have to give up his darling Zophia. He could not bear to think about it. He would enjoy her, breathe her in, experience every part of her, until he was forced to let her go.

They had discussed his fate many times. She did not like it, did not agree that it was worth compromising for a few soldiers or a little gold. This topic provided their only source of conflict, the first scars in an otherwise perfect relationship. Eventually they stopped talking about the issue. Their love was like the city itself: ignoring grim realities and holding on until whatever inevitable end God had in store.

For now, for this moment, there was only Zophia. Zophia and his city. The two things in the world he lived for and would die for. They mounted their horses and rode through the city, trailed at a discreet distance by Constantine's personal guard. They rode down the gently sloping hill of the Acropolis, past the crumbling palaces of the former emperors to the Goths Column and then to the sea wall itself. The sea wall of Constantinople, a single but formidable barrier wrapped continuously around three sides of the peninsula, connecting finally with the massive triple Theodosian land walls.

They rode west above the sea wall, along the Golden Horn, passing the two inner walled harbors of the city. They could look out north across the Horn barely five hundred yards to the walled independent city of Galata, granted to the Genoese in 1273 by the Greek emperor. Galata was much smaller than Constantinople but contained an important port and the stunning rounded Tower of Christ, which dominated the skyline and was built in the fourteenth century. Most of the sea trade now stopped at Galata instead of Constantinople, except for the portion that interacted primarily with the Venetians in the city. The Greeks had lost their commercial power with the decline of the empire itself. They still had a few ships plying the waters of the Mediterranean and the Black Sea, but they had been first challenged, then completely surpassed, by the Italian city-states.

The loss of sea trade further weakened the city, as there was only a trickle of new money into Constantinople. This meager income barely paid the cost to feed the city and left nothing for building new ships, paying soldiers, or maintaining the vital sea and land walls.

The emperor and his consort continued riding west, coming to the Hagia Theodosia, a lesser but important church nestled near the sea walls. They then entered the Petrion district of the city, where Zophia's home was located.

Zophia lived in a simple house near the middle of the district. At one point, this area had bustled with residences and people, but now there were abandoned buildings and open fields everywhere. Zophia's home was covered in foliage and fronted by a large gated courtyard, affording her and Constantine privacy and the ability to come and go without constant attention. The house was built of sandstone and was large but one story. Within, fires crackled, light flickering off rich carpets and dark wood. Icons and an altar decorated one wall of the great room, Zophia's private chapel.

Constantine loved Zophia's home, a retreat away from the busy demands of his office.

They had dinner within, protected from the eyes and sounds of the city except for her servants, who would never have dared betray their conversations or their privacy. They drank wine near the warm fire, holding each other, enjoying each other's comfort and support. Usually they talked about the day, or Constantine would share his frustrations or concerns, but tonight they sat quietly, thoughtfully. They kissed deeply and fell among the blankets, making love more desperately and passionately than usual. They both sensed something coming, something they could not predict and could not control.

As the city fell into twilight, they could linger no longer. Today had been a beautiful day of peace. A perfect day. A rare day without all the busy details of the city and the empire raining down on Constantine.

As they lay in each other's arms, in the darkness and the flickering firelight, they heard a hard banging on the front door. A servant nervously entered Zophia's bedroom and warned that a messenger had arrived with urgent information for the emperor. Constantine dressed quickly and drew his sword. He did not keep a constant guard when he traveled the city. His people loved him and trusted him, but there was always the possibility of an assassin. He cautiously opened the door and then smiled. It was Sphrantzes.

George Sphrantzes wore simple courtier clothing with no armor. He was short and thin, almost frail, with brown hair and blue eyes. He looked older than his forty-two years, his face weathered with worry. Sphrantzes had no formal position in the government but was Constantine's close friend and advisor. He smiled crookedly to his emperor and nodded to Zophia in the background.

Constantine laughed and welcomed Sphrantzes in, clapping him on the back. "Well, my friend, so nice of you to visit today. Perhaps tomorrow would have suited as well. I am trying to enjoy a day of relaxation, as I think you can see."

Sphrantzes did not return the emperor's smile. He seemed to hesitate and then began. "My Lord, it is grave news."

"What sort of news?" asked Zophia.

Sphrantzes glanced at Zophia. "My Lord, perhaps this should be news that I give you alone."

"I trust Zophia with everything," said Constantine, slightly annoyed. "Tell me what has happened."

"It is both fact and rumor. The first is terrible and the second worse."

"Do not be afraid, Sphrantzes," assured Constantine. "I have known little in the way of happy news my whole life. We shall deal with this news as we have all tragedies. Tell me what it is."

"My Lord, just this morning a Venetian vessel was passing through the straits in the Bosporus, past the Turkish forts Rumelihisari and Anadoluhisari. As you know, we have heard rumor that the Ottomans are demanding that each ship stop to be inspected and to pay a fine. The Venetian Captain, an Antonio Rizzo, decided he would not be forced to obey such an arrogant request from the infidels. He sailed through without stopping for payment. The Ottomans fired on the ship, my Lord, and sank it."

Constantine was shaken. He was aware of this ship, which was bound for Constantinople with food and supplies from the Black Sea ports. These supplies were critical to the city that had so few remaining farms or villages to support it. Constantine looked over at Zophia, who stared back with an understanding sadness. Calm. The situation demanded calm and confidence, even among such close friends. He smiled and raised both his hands palms outward and gently lowered them as if he could defuse the situation with this simple gesture.

"Were there any survivors?"

"I believe so, my Lord. I believe most of the men survived, but they were captured by the Ottomans. I don't know what has become of them."

"You said you had both fact and rumor. I assume the ship is your 'fact,' what is rumor?"

Sphrantzes hesitated again, looking Constantine in the eyes. "My Lord, I am hearing through various sources that a large army is massing south of Edirne. That can mean only one thing: They are coming for us."

Constantine felt the anxiety rising through him. Why now? Why would the Turks move so fast? He thought he would get a reprieve when Mehmet became sultan. Certainly the boy had a bad reputation as both unbalanced and arrogant, but wasn't that a bonus? His father, Murad, had been so calculating and strong, a great leader whom Constantine feared but also respected. When Mehmet ascended so young, after such early failures, Constantine was sure it was a gift from God. Surely the Ottoman power base would seek to keep this young hothead under control for many years to come? Mehmet had immediately signed a number of treaties preserving the status quo with the Greeks and many Latin kingdoms. Wasn't this proof that the old guard now controlled the Ottomans?

Why then was an army massing? No point in jumping to any conclusions; the Ottomans' sabers rattled for many reasons. Maybe Halil and the others were letting Mehmet play soldier to keep him busy. Maybe they would raid some small Greek town or village. Constantine couldn't really afford to lose any of the few remaining territories he controlled, but far better that than a full-scale attack on the city. He must wait and see, for now it was time to present the best front, and not allow panic, even in front of Zophia and Sphrantzes.

Constantine turned to Zophia, bowing slightly with a grin. "My dear, thank you for the charming day. Apparently there are some minor matters that require my attention at the palace. I must regretfully cut short what has otherwise been a delightful outing."

Zophia smiled back, knowing exactly what Constantine was doing, but clearly enjoying his strength and poise. "Thank you, my Lord. You are welcome to find your way back here when you are finished."

"I shall certainly do so as soon as possible."

He addressed Sphrantzes. "Let's go."

Sphrantzes bowed slightly to Zophia and turned quickly to the door.

Constantine hurried on horseback with Sphrantzes to his palace at Blachernae. The Palace of Blachernae was connected to the land walls of the city and sat at the extreme northwest corner of the walled peninsula near the Blachernae Gate. The Greek emperors had used this palace for the past two centuries. He had to pass through several large areas of fields and empty buildings. Whole portions of Constantinople had reverted to wilderness, and at times it was difficult to feel one was in a city at all.

The palace was set on a hill and contained multiple terraces and buildings. The entrance was guarded. Constantine dismounted and half walked, half ran to his council room. Sphrantzes had sent additional messengers to the principal councilors of the empire, including the Grand Admiral Loukas Notaras, Constantine's military leader, and the arrogant Cardinal Isidore

Notaras was strong-featured and in his midforties. He was tall, and athletically built, with a full head of graying hair. The Megadux was the emperor's closest friend, and the most important noble in Constantinople.

Cardinal Isidore, at nearly sixty years old, had previously been the head of the church in Moscow. He was short and stocky, with long gray hair and deep wrinkles running down from his eyes to his chin on each side. He wore dark and ragged robes and walked with a slight limp. Isidore was bowed down with his troubles. His tenure in Moscow had been short. He had aggressively advocated union with the Church of Rome and was therefore deposed and imprisoned by the Orthodox Russian leadership. Eventually he made his way back to Rome, where the pope subsequently appointed him as his representative to Constantinople. Isidore had come to Constantinople with the same plan, to reunite the Eastern and Western churches.

Constantine nodded to both men in turn as he made his way into the council chamber and sat down at the head of a long wooden table with two dozen chairs. All of the assembled men bowed formally to the emperor and then took their traditional places at the council table. Servants poured wine and the men shared bread and fruit before they began their business.

"What do we know?" asked Constantine finally.

Loukas Notaras, as military commander and essentially Constantine's second in command, began. "I'm sure Sphrantzes informed you of the sinking of the Venetian ship and of the rumors regarding the army massing near Edirne?"

"Yes, he gave me a brief summary of both issues. Do you know anything else?"

"I can confirm through spies that there were survivors from the Venetian galley, including the captain. Apparently they are being marched to Edirne under heavy guard. I don't think there is any chance we could intercept and free them.

"I don't know anything more at this point about this mysterious army at Edirne. I do know they have had summer camps in that location many times, and they didn't necessarily move on the city. It is a little more unusual that they are massing in the fall. I think we have to take the threat very seriously."

"We've been expecting this for some time, although I was hopeful that Halil and the others could keep this young monster in check." The emperor looked to Sphrantzes. "Do we have any inside information about what is going on with Mehmet?"

"I don't have anyone close on the inside, my Lord, although I'm working to establish one. Our best spies were moved out of the sultan's household when Murad died. I haven't been able to get anyone close enough to find out what's going on in Mehmet's council meetings."

"So we're blind?" Constantine paused. "Loukas, tell me of our defenses. Will the city hold?"

"My Lord, as you are aware, our city walls have fallen into some disrepair. There are cracks and even holes in some of the walls. Many of the towers have not been used in years. Perhaps even more alarming, the great ditch, the foss in front of the outer wall, has been largely filled in over time. We haven't had the resources to dig out the ditch or maintain it, nor to repair the walls. In addition, we don't have enough soldiers, even with volunteers, to adequately man the land walls, let alone the sea walls."

"What resources do we have in the city?"

"We can ask for all of the churches to contribute everything they can, gold, plate, silver, donated coin. We also can ask the same of our citizens. As you know, my Lord, over the past hundred years or more, we have had to make these requests again and again. There simply aren't sufficient resources remaining in the city to gather significant wealth. However, we can make the request, and it will certainly result in some new treasure to pay for soldiers and food."

"But where will the soldiers and food come from?" asked the emperor.

"That's just the problem, my Lord. The sultan has effectively cut off the Black Sea. We are not able to receive aid from our remaining colonies in that area or from the Georgians or Trebizonds. We could sneak some ships past the forts, but this recent sinking will certainly make captains hesitant to run the strait, and I doubt the Ottomans would let soldiers, arms, or grain past, even if the captain paid the fee."

"What about the ambassadors we sent out to the West, to the Venetians, the Genoese, and to Naples? Any word from them?" Constantine had not waited for a crisis to try to prepare the city. He had worked tirelessly since his ascension to prepare Constantinople for a siege. One of the key components was aid from the West, and he had recently sent a new round of ambassadors out to beg assistance from various cities and kingdoms.

"It's still a little early to expect responses, my Lord," answered Notaras. "Our ships could have reached some of the cities and returned, but that doesn't take into consideration time for an audience and nego-tiations. I don't expect to hear from any of our missions for several weeks."

"Any news from my wonderful brothers? Can we not expect help from the Morea?" Constantine's brothers Demetrius and Thomas shared control of the Morea, the ancient Peloponnesus of Greece. The brothers were often at war with one another when they weren't schem-ing to take the throne from Constantine.

"Unfortunately we cannot, my Lord. We have heard from Thomas that the Morea is being pressured by Mehmet as well. It's unclear how long the peninsula can hold out, and it may have fallen already."

Constantine frowned. No help from the East, few resources at home, and no word from the West. They were almost defenseless. If Mehmet arrived immediately, even with a relatively small army, he could overwhelm the few professional soldiers and guards the Emperor possessed in a matter of days, at most, and a matter of hours at least. "What do you suggest?"

"We should send missions to John Hunyadi in Hungary and ask for immediate assistance," said Notaras. "We also should send a mission to the White Sheep in Anatolia. He is no friend of the Ottomans. He might be willing to help us, or at least use the siege of our city as an opportunity to attack the Ottomans."

Constantine considered his friend's advice. The White Sheep, whose kingdom was situated on the Ottomon eastern borders in Asia Minor, was a powerful rival of Mehmet's. Constantine had exchanged messages and gifts with the Muslim leader but previously stopped short of making any formal agreements or alliances. He was concerned about angering Mehmet if the sultan learned of any negotiations. Worse yet if he received aid and ultimately Mehmet was defeated, Constantinople might trade one Muslim threat for another. The situation was desperate however. He had little choice but to explore every possibility and pray for the best.

"I agree on both. I don't know if the White Sheep will help us. Will Muslim turn on Muslim to help a Christian? But we must try. Anything else?"

"My Lord, I know you do not like this subject," said Sphrantzes. "However, you should reconsider my suggestion that you betroth and marry the Georgian Princess Arianna, daughter of George VIII."

Constantine sighed in frustration. "Sphrantzes, we have discussed this time and again. I don't want to be betrothed, and I don't want a wife. Besides, with the strait cut off by these cursed Turkish forts, what is the point?"

"My Lord, the strait is cut off from a single ship carrying supplies, or even a few ships. It is not cut off from a fleet. If you are willing to negotiate a marriage contract, I believe we can work out substantial concessions from the Georgians. A relief fleet with troops and supplies is not out of the question."

Constantine paused before responding. What should he say? He had avoided this issue for a very long time. Zophia would be crushed, devastated. How could he live without her? "I'm still considering that question, Sphrantzes, but let's discuss additional options."

"I don't know why you continue to press him about this," said Notaras. "The emperor has been very clear he doesn't want to entertain a marriage."

"Maybe if you could provide decent defenses for the city, I wouldn't have to press uncomfortable issues on him," retorted Sphrantzes.

Notaras rose out of his seat. "I will not stand for your words! What have you done with your spies and intrigues? Nothing!"

Sphrantzes stood also, and for a moment it appeared the two men would come to blows.

"Enough! Both of you stop at once!" demanded Constantine. "We must fight among ourselves? We don't have enough enemies and enough problems?"

The men sat down. Notaras turned to face Constantine. "My Lord, there is another possibility. You could leave the city. Leave me in command. Sail to Rome. Plead directly to the West. You are more important than the city. You are the empire. This plan would have several advantages. Not only would a direct plea from you be far more effective than ambassadors, but if the city fell in your absence, you could carry on the fight from Morea or some of our island strongholds, or even join John Hunyadi in Hungary. You would be safe."

Constantine was surprised to hear this from Notaras. He was such a noble, honorable man. Flee the city at its moment of greatest need? Constantine was offended. Or was that fair? Had he not thought the same on many occasions? To get out of this noose ever closing in. He could make an appeal to the West. He could gather a mighty army and crush the Ottomans at the gates. Beyond that, could he recapture Edirne? Could he drive the Turks out of the Balkans entirely? He could be more than a savior to his people. He could restore the Greek world to some measure of its former self.

What if the city fell in his absence? He could still raise a mighty army. The remaining Greeks could rally around him. With Constantinople lost, the Latin world would surely rise in a mighty crusade against the Ottomans. And if they didn't, couldn't he just as easily retire in one of his remaining territories or even in Rome as an honored and tragic hero? Zophia could go with him. They could be together for months at a time. If the city fell, there would be no pressure to marry anyone for political purposes. He would be free to marry her. Free to have his life. He had never been able to give in to himself. Ever. He had spent his life in service to his people and his city. He would have everything.

Everything but honor. He shook his head.

"Loukas, my friend, I appreciate your words. I would flatter myself that I am more important than the city. More important than my people. But I am not. Emperors have come and gone over the centuries. Some good, some bad. The city has endured. The city is everything. The city and the people. I will stay. I will live and die within our walls."

Notaras bowed. "As you wish, my Lord."

"As if he has a real choice," added Sphrantzes. "You counsel a coward's path, Notaras."

"I won't hear more of this!" interjected Constantine. "Let us focus on the matter at hand."

"My Lord, will you not take my counsel?"

Constantine looked farther down the table. Cardinal Isidore had spoken.

"You have something to add, Isidore?"

"My Lord, the answer to this problem is simple. All the aid you will ever need is but a moment away. It is time to institute the Union."

The Union. Constantine scrutinized Isidore closely. Why would the cardinal raise this issue now? Did he need more problems? More controversy? He didn't trust Isidore at all. The man was a creature of Rome. But Constantine knew that, as always, as emperor he could do nothing alone. Nothing independently. Isidore had appeared in October with two hundred archers and promises of more aid from the West. But the aid came at a price. A price perhaps too high to pay.

Isidore wanted Constantine to reunite the Western and Eastern churches. More accurately, he was demanding that the emperor put into action what had already been agreed.

The churches had split over several issues of faith in the eleventh century. Since that time, many efforts had been made to heal the schism between the pope in Rome and the patriarch in Constantinople. The Council of Florence, after many starts and stops, had negotiated a Union of the Churches in 1445. The Eastern bishops serving as delegates to this council helped to negotiate the Union.

However, the decision was very unpopular in Constantinople and in the Eastern church. Union meant accepting Western priests and foreign traditions. The mass would be said in Latin instead of Greek. Some people, even leaders in the church, felt the Union would damn the people to hell. For this reason, the provisions had never been formally adopted in Constantinople, despite almost constant pressure from Rome. This awkward situation had created another barrier in negotiating with Rome and in requesting aid.

Constantine faced an impossible position. If he enforced the Union, he would invoke unrest or even open revolt in his people. If he ignored the Union, he risked alienating the pope, whose aid he desperately needed if Constantinople was to survive. He had kept a delicate balance for years, but with the crisis at hand and the pope's representative directly demanding the Union in exchange for aid, he might be out of time.

"My Lord," continued Isidore. "It is time to put into effect what you have already promised and committed to do. You must reunite with the true church. If you do this, the pope will send aid to your defense, and will summon a new crusade of Latin forces to save the city. It is the only way."

"I agree with Isidore," said Sphrantzes. "Why do we not put into effect what has already been promised?" Constantine was surprised that Sphrantzes would support the Union, and more surprised he would do so openly without consulting Constantine first.

"The people will never accept it, and they will hate me for it," answered the emperor.

"The people will learn to live with it," said Sphrantzes. "If they are raped or dead or slaves, they will have less time to worry about the fine points of religious practice."

"How do we know if it will even make a difference, Isidore?" asked the emperor.

"His Holiness has offered ships, gold, and troops. He will declare a new crusade. He has promised he will rally the Hungarians to our side. Did he not provide me resources to recruit the archers I brought to the city with me as papal legate? He will deliver on his promises, I assure you."

"I advise against it, My Lord," said Notaras. "We've heard these promises before. What have we received? A little bread and a few soldiers. At what cost? You don't know how our church, how our people will react. What if they revolt? What if they depose you? You can't sacrifice your people, your soul, for the vague promise of aid."

As always, Constantine faced only bad decisions. What should he do? He couldn't defend the city with only his own resources. It was possible his people would kill him, or refuse to defend the city if he took steps to get what he needed from the pope. In the end it didn't matter. With no help from the West, the city would fall, regardless of the mood of the people. The only hope was papal assistance. He had to do what was necessary. It was a reckless gamble, but he was out of options.

If only his people would see this. If only they would see that they weren't sacrificing their afterlife or their faith by agreeing to the Union. If only they would see that this was the only way to obtain aid from the West, aid that was critical if the city and his people were to survive. He prayed to God and to the Virgin for wisdom and guidance to do the right thing. For now he needed to show strength, and he needed answers.

"I want an immediate survey of our defenses. I want to know the condition of the walls and the condition of our fleet. I also want to know what our food and water supplies are. Don't just survey the public supplies; get information on private stores and what the churches hold. If anyone resists, force your way in. Notaras and Sphrantzes, divide these duties. I want an initial tally by the end of the day tomorrow."

Constantine turned to Cardinal Isidore. "I've decided I will sign the Union of the Churches. I will implement those changes now. I want word sent by a fast ship to the pope. We need food, soldiers, and money immediately. We need a holy crusade against the infidels. We cannot wait weeks or months. It must be now, and it must be immense. I need the Hungarians and all of the West. Tell him he must provide this. Tell him I have given him everything; he must give me everything in return."

CHAPTER THREE

THURSDAY, NOVEMBER 30, 1452

Weeks passed as winter set in. Mehmet rode east on a solitary, windswept road, accompanied only by Zaganos and a few guards trailing behind.

The group was traveling ostensibly on a routine inspection of some of Zaganos's troops, but the trip also allowed Mehmet to speak freely with his favored general without the normal palace spies and courtiers about, and without Halil's prying ears.

As they rode to the coast of the Black Sea, the conversation had been primarily about the logistics of the military. Zaganos reported to Mehmet the number of forces under his command, the condition of the troops, and the number of irregulars that could be readily called up from the various provinces in the event of the need for military action.

"At the present time we have no active military campaigns," reported Zaganos. "However, there are threats from both the north and the south. In the southeast, we have the Persian Empire to contend with. Their numbers are vast, and as you are aware, they follow a heretical form of Islam, a constant threat to our people and our empire. In the south we face the empire of the Mamelukes. They are Muslim like us, but a rival for your power, particularly with their possession of the holy cities of Jerusalem, Mecca, and Medina.

"Probably the greatest immediate threat of attack from Asia is the White Sheep. He has gathered a fairly large force in eastern Anatolia and is apparently communicating with the Greeks as well. We will have to deal with him at some point."

"The White Sheep has ever been a thorn in our side," said Mehmet. "Let him play his games. We will deal with him soon enough."

Zaganos bowed slightly to the sultan and then continued. "To the north and west we face potential threats from the Latin states, including from the pope, who is perhaps your greatest theological enemy as the head of the Christian peoples, but who wields very little power in this world. The Latins are divided and fight each other, and the Venetians and Genoese are more concerned with their right to trade with us than with coming to the aid of the pope against us.

"Our greatest threat lies to the direct north. The Serbians and Bulgarians are divided or conquered, and they are disillusioned by their years of losses at our hands. The Hungarians are our true threat. They are capable of placing large forces in the field. They are brave, organized, and John Hunyadi is a capable leader who could threaten our lands."

"This I know," responded Mehmet. "I am not worried about Hunyadi. He will not attack. Not yet. We beat him too badly last time." In the Battle of Varna in 1444, a large Hungarian force had been defeated by a smaller Ottoman force, primarily because of the stupidity of the Hungarian king, who took over the battle from Hunyadi and was promptly crushed. Hunyadi had returned to his homeland and quickly gathered a new army. He was firmly in control and waiting for another opportunity.

Mehmet feared Hunyadi above all others. A Hungarian army led by him not only could threaten to disrupt a siege of Constantinople, it could also potentially threaten to drive the Ottomans from Europe. He changed the subject.

"What of the Greeks?"

"The Greeks are no real threat. They are divided and weak. To our east there is Trebizond. As you know, Trebizond is a breakaway state from the Greeks. Their empire is little more than the city of and a little land around it. It is ripe fruit for us to pluck when we will.

"The southern portion of the old Greek mainland, what was once known as the Peloponnesus and is now known as the Morea, is divided among the Greek emperor's brothers Demetrius and Thomas. They are jealous of each other, constantly squabbling, and unable to unite together even in the face of our forces. I could march through the entire land in a few days with sufficient forces. We are already pressuring them. They will not come to Constantine's aid."

"Bah! Demetrius and Thomas!" shouted Mehmet, slamming his fist on the table. "They are squabbling women. If only one of them was in charge of the city, I would take it in a day! What of the city, Zaganos? What of Constantinople?"

Zaganos took a deep breath. "I was just getting to that, my Sultan.

"That leaves Constantinople itself, and a few villages. The city has dwindled to less than ninety thousand, according to my sources. They have almost no fleet, very few soldiers, and little food or money. The only thing keeping the city intact is the walls. They can do nothing offensively against you. They can only scheme with other petty principedoms, and of course they can continue to exist in the middle of your empire.

"Constantinople must logically fall, and must become part of our empire. But all of the problems still remain. The walls make it difficult if not impossible to capture the city. If we do choose to attack, we risk wasting our resources and men on a fruitless siege that will sap morale and further damage your reputation. More concerning, a siege will draw in the West, as it has in the past, and we may face not only aid from the Italians but, of more concern, a Hungarian relief force."

Mehmet spat. "Curse these foolish Greeks. Why don't they see reality? What a city Constantinople will be under our rule. A jewel for our empire. I would build such mosques to Allah, such palaces. I would bring people from throughout our lands to make the city great again. Why will they not just leave Constantinople to us? Why won't Constantine see reason, see that his people and his city belong to us?

Better yet, why will he not embrace the true faith along with his people? He must understand they are doomed. I do not wish to destroy his people or his city. I want to make them great again."

Zaganos laughed. "Always with you it is Constantinople, my friend. Is there no other cup to slake your thirst? Never have I met one so young with such single-minded passion. You have a harem with thousands of women. You can sample their delights each evening. You have rooms of gold and treasure. You have enemies whom you can drive from their lands with a sweep of your hand. None of this do you want. You want the impossible." He leaned forward, staring for a moment at the sultan. "Does this make you great or a great fool? I cannot decide."

Mehmet's face reddened. "A great fool? Perhaps if your head is on a pole you will regret that statement."

Zaganos stopped his horse. "A thousand pardons, my Sultan. If you do not wish me to speak the truth, do not ask me questions. I am a simple man, a soldier. I answer the questions that are put to me."

Now it was Mehmet's turn to chuckle. "A simple soldier? I have seen you weave your way through the court with complex and colorful patterns. You would not have risen to your station or survived as long if you walked such a simple path."

"It is Allah's will."

"Or it is *my* will."

"For me, Sultan, they are one and the same." Zaganos bowed slightly in the saddle.

"Well spoken, my *simple* soldier. Have you found a solution to my simple problem?"

"What problem is that?"

"How to capture Constantinople, of course."

Zaganos sighed. "Since you wish to speak of nothing else, then let us speak of that. I have no further solutions for you, my Sultan. My advice remains the same. We cannot easily take the city by sea or by land. We face threats from the west, east, and south. Further, the council will not approve your plan against such obstacles. We should seek other roads and bide our time."

"What if I removed one of these obstacles? What would you say then?"

Zaganos looked at the sultan, puzzled. "What do you mean?"

"Ride with me, Pasha, and I will show you." Mehmet spurred his horse into a gallop, and Zaganos quickly followed, struggling to keep up with the superb young horseman.

They rode at a brisk pace for several hours, resting their horses only briefly and talking little. Zaganos tried to inquire again several times, but the sultan would only respond with a mysterious smile. As twilight approached they crested a tall hill and reached the vast expanse of the Black Sea below them.

Zaganos gasped in surprise. Spread before them in every direction, as far as the eye could see, was a vast shipyard. Thousands of workers streamed busily over at least a hundred ships in various stages of construction. A number of completed ships lay at anchor on freshly built docks extending out into the sea.

"My Sultan, how can this be?" asked Zaganos.

"This is my fleet. Do you like it?"

"I don't know what to say. Of course, it is amazing. A gift from Allah. But I don't understand."

"With a fleet we can attack the single walls of Constantinople by sea, can we not? And we can stop relief fleets from arriving from the west. Does this not address the council's primary concerns? Aid from the West? Invulnerability by sea?"

Zaganos was stunned.

"My Sultan, this fleet may answer those questions, at least some questions. But how did you build it in just a few weeks? This is impossible."

"I started construction of this fleet months ago, Zaganos. I knew the council would never approve my plans unless I overcame all of the obstacles that Halil would put in my way. I knew I would have to make my own destiny in this."

"How will your fleet operate? We do not have sufficient sailors, do we? That is a constant problem for us, our inexperience at sea."

"I have recruited sailors from throughout the Black Sea and the Mediterranean. Our admiral is a Bulgarian named Baltaoglu. He has extensive experience in Western naval strategies and will lead our fleet to victory over the Greeks."

"He is Christian, or was? Can he be trusted?"

"You, too, were Christian, my friend. Can I trust you?"

Zaganos was thoughtful for some time, looking out over the vast construction. Finally he spoke again.

"My Sultan, you have solved only one problem, the problem of the sea. This does not stop aid from the West if it comes in full force, it does not stop Hunyadi, and it does not help us against the land walls. I do not think you will convince Halil. He will brush this aside. He is still far too strong with the council. He thinks he is secure and can challenge you, if not openly, at least through subtle resistance."

Mehmet smiled. "Do not worry my friend. I have other surprises in store for our grand vizier."

THURSDAY, DECEMBER 7, 1452

A week later, Mehmet had returned to Edirne and the palace. The flickering darkness of his room kept him calm. He was awake and alert even at this late hour. The palace slept, all save a few guards and servants. He was filled with anticipation. He had savored this moment for a very long time, his opening move in a game that would risk everything. He was ready, he had prepared and was willing to gamble, even if he was gambling with his life.

He heard a soft knock at his door. "Come," he commanded.

The grand vizier cautiously entered the room. Halil was still dressed in his sleeping robes and looked disoriented and fearful. He carried a plate filled with gold coins, which he proffered to Mehmet.

The sultan smiled to himself. So Halil feared him after all. An ancient custom required that trusted servants of a sultan bring a gold offering if ever they were summoned in the middle of the night. The gold was a last gift, a bribe to show loyalty and to beg for their life. Mehmet was surprised Halil would be afraid. Didn't he control the council against him? Wouldn't the council depose Mehmet and likely kill him if he acted against Halil? *He thinks I'm stupid*, Mehmet realized. *He believes me so reckless that I might kill him without realizing the consequences. How little you understand me, Halil. But you will. You will.*

Mehmet waved aside the gold and beckoned his grand vizier to come farther in and take a seat.

Halil cautiously took his seat, looking around him to see if an assassin would lunge out of the darkness. Mehmet poured Halil some water. Halil took it and drank slowly, as if the liquid were assuredly poisoned. The atmosphere was tense.

"How may I serve you, my Sultan?"

"By now I'm sure you have heard about my little building project on the Black Sea. Surely you will now agree we can proceed with a siege?"

Halil drew himself up to speak. He clearly had considered this issue and prepared his response. "My Lord, I must still respectfully disagree."

"Why? Wasn't the city taken by the Latins by sea? Isn't that the key to the city?"

"With respect, Sultan, we are not the Latins. They have ruled the seas for hundreds of years. They are masters of it. I agree completely with your decision to build a fleet. We should learn the ways of the sea if we are to rule the world. But we cannot simply build these boats and set them on the waters expecting to dominate. We will have to learn the art of warfare over time."

"So you do not think we can take the sea walls?"

"My Lord, the Greeks still have a fleet. There is also a small fleet at Galata across the Golden Horn. Although this is a Genoese rather than a Greek city, we must expect they will rush to the defense of the Greeks in the event of an Ottoman fleet invasion. The Greeks have their terrible Greek fire, which will burn our ships to the waterline. An attack by sea would be hopeless."

"So you believe a fleet does nothing for us?"

"On the contrary, my Sultan, a fleet is a tremendous advantage for us, both now and in the future. Again, I urge you to continue to build the fleet. Use it in the Black Sea against the Greeks and the Georgians. Let the captains and men gain experience. In the meantime, you can generate some victories against the Bulgarians and the Serbs, and against the Greeks in Morea. Once you've won some triumphs, and perhaps have let a decade or so pass, we might be in a position to attack Constantinople.

"Again, I recommend against an attack on the city. Even with everything I have described, you still are in danger of uniting the Latins against us if you lay siege to the city. And no matter what, you still face the land walls. In a thousand years, no one has breached them. How many nations and leaders have fallen beating themselves uselessly against the walls of Constantinople? The city is a curse. Let it rot on the vine.

"Your father tried to take the city and failed. He was *wise* enough to realize that the city had no power over him. He could simply let it fall on its own in its own time. They are insolent, I agree. Raise their tribute even further, the faster to bleed them to submission."

Mehmet looked closely at Halil. "So that is it, is it? We can never move against the city until we can solve the problem of the land walls and stop the Latins from coming to Constantine's aid?"

"Yes, my Lord. You can try, but in my opinion, you must fail. Again, your father was one of our greatest leaders. He won victory after victory. He succeeded in everything he set his hand to, but . . ."

"But he could not take the city."

"No. Even your father could not take it. In the prime of his life, with his people behind him and the full confidence and resources of the Ottomans, he could not take it."

"Thank you, Halil, I will think on what you say."

The grand vizier smiled and rose to his feet, bowing to the sultan. Mehmet rose to walk him out. The grand vizier turned and walked to the door, reaching to open it.

A strong hand stopped Halil. He turned to see Mehmet close to him, menacing. The sultan reached down and took the plate full of gold from Halil. He moved his head near and whispered in the grand vizier's ear, "Give me what I want, Halil. Give me Constantinople."

Halil shuddered. He seemed to hesitate.

The Sultan continued, still whispering. "If I give you peace with the West and I deliver you the walls, you will give me the city."

Halil stared at the sultan for a moment. He seemed about to leave. Finally he nodded once, and turned away, fleeing quickly into the darkness.

FRIDAY, DECEMBER 8, 1452

The following day Mehmet rose early and breakfasted on fruits and bread on his balcony overlooking Edirne. He loved the city. In many ways it was a better capital than Constantinople. Because it lay inland, there could never be a surprise fleet appearing on the horizon to menace the city. Laying siege to Edirne would be difficult, and Mehmet would be able to draw troops both north and south to lift any such effort.

But Edirne was not a great city. Constantinople not only stood strategically between two seas and two continents, it also was a tremendous symbol. The city was the successor to Rome, the seat of the Eastern Roman Empire for a thousand years. The ruler of Constantinople was the successor to the empire itself. The city also contained the great cathedral of St. Sophia, the greatest church in the Christian world. To convert St. Sophia into a mosque to the glory of Allah was worth capturing the city all by itself. To capture the last capital of the Roman Empire and take on the mantle of the Romans would make Mehmet master of both East and West.

From there he could sweep west and capture Rome. He could also sweep north and take Hungary and the German kingdoms. The rest would fall quickly. Europe would be his. He could bring the true faith to these misguided sons of Christ. The Ottomans would rule the world. All of this was in his grasp. He had simply to take the city and all else would fall into place.

He eventually rose, dressed, and made his way to the council hall, where his ministers already awaited him. Zaganos was there, along with the Grand Mufti, and of course Halil. He had assembled his entire council for the first time since September to review the status of the sultanate.

After the bows and exchanges of pleasantries, Mehmet asked Halil to give a summary of the current disposition of the Ottoman forces and the information he had obtained about Constantinople.

Halil bowed again to the sultan. "Thank you, my Lord. I would first note how impressed we all are by your forward thinking in beginning the construction of a fleet. Why you felt the need to do so secretly was somewhat more of a mystery—however it is *of course* your prerogative as Sultan to do as you please."

There was some murmuring, and Mehmet sensed not everyone approved of the vizier's statement. Or rather, a number of ministers approved of the grand vizier's point.

Halil continued. "As discussed, the fleet should be utilized for operations in the Black Sea while we concentrate on some small-scale operations in the Balkans, or perhaps in Anatolia. We then should—"

"Why not attack Constantinople now?" asked the sultan.

Halil looked up at the interruption, taken aback. "I don't understand, my Lord. We just agreed yesterday that it was far too premature to proceed with such a—"

"No, Halil, we agreed that if I could solve the issue of the land walls and ensure peace with the West, then you would wholeheartedly support my proposal to attack the city. Isn't that true?"

The grand vizier didn't respond. He looked around the room slowly as if attempting to determine what to do. He exchanged glances with several council members of the old guard. They could not communicate directly here. Mehmet knew that, which was why he had cornered Halil and why he was springing this plan on them here and now.

"Isn't that true?" demanded Mehmet.

"Of course it is true, my Sultan." Halil chuckled nervously. "But come now, do you have flying carpets to whisk us over the walls?" Several people laughed. Mehmet stared around the room until there was quiet again.

"It is settled then. We will attack."

"But, my Lord, how do you propose to work these miracles?"

Mehmet shouted for a servant, who brought in a parchment rolled up and sealed with wax. Mehmet took the parchment, broke the seal, and displayed it to the room. "This is a treaty from John Hunyadi. I have given him free reign in Hungary and a promise of ten years of peace in exchange for his commitment that he will not come to the aid of the Greeks. He has promised us he will not interfere."

Halil went white with shock. He clearly had not expected this turn of events. "That is quite the surprise, my Lord, but Hunyadi is not the West. He is but part of the problem."

Mehmet pulled out two additional documents concealed in his robes. "Here are treaties from Venice and Genoa. They will not interfere. I have promised them trade rights in the new city under more favorable terms than the Greeks have given them. In addition, they look forward to unrestricted trade through the traditional routes. Our increasing pressure on Constantinople has badly hurt the Latin trade over the years. These infidels would rather sell out their Christian brothers for gold than come to their aid. That is why we will rule them all someday."

Halil was even more surprised. He looked around again, assessing support. He was clearly unprepared for these new developments. Mehmet was very pleased. He had cornered Halil last night and forced him to commit to specifics. Now he was forcing the same thing before the council.

"So, Halil, you can see that I have neutralized to a great extent any potential threat from the West. I know they can be unreliable. I know they may break treaties, but their promises should hold them for a while. At least long enough for us to be able to take the city."

"Our Sultan has assured peace with the West, and he has solved the problems by sea. Can we not now proceed?" asked Zaganos. There was a murmuring of assent from the younger members of the council. "Surely this is Allah's will? It is time."

Halil glared at Zaganos and then returned his attention to the sultan. He bowed. "My Lord, you seem to have thought of everything. How can we not all be impressed with your passion and your cleverness? But of course there remain the land walls. At the end of the day, nothing matters if we cannot breach the walls. And as you know, no hostile army has ever crossed the land walls of Constantinople. Even cannonballs bounce harmlessly off of them. What will we do? Spend a season crashing against them, as we have done over and over? Losing twenty men to every Greek we kill? That is what has happened each and every time in the past. And to what end? Eventually the Latins will break their treaties and come to Constantine's aid. Has not Hunyadi already broken a sacred oath made with your father? How can we trust him now? And what is true of the Latins is even truer of the Persians and even our Muslim brothers in Anatolia. Show but a moment of weakness, and they will strike. They do not yet fear you, my Sultan, as

I've argued again and again. Let us build that fear. Then we can worry about this pestilent city."

"Do you deny you have promised me the city if I can solve the problem of the land walls?"

"I . . . I do not, my Lord, but what does this matter? We talk of fantasies. Let us talk instead of what we can—"

"It is settled, then," said Mehmet. "When I bring you the walls of Constantinople, you will support me, Halil, and all the rest of you will as well."

Mehmet stared out over silence in the council. No one answered. Many could not meet his gaze. He played a very dangerous game. He had maneuvered Halil into a corner, but never is a snake more dangerous than when it has no place to which it can escape.

"All of you, come with me."

Mehmet led the council members out of the throne room and through the twisting halls of the palace. He could hear the whispering behind him.

He enjoyed this moment. A moment of triumph. He had learned so much from the earlier betrayals. Knowledge and secrets gave him power over these men, men in most cases older and with more experience than he. He had learned that it was not enough to be sultan. A sultan was just another man. He could be controlled, even killed, by any group of people who gained power over him. Like the empire itself, if he showed a moment's weakness he would be devoured. He had learned that instead he must be the one to dominate men. He had learned that fear and secrecy, as well as flattery, bribery, and kindness, were tools he must use in equal measure.

He led the men out into a large courtyard. A new person stood waiting, bowing as Mehmet and the council came into view. He was an older man, obviously European, with thinning white hair.

"This is Orban. Orban is a Hungarian with some very special talents. He attempted to offer these services to Constantine recently, but our poor unfortunate friend could not afford them, so he came here instead. He named a sum for his services. I gave him much more than he asked for. I think you will agree this was a wise decision."

Orban bowed again. "The Sultan is too kind to me. Are you ready for the viewing?"

Mehmet nodded.

"Come with me." Orban led the council farther along the courtyard and then through open air corridors to a second courtyard deeper within the palace. The enormous courtyard had been converted to a series of open-air forges. Dozens of men worked at the forges, beating metal over fire into various shapes. However, it was not the forges that held the council's attention. In the center of the courtyard stood a partially assembled cannon. The cannon was enormous, many times larger than any such weapon the Ottomans had previously possessed. It was nearly thirty feet long and three feet in diameter.

Mehmet looked around, savoring this moment. His council was stunned, speechless. Even Zaganos was staring wide-eyed, shaking his head slightly.

"Orban, will this cannon breach the walls of Constantinople?"

"Yes, my Lord. There are no walls made by man that can withstand this cannon. It will lob a cannonball made of stone or iron and weighing two thousand pounds more than a mile. It will assuredly breach the walls. The question is not whether, it is only when. There are drawbacks. This weapon will require at least fifty people to handle it, hundreds to move it, and probably will only be able to be fired ten times a day."

"When will it be ready for a test?"

"Less than sixty days, my Lord. And I am also working on a number of smaller cannon. You will have the greatest artillery force in the world in a matter of months."

Mehmet turned to Halil and the rest of the council. "We will test this cannon, and when the test is successful, we will meet again and we *will* decide to attack the city. It is Allah's will."

Halil stood staring at Mehmet with barely concealed anger. The sultan thought for a moment the older man might leap at him. He couldn't be that stupid, could he? Mehmet savored the vision of the vizier attacking him. He could lop off Halil's head and watch his body shake and roll around on the ground. The sultan silently willed it, praying for his vizier to lunge. Unfortunately he did not.

After a time Halil bowed, turned, and walked away. He was joined by a group of the elder councilors, scurrying away no doubt to plot their next move. Mehmet had outmaneuvered them today. He had won a battle, but not the war. He had permission now to attack Constantinople, assuming Orban's cannon worked. This, however, did not assure him victory. He had simply achieved the right to try where everyone else had failed for a thousand years.

Doubts sprang up even in his excitement. What if he failed to take the city? Had he just brilliantly paved the path to his own doom? He had no other choice. He must live under Halil's boot or he must forge his own path. He would take all or he would lose all. Allah protect him.

CHAPTER FOUR

TUESDAY, DECEMBER 12, 1452

Constantine lay in bed with Zophia, his head on her bare stomach. They clung to each other in the darkness, afraid each moment might be their last. He needed her strength, her companionship, and he dreaded the news he had to share with her, news he had held from her far too long. He could not wait any longer. She would know tonight and he feared it would change everything. He had to tell her now.

"Zophia, dear, you know how much I love you."

"Mmm, yes, you just showed me again." She said sleepily, with satisfaction.

"I have something I must tell you, and I'm afraid you are going to be unhappy with me."

He felt her stiffen. "What is it?" she asked.

"I . . ."

"Don't tell me you have given in to that bastard Sphrantzes and you are going to marry that whore of a princess?" She pushed the sheets away and got out of bed, standing and staring accusingly at him.

"No, no, it's not that, it's . . ."

"What is it then?" She still sounded angry, although Constantine could tell she was relieved.

"Perhaps something just as bad. My dear, I have been trying to tell you about this for days. I haven't been able to find the words. I don't know how to make this better so I am just going to say it. Tonight at St. Sophia, Isidore is implementing the Union of the Churches, on my authority. He will be giving the Latin mass."

Zophia took a couple of steps back and turned as pale as the sheet she was holding. She looked as if Constantine had struck her a blow.

"No, Constantine. What terrible news. How could you do such a thing! You tell me you are not marrying a princess. You have made my body happy. But now instead you wish to destroy my soul? How could you! We will give in to these wretches? To what end? We give up our souls to eternal damnation? For what? A few more years of life on earth? This city will fall eventually, Constantine. You must know that. It is only a matter of time. You cannot do this. The people love you. They trust you. If you do this, you lose them, you lose everything. You cannot protect this city forever. But you can protect the people."

"I have to, Zophia. It's not even my decision. Our representatives at the Council of Florence already endorsed this . . ."

"Endorsed it, yes. Implemented it? No. It's been almost a decade, Constantine. In all of that time, there has been no effort to actually make the people follow the Latin ceremonies. The people will rebel. At the best, they will refuse to defend the city and they will never forgive you. At the worst, they will depose and kill you. You must stop the Union."

Constantine rose out of bed and slowly walked toward Zophia, putting his arms on her shoulders. "My dear, you do not know what you say. Do we not possess the Doctrine of Energies? We Easterners have always taken doctrine with a grain of salt, yes? If we do not agree with every part of the Latin mass, we can take the good and ignore the bad. Is that not our way?

"I know the people will be angry. Maybe they will even hate me. I want to save them. I want to save the city. I need Western aid. You have no idea how weak we are. How poor. You must believe in me. You must trust me. I cannot do this without you, Zophia."

"Constantine, I'm begging you not to do this. You won't lose me if you let this happen, but you will lose a part of me. I love you, I will stay with you, but I beg you to keep our faith. If it is God's will to let the city fall, then let it happen. At least we die a pure death, untarnished. I know you have had to live a life of compromise, but some compromises cannot be made. Please, dearest, please do not."

"I love you. I love you." He was crying now, shaking uncontrollably. She held him tightly; he could feel her love and comfort. They did not speak for a while. Finally she let him go and stood near him, staring deeply into his eyes. "Zophia, my dear, I must do this. Please pray for me; please support me."

He could see her deep disappointment. He was torn apart inside. Was there never an easy answer for him? Could he not have the luxury of one choice that did not cost him dearly? But he knew he had to do this. Could he let the Turks in to rape and enslave Zophia? He did not feel the Union destroyed his faith or the faith of the people. It was a compromise when nothing but compromises were available. Five hundred years ago, if a pope had demanded something of a Greek emperor, the emperor might well march on Rome with a massive army and sack the city, once again imposing the imperial will on the Latin church. Those days had passed. The West was rising and the East was all but gone.

Zophia was right. He should not force this change on the people. She was always right. But he had no choice. He knew in his heart that Mehmet was coming. He had no money, no men, and the walls were crumbled and in disrepair. If he did not force this, then the city had no chance. He must live with the disappointment of the people. In time they would forgive him.

"I'm so sorry. I know you are right, but I must do this. Will you come with me tonight to St. Sophia? Will you stand by my side through this mass? I don't know if I can face it without you. You talk of souls,

Zophia. You are my soul. Please come with me. I know I am asking too much of you."

She hugged him again, sobbing. "I can't, my dear. I can't be there for you in this. I'm so sorry. I love you so much, but I can't sacrifice my soul, even for you. Go do this if you must. When you are done, I will be here. Hurry back and I will do everything I can to make things better for you."

Constantine held her tightly. It was unfair to ask her to go with him. This was his shame, not hers. Was she right? Should he just let the city fall, or leave it to God? How could he do that? His entire life had been devoted to keeping the city safe, his people safe. He had done this against impossible odds, without real allies or friends. He had no money. No resources. Betrayal everywhere. The Ottomans constantly required additional annual tributes, the relinquishment of more towns. How could he stop fighting now?

"I understand, dear. I'm not mad. I love you. I will face this alone. I deserve nothing better. I will face this, and I will come back to you. I will need you terribly tonight."

She smiled. "I will be waiting for you."

Hours later he reappeared at her door. He was grief stricken, exhausted, broken. He walked stiffly inside and into her arms. She kissed him deeply, and he could feel her taking away the pain, covering him in her love.

"Tell me," she said.

"It was worse than I could even imagine. Isidore announced the Union at the beginning of mass and invoked the name of the Pope. You could hear the gasps ringing through the cathedral. I saw people staring at me, people I knew. I have never been looked at like that before. They were wounded, dismayed. They weren't angry. They were hurt. People started to leave. Notaras came over and placed a hand on my shoulder. He gave me a slight squeeze, but then he left as well. By the end of the mass, there was almost nobody left."

"I'm so sorry."

"That's not the worst. As I was riding over here people turned away from me. They always cheer and smile. Now they won't meet my eyes. You were wrong, Zophia—they do not hate me. They aren't angry. They are crushed. They are betrayed."

"It is a terrible thing you have had to do, Constantine. But if I was wrong about the people's reaction, perhaps I will also be wrong about the ultimate effect. If the people are only sad, hopefully they will forgive you. Let us pray they do, and pray that we receive the aid you have paid so dearly for."

"The aid will come. The pope has promised it." Constantine wondered if he truly believed that. The Greeks had been forced for two hundred years to beg for help from the West. They received only scraps, and it seemed less with each passing year. Still, any crumbs would weigh heavily in the defense of the city. If you have nothing, a trickle is as much as a flood. He prayed silently that the Union would have a meaningful effect, and that for once the aid from the West would be significant and immediate.

MONDAY, JANUARY 15, 1453

The New Year came and passed. After their initial shock regarding the Union, the people had seemed to settle down into a dull melancholy. Constantine, however, noticed a definite change in his relationship with the populace. They still loved him, they would still work with him, but they treated him like a wounded child treats a parent who has punished them for something they did not do. He felt their sadness in everything he did, and even in his relationship with Zophia. She loved him, she had repeatedly voiced her support for him, but she was disappointed. She was a little more distant. Some of the fire and passion of their love had died with the Union.

Constantine rode through the city alone under a cold, windy drizzle, considering this issue. He had nothing yet to show for his sacrifice. After the mass, he had immediately sent a ship with an ambassador to Rome. He was very hopeful that he would now receive the full support and resources of the papacy, which carried with it the promise of aid from all the Latin states. But it would be months before news would reach him from this ambassador, and perhaps even longer before any material aid would arrive.

Fortunately, the church was still cooperating with him. The Eastern clergy would no longer set foot in St. Sophia, nor would most of the people, but he was receiving some money and supplies from the various churches in the city, which he was able to then turn over to Notaras to help pay for soldiers, to buy food, and to work on the city walls. In even better news, the Turks had never left their camps near Edirne. Constantine now hoped that this had just been a ruse on Mehmet's part, and that the Sultan had no intention of attacking the city. With any luck, he would be able to repair the walls, build his food reserves, hire additional mercenaries to protect the city, and wait for a crusade from the West and Hungary to crush Mehmet. With tremendous luck, that would mean wiping out the Ottoman presence in Europe as a whole.

Grand Admiral Notaras had also begun work on a sea defense that had served the city well in the past. The extreme tip of Constantinople jutted out to the north toward the shores of Galata, across the Golden Horn from the city. Notaras was reconstructing an enormous chain stretching from Constantinople on one side to be attached to the walls across the Horn at Galata. The chain consisted of huge iron links, connected periodically to wooden booms. When the chain was completed, it would cut off the Golden Horn, vastly reducing the amount of sea wall that would have to be defended and allowing ships and supplies to flow freely from Constantinople to Galata. The Genoese, who controlled the independent city, had agreed to connect the chain to the wall of Galata at substantial risk to their own city, as the Ottomans could hardly fail to note their cooperation with the Greeks.

Constantine finally felt he could breathe. Aid from the West must appear soon, and he was making progress with the city defenses. And while he feared the worst, it was possible the Turks might not be coming after all.

Constantine completed his tour of the city. Drenched, he eventually reached the palace. He changed his clothes, ate a small meal, and entered the council hall for an update. Sphrantzes and Notaras were already waiting for him. Constantine met with these two close confidants on a daily basis, but convened his greater council for only a weekly meeting.

"How's the weather?" asked Notaras.

"Lovely." Constantine laughed. "It's Greek weather. The Turks would never attack us under these conditions. The roads are a muddy mess."

Constantine noticed Sphrantzes did not join in the joke. He stared at the table without comment, flicking fruit back and forth across his plate.

"What's wrong, my friend?" Constantine asked, grabbing a fig off Sphrantzes's plate and tossing it in the air in an attempt to lighten the mood.

"I bear terrible news, my Lord."

Constantine felt his stomach heave. What now? Couldn't he enjoy a moment with things going at least a little right? "What is it?" he demanded.

"I wish I had only one piece of bad news, my Lord, but I have two."

"What could it be now?" repeated the Emperor.

"First, my Lord, I have news of the Venetians captured last fall when their ship was sunk. They were ushered before Mehmet after a period of imprisonment. Mehmet ordered them beheaded. They were all executed."

"Terrible. Spread the news through the city. The people must remember what we are dealing with, and what will happen to them if the city ever falls. I hope that's the worst news."

"No, my Lord, unfortunately it is not. The other news is far graver. Apparently that Hungarian Orban who came here last year searching for work has instead been retained by the Turks. He has constructed a number of cannon, including a huge monster, larger than any cannon ever constructed. This cannon was tested ten days ago. It lobbed a giant ball a mile or more and caused a huge crater outside Edirne. This weapon could potentially tear our walls apart. Without our walls, we cannot hold the city. I have to surmise that the construction of this monstrosity can only be for the purpose of attacking the city. I predict the Turks will move against us in March or April, as soon as the roads are sufficiently dry and firm."

Constantine could not believe it. Must his life be filled with impossible odds and unfortunate surprises? He knew the Turks had cannon, but they were small and unreliable. While they made tremendous noise, they blew up and killed their crews more often than they did any real damage. These smaller cannon might have posed a risk to some of the buildings beyond the walls, or against his forces in the open field, but not against the city walls themselves. Constantinople could withstand any siege, against any size army, if the walls remained intact. But if the walls were breached, the city would fall to the Turks. He had nothing like the number of troops he would expect Mehmet to have. He might be able to field fifteen or twenty thousand men against probably two to three times that number. They would never be able to survive in the open against the Turks. Constantine considered all of this while he kept his face impassive. He knew he must encourage even his closest advisors.

"Thoughts on this, Notaras?"

Notaras had remained silent thus far, considering the question before he answered.

"I still don't think these rumors are guaranteed to be true. Even if the cannon *was* actually as powerful as Sphrantzes says, they might be intending to use it for the defense of Edirne, or for operations to the north or even in Anatolia. But let's assume Mehmet intends to use it against the city. No weapon has ever made any real impression on our walls. They would have to transport the cannon to the city, a distance of almost one hundred and fifty miles. Even when it gets here, we don't know if it will work. It might explode at the first shot. Finally, if it does work, that doesn't mean it will breach the walls. I have no idea what kind of cannon would be needed to break down our walls. Perhaps no cannon could do so.

"It is grave news, my Lord, but it is not the end of all things. It is but one piece of bad news among so much that we have had, yet we still sit here and Mehmet still cannot get in. We must plan, we must pray, and if the cannon destroys the walls, then we must fight our best and hope for a miracle."

Constantine nodded in agreement. He smiled to himself. They all knew how desperate the situation now was. But Notaras was correct: The circumstances had been so grave for so long, yet they still possessed the city. He must pray for further miracles.

"My Lord, surely now you will agree to at least begin discussions with the Georgians regarding marriage and potential aid," said Sphrantzes. "Clearly the situation has changed. We need support now."

"You're an idiot!" said Notaras. "The Emperor has refused you again and again. Why do you persist, when you know it only causes him pain?"

"Loukas, my friend, don't blame Sphrantzes for looking for solutions. I must seek aid and miracles where I can find them."

Constantine thought again about the marriage proposal, as he had done over and over. Sphrantzes had been pushing a marriage for more than a year now. The King of Georgia was not all-powerful, but he possessed a sizable army and a fleet. If Constantine married his daughter, surely he could expect aid in the event of an attack, particularly if the Princess was already living in Constantinople when the siege began.

The problem was Zophia. If he made this proposal, he would lose her. She was the only person in his life he truly loved. The only person he could share with, to whom he could show his true self. Must he give that up as well? He realized with great reluctance that he could not ignore any possible chance for aid. It would take some time to make the arrangements. He could always retract the offer later if the city was safe.

He made his decision.

"You may send an inquiry to the Georgians, and find out what aid they would send if I married the Princess Ariana. They must understand this aid would have to be immediate. Under no condition is anyone to speak of this publicly. We will wait to hear back from them before we make any final decisions on the subject."

Both men nodded, clearly understanding that Constantine did not want this information to get back to Zophia. He was greatly conflicted about this decision but also stunned by the news of the new threat to the city walls. Could he ignore any possible avenue of relief for Zophia's sake? She would probably never know, and if he ultimately had to tell her, at least he could delay that disclosure until he knew whether it would be worth the sacrifice. He knew he was betraying her a second time. He hoped she would forgive him and understand why. But he knew she would not. Was it wrong to keep the information from her until he knew more? Of course it was. It was wrong, and it was selfish. He needed her, though. Needed her as long as she could be by his side. He wanted one person in the world who would love him regardless of his decisions. He knew this was naïve. Constantine just hoped that if she ever learned the truth, she would forgive him, even if she never talked to him again.

MONDAY, JANUARY 29, 1453

January came near its end with no sign of any aid. The church and public donations had stagnated. Work on the land walls had to be greatly cut back in order to save money. Constantine still had several crews rebuilding portions of the wall, but no work could yet be done on the Foss, and there were still large cracks and even several holes in the walls. He was upset with himself for not completing this reconstruction years ago, but there were never enough resources, and always crises to deal with. What little money he was able to generate from taxes and trade tariffs was applied to the substantial annual tribute he paid to the sultan, supposedly to keep the Turks at bay.

He spent the morning inspecting the work on the land walls and looking out over the valley beyond the walls, searching for Turkish scouts. After the inspection, he made his way to Zophia's house for lunch and invited her to ride on an inspection of the sea walls near the tip of the city.

They rode slowly through Constantinople, taking their time, enjoying each other's company. The sun was out and warm on their faces, unusually so for the time of year. They rode past the towering St. Sophia, the great cathedral, the Church of the Holy Wisdom. St. Sophia had been the largest building in the world for more than a thousand years. It towered above the city, the massive dome rising, as if suspended from heaven, more than 180 feet above the marble floor at the center of the sanctuary.

Eventually they arrived at the Acropolis near the crumbling ancient palace of the city, where they could look out over the walls to the Asiatic shore. The water was serene on the light-winded day. They looked north over the Golden Horn to the walls of Galata. They could make out the sea chain, nearly completed now, stretching out over the Horn. To the northeast, the Bosporus extended across to Asia. To the south, the Sea of Marmara reached out of sight on its long path to the Gallipoli Peninsula and out to the Aegean Sea.

To his surprise, Constantine noticed several masts on the extreme horizon to the south. He pointed them out excitedly to Zophia.

"Oh no, could it be the Turks?" she asked.

"Not coming from that direction, dear. This could be what we are waiting for, a relief fleet from the pope! We are saved!"

They stood together counting the ships as they appeared on the horizon. Constantine's hopes fell as he saw there were only three. Still, could this be an advance guard of a much larger fleet.

They sat for hours together, laughing, hopeful, watching the ships move closer and closer to the city. Eventually the galleys moved past the point of the peninsula and tacked to the southwest into the Horn until eventually arriving at the city harbor.

Constantine and Zophia rode from the Acropolis along the sea walls and watched the ships dock. They held back for a few minutes to make sure the passengers were in fact friendly, then they dismounted and made their way to the pier.

"Who is in charge here?" asked Constantine.

A tall, middle-aged man with dark hair and a beard stepped off the ship. "I am."

"Who are you?"

"I am Giovanni Longo di Giustiniani; who are you?"

"He's the emperor," answered Zophia.

Giovanni was obviously surprised to meet the emperor right at the dockside. He bowed low and ordered the men on the ships to do the same. He then stepped forward and bowed low to Constantine.

"Where do you come from?" asked Constantine. "Did the pope send you?"

"The pope? No. I am Genoese, but I didn't come from Genoa. I came of my own accord. I have late been of the island of Chios. I am a soldier and have fought in many battles. I have heard rumors of the danger to Constantinople and I raised a company of men to come to the relief of the city."

Constantine was surprised. A private citizen had raised a force for the city without any requirement from a king or prince? He was both pleased at the admirable effort of Giovanni and hopeful that if the threat to the city had moved this man to assist, additional help must be on the way from other individuals and leaders.

"Your help is much appreciated! How many men have you brought with you?"

"I have some seven hundred souls, ready for battle, Emperor. I have also brought money collected from a variety of benefactors. Many wealthy people on Chios donated to the cause, even if they were unable to assist in the actual battle."

Constantine smiled, relief flooding over him. He kept his composure as best he could, but he could not help showing his delight. Seven hundred men, plus money! Might they be spies? Ottomans in disguise sent to infiltrate the city? He doubted it, but he would have them watched carefully for a few days nonetheless. Even with this nagging doubt he felt renewed confidence. He could resume work on the walls, and the seven hundred men would add substantially to his military force. He wasn't sure yet exactly how many men he had for the defense of the city, but he had Sphrantzes working on a count and hoped to have accurate numbers soon.

Zophia smiled encouragement to him. He could feel her happiness too. She looked so beautiful when she was happy. He felt a tinge of guilt. It had been premature for him to send a messenger to the Georgians. Now that the aid was coming in, he hoped he could soon send a second message, saying that he had reconsidered. Zophia never needed to know he had looked into marriage.

"Your help is greatly appreciated, Giovanni. We need all the men we can find, particularly with battle experience. We may also be facing mighty cannon, which, if they are effective, we have no defense for, even with our land walls."

"My Lord, I have extensive siege experience, including with cannon. If you let me work with your engineers, I know many tricks for strengthening walls against cannon fire, and methods for quickly rebuilding breaches."

Giovanni's arrival had to be a miracle from God, thought Constantine. He needed aid, and a private citizen, with no ties to the city, appeared, having raised seven hundred men and money for Constantinople. Constantine faced the destruction of the city's legendary land walls to cannon fire, and this same man had experience in defending against that very problem. The emperor closed his eyes for a moment and uttered a silent prayer to God.

Constantine ordered a horse for Giovanni. He kissed Zophia and bade her farewell, taking off with the Genoan to immediately inspect the walls and other defenses of the city. He felt hope for the first time in a very long time.

CHAPTER FIVE

THURSDAY, FEBRUARY 1, 1453

Pope Nicholas V sat in his meeting hall in the Lateran Palace with a number of his ministers, receiving ambassadors and other dignitaries. Nicholas had become pope in 1447. He had attended the Council of Florence, where the Union of the Churches had been announced. He had worked hard to begin rebuilding the ruins of Rome, including work on his palace, on the Basilica of St. Peter, and on the Aqua Virgo aqueduct.

Rome was an eerie city in 1453, near-deserted. Once home to a population well over a million, the city now housed fewer than fifty thousand. Travelers were required to ride or walk through miles of ruins until they finally reached the central inhabited portion of the city.

Nicholas was working hard to restore Rome's former glory, for the greater glory of God. He was currently meeting with the Venetian ambassador to discuss another shadow city: Constantinople. "Tell me, what have you heard of our Greek cousins?"

"Holy Father, grim news from our representatives to the Greeks. The new sultan, who we all had such hopes would be busy for years consolidating his position, has instead already gathered an army near Edirne. There are rumors he is building cannon, including a behemoth. Constantine fears an attack at any moment and is doing everything he can to prepare the defenses of the city."

"And the Union, what of the Union? Is it true that Constantine has implemented it?"

"That is true, Holy Father."

"How have the people received the Union?"

"As might be expected, they are somewhat slow to embrace the true church. Isidore has taken over the main cathedral and leads daily masses under the Latin Rite, but few Greeks are actually attending."

"And Constantine?"

"He attends daily. He, for one, has been very honorable in his commitment. I daresay from our reports, he is not thrilled with the situation, but he has been true to his word."

"Not thrilled, aye? Well, he must do better. I am happy to hear that he is following the agreement, but he is also responsible for his people. He has not done *enough*; he must force them to attend. In a year or two, they will forget the old ways, and the true Union will be complete."

"That is sound reasoning, Holy Father. But what should we do now? What about the city?"

What to do about Constantinople? That was the question ever on Nicholas's mind. He had been prepared to do nothing. He had his own problems. Rome had suffered a huge revolt recently that he had had to put down with some bloodshed. He was surrounded by rival delegates from the Italian cities, all independent, all bitter rivals, and none to be trusted. Even more powerful were the great kingdoms: France, the Holy Roman Empire, and the Spanish kingdoms. The only power the pope held over these various princes was religious. It was a significant power, but not always omnipotent. Any of these sovereigns posed a significant potential threat to Rome.

And then there were the Turks, the greatest threat of all. Those terrible infidels. They had power far greater than any individual Christian kingdom, or even many kingdoms combined. They had either immediately or eventually crushed every force and every crusade brought against them. They were deep into the Balkans already: not deep enough to threaten Italy, but only the Hungarians and the Greeks stood in their way. Once Constantinople fell, only John Hunyadi and the Hungarians would remain as a bulwark. Still, the Hungarians were the real Christian power in the Balkans. The Greeks were hardly more than the walls of their city and a few isolated islands.

That was the reality, was it not? Any real defense of Europe must fall to the Hungarians. He must certainly do something for Constantinople, but not everything. And with God's will, the city would survive as it had miraculously done so many times. The pope turned from his contemplation to speak.

"I wrote to Venice about a relief fleet. I proposed that Venice provide a number of galleys and several thousand men-at-arms on behalf of Rome. Have you given consideration to this request?"

"Ah, yes, Holy Father, this request was debated at some length. We are prepared to assist in provisioning a relief fleet for the city, but there is the rather delicate issue of payment."

"What do you mean?"

"Well, with all respect, Your Holiness, your predecessor also requested several military aid campaigns for the Hungarians and the Greeks. Unfortunately, those bills have not yet been paid."

Nicholas was shocked. He was unaware there were debts still owed to the Venetians. "How much is due?"

"They are owed, including interest, a total of forty-two thousand ducats."

The number astounded Nicholas. He had limited funds available from the treasury, another gift from the last pope, who had spent more than he'd earned. He was stretched thin. Could he afford to pay out of his dwindling reserves to save the Greeks? What would be the cost if he did not?

"Surely now is not the time for squabbling over petty debts. If the noble Doge would simply give us some time, I'm sure we can come up with a payment plan."

The ambassador looked uncomfortable. "Father, it is most difficult for me to raise this point with Your Holiness, but I am not authorized to extend additional credit. Unfortunately, with all of our international commitments, we are simply too pressed to allow any person or state to become too deeply indebted, even the Holy See. A thousand apologies."

Nicholas had expected this answer, but he had to try. If he had been able to delay the repayment at least by a year or two, it would have been helpful. The question was whether to commit his precious resources to help the Greeks at all or not. He paused and considered the issue for a few more moments, then made his decision.

"The church must support those who support it. The return of the Eastern Church into the fold is too important for us to treat lightly. We will pay the past debt immediately, along with thirty percent of the estimated cost of a new fleet. I also ask that the Venetians contribute another force at their own cost. I will ask the same of your sister cities."

"Sister cities, indeed! A band of robbers all. You can certainly ask them, Your Holiness, but I doubt you'll get anything but excuses. Remember that it was the Genoese who ferried Mehmet's father back over the Bosporus to Europe and saved the Turks when we finally had them trapped in Asia. If you would only be willing to wholly support *our* cause, the Venetians could unite Italy for the greater glory of the church. I am sure any debts could easily be overlooked, and even forgiven, under such a circumstance. We could also provide troops to protect your lands, allowing you to focus on the spiritual world."

Nicholas had heard this speech dozens of times from different Italian ambassadors. He grew angry thinking of the debts his foolish predecessor had left him. If he didn't keep the Papal State strong, it would be swept up by one of these petty states one day. *Your protection!* Hah! *Your control, you mean.* As for supporting one of these vipers over another, any of them would kill him and sacrifice the church for power or even for a little gold.

"Thank you, Ambassador, but it is not my place to worry about kingdoms of this earth, except for our own humble lands near Rome. I very much appreciate the gesture, but we will certainly pay our debts."

The ambassador bowed. "I appreciate your handling of this sensitive matter, Holy Father. I am very encouraged, and I will do everything I can to secure an independent commitment from Venice. I will communicate back to you as quickly as possible with our progress."

Venice would build its own fleet and nothing else, unless Venice would profit directly. The same was true of Genoa, Milan, and all the rest. Still, even at a cost, the pope was providing aid to the Greeks without having to weaken his own limited military forces.

"Thank you, and may God go with you."

"And also with you, Father."

TUESDAY, FEBRUARY 6, 1453

John Hunyadi rode down a forest trail in the mountains of Hungary, traveling back from Poznony, where he had met with the Holy Roman Emperor. He had recently been named Commanding General of the Hungarian Kingdom by King Ladislaus. He rode his horse with absolute control, his muscles rippling beneath a shirt of mail.

Hunyadi was very aware of his importance to the Christian cause. He was the only commander with any real experience or success fighting the Ottomans. He knew them and he properly feared them.

He thought back on his battles with the Ottomans. He had led his knights to a victory in 1441 at Semendria against the Turkish commander Ishak Bey. He followed up this battle in 1442 with a miraculous victory against an Ottoman invasion force of eighty thousand. He had stopped this army with fewer than fifteen thousand Hungarians.

In 1444, Hunyadi led a large Hungarian force along with the king of Hungary against Sultan Murad at Varna. Hunyadi entered the battle with only a portion of his men but was still able to hold his own against a huge Ottoman army. He would have won the day and perhaps driven the Turks from Europe, but the king had taken command from Hunyadi and rashly charged the Ottoman center, losing the bulk of the Hungarian cavalry and his own life in the process.

Hunyadi had eluded the Ottomans and escaped back to Hungary. Since the battle, he had assisted in internal politics and had done everything he could to keep his people protected and strong. He still stung from the loss at Varna and would welcome a viable opportunity to attack the Ottomans again, but his first priority had to be his flock. He could not afford to gamble the flower of Hungary's youth again without significant cause.

Hunyadi had sat back during the past few years after Mehmet took the reins of power. He was ready to strike at the proper moment, but he wanted to watch this new sultan to see how he acted and reacted, what moves he made, what his strengths and weaknesses were. At thirty-six, Hunyadi was in the prime of his life, respected and feared. He was patient, waiting for the moment when he could strike again against the Turks.

As if Mehmet could sense this, he had recently contacted the Hungarian and requested neutrality in exchange for an agreement that the Ottomans would not invade Hungary again. Hunyadi had agreed but did not consider himself bound to agreements with an infidel. He would not have agreed at all except that Constantinople seemed so vulnerable, situated hundreds of miles within Ottoman territory and with few defenders or resources. If Hunyadi believed the city could hold, or even better, if the Italians would commit substantial resources to a new crusade, he would consider a new attack on the Turks.

He thought this through as he rode south with a few trusted retainers. Of course he had many problems of his own. Hungary faced challenges not only from the Ottomans but also from the Germans to the north and from the Italians. Guarding a nation surrounded by enemies with only partial natural barriers, he did not have a free hand to act without ensuring the safety of his people.

A lone horseman appeared in the distance. Hunyadi and his men halted, several moving in front of their leader and drawing their swords. The approaching horseman put his hands in the air to show he meant no threat. He called out to them. "I seek the Lord John Hunyadi. Are you Lord Hunyadi?"

"Who asks?"

"I am Gregory. I serve the emperor in Constantinople."

Hunyadi raised a pale hand and drew a lock of salt-and-pepper hair out of his eyes. He observed the Greek closely. He was young, probably twenty or less, with sandy blond hair. He was thin, and his armor and cloak seemed to swim on him. *A daring lad.* This Gregory had ridden alone hundreds of miles through hostile territory, an act of bravery that immediately endeared him to the Hungarian leader. He was careful not to show these emotions on his face.

"Approach."

Gregory rode forward slowly, keeping his hands in view. When he was within a few feet of Hunyadi, he halted his horse and bowed in the saddle. The Hungarian leader nodded slightly in response.

"What can I do for you?" asked Hunyadi, speaking Greek.

"Constantine sends his regards. He regrets he was unable to join you in your previous endeavors, as he was otherwise indisposed in the Morea."

Hunyadi knew Constantine by reputation. Gregory referred to Constantine's previous position as the ruler of the Peloponnesus. Constantine had been a capable military commander and administrator on the Greek mainland, even before ascending to the throne.

He also knew Constantine had almost insurmountable difficulties. In addition, he was a potential rival. If Hunyadi was successful at driving the Turks out of Europe, would that not mean a resurgent Greek Empire? He might replace a Turkish threat with a Greek one, and then Constantine's capabilities could quickly become a liability for Hunyadi and his people. The Hungarian leader could not afford to be idealistic. He chose his words carefully.

"I am not offended that Constantine could not join me from the Morea. He kept the Turks busy there, and that helped us indirectly. I've always admired your emperor and wished he had more tools to work with. I have watched his frustrations from afar."

"My emperor would like to invite you to become much more closely acquainted."

Hunyadi raised an eyebrow in mock surprise. He recognized where this conversation was going and his mind raced. He knew what he wanted to do, but was it the right time? Was it the right decision? He had overextended his lines stretching to Varna with disastrous results. He might not survive another daring raid into Ottoman territory, and more importantly, he might fatally weaken his own people if he failed. If he succeeded, then what?

"How might that be accomplished?" he asked.

"You are probably aware that the Ottomans appear prepared to attack Constantinople again. They have gathered a large force."

"Yes, I have heard; I've even heard from Mehmet. I have assured him in writing that I will not get involved."

"Surely you would not sit back and let the city fall?"

Hunyadi smiled to himself again. He liked this young man's nerve. On the surface he frowned and feigned offense. "I keep my own counsel and decide what I will and will not do, Gregory. Your empire has not always been an ally. What possible advantage can I gain by action?"

"I know we haven't always fought together, my Lord, but you also speak of days long gone by, days that will not likely ever return. We Greeks do not seek domination any longer. We just wish to be free in our own lands. Long now have the Turks kept all attention, yours and ours. We all fight to stop them from taking our lands. Constantinople has served as a buffer. If it is taken, where will Mehmet look next?"

Of course the Greek was correct. Constantinople had long served as a distraction to the Ottomans, with many seasons occupied by fighting Greeks or laying siege to the city. With the Greeks gone, the Ottomans would certainly look to Hungary next. But Hunyadi was not prepared to admit this.

"Perhaps Mehmet would focus on Italy?"

"Perhaps. But the Italians are masters of the sea. The Ottomans are masters of land. It is far easier for Mehmet to look north, to Buda and Pest and the crown of St. Stephen."

"True enough, at least until they are at the top of the Italian boot, aye?"

"At least until then. But can we afford to let them get there? And how much do you really have to fear from the Greeks? If they did manage to defeat the Ottomans, even if the Turks were driven from Europe and all the Greek dreams came true, would they really be a threat? They have not been a danger to Hungary for more than two centuries. How much longer would it take before they would be again? Another two hundred years? And of course they would owe you a tremendous debt."

Hunyadi smiled. "I have seen many debts go unpaid. I will not put too much stock in future promises of Greek goodwill. But I am more than somewhat interested in the future of my Turkish neighbors. What I am *not* interested in is another terrible defeat deep in Ottoman territory. Therefore, you will have to explain to me how such a defeat might be avoided."

"First of all, if Mehmet does come against the city, as it appears is likely, he will be fully committed before the walls of Constantinople. That was certainly not the case at Varna."

"True, but what if he lifts the siege to attack my forces?"

"We will send out a force to attack him from behind. He will be hit from both directions."

"That is a slight advantage perhaps, although I do not know how many Greeks are left to fight outside your crumbling walls. What else can you promise me?"

"We will have significant aid from the Italians."

Hunyadi snorted defensively in derision. "Now you are telling me tales I have heard before. I have had the promise of aid from the Italians on many occasions. I experienced Italian aid firsthand before Varna, when the Genoese sold out their Christian brothers and ferried Murad and his armies across the Bosporus in exchange for a huge sum of gold. Besides, why would the Italians help you? They look at you as heretics yourselves, hardly better than infidels."

"We have agreed to Union with the West. Constantine has declared it. The Latin mass is celebrated in St. Sophia."

Hunyadi was impressed. He had not expected that. Still, Italians betrayed other Latins as quickly as they did the Greeks. He would need more than that. "Give my compliments to Constantine for his bold decision. Convey to him that I will carefully consider this situation. The key for me will be *actual* Italian aid, not Greek promises and not Italian ones. If there is substantial aid from the West, then I will consider coming."

"I hate to ask, my Lord, but I need to be able to tell Constantine. How many men could you muster?"

Hunyadi smiled to himself again. He needed more men like this one. Maybe he should detain him and not let him waste himself dying in the city or somewhere along the way home. He was very bold. Such impertinent questions could land the messenger's head on the ground. He motioned and instantly Gregory was surrounded by men, weapons drawn. Still the Greek didn't move. *My first gift to the emperor will be returning this man to him. Assuming he is a Greek and not Mehmet's spy. I would make sure of that.* "I'm sending these men with you for your protection. They will ensure you return to the city in safety. Tell Constantine I will rally between twenty thousand and thirty thousand men. Brave souls all. But only if I come."

FRIDAY, FEBRUARY 9, 1453

Mehmet unfolded the letter again in the flickering firelight of his bed-chamber, carefully rereading the contents. He was still processing the message. Was this real or just another of the tricks for which the Greeks were so famous?

He knew the author vaguely, primarily by reputation, although he had met him a time or two in the past. Could he be trusted? Even if the letter was authentic, what was the purpose? Was it simply to ferret out his intentions?

The sultan spent several more hours carefully considering what he should do. He could not afford to reveal his plans, but he decided finally that neither could he pass up this opportunity, whatever the risk. Finally he carefully crafted his reply.

Thank you for your letter and offer. I do not know when or if I will be near the city of Constantinople again in the future, but if I am I would be happy to meet with you as you suggest. I do not know what information you could possibly supply me, as I am a peaceful man and have no intentions on your city, but I would be happy to exchange a meal with you and hear your ideas for the future of our two peoples.

Mehmet read his response over and over, carefully checking the words to be sure he had not provided any hints about his future intentions. Satisfied that the letter opened up the possibility of a meeting but revealed nothing else, he carefully sealed it and ordered one of his most trusted messengers to his room. He passed the message on and gave instructions to take the note with the greatest secrecy to Constantinople and to deliver it in private. The messenger bowed and left silently.

Mehmet smiled to himself. He enjoyed these games of intrigue, even if they went nowhere. If the message was a fake, he would lose nothing. If the contact was real, he now had potential access to vital information about his enemy and about Constantinople. The sultan lay down, satisfied with his night of labor, and fell into an immediate sleep.

CHAPTER SIX

SATURDAY, MARCH 17, 1453

Giovanni, Constantine, Sphrantzes, and Loukas Notaras were mounted outside the city walls, examining the work that Giovanni had accomplished since arriving in the city.

Giovanni was supervising the excavation of the Foss, the giant ditch that had formed the outer portion of the triple defenses of the land wall. Over time, the Foss had filled in until it was useless, not much more than a narrow ditch thick with grass. The Genoese leader, with the assistance of a troop of engineers, had worked day and night to restore the ditch. Stretching along with the walls from the Golden Horn to the Sea of Marmara, a distance of three and a half miles, the restored Foss was sixty feet wide and twenty feet deep. It extended out sixty feet from the outer Theodosian Wall. When the work was completed, the ditch would keep Mehmet's soldiers from reaching the first set of walls and would present a difficult obstacle while also leaving his men vulnerable to arrow and musket attack from the walls.

Once past the Foss, any attacker faced the imposing outer wall. The outer wall was six feet thick and twenty-five to thirty feet high, with taller towers spaced every hundred and fifty feet. The outer and inner walls were separated by a terrace. The inner and even more massive wall was on average fifteen feet thick and thirty feet high. The inner wall contained ninety-six towers spread along the distance of the wall, with a typical height of sixty feet. Both the inner and outer walls comprised nine main gates and a number of posterns that could be used for surprise sorties by the Greeks once the Ottomans were attacking.

The main gates into the city were the Charisius Gate, at the top of the sixth hill of the city, and the Gate of St. Romanus, which sat at the top of the seventh hill, with the Lycus Valley between them. These gates would likely be the main focus of the Ottoman attacks and were therefore being reinforced and rebuilt first.

Because of the limited forces available, only the outer wall was being heavily defended by the Greeks. The inner wall, which was even more formidable and would likely make the city impossible to breach, simply required too many men for Constantine to defend. This reality was yet one of many limitations he was faced with, along with limited food, a tiny fleet, and virtually no money.

"You are doing great work, Giovanni," said Constantine. "Besides the ditch, what progress have you made on the walls?"

"I am about halfway done rebuilding the walls in the areas where they were badly damaged. I also have reinforced the walls and towers with logs and dirt, which will allow them to receive and absorb the shock of larger cannonballs. Unfortunately, our resources are still very limited, and I do not know how much time we will have. Certainly the ditch will be completed before Mehmet could launch any kind of attack. As to the walls, there are no obvious breaches, but effective cannon could knock holes. We will have to be ready with reserves to keep any attackers contained until nightfall, when I can rebuild and reinforce any actual breach. With any luck at all, even with cannon, we will be able to hold the siege for a long time, years even, assuming the city has ample food."

"Don't worry about our food supplies," said Constantine. "We own the seas. The Turks have no navy to speak of. They may have been able to cut off the Black Sea, but I can reinforce the city from the Sea of

Marmara pretty much at will. As long as supplies are sent from the West, the city will have plenty to eat for as long as we need it."

"What about the Dardanelles? Do not the Turks control both sides of the straits into the Sea of Marmara?"

"They do, but as you saw when you came through, they have not closed off the straits like they have the Bosporus. And even if they tried to cut them off with forts and cannon, a fort or two may be able to stop a single ship, but never a fleet. We will be able to supply the city so long as the West actually does send aid to us."

"I think we are in an excellent position then, my Lord."

"Thank you, Giovanni. Truly you have been the miracle from God we awaited."

Sphrantzes and Notaras added their assent, and the Greeks rode back through the gates to the palace. They made their way to the emperor's council hall and after a light meal and some wine, sat down to further discuss the situation.

"He certainly has done more for us than we could have done ourselves," said Constantine.

"I am amazed at his ability," said Notaras. "I had my doubts when he first arrived, but he has knowledge none of us possess. What fortune to have someone with significant previous experience in siege warfare."

"That observation brings up a difficult issue," said Sphrantzes.

"What issue is that?"

"Well, my Lord, our friend Notaras is the commander of our forces in the city, but by his own admission is no expert in siege warfare."

"What are you trying to say, Sphrantzes?" asked Notaras.

"Candidly, and I beg your pardon, I am trying to say that I believe our emperor should appoint Giovanni overall commander of the city's defenses. I know you are going to be angry about this, Notaras, but really, we need to use the resources we have. You are more of a sailor than a soldier, and you will be needed in the Golden Horn against any navy that Mehmet might put together. We cannot afford to make mistakes in the land defenses. If Giovanni has to find you for permission to deal with an emergency, it might be too late. He has stressed again and again that it will be critical to close any breach the moment it happens. We cannot have him looking for permission from Notaras at the moment he should be commanding the attack. Not only that, but what if a local commander challenged Giovanni's authority? People need to know who is in charge, and his orders must be answered immediately and without question."

Constantine could tell Notaras was furious. He had started to interrupt Sphrantzes several times.

"What you propose is unprecedented, Sphrantzes," fumed Notaras. "I am the Megadux. It is my right and my responsibility to command *all* military forces in the city. You propose that I command the navy. What navy? Our tiny collection of ships? And against what? A couple of ramshackle boats the sultan cobbles together? I will defend the city! Giovanni can work with me. I will give orders to all our forces that he is to be obeyed as if I gave the order. *That* will be enough for everyone concerned."

"And what about the Genoese?" asked Sphrantzes. "They control Galata. We need their aid. We have a Genoan soldier, a famous one, right here in the city, right now. He knows more about warfare than all of us together. If we give him command of the defenses, it is very likely that the Genoese in Galata will come to our aid as well. Is that not another reason to give him the command?"

"You scheme and scheme against me, Sphrantzes, but you will not win out this time. Tell him, Constantine."

Constantine looked at his two friends, unsure what to say. Damn Sphrantzes! His dislike of Notaras and constant needling created dissent in Constantine's most intimate circle of friends and advisors. If he did not need Sphrantzes, and did not trust him, he would have excluded him from these meetings entirely. But Sphrantzes was cunning and practical. He had resources nobody else possessed, including spies in the Turkish camp. Admittedly, he also created problems. At the present time he had raised an issue Constantine had already inwardly considered. There were obvious and significant advantages to naming Giovanni the overall commander of the defenses. However, Constantine had intended to raise the topic with Notaras in private, and then very subtly. Now Sphrantzes had forced the issue and put the Megadux on the defensive. Now he would have to hurt his closest friend. Notaras did not deserve this; he had shown nothing but loyalty and hard work. Once again, Constantine would have to compromise a friend for the necessities of the city.

He looked at Notaras and smiled. His friend was looking at him, trying to read his expression. Constantine could see the color draining out of his face. He knew what was coming.

"Loukas, my friend. I don't agree with how this was addressed at all." He looked sternly at Sphrantzes. "However, I have been considering this issue, and I have a tremendous favor to ask of you. You know that we need every bit of aid that we can put together?"

Notaras squared his shoulders. "Yes, my Lord, I know that, but—"

"I have considered this, and I do want you to understand this decision has nothing to do with Sphrantzes. I must ask a boon of you. I wish to offer the defenses of the city to Giovanni, and the island of Lemnos as his hereditary possession if we are attacked and succeed in defending the city. I know this comes as a hard blow to you. This decision has nothing to do with your abilities. But I do feel that we may be able to obtain additional aid from Galata if we elevate a Genoan to this position. And I also believe it will be critical if we are attacked to be able to instantly defend against breaches of the walls. And after all, my friend, you *are* more of a sailor than a soldier."

Notaras looked at Sphrantzes and Constantine. He stood up and bowed to the emperor.

"Don't go, Loukas . . ."

"I accept this, my Lord. I don't have to like it. I will do whatever you wish in defense of the city. I believe you are making a mistake. You may find that others agree. I also worry about the Venetians. You may learn that they do not agree at all with this decision."

Notaras bowed again to the emperor and walked briskly out, without acknowledging Sphrantzes. Of course Notaras also had raised an important issue: The great weakness in the argument of appointing Giovanni was the Venetians. The Venetians and Genoese were ancient enemies, constantly at war, battling at sea and for control of trade with the East. Venice kept an important presence in Constantinople, including several thousand men-at-arms. The city-state also had nearly a dozen ships in the harbor of the city, ships that could aid significantly in the defense or be used to obtain provisions from Italy or the Greek islands. If the Venetians left the city, Constantinople would be greatly weakened, and certainly he would have lost all the benefit of appointing Giovanni as the leader of the defense. As always, he was forced to pick between impossible solutions. Regardless, he would have to proceed. For now he would chastise Sphrantzes for his impertinent outburst.

Constantine turned to his other advisor. "Why do you needle him so? I should turn you out in the street! I need Notaras, and I need him loyal and happy. You have taken him down at a critical time when a gentler approach would have served far better!"

"I apologize, my Lord. I thought it would help to raise a difficult issue. Notaras is now mostly angry at me, *not* at you. We both know this decision had to be made. Better for me to take the blame. If you had raised it, he would have been less angry at first, but would have resented you more for it later. Now he will blame me, and over time he will rationalize that you had nothing to do with the decision."

Constantine had not considered this. Sphrantzes was shrewd. Constantine often disliked him, but in the end his decisions were usually the best ones. He calmed down.

"As usual, you see more than all of us, Sphrantzes. Still, you should tell me ahead of time when you are springing one of your plans. I could have been prepared for the action and reconciled myself without having such a surprise."

"Again, my Lord, I thought genuine surprise would be better than requiring you to act. However, you are right. You are Lord and master here, and I presumed to act on my own accord."

"I suppose at the end of the day I cannot be mad at you. If we had the armies and wealth of old, we would not have to devour ourselves in desperation to seek any minor advantage. The people already hate me for the Union. Why shouldn't I anger my closest friends as well?"

"We shall endure, my Lord. And when this is over, we will not have to compromise for anyone."

The decision was announced throughout the city the next day. As Sphrantzes had predicted, the Genoese were delighted. They confirmed the decision to allow the sea chain to connect to the walls of Galata. They also offered private support and resources. Unfortunately, the smaller city across the Horn decided it had to maintain neutrality, at least officially.

The Venetians reacted very differently. A delegation including the Bailey, the representative of the Venetian government, came to Constantine, complaining about this official insult to their importance and contributions. The following day, a small fleet with eight hundred Venetians fled the city, heading for home. Fortunately, that was the end of the row. The remaining citizens of Venice pledged their support to Constantine and agreed reluctantly to work with Giovanni.

The Greeks were also unhappy with the decision, and Constantine could feel another strand connecting him to his people severed in the name of need. He accepted this strain, like the tension over the Union, with the same stoic fortitude. If the city was attacked and did survive, he was sure all would be forgiven. If the city fell, it would not matter.

SUNDAY, APRIL 1, 1453 (Easter)

Constantine woke exhausted. He shivered despite numerous blankets and Zophia's warmth next to him. He felt a slight tremble in the bed. The trembling increased and he realized it was another earthquake. He woke Zophia and pulled her out of the bed. They ran across the room and fell, naked, under a heavy table. The rumbling increased; a clay pitcher fell off the table and crashed to the floor. Zophia held tightly on to Constantine. After about a minute, the trembling subsided and they were able to come out.

"Why are we having these earthquakes, Constantine? What can they mean?"

The emperor was unsure. Earthquakes were unusual in the city, but this winter and early spring had seen many. The weather was also unusual for spring, cold and rainy. He knew the deeply religious people saw these unusual patterns as terrible omens. He had even heard that some blamed him for the city's ill luck, because of the Union of the Churches. Could it be his fault? What did God want from him? Was he to do nothing to save the city? If not, why was he put in this position? Was he simply cursed?

"I do not know what they mean, Zophia. At such a time as this, I think we have to look at our blessings." He smiled and kissed her. "There certainly is enough bad to worry about. I thank God for the primary blessing in my life, which of course is you."

She smiled back. "I agree. I've prayed all winter to the Virgin and to God that we would make it to this Easter morning. With God's grace, we have survived thus far. We have much to be thankful for."

"I hate to agree with you, but I suppose I must. When I heard about the Turks massing at Edirne this past fall, I thought they might attack before winter set in. Now I start to wonder if they might actually leave us alone, at least for another year."

She kissed him back. "Don't push your luck, my love. Let us be content with Easter and go from there."

"Before we are stuck in mass for hours, I have some other ideas for now . . ."

She laughed. "I suppose I must submit to your royal commands."

Later the couple left and went for a ride through the city. Despite the earthquake, the populace seemed to be in good spirits and greeted the emperor with waves and even applause. After the initial strain and unhappiness about the Union, the people had slowly warmed back up to their emperor. Their reaction to him on this particular day was even more enthusiastic. Perhaps Zophia was not the only person who had prayed that the city would be delivered to Easter.

Finally they arrived at the cathedral itself. Zophia kissed Constantine and rode slowly away. She had proved stubbornly unwilling to support him on the Union, even these many months later.

Constantine entered St. Sophia through the Imperial Gate, the massive doors just past the narthex that allowed entrance into the sanctuary. He stood and admired the great interior of the cathedral. The dome stood as if suspended from heaven, almost two hundred feet high. The sanctuary was filled with ornate mosaics and paintings in gilded frames, along with the gold and silver pitchers, candelabras, and crosses. At the top of the dome, a huge mosaic of Jesus stared down at the worn marble floor below, with paintings of four archangels on the four massive supporting arches.

Constantine noted that even for this Easter celebration, very few Greeks were in attendance. The attendees were mostly Italians and Isidore's minions. He climbed slowly up to the traditional imperial balcony above the sanctuary. He had difficulty concentrating on the mass. Constantine hoped that his people would have their souls filled on this most important day, wherever they had to go to do so. He realized he was proud of his people. He had to compromise, but they did not. And while they might be upset with him, at some level they seemed to understand that these sacrifices needed to be made.

Not that the sacrifice seemed worth it at this point. After the initial wave of enthusiasm when Giovanni arrived, the city had received little aid from the West. A few private individuals and ships had arrived, but no relief came from Rome or any other city or state. Constantine rode out faithfully each morning and each evening to the rise of land near the Acropolis, looking out over the sea walls, straining his eyes down the Marmara in hopes of spotting another fleet. The Pope had promised aid, and the sooner it arrived the better. He just hoped any assistance would arrive before the Turks besieged the city, if that was in fact their intent.

On the other hand, the city was in far better condition now to deal with any attack that might come. Giovanni had worked miracles with the walls. The Genoese in Galata, while neutral, had supplied individual soldiers and some food and supplies. The remaining Venetians had pledged their support and loyalty after the flight of the eight hundred citizens in February. In addition, there were various companies and individuals from other Frankish cities and even purportedly a visitor from the land of Scots.

A Turkish prince, Orhan, also lived in the city with his household. He was a pretender to the sultan's throne. He lived in Constantinople with financial support from the sultan, who paid to keep him out of royal business.

The previous emperor, and even Constantine, had used Orhan as a threat at times to the sultans, suggesting that if the Ottomans did not meet the demands of the Emperors, then they would turn Orhan loose and support him for the throne. Certainly this threat was unlikely during Murad's reign, but Mehmet's control of the throne was far more tenuous. If the city fell, the sultan would most assuredly kill Orhan. For this reason, Constantine could depend on Orhan's loyal support, and the support of his household.

Isidore was really working himself up today, Constantine noted. He chastised the Greeks for failing to truly embrace the Union. Constantine had to smile to himself. To whom was he preaching? The Venetians? The Genoese? Constantine was practically the only Greek there. Perhaps Isidore was directing this message to him. If so, the emperor's response was simple: *Where is your aid, Isidore? I did not sell my people's souls for two hundred archers and a little grain. If you want the Union to take root, perhaps some more material aid would be beneficial.* Constantine mused at what a strange and sad place his empire had become, begging the beggars in the west to come and save him.

The fiery lecture ended, and Isidore began the Holy Communion. Constantine rose and quietly left the Cathedral. He did not feel like receiving the Host from a Frank today, or even a Russian for that matter. Still, he felt a strange warmth and comfort. He had made it through a difficult winter, a winter constituting another few impossible months in an impossible life. By all accounts, he should have been killed years ago, when he was a hostage of Murad, Mehmet's father, or in the multitude of court intrigues and the competition for the hollow throne of the Greeks. Even during his time as the leader in the Peloponnesus, he could have died in battle or at the hands of an assassin a dozen or more times. He lived for this crumbling city and a few scraps of territory remaining to the Greeks.

What would Constantine have done with a powerful empire instead of this empty, dead shell? He had fantasized about this before. He would have married Zophia, certainly; he could have chosen anyone he wanted. Had not the great Justinian married a prostitute and made her empress with equal power? He would not have been dependent on foreign aid. He certainly would not have ordered the Union of the Churches.

Would he have been a great conqueror, leading Greek armies on the field of battle and acquiring huge new territories to bow before him and Constantinople? No, that was not like him. He would have been a man of peace, content to keep the empire and its people safe. He would have accumulated treasury reserves, maintained the city's defenses, and perhaps built another great monumental work within the city, maybe another great cathedral to mirror his St. Sophia.

Such speculation was maddening. He did not, would not ever have the power and resources of his ancestors. He must make do with far less.

On the other hand, in many ways the city was more prepared now than it had been in the previous hundred years. He still was not sure how many soldiers he had available, but he estimated the total must be close to twenty thousand. Assuming the Turks actually attacked, if Mehmet fielded double or triple that number, he was sure the city could easily hold. With some luck, *he* might even attack Mehmet after a month or two of siege, and deal the Turks a blow that would make them hesitate for a generation or two. He even fantasized about the remote possibility that Hunyadi and the Italians would join him and drive the infidels from the shores of Europe for good. He would go down in history as the greatest emperor in hundreds of years, maybe ever.

Had Augustus or Justinian faced odds like these? Or even the original Roman Emperor Constantine, who created this city from the town of Byzantium? He wondered if Gregory had reached Hunyadi again. He thought it very unlikely that the Hungarian leader would join him, but with the promise of aid from the Pope, perhaps he would. Even the threat to the Turks of an attack from the Hungarians might be enough to save the city, at least for another year.

Constantine stood outside St. Sophia, turning to admire the great cathedral. The church rose sharply into the sky. He admired the huge dome sparkling in the heavens, with the gold cross at the top. How many invading armies had looked with impotent frustration at this dome, hidden behind the impregnable walls of the city? He thanked God for his fortune and for protecting Constantinople.

As he finished his prayer, he heard the thudding of hooves and looked up to see Sphrantzes reining his horse in sharply. Constantine smiled ruefully again to himself. He had felt so at peace, and of course such moments had never been meant to last for him. He lived crisis to crisis. Such was his fate.

"Sphrantzes, my friend, happy Easter to you. What requires you to me in such haste? Did you bring me an Easter gift?"

"My Lord, a huge fleet approaches!"

Constantine smiled larger. It was after all the perfect Easter present, aid from the West at last!

"Can you tell whether they are Roman or Venetian, or are they from some other city sending aid?"

"I'm sorry, my Lord, they are not friendly. A huge Turkish fleet. They are coming up out of the Bosporus. They are too numerous to count."

Constantine felt his joy drain out of him and turn to cold despair. A Turkish fleet? How could that be? The Ottomans had certainly had a small navy in the past, but not in recent memory. Mehmet's father was almost ruined by the lack of a fleet when he was caught on the Asian side of the Bosporus without sufficient ships to ferry his forces back to Europe in the face of Hunyadi's invasion. Only Genoese greed had saved him. Now the Turks had a new navy? How had they built it so quickly, and how had Constantine not learned about it ahead of time? This news was unexpected and terrible. However this disaster had come to pass, the reality was here, and Constantine had to face it.

"Is the sea chain in place?"

"Yes, my Lord. Notaras has kept it in place constantly, except when we have ships coming or going."

"Let us go look at it for ourselves."

The emperor still held out hope that Sphrantzes was mistaken. A fleet coming out of the Bosporus did not necessarily mean a Turkish navy. The Georgians or Trebizonds might have sent a fleet to the city. Yes, these could be relief ships.

Constantine had his horse brought to him and he quickly mounted, taking off at a gallop toward the Acropolis. Fortunately St. Sophia was close to the northeastern tip of the city. Constantine was there in a matter of minutes.

Crowds had gathered and were looking out over the sea walls at the ships floating up the Bosporus toward the city. Constantine immediately saw that Sphrantzes was right. The ships flew the red banners of the Ottomans. This was an Ottoman fleet, a huge fleet. Constantine could not believe it. When had the Sultan created such a navy? There seemed to be hundreds of ships on the horizon, all heading toward the city.

He watched for hours. Zophia, Sphrantzes, Notaras, and even Giovanni all joined him to watch the ships coming closer to the city. Notaras had sent the small Greek fleet out into the Horn near the sea chain, not to challenge the Turkish forces, but to make sure they were in position in case the Turks mounted an attack on the chain itself.

Fortunately, it appeared the Ottomans were not yet ready to attack. The ships came near the chain and then turned to the south and eventually circled around, sailing in an oval pattern back past Galata on their left and down the Bosporus, where they anchored about five miles from the city. For now the Turks made no effort to menace the chain or the tiny Greek fleet standing off in the Horn.

Zophia kept her horse near Constantine's so she could hold the emperor's hand and rub his arm supportively. Tears flowed down her face and she whispered comforting words to him, words of support and love that fell on deaf ears as he contemplated this terrible turn of events.

What could he do against this fleet? He had not considered an attack by sea as a threat at all, let alone a serious one. This changed everything for the worse in an already desperate situation. Even with the sea chain, Constantinople had miles and miles exposed to the sea on the Marmara side. There were sea walls to defend the city, but they were not nearly as intricate or as strong as the land walls. These sea walls would certainly slow down any attack, but he would now have to keep soldiers posted along the perimeter of the entire city to defend against a sudden naval onslaught.

Additionally, the Turkish ships would be able to stop any aid from reaching the city, unless a relief fleet was similarly sized. Constantine had counted on supplies and reinforcements coming from the sea. Without this relief, the city could not stand a prolonged siege.

Constantinople held all the water it would ever need in a huge system of underground cisterns, but the city also needed food, particularly livestock and grain. Constantine had counted on additional sustenance arriving from the Greek islands and also hopefully from Italy. Without these fresh reserves, the city could last only a couple of months, and then only by carefully rationing the food supply. The morale of the people was critical during a siege, and now the people would be hungry as well as fearful.

The appearance of the Ottoman fleet also answered a final question for Constantine. The massing of troops at Edirne and the building of cannon was not for the purpose of an attack somewhere else. The Turks were coming to Constantinople. They were not coming to bargain for more tribute. The sultan was coming to take the city once and for all. Feeling sick, Constantine gave his friends the best possible look of encouragement and slowly turned his horse away, heading toward the palace to consider the defense of the city.

He'd had such hopes that Easter would be a beginning, but instead it was clearly an end, an end to the hope that they would be left alone for another year. Instead they would finally confront their fears. They would face the massive Ottoman military machine at land and at sea, with only the walls to protect them.

WEDNESDAY, APRIL 4, 1453

Constantine stood in a tower high above the city, one of the ninety-six towers along the inner wall of the massive land fortifications. Each tower was intended as an individual castle that would have to be attacked and defeated by any force that besieged it.

Constantine stared grimly out over the plains and watched the Ottomans slowly moving their forces into place. He was amazed. He had never seen so many men, and they moved with great organization to the sounds of drums and music. The Ottomans were legendary for their ability to move quickly and quietly, but today they announced their arrival with tremendous fanfare. They wanted to be seen.

There were tens of thousands, perhaps hundreds of thousands. He had Sphrantzes working on an accurate estimate from his spies within the Ottoman camp, but he would not know for hours, perhaps days, how many men he was facing. Giovanni stood next to him, carefully watching the disposition of the Turkish forces and the positions of the cannon that were being slowly dragged into place and secured by their crews.

"There seem to be far more than we estimated, my Lord. I would say several hundred thousand."

Several hundred thousand. The number was staggering. Constantine did not know such an army could even exist in the world. The greatest Christian army he was aware of was the Hungarian one under Hunyadi, and he could muster perhaps thirty thousand to forty thousand men in the field. How could anyone stand up to two hundred thousand?

Then he remembered that the city had withstood a score of sieges in the past. The walls were the great equalizer, and as long as the walls held, the city would hold. If they held long enough, Mehmet's men would grow frustrated, and they would leave, like every army before them had done.

Over the past few days, the Turks had spread out all along the city walls, and in the plains directly in front of Galata. The vast majority of the Ottoman forces seemed to be gathering on the crest of the two hills before the Charisius Gate and the Gate of St. Romanus, and in the Lycus Valley between them.

Constantine asked, "What of our own forces? How have you set up the defenses of the city?"

"My Lord, I set up our main defenses along the land wall, of course, and I divided up responsibility among our various nationalities and leaders. You and I will field the main force of Greeks and my Genoese here in the Lycus Valley, where we can defend the wall and both primary gates. To our left, there is a mixed force of Greeks and Italians defending the rest of the wall to the Sea of Marmara. To our right, the Venetian Bailey Minotto is defending your palace and the walls all the way to the Golden Horn. The Horn itself is defended by our fleet and also by Venetians and Genoese, and two shiploads of sailors from Crete. The Acropolis is defended by Isidore and two hundred archers. The Marmara side of the sea walls is defended by Orhan and his Turkish retainers and then by some Greek monks. As you know, our best armed and skilled fighters are here with us, including the large mobile reserve force I have created."

As they surveyed the enemy disposition Sphrantzes joined them.

"Sphrantzes, have you come to enjoy the view?"

"Not quite, my Lord. I have several items to discuss with you in private."

Constantine motioned Sphrantzes over to the opposite end of the tower, facing into the city.

"What is it now?"

"My Lord, I have completed a tally of the forces in the city."

"What are we working with? I'm hoping you have some good news for me. Did we make twenty thousand?"

"We have seven thousand defenders for the city."

"What? How can that be possible? We received reinforcements. All of the previous estimates were in the ten thousand to fifteen thousand range."

"I'm sorry, my Lord, but I have made a very careful census and there are only seven thousand."

Constantine leaned against a tower wall for support. Seven thousand! How could he defend the city with seven thousand soldiers against two hundred thousand or more? Constantine was overwhelmed. Did he have to live a cursed life? Why was there never any good news? What had he ever done to deserve this? His ancestors had ruled over a city with half a million residents. Huge Greek armies and fleets had roamed every direction on the compass, extending the power of the empire and bringing back the riches of the world. With a tenth of the former might, he could easily defend the city. What could he do now? Should he just open the gates and be done with it? Should he negotiate a surrender?

He forced himself to breathe and keep his emotions under control. He hoped the internal struggle had not shown on his face. He had to keep his composure and give as much encouragement as he could muster.

"It will be all right, Sphrantzes. I appreciate your hard work gathering this information. I am going to ride out to the sea wall defenses and inspect the forces there. Please let Giovanni know the number, but nobody else. We must keep this confidential."

Constantine maintained his composure and left the tower. He mounted and rode stoically through the streets, greeting his fellow Greeks and providing as much encouragement as he could. The atmosphere in the city had changed noticeably since the arrival of the fleet, and more so after the army appeared. The people were afraid. He could see it in their eyes. The crisis had seemed to draw them back to him. He did not encounter the disapproving looks he had seen on so many faces since the announcement of the Union, and he felt that all would be forgiven if the city was held successfully.

He eventually made his way to Zophia's house. She was surprised and delighted to see him.

"My Lord, to what do I owe this visit on such a day?"

"May I come in?"

"Of course, my love, come in."

Constantine went in and sat down heavily in a chair. "Do you have anything to drink? Something strong?" He saw Zophia's look of concern.

"I know it's not my habit, but today I need a little bit to take my mind off everything."

She didn't bother to summon a servant but instead searched the kitchen herself and finally came across a dusty bottle. She filled two glasses and brought one to Constantine. He gulped it down, scowling at the harshness of the drink. She put a gentle hand on his. He poured another glass and quickly drank it, his hands shaking uncontrollably.

"What is wrong?"

"I cannot hold the city."

"What do you mean?"

"It is impossible. I have done everything I could. I even sold my soul and the city for the Union, but it does not make any difference. I cannot hold it."

Tears streamed down his face. He needed to tell someone his fears. He had held them in for so long, hiding the full truth even from Zophia these many months. Now it was all coming out. He fell to his knees and wrapped his arms around her legs, sobbing, holding her close. He felt her hands on his back and neck, rocking him back and forth, not understanding but holding him in support.

"Constantine, I have never seen you like this. Why are you feeling this way?"

"I always feel this way. But I try to maintain hope for the city. I do not see any hope now. No real aid has come from the West. Now there is a huge Turkish fleet that will stop any aid from reaching the city, even food, let alone more men. The Ottoman army is immense, many times larger than I expected. And they have cannon. Giovanni has worked miracles and I have no doubt he will be able to repel some of the breaches, but for how long? How long before we have lost too many men? Sphrantzes just told me we have only seven thousand men for the defense of the city. I thought we had fifteen thousand or more. I cannot hold the city with seven thousand men. It cannot be done."

Zophia held him more tightly, letting him fall apart for a few minutes, giving him strength.

"Constantine, my love, you know what you have to do. There is always hope. God can and will deliver this city if that is his plan. You are the people's strength. If you lose faith, the city *will* fall. I know I am the only person you can show your fear to. It must remain that way. You must dry your tears, show your courage, and lead your people. But I ask you, for me, do not give up your faith."

He squeezed her tightly, kissing her. She was right, of course. She was always right. For this moment, this brief moment, he wanted to forget it all, let it all go. But he knew he could not. He knew he had to be strong for his people. That was why he had fled the walls to come here, so he could have his moment of weakness to better brace himself for what he must do.

"And you must restore the church, Constantine."

"What?"

He hadn't expected this. She never involved herself in his political decisions. He needed her support right now, not further judgment. Why would she choose this greatest moment of weakness to bring this up?

She repeated, "Constantine, you must restore the church. This Union has divided the city. It has brought no aid. God will destroy the city because of it. I ask for the people. Restore their faith, and their faith in you."

"Why would you bring this up now? After all these months? You know how difficult this decision was to make. If I go back now, the people would see the *only* reason I made this decision was for aid. I would look like a beggar. And aid may still come!"

He rose, angry.

"I came to you for support. You are the person on whom I depend. What do you seek from me? Compromise! I will be strong for the people, Zophia, I assure you! I will do and have done everything I need to do. You think I've gone too far? I've gone farther than you realize."

"What do you mean?" she asked.

"It . . . it doesn't matter."

"Don't leave it there. Tell me what you meant."

Constantine hesitated and then answered. "I even sent an ambassador to Georgia to consider a betrothal. I told you, the city must come first. Not you, not the people's stubborn faith!"

He immediately regretted his outburst.

"You did what?" Now she was angry as well. "When?"

"Several months ago. Not that it matters, because it is but one more desperate gamble that will bear no fruit. Everything I do comes to nothing. That is my lot in life, as if you did not know it!"

"You broke your promise to me and you kept it secret for two months? You have come here and laughed with me and made love to me while you held this from me. Does this mean nothing to you? Do I mean nothing? And you did not have the courage to tell me?"

He knew he had made a terrible mistake. A terrible mistake to send the betrothal request, and a terrible mistake to tell her. But she knew now, and he could not take it back.

"Zophia, I'm sorry. I wanted to tell you. I already decided, regardless of the answer, that I would not marry her," he added helplessly. He wondered if that statement was true, or just another lie told in the name of saving the city. What had become of him that he didn't even know what was the truth anymore? He realized how much of himself and his own integrity he had lost in the last few years, ostensibly all for his city and his people.

She rushed forward and struck him across the face, a stinging blow that nearly knocked him off his feet. "Get out! Get out and don't come back. You have sold your soul and yourself! For what? Scraps! The scraps of these Italians! Oh, what our great empire has become, that we are now the beggars and puppets of petty princedoms. For a ship or two, a few hundred men, a few thousand coins. To what end? To save a city that has decayed to nothing for a few more years? We are lost, Constantine! You are lost! Go to your city and save it. I will keep my soul, my body, and my honor!"

Constantine tried to touch her but she pushed him away. "Please, Zophia, listen to me. You need to understand—"

"Get out!" she screamed again. She turned and fled the room. Constantine started to follow her. He heard sobbing in her bedroom.

"Leave! I told you to leave! I don't want to see you!"

He turned and left Zophia's home. He made his way back to his horse, tied to a tree near her front door. He adjusted the straps of his saddle as he distractedly leaned against his mount for support.

Now everything was lost for him. He had already lost his people and now he had lost his love, the only person he could depend on and to whom he could show his private self. He would face the long weeks, months, or even years of siege alone. For every moment of despair and dread, he would be alone, without anyone to turn to. He turned and took a half step back toward Zophia's house. He would return and beg her for her support and forgiveness.

He stopped himself. He knew she would not forgive him. Perhaps in the future, but not today, not for a long time to come.

She was right, of course, right about everything, as always. He had sold everything, compromised everything. Compromise was all he knew; it was all he had ever known.

CHAPTER SEVEN

FRIDAY, APRIL 6, 1453

Mehmet smiled. He stood outside his enormous silk tent and gazed at Constantinople. For eight hundred years, the armies of Islam had dashed themselves fruitlessly against these walls. Even his father, the great Murad, who had succeeded in virtually everything he had attempted, had failed here. And here he was in front of the great city. He not only had more men available than his father ever had, he also had a fleet, and his great cannon. If it was Allah's will, he could not lose.

He was trembling with excitement, but he had to keep his control. He knew he was gambling everything. If he failed, or even if success was delayed, Halil would, in all likelihood, succeed in having him removed. Removal meant death. He thought of Halil, and the familiar fears flowed through him. He hated his grand vizier, hated and feared him above all things. Halil was here with him, of course, here with the army. He was watching Mehmet's every move, waiting for every small mistake to whisper poison into the ears of the council. His influence would ensure that Mehmet had the least amount of time possible to win victory. Again Mehmet considered killing the vizier. If he did, what would happen? Would the council destroy him immediately? Would his guards even carry out the order?

The risk was too great. He did not need to move against Halil right now. He had all the pieces in place; he just needed to fulfill his destiny. He was ready for the great chess game to begin.

The first move in that game was to offer peace. This was a pragmatic decision and also required. The offer was pragmatic because if Constantinople simply opened its doors, he would win an easy victory and accomplish everything he desired at no risk of any kind. His wisdom in pushing the attack would be shown with no effort at all. He seriously doubted the Greeks would surrender without a fight, but it certainly was worth a try.

He also was required by Islamic law to make the offer of peace. Any city that voluntarily surrendered before the siege began must be allowed to do so, and under such a situation the citizens were allowed to keep their possessions and also their churches. Mehmet wrote to Constantine with an appeal to voluntarily open the gates to the Ottomans:

Constantine:

I appeal to you before Allah to consider the welfare of your people. You are a great and sensible leader, and have done well to maintain your position and keep the city safe. However, it is Allah's will that Constantinople become part of the great Ottoman Empire. If you will open up the gates, I will ensure that no harm will come to any person within the city. Your people will retain all current churches and cathedrals for their religion. They will retain all property. You and your household will be given safe passage to Morea, or any other territory. There you will be unhindered for the rest of your lifetime. You will pay no tribute, and I will pay you an annual sum of 10,000 ducats for your retirement.

I pray you will see reason. If you do not accept these terms, I will be forced to capture the city. Your people will lose all of their property and churches. They will be sold into slavery. As you are aware, I must grant three days of pillaging to my men if they capture Constantinople by force. Your people will suffer terribly under such a circumstance. Many will be killed, and your women will be dishonored. This, of course, would be beyond my control.

I appeal to your good reason and to the safety of your people, and humbly ask that you accept these terms of surrender. I will be generous to your people and to you. Once the siege begins, I must carry through to the end, and cannot again make this offer. I pray Allah will guide you in a proper path for your people.

Mehmet.

Mehmet directed a courier to carry this message to the city under a flag of truce. He did not expect Constantine would see reason, but this offer would surely create a debate and uncertainty among the emperor's closest advisors. More important, he would have satisfied his requirements before Islam to offer terms before beginning a siege.

He waited the rest of the day in his tent. He passed the time in silent reflection and prayer, kneeling rigidly, his mind contemplating the siege and the future suffering of his army. He prayed that Allah would spare his people and bring them quick victory in the event Constantine refused his generous offer. He prayed that Allah would show the Christian emperor the wisdom of the proposal, and even better, that Constantine would convert to Islam along with his people.

In the early afternoon, he received a reply.

Mehmet:

Thank you for your generous terms. Unfortunately, it is the will of God that I protect my Christian subjects and this city, which was built by Constantine, the first Christian emperor. I must continue to do so. I know you realize the city has never fallen, except by the unexpected treachery of the Italians.

I do not believe you have the ability to capture the city, which is protected by more than 30,000 Greek soldiers and allies. You should also know that I expect relief from the pope, who has called a mighty crusade. John Hunyadi also is prepared to march against you again from Hungary.

I would suggest you retreat as soon as possible before I have to proceed on the offensive.

I am willing to increase the annual tribute to you by 20 percent, and I will agree to a five-year truce if you are willing to immediately remove your men from the vicinity of the city, along with your fleet.

Constantine

Mehmet smiled. *You are lying to me, Constantine.* He had confirmation that there were far fewer defenders. He also knew John Hunyadi was not preparing to attack, since they had signed a treaty.

He was worried about the pope. The pope would never negotiate with the sultan, at least so long as Rome was not directly threatened. It was possible he was sending a relief force. Could it breach the Ottoman navy? Could a fleet arrive in time to change the tide of battle? These were worries indeed. Then again, what troops did the pope possess? He would have to find support from the other Italian cities. These cities were not only constantly at war with one another, they also traded for profit with Mehmet. It was unlikely they would unite to save Constantinople. Unlikely, but not impossible. Another worry.

He wrote a second note and provided copies of his offer to Constantine and the emperor's response to Halil, Zaganos, and other top ministers. He wanted everyone to know he had followed the formalities. He did not disclose his knowledge of the city defenders. He did not want to reveal his spy. And let them worry that there were indeed thirty thousand defenders, the better to be revealed later, to his advantage. Surely Halil would try to use this information against him, and if he could show his grand vizier was wrong it would strengthen his own position.

For now, it was time to demonstrate the power of his cannon. He sent additional messengers to request that all his top commanders and ministers be present at his tent one hour after sunset.

He knew he must constantly keep the momentum of victory going or Halil would feed doubts to the council. So far his ministers had been busy with the long travel to the city and with the placement of troops and supplies. Halil too had been busy with administrative tasks associated with the coming attack, but soon everything would settle and the grand vizier would have more time to infect the council with his poison. The Sultan needed to set the tone for the siege with another display of his planning and innovation, and he intended to do so immediately.

At the appointed hour, Mehmet and many of the council members and commanders gathered before Mehmet's tent. The sultan then led them a short distance toward Constantinople, where they found Orban's twenty-five huge cannon in a line almost directly between Mehmet's tent and the city walls. The main cannon had been nicknamed the Basilisk, after the mythical lizard that could turn people into stone with a single gaze. The Basilisk was in position a bare two hundred yards from the outer city wall. The muzzle extended out from the wooden cradle to which it was secured. The Turks had buried the base of the cannon into the earth so it would absorb the shock of firing without blowing the weapon backward.

Orban greeted the council members and then immediately set to work loading the Basilisk while explaining how the weapon functioned. Orban had forged not only the mighty main cannon but also two dozen lesser cannon, all of which had been laboriously dragged the 150 miles from Edirne to Constantinople. All the cannon were now in position in a more or less straight line extending out with a dozen on each side of the main cannon. Crews were busy loading each of the weapons.

After about an hour, all of the cannon were loaded and ready to be fired. The bombardment of Constantinople would be unprecedented, and Mehmet intended it to continue around the clock, but it would also be very slow because of the reloading time.

Mehmet led the group of spectators back about fifty yards so they could observe the firing from a safe distance. Once everyone was in position, Orban looked to the sultan for the signal to fire. Mehmet nodded to Orban and then quickly raised and lowered his arm. Orban turned and waved a red flag. The crews almost simultaneously placed torch to cannon.

There was a rapid repeating and thunderous roar. Mehmet had never heard anything so loud and terrifying. Almost at once he could see explosions of dust and smoke against the outer land walls of the city. His ears rang and he felt sick to his stomach from the concussion. Eventually the smoke dissipated and he was able to see the result of his first bombardment. Where he expected massive holes through the wall, other than some noticeable depressions in the stone and some dusty smoke, there was no visible damage at all! He looked at Halil and saw a satisfied grin that quickly turned to a frown once the vizier's eyes met Mehmet's.

Mehmet grew angry. He had expected a display of tremendous power, and instead his mighty cannon had made a huge noise and produced a few puffs of dust. He motioned for Orban to come back to him, and the Hungarian hurried to comply.

"What happened?" he demanded of Orban.

"My Lord, you must have some patience. These cannon will surely reduce the walls in time, but remember, they are the greatest land walls in the world. Even cannon will not breach them on the first shot."

Mehmet also noticed frantic movement near the great cannon. "What is going on over there?"

"I do not know, my Lord, I will find out," answered Orban. The Hungarian hurried over to the cannon. Mehmet stepped away from the crowd and motioned Zaganos over.

"I do not need this failure, Zaganos. This show was supposed to impress the council. Instead we've only proved just how powerful the walls are. I should rid this Hungarian of his head. I'm tired of idiots and fools wasting my time and risking my life!"

Mehmet started to draw his sword, but Zaganos stopped him and blocked the view of the others while he whispered to the sultan.

"My Lord, patience. These things take time. The cannon can be fired many times per day. It may take days, weeks, or even months, but we have that much time."

Mehmet snatched his hand away from Zaganos, although he did not attempt to draw his sword again.

"We do not have time! Not with Halil, we do not. He works against my every move. Look at him, like a hen worrying with her flock. He will not give me months. I risk everything in this, Zaganos. You know that. I had hoped Constantine might yield the city. He will not. This was not unexpected, but I intended to show the power of our cannon. I did not expect we would destroy the walls with one volley, but the walls show no damage at all. That fool lied to me. He promised he would give me the walls."

"Like Orban said, my Sultan, these things take time. He never promised immediate results. Perhaps we assumed the effect would be quick, but he never said so. He did promise the walls would not stand up to the bombardment. Let us not be hasty. Look, he comes back. Let us ask him when we can likely expect results."

Orban looked pale and nervous when he returned.

"What is it, Orban?"

"Bad news, I'm afraid, my Lord. The Basilisk has cracked in several places. This does happen sometimes. It will take a number of days to repair, at best a week. I suggest that we hold off on any assault or use of the other cannon until this one is repaired."

"Why would we wait a further second?"

"I cannot guarantee any of the other cannon can breach the walls. They were designed to weaken—to assist the great cannon. They were *not* designed to operate without the Basilisk."

Mehmet exploded and struck Orban to the ground with a blow from his gauntleted hand. "Fool! You promise me a cannon, and it blows up on the first shot. I should have your head now!"

The sultan removed his sword and held it against Orban's neck hard enough that a trickle of blood ran down the Hungarian's left shoulder. He pulled the blade up and swung it down with all his might.

His sword was stopped by Zaganos, who had drawn his own sword at the last moment and blocked the blow.

Mehmet pulled the sword up and turned to Zaganos, ready to strike at his friend for this insolence, but the pasha dropped his weapon and lowered his head. This act of submission calmed Mehmet down. He lowered his own sword.

"Please, my Lord," begged Orban. "These things happen. I will have the cannon repaired quickly. You must understand that even a small fracture in the casting process can cause a cannon to splinter when it is fired. This is to be expected and can be easily repaired."

Mehmet still lusted to kill the Hungarian who had so embarrassed him. He was further humiliated by his show of anger and loss of control. He could hear the murmuring of the council members behind him, and he was sure that Halil and the other senior members would discuss this failure at length.

"Please, Sultan, let him fix the cannon," whispered Zaganos. "If you do not, we have nobody skilled enough to maintain these weapons. We need him. Remember what we are doing here. We must stay focused. A few days will not make the difference."

Mehmet turned back to the Hungarian. "I want it repaired in two days, Orban! I'll spare your life for now. Two days, or I may not be so generous again!"

Mehmet sheathed his sword. He was still seething inside. Did Allah curse him after all? Would he again be the laughingstock of Halil and the council? He remembered facing his father when his power was taken away the last time. The disappointment in his father's eyes, Halil standing by with that same knowing grin. No! He would not go down in history as a young fool who was removed from power before he had even begun. He would be the greatest Ottoman of all. It was his destiny. It was Allah's will.

But he needed a victory now. What could he do? If he waited, Halil might make a move against him or demand that they withdraw from the city before the siege had even properly begun. He dismissed the assembled men and returned to his tent.

It was too early to test his fleet against the sea chain. He needed a victory on land. He pulled out his maps and studied them carefully, considering what might be done. Should he attack the walls without waiting for the cannon? If he lost a large number of men immediately with no gain, he would be worse off. He could set to work on filling in the Foss. That would certainly help the siege in the long run, but filling in ditches could hardly raise the men's morale. He studied the map for several hours and then formed a solution. He smiled to himself. He knew just what to do.

Later that evening, Mehmet met with Zaganos in his tent over apple tea. The men did not discuss Mehmet's outburst, although the sultan was sure his older friend would have liked to have lectured him on the topic. One of the benefits of being sultan was not having to suffer rebukes, even if they were perhaps deserved. After they had drunk their tea and enjoyed some light refreshment, Mehmet got down to business.

"I have a task for you, my friend."

"What is it, my Lord?"

"I want you to take some men and lay siege to the Greek castle at Therapia over on the Bosporus. I will do the same with the Greek castle at Studius."

"Certainly, my Lord, but may I ask why?"

"Of course. I cannot afford to sit idly by. So far our men lie helpless outside the city walls, like every army in the history of this city. My ships are stuck outside their accursed sea chain and my cannon cannot breach the walls or even be used until our primary cannon is repaired. I must have momentum. Halil will not give me the benefit of the doubt. He could move against me at any time. If we attack these two castles, we keep people occupied, and they should fall relatively easily, yes?"

"I would think so, my Lord." Mehmet could tell by the look on Zaganos's face that his friend was impressed by the suggestion. "As always, you surprise me. Just as with the fleet, you have come up with a solution to a problem where I saw only difficulties."

Mehmet enjoyed the flattery, although he wondered if it was fully genuine. He respected and trusted Zaganos, to a degree. But he had been betrayed multiple times already by those he trusted most. He would not make that mistake again. He would err on the side of caution, and if that kept Zaganos at arms' length, so be it. At least if Zaganos stabbed him in the back, he would see it coming and be prepared.

"It is settled, then. Go tomorrow at dawn. I shall do the same. If Allah wills it, we shall both be quickly victorious, and we will have something to show for our efforts. By the time we are done, we will hopefully have our cannon repaired and be prepared for more extensive attacks."

The following morning Mehmet rose early, gathered some of his guards, and went to the Janissary camp nearby. The Janissaries were the sultan's elite troops, a unique part of the Ottoman army, and in fact unique in the world. As opposed to the other armies he faced and the bulk of his own army, which were formed by gathering retainers from local areas on a seasonal basis, the Janissaries were a standing army.

Mehmet's father had first formed the Janissary corps. It was populated by men who had been captured as young Christian children and removed from their families as a blood tax. They were forcibly converted to Islam and trained as a private brotherhood of elite soldiers, fiercely loyal to the sultan and their own men and officers. They possessed the best training, armor, and weapons, and they were used by the sultan for the most important and most dangerous attacks.

Mehmet greeted their commander. "I am in need of five hundred of your best men. I intend to lead an attack on the castle at Studius. I need archers and swordsmen. I should be back in the next few days."

"Yes, my Lord, I will gather a force for you. Would you like assistance in the siege?"

"I don't think that is necessary. I want to savor this attack for myself."

Mehmet waited several hours for the men to be gathered and then to form ranks. They were superbly dressed in chain mail armor with high-quality swords. The men wore the distinct white hats that marked them as members of the Janissary corps. They lined up quickly and then remained silent and stone frozen, awaiting the next command. The Jannisary were superbly disciplined. Mehmet admired them for a few minutes and then ordered them to follow him. He dismounted from his horse to lead them personally on foot.

He led them along the land walls of Constantinople up and down the several hills that formed the city. Once they reached the Sea of Marmara they travelled down the coast away from the city to the village of Studius. Studius was situated very close to Constantinople and one of the few territories still claimed by the Greeks. The village stood on the shores of the Sea of Marmara, nothing more than a collection of huts that formed a trading center for the nearby farms.

A small castle stood near the village, overlooking the Sea of Marmara and serving as a rallying point for the village for protection at times such as these when hostile forces approached. As Mehmet came nearer he heard bells frantically pealing. He saw Greek peasants and a few soldiers running from the village houses into the castle. He reached the castle walls within minutes, staying back about fifty yards. The castle walls, which constituted little more than a stone enclosure, were about twenty feet high but did not contain towers or any other intricate defenses. A reinforced wooden gate, closed now, guarded the entrance to the fortification.

Mehmet did not consider a small village subject to the same rules of surrender as a city like Constantinople. He would simply strike. He ordered his Janissaries to surround the castle and sent a messenger to hurry up the battering ram that was being brought up on wheels. While they waited, his men moved into place, completely surrounding the castle but remaining a distance away. The archers kept their bows partially drawn, ready to shoot any Greeks who might appear on the walls.

Mehmet sent a smaller force of Janissaries toward the village. He watched a woman run in fear from one house to another.

The Janissaries entered the village and began moving quickly from door to door. Soon the sound of screaming emanated from the houses as the Turks killed the inhabitants. Several soldiers carried torches, which they threw onto the roofs of houses, setting them ablaze. The cries of terror and pain grew to a steady thrum and then slowly subsided as the Turks completed the task. The entire village was put to the sword and consumed by fire in less than ten minutes.

Mehmet watched as impassively as he could. He had to appear uncaring. This was war, and his men needed a victory. The cries bothered him but a little. These were not only men but also women and children. He had ordered many deaths in his short life, and had even killed because of anger, irritation, or to prove a point. He did not relish the killing except when his blood was up; he saw it as a necessary evil in a harsh world.

The destruction of this village and castle would appear a victory for his men. But it would also anger the Greeks and instill fear in them. He wished that Constantine had understood the wisdom of surrender. He truly would have welcomed him and his people and added them to his empire. Constantine was forcing this violence on his people. He must pay the butcher's bill.

The ram was in place by noon. Mehmet ordered an immediate assault on the gate. The ram was a simple wooden log, twelve inches in diameter and twenty feet long. It was attached to a wooden cradle by a series of chains. The cradle was in turn mounted on a wheeled trailer. The tip of the ram was encased in a crude iron hood that was fastened to the wooden end with thick nails. It would not last in sustained combat, but it would do tremendous damage to even a substantial city gate, let alone the primitive wooden structure attached to this enclosure.

Mehmet had ordered dozens of these devices prepared for the main assault on Constantinople.

A group of Janissaries wheeled the ram forward. Others walked close by, with shields tipped up and over to protect the ram-bearers. Several Greeks attempted to fire from the walls above the gate, but they were driven back or killed immediately by a volley of arrows sent from the waiting archers below.

The sultan's men struggled together and pulled the ram back, then released it. The ram sprang forward on the chains and crashed into the gate. The gate shuddered but held. They pulled the ram back a second time and released it again. This time the gate splintered in several places. The Janissaries drew the device back a third time, and shouting, drove it forward as hard as they could. The ram crashed through the wooden gate, leaving a hole the size of several men, although the bottom of the gate was still attached up to waist height.

Arrows flew out of the hole, striking three of the Janissaries, who fell back dead or badly wounded. The rest drew their swords and, shouting to Allah, began climbing through the hole, fighting the Greeks. The combat at the gate was furious for a few minutes, but soon, enough of the Janissaries had battled through that the fighting moved inside. Eventually the shattered gates were ripped open from within, allowing more of the Janissaries to rush into the castle. The clash of battle grew louder as the Greeks tried desperately to defend their keep against the rush and press of Mehmet's elite forces.

The sultan's blood was up. He drew his own sword and was preparing to join the fray, but the sound of battle was already unfortunately beginning to dim. He motioned for his guards to follow him. He entered the castle, stepping over the bodies of Turk and Greek. The sandy castle grounds were awash in blood and bodies. A few Greeks remained alive but had dropped their weapons and surrendered.

As Mehmet walked among the bodies, he felt a sharp burning pain in his leg. He turned and saw that one of the wounded Greeks had plunged his dagger into the sultan's shin. The blade had been deflected by the bone and slipped along the skin line, causing a long superficial cut. Mehmet drew his sword again and hacked the head off the soldier. His men cheered, and Mehmet looked around in elation. The burning pain felt good amid the approval of his men. He tore a strip of fabric from his cloak and tied it around the wound, then continued on.

Further in, he found a group of Janissaries surrounding a group of Greek prisoners. The Greeks were disarmed and on their knees, their heads bowed. Mehmet counted the prisoners. There were thirty-six of them.

He smiled approvingly. He had his victory. The Janissaries were smiling, too, and cheering their sultan. He ordered the prisoners chained and the castle burned to the ground like the village before it. He then ordered his men to reform ranks and began the march back to his headquarters, with the prisoners in tow. He limped a little, but he hardly noticed the injury as he basked in his victory.

As Mehmet's contingent marched, the men encamped before the city realized what had happened. They could see the smoke behind the column, and the prisoners with bent heads. The Turks banged their weapons to their shields and against their armor, shouting the sultan's name. Mehmet had a hard time containing himself. He had been cheered before, but really more out of fear than anything else. This salute was something different. The men were cheering him as a victor. In the Ottoman world, the leader who brought victory was the leader worthy of love and respect. He had always known this fact, but never really experienced it. He thought he would burst from pride. This was what Allah intended for him. Not to be humiliated and killed. Not to be the laughingstock of Halil and his cronies. He was born to conquer. And before him was the greatest conquest of all: Constantinople. Let them doubt him. He would prove it to them all, and then he would punish the doubters.

He arrived back at his tent in the late afternoon. He had no word yet from Zaganos and assumed the siege at Therapia was still ongoing. The cheers continued for some time and then faded slowly away, still music in his ears.

The Janissary captain reported overall casualties, which were few, and asked what should be done with the prisoners. Mehmet thought for a while. Would Constantine trade these prisoners for the city? No. He already was gambling with the entire population inside. Could anything be gained by turning the men over to Constantine? They would certainly tell about the castle falling, which might spread fear. But castles came and went. Constantine would only compare the feeble walls of Studius to the impenetrable walls of Constantinople.

Should he hold the men and possibly exchange them later? But exchange them for whom? If Zaganos or someone else important were captured, it would likely mean the sultan had failed in taking the city. He would not want to free anyone who had let him down in the first place, and likely he would not be alive to consider the issue. He would think on this question and see how things developed.

As the sun set, the sultan enjoyed the sights and sounds of his camp as the soldiers made fires and dinner, the light of the campfires flickering off the land walls of Constantinople, so near his grasp. He ate his own meal in the quiet. Soon he was asleep, feeling more satisfied than he could ever remember and dreaming of capturing Constantinople as he slipped into the darkness.

MONDAY, APRIL 9, 1453

The next morning Mehmet woke very well rested. He felt confident of victory and hoped today would bring more good news from Zaganos about the castle at Therapia. He received an early-morning update from his friend, indicating that the castle was still holding out, but that he anticipated it would fall in the next twenty-four hours.

Mehmet decided he did not want to wait another day for any action. What could he do to continue the momentum from yesterday? With the cannon still under repair, an attack on the land walls would likely end in failure and simply take away his victory from the day before. He thought through things over breakfast and then ordered his horse brought over. He had an idea for another bold action.

He rode north with twenty guards along the line of his camp. Mehmet soon encountered the Golden Horn and rode along its shore until he finally reached the end. The sultan turned south and moved first up a ridge, then down again, to the Bosporus, past Galata, where his fleet was anchored.

He found Admiral Baltaoglu.

"Greetings," said the admiral, startled that the sultan had suddenly appeared at his tent unannounced. "What may I do for you, my Sultan?"

"Greetings. I would like you to attack the Golden Horn."

The admiral looked surprised but quickly recovered. "Certainly, Sultan, when would you like me to do so? I can be ready within seventy-two hours."

"I want you to attack them now."

"Now, Sire? That's not possible. I need to scout the sea chain and spend some time learning the currents and the wind patterns. I do not have a good understanding of the Greek fleet. I would be happy to attack in three days."

Mehmet was growing angry. "You did not hear me, Admiral. You will attack this instant! I did not put you in charge to hear excuses from you. Yesterday I took a castle and a village with no thought or preparation at all. I just did it. You will show the same courage or I will find someone who will! Do you understand me?"

Baltaoglu went pale. "Sultan, please," he stammered. "You do not understand. Naval warfare is not something to be left to chance and hope. The ships must be properly prepared. The positions must be scouted and understood, and the currents and wind conditions analyzed. I beg you, Sultan, please do not force us into disaster."

Mehmet lashed out and struck the admiral in the face, knocking him to the ground. He drew his sword and stood over him.

Baltaoglu raised his arms as if to ward off the blow. "Please, Sultan, please do not! I will ready the ships immediately!"

Mehmet calmed down enough to sheathe his sword. "If the ships are not put to sea in the next hour, Baltaoglu, then I will replace you, and only your head will accompany the attack. No more excuses."

Baltaoglu rose slowly to his feet and, still bowing, turned quickly and fled toward the ships, shouting orders. Soon the fleet and the surrounding tents were busy as a hive, with men and equipment moving in every direction. The ships were not ready in an hour as promised, but within two hours the first ship departed the moorings, and soon the entire fleet was moving slowly up the Bosporus toward Galata.

Mehmet was pleased enough that he did not even mind the extra hour. He mounted his horse and rode along the shore of the Bosporus, shouting encouragement to the fleet he had built with his own willpower and forethought. He kept riding toward Constantinople and soon was passing the walls of Galata on his right, until he was at the point of the peninsula directly across from Constantinople.

By the time Mehmet was in position, the fleet was already floating past him on the way to the Golden Horn. He saluted the ships as they passed, proud of this massive fleet and of his men, many of whom had little experience with ships but had signed up when he needed volunteers.

The Turks pulled hard at their oars, moving the ships forward slowly toward Constantinople. Mehmet could see a buzz of activity in the Greek city, not only in the harbor, where a small fleet of ships was obviously getting ready to set sail, but also above the sea walls, where soldiers and regular citizens were moving about, obviously reacting to the appearance of the fleet.

The massive fleet moved slowly around the tip of Galata, banners snapping in the wind. The sailors and soldiers were pacing the decks, fingering their weapons, ready for a fight. Some of the sailors held muskets on poles and even a few small cannon. Others had bows and long throwing spears.

Mehmet could hardly contain his excitement as he paced his horse back and forth along the shore, shouting encouragement to the ships.

The sea chain was visible across the entire strait of the Horn, connected to a series of wooden booms. No ship could pass the chain when it was intact, but the weakness of the chain was the booms themselves. If his fleet could get close enough, then Mehmet's men could climb onto the booms, hack them apart, and then they would be within the Horn itself. If they could break into the Horn and destroy Constantine's navy, they would be able to attack the vulnerable inner harbors and potentially take the city immediately. They just needed a few minutes against the chain to be successful. That would mean neutralizing the Greek fleet, which seemed to Mehmet a simple task, as it appeared to be pitifully small.

As the fleet moved slowly toward the chain, Mehmet could see a number of these Greek ships leaving the two interior harbors and floating out toward the chain as well. They had a fairly strong backwind and with sails were moving very quickly. He realized with displeasure that they would arrive at the chains first. No matter; there were only ten or so, against his hundreds.

The Greek ships floated out quickly, aided by both oar and sail power. They arrived at the chain and spread out, adjusting their sails to float a few yards away from the chain. He was surprised by the speed of the Greek fleet and also the obvious skill with which the ships were handled, but ten could not stand up to two hundred. Mehmet watched anxiously as the minutes passed, and the first Turkish ships arrived to challenge the chain. Soon they would be up against the booms and in range of the Greek ships.

He was shocked to see streams of fire exploding from several of the Greek ships. In moments the first Turkish vessels were engulfed in flames. This sight was the famous "Greek fire," a petroleum-based and pressurized fire that could be shot from a tube. It could be directed at a distance and would quickly engulf any wooden ship, killing or badly wounding anyone who was exposed.

The Greek fire had a devastating effect on the lead ships. Sailors writhed in the fire, jumping overboard into the water. One ship crashed into the chain and then drifted off toward Constantinople, unfortunately failing to set a wooden boom on fire as it smashed alongside it.

Mehmet's fleet tacked sharply to the port side toward the city as more Greek ships shot the fire at them. Several more were hit and ignited, but the others had turned quickly enough to be out of range. The maneuver had been swiftly executed and no doubt protected the fleet, but it also meant the ships were not able to attack the sea chain.

The sultan was furious. Why were these cowards floating away? So a few ships were burned! So what if they lost half the ships and all the men? He had more men. He needed this sea chain down. He needed access to the Horn. Why was he surrounded by fools and cowards? He screamed out at the ships, ordering them to turn around and attack. The fleet was traveling away from him and out of earshot. If they returned without any further attempt, he promised himself he would flay the skin from Admiral Baltaoglu the moment he docked to teach these sailors a lesson.

Perhaps sensing the rage of the ultan, the fleet executed a full circle and headed gradually back to the chain. This time the ships spread out well away and approached on a broad front, forcing the Greek ships to break formation and attack single targets.

The Greek ships shot their fire again, burning a number of Turkish vessels immediately. However, there were not enough ships in the Greek force to stop all of Mehmet's fleet, and one Turkish ship smashed into the chain with a grating crash. Sailors were quickly lowered over the side and directly onto the boom. They began hacking furiously at the wood with axes.

Mehmet called out to the men, encouraging them to break the chain. He could see the Greek ships turning and moving quickly toward the men on the booms. His men could see it, too. They redoubled their efforts, trying to break the chain loose and escape back to the ship before the Greeks were in range. The sultan could not see how much progress they were making, but the axes seemed to be cutting ever deeper. He hoped they would break through the wood and set the chain free in time.

Fire streamed out of the Greek ship, landing about twenty yards short of the boom. A great cry came up from the Turks. The boom split in two. The chain was broken. They were through!

The Greek ship shot fire out again. This time it hit the mark, and the Turkish vessel exploded in flame. The Greek fire completely engulfed the ship in moments. The burning vessel drifted away from the chain, falling apart as screaming men tried uselessly to extinguish the devouring flames by jumping into the water. Even in the water they burned, writhing in agony as they roasted under the fire that would not go out.

The Greek ships were closing on the point of the broken chain, threatening the Turkish ships just outside their range. Several of the sultan's ships tried to move closer but were hampered by their burning sister ship and by the looming Greek fleet. Another ship was doused in the fire when it tried to approach, and soon the Turkish fleet turned away, the admiral apparently deciding they had tried enough for one day.

Mehmet screamed out at the fleet, ordering them back. Again, the ships were too far away to hear him. He spurred his horse and rode north along the Bosporus, arriving at the fleet harbor long before the ships. He paced his horse back and forth near the docks, fuming. He wanted the head of the admiral. They had broken the chain. They were through! All they had to do was send all of the ships in together at the same time and the fleet would have made it into the Horn.

Finally the ships made their way back to their moorings. Mehmet dismounted and hurried to the admiral's ship. Admiral Baltaoglu saw Mehmet and waved. He was smiling, obviously proud of the day's work. "My Sultan, great news," he announced as he hopped overboard and down to the dock. "We have tested the defenses of the enemy and very nearly broken through on our first day."

Mehmet charged the Bulgarian and struck him to the ground for a second time. "You did break through, you fool! How could you flee from victory?" He drew his sword, fuming, his blood boiling in anger.

The admiral prostrated himself, face and hands pressed against the dock. "We could not break through today, my Lord. There were too many ships with the Greek fire. We did break one boom, but the gap was not even wide enough for a single ship to pass through. We lost twenty ships today. If we had tried to force our way through, we might have lost the entire fleet!"

Mehmet fingered the pommel of his sword, debating what to do. He wanted to see this fool's head rolling around on the dock. Was he telling the truth? He had not considered whether more than one boom would have to be breached to get the fleet through. Would they have lost the entire fleet? He knew so little about the sea and proper sea tactics. He would have to remedy that as soon as possible after the siege.

For now, what should he do? Should he believe this man or kill him? Even if he did believe him, would killing him make the next commander more effective, or would it just make him reckless? He had taught himself that when he did not know what to do, he had to be patient.

He knew what it was to be too rash, to push too hard. When he had assumed the throne at twelve he had wanted to do everything at once, and he had lost everything because of it. He had demanded that his orders be followed, and when he was ignored, he had started executing the leaders. Halil had stepped in and had him physically restrained, and soon his father had been called back to take charge of the Empire. Patience for now, he counseled himself. He had time to kill this fool whenever he wanted.

"Get up! I expect you to follow my orders in the future. I ordered you to break through the sea chain! You have failed me. Your next failure will be paid for with your head. Now get out of my sight!"

The admiral bowed low again and backed slowly away. Mehmet felt calmer. He was sure he had made the right decision by not killing Admiral Baltaoglu. The admiral certainly would do everything in his power to follow orders from now on. If he failed the sultan again, Mehmet would get the chance to remove the admiral's head, which would give him joy. If the Admiral succeeded, then Mehmet would reward him and be glad he had spared his life.

He remounted and began the long ride around the west side of Galata and then around the end of the Golden Horn. He was still frustrated with the failure to break through the chain. He was convinced the city would have fallen if they had only broken through. Still, he must have given the Greeks a tremendous blow to their confidence, and another major issue for Constantine to worry about.

What *did* Constantine worry about? He often considered this question. How did Constantine think? He knew a great deal about the Emperor from others who had known him, from his spies. However, it was not the same as knowing him personally. What did Constantine think about Mehmet's massive army? What about the surprise fleet and the cannon? Surely he must realize that Constantinople was in greater danger than at any time during its history. Yet he wouldn't surrender. Why not?

There was no dishonor in surrender in an impossible situation. And the terms Mehmet had offered were fair. Everything would be so much easier if the city simply gave up. Then there was no risk. Yet somehow Mehmet felt the emperor would never yield. He would have to take the city or fail trying. It would be Constantine's life or his.

In a sense he admired the emperor. Mehmet knew what it was like to have everything taken away, to feel powerless. Mehmet had always had the resources of the most powerful empire in the world in his hands, but he had never been able to lead it. He had always been dominated by Halil, manipulated by a grand vizier who controlled the empire while he pretended to give power to Mehmet. Halil had essentially succeeded Murad, and Mehmet wondered if the grand vizier had even manipulated that situation, eroding Mehmet's authority before Murad died by showing he was unfit to rule.

Why can I not just kill him? Mehmet plotted the death of Halil every day. He wanted him dead so badly. But it would be no good to kill Halil simply to be usurped and executed immediately thereafter. Patience. He knew the key to Halil's fate: Mehmet must become the true sultan in the eyes of his people. Once he accomplished this goal he would have everything he needed, and he would take his sweet revenge.

Mehmet returned to his tent exhausted and frustrated. He had hoped for another quick victory. Instead the Greeks had inflicted a humiliating defeat on the sultan's new navy. He had banked heavily on this fleet's ability to dominate the Greeks, and to attack the Golden Horn. Instead, he had been surprised by the sea chain, and now he saw that the chain enabled the Greeks to protect the Golden Horn with only a few defensive ships to keep the Turks away from the wooden booms.

The effectiveness of his fleet was vastly reduced. If the Greek ships could truly burn his entire fleet while it attacked the sea chain, then there was little point in attempting this tactic again. He could still hope to stop a fleet of reinforcing ships, but the most vulnerable parts of the city, the sea walls and harbors within the Golden Horn, were protected by the chain, and perhaps out of his reach.

Part of his master plan was unraveling, and he did not yet know how to deal with it. Why was there no one else for him to consult on this? Again he was frustrated by his weakness at sea, by the lack of knowledge of his council and top advisors on naval affairs. He must change that for himself and he must find experts to promote. But all of that would have to wait.

On his arrival back in the main camp, he was met with some good news. Zaganos had returned and had succeeded in destroying the castle at Therapia, capturing an additional forty Greek prisoners. Combined with Mehmet's total this brought the number of prisoners to seventy-six.

Mehmet congratulated his friend and invited him to dine with him. They were soon drinking apple tea and eating lamb and rice while they shared stories about their two successful attacks. Mehmet also discussed the naval attack with Zaganos in detail and explained his frustration with his lack of experience and knowledge regarding the sea. Zaganos agreed that something must be done to change the situation, and suggested that some Italian captains be bribed to change sides and bring their ships, crews, and knowledge to the Ottoman camp. Of course, this change would have to wait for the result of the siege one way or another.

Mehmet also discussed the issue of the prisoners. They debated what to do for several hours, and as dawn broke on April 10, he had made up his mind.

As usual, he had conceived of a plan that would wring the maximum benefit from the situation, regardless of how barbaric. He needed to capitalize on the capture of these Greeks and also do something to eradicate yesterday's naval failure in the minds of his own men, and the Greeks, for that matter. The citizens of Constantinople needed to know fear. Fear was the best medicine for these stubborn Greeks.

He summoned a nearby guard and scribbled out a message. "Give this message to the Janissaries: Tell them to impale all of the prisoners.

I want it done now, halfway between my tent and the walls." The guard bowed and left.

"Impalement, my Lord? A cruel death, even for an infidel. Will this not only encourage the Greeks to resist you even more? We discussed so many different options last night. You never even mentioned this. Why did not we discuss this before you made the decision?"

Mehmet felt his anger rise swiftly, as it always did when he was challenged. "It is not your place to question me, Zaganos. You are my servant, here at my pleasure. I am not here at yours."

Zaganos bowed. "That is of course true, my Lord, and need not even be said. However, you have often asked my advice, and I cannot give you advice if I do not know what you are doing. Last night we agreed to release the prisoners as a show of good faith. Impalement will only anger the Greeks and harden their hearts to the possibility of surrender. They must not think us barbarians."

"I think not, my friend. The Greeks think us barbarians already. Let their worst fears be realized. I have offered peace if only Constantine will surrender the city. He has refused, but others must be questioning him about this decision. If the population is terrified of what will happen to them if we do assault the city, perhaps they will put pressure on him to surrender now. We are not truly foreigners, are we? We have millions of Greeks already living in our empire. They have religious freedom, provided they pay their taxes. Have we not heard from many of them that they are happier now than they were under the Latin and Greek masters? Are they not safer? Are they not actually freer to practice their own religious beliefs without interference?

"They know our tolerance, and perhaps that is why they refuse to surrender. Perhaps they believe they will be treated gently if we ever manage to break into the city. But they need to also know to fear. If they fear us and respect us, they may choose our mercy rather than our fury."

"I am afraid that they will more than fear us, my Sultan. I am afraid that this act of impalement will make them angry as well. If they feel they will all die horribly if the city falls, then I believe they will fight all the more desperately to keep us out."

"You may be right, but I do not think so. I will trust my instincts in this. I would rather have their fear than their love, at least for now. Let them be afraid."

Mehmet discussed a few more details with Zaganos, then dismissed his friend back to his position on the opposite side of the Golden Horn, facing Galata.

Mehmet knew Zaganos was frustrated about his assignment. The commander of the men near Galata led more of a containing force than a true part of the siege: He could not take an active part in the actual assault on the city. Mehmet had placed Zaganos there on purpose. The convert was his friend and his closest advisor, but he would not become a rival. Zaganos was also his greatest general, and widely popular. If he led the assault that took the city, his fame would grow even greater.

Mehmet would be the conqueror, and nobody else. This result was a necessity, an assurance of his own survival. If necessary, his great general, Zaganos, was close by, but Mehmet would play that card when and if he needed to.

Mehmet returned to his tent and prayed. He relaxed, letting the worries of the day and the night pass away from him. He prayed for the Greek prisoners, the men who would suffer so terribly, even if they were infidels. He prayed that Allah would help Constantine see the wisdom of giving him the city. He prayed that the city would fall, and that he would be able to restore Constantinople's former greatness, to the glory of the Ottomans and Allah. He did not enjoy causing pain this way. It was necessary. Mehmet used cruelty like any other tool of survival. This was a game he had learned very early.

Later he heard the first screaming. He kept his eyes closed and sat motionless in his tent, listening to the increasing horror, the pounding sound of mallet to stake, the terrible screams of the prisoners as sharpened poles were slowly hammered through their bodies. After several hours, the sounds began to dim. He came out of the tent. Before him, a distance toward Constantinople, he counted seventy-six stakes, rising like thorns from the plains before the city, buried upright in the ground. On each pole, near the top, was one of the prisoners, skewered from their anus through their entire body and out their mouth. The bodies still writhed. An occasional moan or even scream came from the Greeks. Mehmet watched the men, and also looked out over the distance to the city walls, where he could see many Greeks gathered, grimly watching, some with hands to their faces, wailing in grief. Mehmet smiled again. They would know fear.

CHAPTER EIGHT

MONDAY, APRIL 9, 1453

John Hunyadi greeted the weary traveler and welcomed him to his table. Unlike many noblemen, Hunyadi dined informally with members of his household at a large table near the kitchens. His hall contained a formal dining room as well, but he rarely used it, preferring to eat with his men. The conversation at the table was loud and raucous as usual, with much drinking and joking.

Hunyadi grabbed an extra chair from against the stone wall and pulled it up next to him. He beckoned Gregory to sit down and enjoy a meal. The young Greek wished to talk immediately, but Hunyadi ordered him to eat and drink first; messages could wait. He smiled to himself. He still found himself liking this Greek. He reminded Hunyadi of himself as a young man.

Gregory was ravenous and dug in immediately. His manners might have been considered uncouth in another setting, but here he was just one more tired warrior grabbing food and grunting as he chewed and swallowed. He drank several cups of wine and soon was slowing down on his meal.

When Hunyadi judged it the right time, he opened the conversation. "So, my young friend, what news do you have from Constantinople?"

"Grave news, my Lord."

"How so?"

"The Turks are definitely coming to the city. They were building a huge cannon in Edirne, and they kept their forces in camp even into the early winter. But the cannon they built was, according to our sources, far too large to transport any great distance for an extended campaign. It was built to haul the hundred and fifty miles to Constantinople."

Hunyadi was not surprised to learn the Ottoman's might be contemplating an attack. He had received confirmation of much the same information from his own sources. The cannon was a surprise to him. Not that it particularly concerned him; cannon were made for siege warfare and were practically useless in a pitched running battle. They were too slow to reload and fire. Much like the gunpowder weapons that every army now possessed, they made far more noise than damage.

"You tell me things of which I am already aware, Gregory. The question is, what do you want me to do about it?" He already knew the answer.

"My emperor requests that you bring your army down into Thrace. By the time you would arrive, the Turks should be fully surrounding Constantinople. If you move with speed you would able to smash them against the walls, and together we can annihilate the Ottomans once and for all and drive them from Europe."

Hunyadi smiled again to himself. He admired the pluck of this young Greek and he had to be careful not to show him too much. He frowned and made a show of concern. "Gregory, I will gently remind you that you have sung this tune for me before. What you propose has tremendous risk for me; in fact, it offers as much risk as it does opportunity. And I may risk destroying one enemy to simply supplant it with another."

"In regards to the first, my Lord, I can confirm that we are expecting significant aid from the Italians. As you know, Constantine has ordered the implementation of the Union of the Churches."

"I am sure his people love him for that . . ."

"You are wise, my Lord. The decision has caused some political friction among the Greeks, but it has assured us aid from the West. We will have significant aid from the Italians, including a fleet. With your forces on land and their dominance at sea, we can certainly defeat the Ottomans."

"What you tell me, if it is true, at least provides some encouragement. The question is, what is in it for me?"

"My Lord, I have an answer to that question as well. My emperor has requested that I offer you all of the lands to the south of your kingdom, all the way to the lands of the Greek speakers. He will also offer a fifty-year treaty of alliance."

Hunyadi threw his head back and laughed heartily. "So you will offer me lands you do not control? How generous of Constantine. Not to mention the lands are full of Serbs who hate us more than they hate the Ottomans. I am sure they will not mind if I just swoop down and take their territories!"

Inside, Hunyadi thought differently. The Serbs would be difficult, but if they could drive the Turks out of Europe, Constantine was offering him huge tracts of territory. He would secure a substantial buffer against any future attacks, including from the Greeks. A fifty-year alliance would also ensure peace on his southern border. He could protect his people, which was all he had ever wanted to do. Then he would only have the damned Germans to deal with. All of this flashed through the Hungarian's mind.

Gregory started to protest, but Hunyadi raised his hand. "Now, now, my friend, I jest with you. Your Emperor needs our help; I know that. I do not think his offer is beyond consideration. I appreciate this opportunity to dine with you again. You must be weary from the road but perhaps ready for some entertainment."

Hunyadi snapped his fingers and several young maidens rose from the table and moved over to Gregory, one sitting on his lap and giggling. The Hungarian rose. "I, on the other hand, am too old for frivolity. I must be off to bed. I trust my young warriors and maidens will keep you entertained."

Hunyadi bowed and left the table. He kept his face impassive as he walked slowly through the hallway to his private bedchamber. Only when the door was closed and he was truly alone did he relax. He pulled a letter out of his pocket and read it again. The letter was from Pope Nicholas, and it offered him a huge payment in gold from the Venetians and Genoese if he would bring his army in aid of Constantinople. Riches, land, and security. All this and a chance at long last to vanquish his lifelong enemies.

He would wait until morning. Gregory would be hungover and exhausted from a night with a couple of the local prostitutes. He would wake him up early and demand 10 percent of the trade revenue coming through Constantinople for the next ten years as an additional prize. Gregory would gratefully accept, and Hunyadi would have secured all he wanted and more. He probably would have attacked under the present conditions with no assurances from anyone. But it made sense to get paid as well.

He sat up late into the night composing a letter back to Nicholas that he would send by his fastest rider and ship first thing in the morning.

TUESDAY, APRIL 17, 1453

Captain Uberti stood on the deck of his war galley in the harbor of Venice. He had been appointed commander of a relief fleet financed by the pope and provided by the Venetians. His fleet consisted of twelve war galleys and two thousand Venetian soldiers. He had received orders in early March from the doge and had been busy since that time outfitting his ships and securing the necessary men-at-arms.

The captain had received a huge sum of gold from the treasury with which to pay the men and secure the ships. He stood to make a personal fortune from the expedition, regardless of the result. He was prepared to sail in the next several days. He had some grain, gold, powder, and the ships and men for the city. All he was required to do was unload the provisions and men and drive any Turkish fleet away.

The Turks had not had a fleet of any significance in his memory, so he was not worried about that part of his orders. The greatest concern would be passing the narrow straits at the Dardanelles. The Ottomans controlled the land on both sides, and if there was insufficient wind, he might lose a portion of his fleet running the narrow channel before the Sea of Marmara opened up again.

Uberti observed a rider coming down to the quay. He was dressed in the livery of the Senate of Venice. A messenger. The rider dismounted and quickly made his way up the gangway and onto his galley. When he saw Uberti, he bowed low.

"What may I do for you?"

"A message from the Senate, my Lord, for your eyes only."

"Give it here." Uberti took the note and read it quickly. The Senate had received word from John Hunyadi that he was gathering an army and would be proceeding south to attack the Turks while they were busy laying siege to Constantinople. The Senate was concerned that the Hungarians might capture all of Europe if they were successful, and potentially gain control of the trade routes from the Black Sea. The pope, however, wanted action, and the Venetians must be sensitive to the political situation in Italy.

Uberti was to proceed with his fleet to Constantinople, but not too quickly. The Senate was cancelling the second phase of the operation. Uberti knew a second and more substantial fleet had been planned for the summer. His fleet was designed to reinforce, not necessarily to conquer. The commander was to conduct a tour of Greek islands, stopping at several ports with the appearance of adding forces and provisions. The real purpose was to slow down the reinforcement.

Uberti understood the point immediately. If the Hungarians were defeated by the Turks, or at least badly damaged, they would not be in a position to dominate the Balkans and the trade routes. Then they would need the Genoese and Venetians to assist them in defending their gains, and so would the Greeks. The status quo would remain, with the Italians dominating trade. If the Turks were eliminated as a factor in the meantime, so much the better. If not, they had dealt with the Turks for a century and had only been made richer for the effort. The Turks needed them and always would.

Uberti shook his head. He was sick of the perfidy and infighting of his Italian brethren. He saw the Turks as the primary threat to his people. Right now the Venetians and others were playing the Greeks and the Hungarians against each other as they had for a century. But the Greeks were almost gone as a buffer, and the Hungarians were not far behind. When these buffers were gone, then who would stop the Turks? They would be at the Venetians' door and the Italians were divided and weak, relying on their fleets and mercenaries rather than their own internal strength.

What should he do? Could he refuse these orders? What if he did? Someone else would immediately take the fleet over, and he would be dismissed, or even worse. He could ignore the orders and rush to Constantinople. Could his two thousand men make the difference against tens of thousands of Turks? Even if he could, what would be the benefit to him? He would still be punished, and perhaps many of his men with him.

There was little he could do about it. He would make his money, and when the time came he would be in a position to flee to greener pastures or bluer seas. At least Lecanella and a few ships would arrive in Constantinople shortly. They would be of some help. His hands were tied.

"Do you understand the instructions?"

"Yes, I do."

"I was required to ensure that you read and fully understood the instructions. I do not know the content of this message, but I was told if you dispute the orders, you are to return to the Senate house with me."

"I understand the instructions, and I will follow them. It will not be the first time I have followed orders I do not agree with. You may tell the Senate I am their humble servant, as always."

He thanked the messenger and dismissed him. He then turned and spoke with several of his key crew members, ordering an immediate forty-eight-hour furlough for the men. Let them rest up, no need to rush now. He watched the rider depart back to the Senate, and prayed that in the coming years there would still be a Senate to return to.

CHAPTER NINE

Constantine stood on the city walls near Blachernae with Notaras, Sphrantzes, and Giovanni. They looked out over the massive Ottoman camp. The rotting corpses of the Greeks still stood staked in the ground on the two ridges and in the Lycus Valley before him.

Constantine remembered standing in this same place only eight days before, watching the terrible impalement play out. The men were speechless as the agonizing screams of the captured Greeks floated over the valley to them.

They had stood for more than an hour, watching. They were previously informed by messenger what was occurring, and they had rushed from various parts of the city to the command tower. When they arrived, about half of the Greeks were already fully impaled and hanging in the air. They had watched the Turks cruelly impale the remaining prisoners. Giovanni, who was unused to the Turks' brutality and had never seen an impalement, had run to the end of the tower facing the city and vomited.

Constantine had much experience with the Turks, having fought them on a number of occasions, particularly on the ancient Greek mainland and in the Peloponnesus. While he had made much of the recent impalements in order to stir up anger among his people, he knew the Turks were not particularly barbaric. The Romans and their

successors the Greeks had employed beheadings, torture, and even cru-
cifixion regularly with not only enemies but their own populace. The
sophistication of his people had not reduced their cruelty, but rather
enhanced it, giving it a mathematical and scientific edge.

Constantine had been somewhat surprised that Mehmet had
resorted to impalement. He felt the decision showed his youth and was
nothing if not counterproductive to the sultan's cause. The people in
the city were horrified, terrified. The word had spread throughout
Constantinople that this was what could be expected if the Turks won
the day. The impalements had strengthened, not weakened, the resolve
of the people. Mehmet probably thought he would scare the city into
subjugation. He had badly miscalculated.

The true tragedy of the situation was the agonizing loss of life.
Constantine knew the two villages of Therapia and Studius well. He
had visited them each multiple times and even knew some of the people personally. They were all dead, and these few unlucky souls had
died even more terribly than the rest in front of him.

This terror had shaken them all badly, but also given them even
more resolve. And in the past week, this resolve had even turned to
hope. The initial moves of the sultan had been played out, and the city
showed no evidence of falling, even of bending. Constantine had been
shocked by the appearance of the huge Turkish navy, and feared the
city might be crushed immediately, but other than potentially cutting
off future aid, thus far the fleet was impotent. Notaras's insistence that
the sea chain be rebuilt had cut off the most vulnerable part of the city
from the sultan, and the recent attack on the chain was an unqualified
defeat for the sultan. Notaras, with the sea chain and his tiny fleet,
appeared able to keep the Turks at bay indefinitely.

Perhaps even more important, the cannon had thus far had no
meaningful impact on the city walls. Constantine had learned through
Sphrantzes that the main cannon had cracked at the first shot. He was
not sure if the sultan was giving up on the cannon, or just waiting to

repair the behemoth, but its silence had to be discouraging to the sultan. Of course, one volley did not make a siege. Constantine had little experience with siege cannon, but Giovanni had assured him that it was not a matter of if they would break the walls, but when.

That fact would have left Constantine hopeless except that Giovanni assured him that a breach was not the end of the world. So long as the Greeks and Italians could keep a fast mobile reserve in position with well-armed, elite men, they could plug the hole and wait until darkness to rebuild the wall with wooden palisades. Additionally, even if the Turks were able to break through the outer wall, they would still have to breach the larger, taller inner wall.

Although Constantine did not have the forces to guard this wall effectively, there still was no easy way into the city once the outer wall was breached. Men could be rushed to the point of attack, and also mount the inner wall to rain arrows and gunfire down on the attacking force. In some ways, a breach of the outer wall placed the attacking force in an even more dangerous position. A series of small doors, well hidden at angles, would allow Constantine and his men to appear as if from thin air to attack anyone who breached it.

After almost two weeks of the siege, Constantine felt a confident and calming peace. At this point, every day was a miracle, and God had already given the emperor twelve. He hoped that if the city could hold out a few more weeks, or at the longest a few months, the Turks would leave, and perhaps Mehmet would be discouraged for years to come.

Constantine had plans to rebuild the Greek military forces from the islands and the Morea, and to use the new alliance with Rome to cobble together a crusade of Italians, Greeks, and Hungarians to hit Mehmet from Constantinople in the south and from Hungary in the north. If Hunyadi came immediately, as Constantine had requested, they might even be able to attack during the siege itself. There was every possibility, given enough time to plan, that the Turks would be pushed back and weakened in Europe, if not driven out entirely. Millions of enslaved

Greeks would be freed. The power of the empire could be restored. He could marry Zophia.

Zophia. He was looking at the end of the world, or possibly the beginning, and his thoughts always returned to Zophia. He had not spoken with her since he had revealed the marriage embassy to Georgia. He had attempted to send her notes, gifts, everything. He could send men and have her summoned to the palace, but he knew that would only exacerbate the problem.

She was so stubborn. Did she not realize he needed her so badly? This siege was tearing him apart. The city teetered between destruction and salvation, sometimes by the minute. He could not sleep. He felt exhausted, his nerves frayed. He also felt an unexpected excitement. Battling for his life and the lives of his people carried a thrill he had never experienced before. He needed to share these thoughts with her, to be with her, love her, sleep by her side. He always slept so much better in her bed, as if she protected him in some way he had never been able to understand.

But he knew she would not see him. She was stronger than any person he had ever met. For her, there were no gray areas, there was only right and wrong. She might forgive without forgetting his decision to push through the Union of the Churches, but she would never be with him while he was seeking betrothal with another woman, regardless of the reason. For Zophia, he was hers alone, or she would not have him at all.

Constantine saw a sudden flash from the Turkish line, then another and another. He felt a rumbling vibration through the floor of his tower and then heard a tremendous series of explosions. The cannon! The giant cannon had finally been repaired and was being fired again. He looked out to assess the walls and was horrified to see a breach in the outer wall. They had breached the wall!

The Turks were screaming loudly in excitement and began streaming forward, sending arrows at the inner wall and rushing toward the city with weapons raised. Constantine had hoped the Foss would continue to serve as a factor in the fight, but it had not. The Turks—at considerable loss of life from arrows and musket fire from the walls— had worked day after day and had filled in small sections of the ditch. The Foss still served as a bottleneck point, where men had to slow down to make their way across the narrow sections that were filled in, but it no longer was a true barrier to the wall.

As Constantine watched, this was exactly what was happening. Men were jamming together at three or four points on the Foss and working their way across. Once they reached the near side they rushed forward toward the breach in the wall, screaming with weapons raised. Some stopped to fire arrows over the wall or at Greek archers on the outer wall. The defenders were killing a number of the Turks, particularly as they moved closer to the breach, but there were soon hundreds of Ottomans past the Foss, and they were all running as quickly as possible to gain the breach in the wall.

Constantine turned to Giovanni, who was already shouting commands. He sent as many archers forward as possible. They began raining arrows down on the advancing Turks, killing many and pinning them down outside the hole, at least for the moment. The Turks were also charging with tall siege ladders, slamming them up against the walls and attempting to climb up and over. Archers shot Turks as they attempted to climb, but they themselves were also shot off the wall by Turkish arrows fired from below.

Constantine felt an enormous rumble and was knocked to the hard ground of the tower. He pulled himself up and looked out. A cannonball had struck the base of the inner wall. Several men standing near Constantine had been blown out of the tower by the concussion of the cannonball, and had fallen to their death below.

Constantine felt pain in his head and placed a finger on his forehead, coming away with blood. His ears rang, and he was having difficulty concentrating. What was happening? A few volleys of the cannon and his walls were disappearing? Why had the first volley so many days ago done almost no damage? He realized now with horror that he had been lucky the first time, that the walls could not stand up to the cannon in the long term. They could be breached. He was also terrified to realize that the Turks were coming and his men must defend against the surge or they might soon break into the city itself.

Giovanni had already disappeared, heading down to the city level to rally his reserve force. Constantine shouted at the archers to keep a steady stream of fire at the Turks storming the breach, and he quickly climbed down with Notaras and Sphrantzes. He sent Sphrantzes into the city to rally additional reinforcements. Then, with Notaras and a few guards, Constantine went through one of the small doors in the inner wall that led into the gap between the walls. His body coursed with excitement but also with fear, and he realized that without quick action, the city could be only an hour away from falling.

As he arrived at the breaking point, he recognized with some relief that the breach was small so far, only the width of a few men. The Turks were already pressing in, but they had been met by several hundred heavily armed and armored Greeks and Italians commanded by Giovanni.

Giovanni had created this elite reserve force and trained it over the winter to quickly respond to a breach in the walls and to battle at that point as a last defense. Constantine was prepared to fight, but there was already a press of men surrounding the breach, so he watched, ready to assist.

He was impressed with the tactics utilized by Giovanni. The archers above in the towers kept a steady rain of arrows flying down on the Turks below. This left many dead and also blocked other Turks from pressing forward and slowed down the momentum of the attack. The Turks who appeared within the actual breach were only able to enter the gap between the walls a few at a time and were immediately met by the reserve force. The fighters out front would engage their enemies for a few minutes, then at Giovanni's command, they would step back, and a new line of fresh men would step in. The men of Constantinople were taking casualties, but only slowly, and thus far they held their ground.

The battle continued on for hours, or so it seemed to Constantine, although in the heat of combat he could not be sure of the actual passage of time. Turkish dead piled up on both sides and in front of the breach, further plugging the small hole. Miraculously, the cannon, despite ongoing volleys, failed to breach the outer wall again, although cracks appeared in many places.

Slowly the barrage wore on, with the smell of battle, blood, and dust filling the city. Finally, when it seemed the fighting would go on forever, the pressure began to slowly ease, then finally ended. Light began to fail, and the Turks retreated from the walls and streamed slowly back into their camps outside the city. Constantinople had survived to fight another day.

Constantine found Giovanni in the failing light and clasped him on the back, congratulating him on his victory. Giovanni bowed and then went to work organizing aid to the wounded.

As darkness fell, Giovanni set his men to repairing the breach to the outer wall. The original concrete and limestone walls could not be rebuilt overnight, but Giovanni plugged the breach with a heavy wood palisade. The wall was reinforced with long beams placed at perpendicular angles against the flat surface. The Genoan commander assured Constantine that the wooden structure was nearly as strong as the walls themselves and could be quickly replaced when additional damage occurred. Giovanni employed a huge force of several hundred Greek citizens whom he had trained and drilled these many winter months in rebuilding siege defenses. All the hard work paid off. Constantine congratulated himself again in having the foresight to put Giovanni in charge of the defenses, even over the objection of his friend Notaras.

When some time had passed and the work looked well organized, Constantine pulled Giovanni aside to discuss the day's battle.

"How close did they come to breaking through?" he asked the Genoan.

"That is a matter of how you look at it, my Lord," said Giovanni, managing a wry smile. "They did not come very close to getting into the city at all, in terms of the one breach they did make. As you saw, we quickly brought our reserves into position and once they were there, the Turks had no chance of breaking in.

"But of course, there are many variables. We were very fortunate that the breach was small, and also that it occurred so close to our command tower. I was able to quickly bring the forces to this point, so we were only fighting a few Turks at any given time. We had almost a perfect problem to solve here."

"But it is true that other things could have gone wrong?"

"Many things, my Lord. If a breach occurred somewhere farther along the walls, we would take some time to arrive there. Let us say that a hundred or more Turks made it through the hole and spread out. Now our reserve force is fighting on a more widespread front, with more Turks pouring in behind them. In that situation, we could probably fight for some hours, and we might even plug the hole again, but there would be no guarantee."

"And multiple breaches?"

"Exactly. If there are multiple breaches, we might end up spread too thin. I think we could handle two at the same time, but three or four? That was my main worry today. After the first hole was blown through so quickly, I was sure that there would be multiple breaches during the day."

"And then the city would fall?"

"I do not like to think that way, my Lord. I have not lost a city or a castle yet, and there have been times when I was sure that I would. I think we have to focus on what *did* happen. Whether it was the will of God, or whatever the reason for our miracle, the walls did not fall today. The Turks did not achieve multiple breaches. The city still stands.

"I have to think this is a blow to the sultan. Siege warfare is as much mental battle as physical. The attacking force can only sit outside for so long, and can only suffer so many failed attacks, before it gives up and leaves. Granted, there have been sieges that lasted for years, but mostly they are a matter of a season or two. And usually there are not constant attacks; usually it is only a few here and there. We have fought off the first attack, and the second, if you consider Notaras's victory at the sea boom. I feel confident we can hold the city, my Lord, given a little luck and of course divine assistance."

Constantine was encouraged. He had been so sure the city was going to fall today after the shock of the breach. During the battle itself he had felt a strange calm, almost an internal peace. He simply watched the events unfold. But once the Turks had retreated, he felt an overwhelming exhaustion and noticed his hands trembled so badly he had to hide them behind his back.

"I know one thing, my friend: The city would have already fallen if it was not for you. Without your help, we would never have had the walls repaired, and we certainly would not have been prepared for what happened today. When you suggested keeping back a force away from the walls I was skeptical, because we are so shorthanded. Now I understand."

Giovanni bowed and smiled. "My Lord, I am happy I can be of service. I have been a soldier all my life. Truth be told, I have never been in a siege like this, with so much at stake. I know we can defend the city and drive back the Turks. Again, if it is God's will."

"It must be God's will. Is this not God's city? The first great Christian city? We have lost Jerusalem, but it was never truly our city; it was the city of the Jews and now of the Arabs. Alexandria was the city of the Egyptians and our pagan Greek ancestors. Even Rome was built and dedicated to false gods. Constantinople was built by Constantine the Great, dedicated to Christ and to the Virgin. There have been so many times when it seemed the city would fall to infidels, but it never has, unless you count my Latin cousins, whom we have forgiven, if not forgotten. Thank you again, Giovanni; you will be richly rewarded when we have driven the Turks back. You will be Lord of Lemnos, and will be a hero of the Greeks. In fact, you already are."

Giovanni bowed again, and Constantine left the walls, wearily mounting his horse and making his way slowly through the quiet streets of the city. They were unusually deserted, as if the struggle of the day had exhausted the entire population. He wandered through the city for a time, enjoying the relief of their salvation. He eventually made his way to Zophia's house. He knocked on the door and waited for an answer. He heard her voice within asking who was there, and he answered. After some hesitation, she opened the door, although she did not invite him in. She was dressed in a silk sleeping robe. She was so beautiful, and he missed her so much. He felt his heart nearly bursting.

"So we survived another day," she commented. "I'm glad you're still alive."

"May I come in?"

"I'm sorry. I cannot let you in."

"Won't you please? I beg of you, I have so many things I want to tell you. Please, Zophia, I am so sorry. Please let me explain."

"What do you want to explain to me that we have not already discussed? I understand why you felt forced to do this. You made your choice, and I understand why you made it. I have also made my choice. I never hid my feelings about this. You understood them. What are you asking now, that I pretend you are not going to marry someone else? Should I become your whore? Should I sit here at night, waiting for you to sneak out of your bed and come to me? I cannot do it, Constantine. I will not."

"I know, Zophia, I know. But can I not at least come in and talk to you? Cannot you at least be my friend? You know there is no one else I can talk to. This marriage proposal will not even happen. It is Sphrantzes's dream."

"I am sorry, my love. I love you, you know I do, but I cannot do it. If you come in, I will kiss you. If I kiss you, I will be with you. I cannot stop myself. You are everything to me. But I cannot. I cannot see you, and I cannot spend time with you. You have made your choice, and I must be true to mine."

Constantine looked at her. Why could they not just leave, sail away from this city and the stupid "empire" that hardly extended beyond the walls of Constantinople?

"We could just leave together. Just you and me. I have some secret personal funds left. We could climb aboard a ship and go into exile. We would be welcome in Rome, or anywhere in Italy for that matter. We could live together, marry, have children together."

She laughed. "Who is dreaming now? I know you, my love. You may give everything *for* your city, but you will not sacrifice Constantinople for anything or anyone."

He smiled back. "I suppose you're right. You always have known me better than anyone else. But that is why I need you now. I need your support. I can get through all of this with you, but not without you."

"I am easily yours, Constantine. Send a second messenger canceling your betrothal negotiation, and I am yours the second he departs. Even simply announce to the city that you will marry me. Do so, and I am yours in an instant. But I won't be your second woman. It would destroy me, and I would have nothing to give you, no way to support you."

Why didn't he do just what she suggested? The ship he had sent into the Black Sea probably had been sunk by the Turks in any event. If it was not, there was no guarantee that the Georgians would offer enough to make it worthwhile, or that any aid could come in time. But what if it could? What if it was the final aid that tipped the advantage to the Greeks? If only the pope's assistance were delivered. If only the Turks simply abandoned the siege.

"You do not have to answer, dearest. I already know you will not give up even a small chance for your city. Know that I love you for it. But please, please, let me be. We both must suffer alone."

She pulled him to her and kissed him. He could taste her sweet lips, smell her hair. He held her close, not wanting to let go. They stood together for long minutes before she finally pulled away. "Go, my Prince. Go save Constantinople. I will be here, praying for our city. Praying for you. Praying for us."

Tears streamed down her face. She looked so pale—unwell. "Are you sick, my dearest? What is wrong with you?" He reached for her again, but she pushed his hands away.

"I have been ill. I'm . . . I'm sure it is simply this siege. We all suffer. We suffer God's displeasure. Please, you must go, Constantine. I cannot be here with you any longer. I'm sorry."

She shut the door slowly, and Constantine stood outside for a long while, regaining his composure. Thank God she still loved him, still understood him. He so desperately wanted her to give in, but he loved her for the person she was, and Zophia would never compromise her beliefs. He mounted, turned his horse slowly, and rode onward.

Soon he could make out the towering dome of St. Sophia against the skyline. He smiled. He had come to his other woman, the heart of his city. His great cathedral. He dismounted and walked silently through the darkness, moving among the shadows to avoid the occasional passerby. He wanted to be alone.

He entered the church quietly and crept up the stairs in the near darkness. He had to feel along the wall to make sure he was heading in the right direction. Soon he had felt his way to the second floor. He walked on to the imperial platform. He had gone undetected as he had hoped, and he dropped down softly, kneeling in the darkness lit only by the candles below. He closed his eyes and prayed.

He thanked God for saving his city again, for the miracles of the day. He prayed that God would continue to protect Constantinople, and would lead the Turks to lift the siege and leave the city. He thanked God for Zophia, for her courage and strength. He prayed they would be together again. He thanked God for Giovanni, and for the brave men who had died or been wounded today. Finally he prayed for his people, and asked God and the Virgin to deliver them in safety.

Constantine arrived back at the palace shortly before midnight. He bathed hurriedly, changed clothes, and joined Notaras, Giovanni, and Sphrantzes for a late dinner and council. They discussed in detail the attack on the city, and Constantine again praised Giovanni in front of the others. Notaras updated them on the naval situation, which had remained static since the victory at the sea boom. Sphrantzes had the most important news.

"I have finally established a connection within the Ottoman camp. The highest possible connection. I have learned some very interesting things. Apparently the decision to attack Constantinople was on its surface unanimous, but there are many ministers and advisors who felt it was a mistake. This faction, which includes the Grand Vizier Halil, is looking for a way out. The failure at the sea chain was already seen by this group of dissenters as a possible reason to put pressure on Mehmet to lift the siege. The failure today at the land wall must surely be another significant disappointment."

"So you are saying they might be willing to just walk away?" asked Constantine.

"Correct, assuming there is enough pressure on Mehmet. There is even some talk of replacing him if they do push the point and he won't agree. You have to remember, he's still a child as far as Halil and the rest perceive him. A petulant child at that. But they also have to be careful and then swiftly decisive. Technically, he is all-powerful. He certainly could order any one of them killed, and the order would probably be carried out before anyone could stop him."

"Where are you hearing all of this?" asked Notaras.

"I would rather not say, as I do not want our spy to be compromised."

"Sphrantzes, who is going to say something? Would it be me or Constantine? We're not at a supreme council here."

Sphrantzes hesitated and looked to Constantine. The emperor nodded.

"Halil."

"What?" demanded Constantine. "The grand vizier told you this? Why would he tell you, or any Greek, anything?"

"A couple of reasons, I think. First, he believes that capturing Constantinople will be a waving banner that will bring all of the West against them. He wants to avoid that at all cost. Second, he cannot stand Mehmet. You will remember he was instrumental in removing Mehmet from power before. Third, he is in our pay."

"He is accepting bribes?"

"Yes, he is, and it is not the first time. Apparently he accepted gifts from the previous emperor as well."

"I have a hard time believing this," said Notaras.

"It is true. And he is reaching out to us again for assistance. He has a request."

"What request?"

"He is asking that we renew our offer to increase tribute in exchange for the Ottomans lifting the siege. He believes that given the recent failures, he should have enough power to pressure Mehmet to lift the siege."

"We already made that offer, and it was rejected."

"Yes, my Lord, but now Mehmet has experienced several failures. I think he believed the city would fall very quickly. Now is the time to renew the offer and see what happens."

"Notaras, what do you think?"

"Well, my Lord, I have some serious reservations about the source and quality of Sphrantzes's information. As you know, I do not like these secrets and spies." Sphrantzes was about to interrupt him, but Notaras raised his hand. "However, I do not see any harm in renewing the offer. If Mehmet declines, then at the worst, he has said no twice to the same thing. If he accepts, then they will leave the city. And who knows, perhaps Halil would be able to remove Mehmet. It is really a free opportunity to see what happens."

"We are in rare agreement, Notaras," said Sphrantzes, "even if I do not agree at all with the way you approach the problem."

James D. Shipman

Constantine looked at his two friends for a few moments. "It is settled, then. We will renew our previous offer and see what ultimately comes of it. I agree that there can hardly be a negative effect. Any other updates, Sphrantzes?"

"We haven't heard anything from the pope yet, or from the Georgians. I believe we would have heard back if the Turks had sunk our ship sent to Georgia. It is always possible, I suppose, that it was sunk in the Black Sea away from land, but that is somewhat unlikely as we can maneuver more effectively with wind power, which allows for speed and maneuverability in open water. If all went well, our ambassador should be there or hopefully on the way back by now."

"Nothing back from the pope? How frustrating. I had hoped we would have a relief fleet by now. Still, I can only assume it is a matter of days before we receive at least a vanguard fleet. It would be nice to hear from Gregory as well about Hunyadi. I wonder if the pope sent him a message as I requested.

"We wait still. Perhaps we will not have to worry about it at all. Perhaps this peace gesture will end our problems. Tell me, Sphrantzes, and I apologize for returning to an earlier issue, but is there any possibility that we could simply wait a little longer, and not increase our tribute? We can scarcely afford an increase."

"My Lord, I think we have to take the option of making an offer. Halil has directly requested our assistance. It is likely he would be instrumental in any future regime; it is even possible he himself could replace Mehmet. We need to look to future cooperation as well as short-term strategy."

"All right, Sphrantzes, send the message. This is under the same terms as before but let's offer some additional annual tribute to sweeten the pot for the dissenters. Let us see whether our young cub has bitten off more than he can chew."

CHAPTER TEN

WEDNESDAY, APRIL 18, 1453

Mehmet watched the darkness fall and his men stumble back from the land walls, exhausted, many of them wounded. He could see the frustration in their faces. He felt the same. They had been so close! The walls had shattered under the first few cannon volleys. When the giant cannon blew a breach in the outer wall, he thought the city was his. He immediately ordered his Janissaries into the breach, to battle through and take the city. He watched, expecting his forces to stream through the hole. Instead, he witnessed hours of logjammed pushing at the breach. The bodies piled up, and his elite forces made no real progress. As darkness approached they began losing momentum, and he was finally forced to order a retreat.

Was he cursed? This was to be his moment. But like at so many "almost" moments, his men failed him. They had failed at the sea chain, failed in the initial cannon volley on April 6, and failed him now in this critical attack.

Perhaps he should kill some of the attackers as a lesson for the rest? No, what could it prove? He had watched the attack. The men had fought as courageously and aggressively as was possible. The breach was simply too small, and apparently the Greeks on the other side had fought even more desperately than his own men. He needed a bigger breach, or multiple breaches.

He had been unlucky. Life at times depended on good or ill fortune. Unfortunately he had no time for luck. He had gambled everything on this venture. His council had reluctantly approved it, but he knew he had pushed it through far earlier than anyone advised. He needed results, and he needed them now, before Halil could rally his enemies against him.

Zaganos was back with him. The sultan had called him over at the moment of the first breach, not to lead an attack but to watch his moment of triumph. Halil had appeared as well, and looked dejected at first, until it became obvious the attack would fail. Now all three stood together, watching the retreat.

"A noble attempt, my Lord," said Halil. "Surely we will succeed next time."

Zaganos added, "I agree, my Sultan. It was but a moment's fortune that the Greeks held out this time. The cannon will make other breaches, and we will battle through. Perhaps we should wait next time for a bigger breach?"

"Yes. Next time we will succeed," said Mehmet, not really sure he felt that way. "I agree that we will need a bigger breach. All of our advantages are taken away by a small hole in the walls. The Greeks are able to bring equal numbers and to fight us to a standstill. I also suspect we will wake up tomorrow and find the breach has been repaired. I understand that this Giovanni Longo who leads the Greek forces has substantial experience in siege warfare."

"Yes, bad luck he arrived so shortly before the siege," said Zaganos.

"Well, let us not dwell too deeply on a minor setback. Let us have our evening meal and talk about the future."

The men followed the sultan into his tent, and they were soon dining on a rich variety of food and drink. Mehmet had spared no comfort in his tent and had assured that a steady supply of food was brought from Edirne for both his troops and himself. They enjoyed their meal and then stayed up late into the night, discussing the strategy of the siege and also the past and future of the Ottoman people.

Mehmet noticed Halil would not speak about the future in any detail. He smiled to himself. *There is no sense dwelling too much on the future, is there, my friend? Neither of us intends to share it with the other. So be it. You can serve my father again in paradise, since you will not serve me in this world.*

In the early morning, a messenger disturbed them and handed Halil a note. The grand vizier read it.

"Well, this is very interesting news, my Lord."

"What is?"

"I have received a letter from Constantine. He offers substantially the same terms he offered on the first day of the siege. But he will increase his tribute to you if you lift the siege."

Mehmet was incensed. He did not need additional pressure. "Bah," he said. "They offer us a little more money but nothing else after we almost take the city. He is afraid. He should be begging me for any terms of mercy and handing the city to me now. He knows it is just a matter of days."

"With all respect, my Lord, I would beg you to consider the offer more closely. You were brilliant to have developed your navy and also these cannon before the siege. But again, we find Constantinople somehow escapes us. The Greeks block us at sea with the sea chain. Your cannon have shown some benefit, but they have not opened up a usable breach. Your men must be exhausted and frustrated by the attack today. I certainly would not say that we are in a position where we *must* lift the siege now, but if another month goes by with no additional progress, the men will grow very restless. If we are forced to lift the siege, you certainly will get no more money from Constantine. Instead he will cut off all tribute. He will have defied you, and in defying you he will have won sympathy from the West.

"We know he already agreed to their ridiculous church union, as if one infidel's church is better than another. Their differences may seem silly and incomprehensible to us, but apparently the pope is very impressed with their decision to implement this Union. We could face considerable forces from the West, even from Hungary, in just a few short months."

Mehmet had expected this argument. "I am not surprised to hear this from you. But again, I disagree. There is no point in putting our attack off for another season. We do not need the money from the Greeks. There is far more wealth available by taking and rebuilding the city. We can then regulate the trade from the Black Sea, and we will be in an even better position to deal with the Venetians, Genoese, and the rest.

"The key argument is aid from the West. I do not think any measureable aid can come in time. Our cannon will blow another hole or two in the walls tomorrow. When they do, we will rush in and take the city."

He realized he should placate Halil somewhat, and stall for time. "I will hold off on any decision for a few days, and see what our progress is. Hopefully, by the end of the day tomorrow, the city will be ours and our problems will be solved."

Halil was pleased with the decision. "Thank you, my Lord. I think you should carefully consider the offer, and I agree another day or two should make no difference. I sincerely hope you are successful in taking the city before we have to respond to Constantine."

No you do not, thought Mehmet. *You want me to fail. Beyond that, you know what will happen if I succeed. You are positioning yourself to destroy me, now that you know I cannot be led.*

Mehmet felt grim satisfaction that he understood Halil so well but also a nagging disappointment he had felt many times in the past and could never force himself to subdue. There was a part of him that yearned for Halil's acceptance. Why would the Grand Vizier not respect him and follow his commands? Must it always be the disgruntled Halil, sitting back disapprovingly and waiting for his moment to intervene? He hated Halil deeply. Hated himself for needing his approval. When

Halil's head sat on a pole on the palace walls, he would think of him no more, he promised himself. For now he needed to deal with his grand vizier as best as he was able.

"What do you think, Zaganos?"

"I think you have a wise plan, my Lord," said Zaganos. "With Allah's will, we will break through the city today or tomorrow. If not, we will consider the terms again."

Mehmet was satisfied. He dismissed them and took a few short hours of sleep. In the midmorning, he arose and ordered a renewal of the bombardment. He noted that Constantine had succeeded in rebuilding portions of the wall overnight, which he had known would happen, although he was surprised by the extent of the repairs. This bastard Giovanni truly was a misfortune on his plans. He must keep the Genoan busy.

Mehmet's cannon kept up a continuous attack on the walls for the rest of the day, but while the barrage caused cracks and chips all along the outer wall for several hundred yards on either side of the sultan's command tent, the cannon failed to significantly breach the walls again as it had done so spectacularly the day before.

Mehmet met with Orban at the end of the day. He ordered that the cannon fire be concentrated on a small area of the land wall the next day. He hoped by firing all of the cannon simultaneously at a small portion of the wall, he would force a more significant breach. He also ordered his Janissaries to form at dawn and prepare to storm the city. He then fell into a restless sleep.

FRIDAY, APRIL 20, 1453

Mehmet was awakened at sunrise, but not by cannon fire. A frantic messenger begged permission to enter. The sultan beckoned him inside and opened the message. A hastily scrawled note from Zaganos informed him that ships had arrived in the Sea of Marmara and were heading toward the Golden Horn. A relief fleet from the West.

Mehmet rushed out of bed. He ordered the messenger to leave his tent. He felt shaken, dizzy. Was he to lose everything after all of his plans? He had worked so hard and he had nearly taken the city only two days before. Now he faced a relief fleet that could be bringing supplies, food, and thousands of men to defend the city. He finished dressing and quickly left his tent. His guards were already mounted and his horse had been saddled. He leapt on his mount and took off at a gallop toward Galata.

He arrived on the Bosporus shore several hours later. Zaganos was anxiously waiting for him. Mehmet looked out past the Galata walls and in to the Sea of Marmara. He strained his eyes to see at first but eventually could make out a few masts in the distance. Much closer, he saw ships of his fleet sailing out of the Bosporus to intercept the enemy fleet. He was relieved to see that the number of enemy ships seemed small, only three or four that he could make out.

"I see you ordered the fleet to attack, Zaganos. Thank you, that was exactly my order."

"I assumed as much, my Lord. I kicked that fat Baltaoglu out of his tent and sent him after the Italians. He moved very quickly. I think you may have made your point with him the last time around!" Zaganos smirked.

"Do we know how many ships are out there?" asked the Sultan.

"Well, as you can see, there appear to be only a few. I would think this is just a small enterprise, unless it is the vanguard of a larger fleet."

Mehmet was greatly relieved, at least for now. This did not appear to be some great navy with thousands of reinforcements. There might be a few hundred men aboard, and perhaps food and supplies, but nothing that could hold back his army if they were able to break through the walls. In addition, he saw real opportunity here. Just as the razing of the small castles in the first days of the siege had raised the morale of the land troops, the destruction of these ships could serve a similar purpose. If his fleet could sink the enemy ships, particularly in full sight of Constantinople, he would strike a great blow to the morale of the Greeks and restore his own men's faith in the siege.

"What orders did you give Baltaoglu?" Mehmet asked anxiously.

"I ordered him to sink all of the ships before they gained the city. Was that incorrect, Sultan?"

"No, that is excellent. Good thinking, Zaganos. Is there any chance they can escape us?"

"As you know, I really have no idea. But I cannot imagine how they would. I think you will have a victory to celebrate today."

Mehmet was pleased and excited. He impatiently watched the loading of the fleet. Men struggled in small groups to carry cannon onto the ships. Groups of soldiers, including Janissaries, were also boarding to reinforce the complement of sailors. The men were armed to the teeth with bows, spears, swords, and firearms. The sultan shouted encouragement to the men and received confident cheers in return. Soon the majority of the ships departed. Mehmet remounted his horse with Zaganos and his guard to find a place to watch the impending battle.

They rode together along the shore near the walls of Galata, moving as close as they could to the Golden Horn so they could observe the destruction of the fleet. They arrived at the high ground with a commanding view of the Golden Horn and the ships. They were close enough to the ships that Mehmet was able to shout orders to Baltaoglu as he floated by. "Take the ships, Admiral, or do not come back!" He received a grim bow in response.

The Italian galleys drew closer to the city. Mehmet was able to make out the red cross and white background of the city of Genoa. There were three merchant galleys and what appeared to be a heavy transport that flew the imperial double-headed eagle symbol of the Greeks. No additional ships had appeared on the horizon, so Mehmet was satisfied that this small relief fleet was all that was coming at the present time.

As the Ottoman ships moved out to meet the Italians, Mehmet could hardly contain himself. He had at least one hundred vessels heading out to intercept them. One hundred against four. He looked out over the Horn to Constantinople. Hundreds, perhaps thousands, of people had gathered on rooftops and at the Acropolis and the crumbling Hippodrome to watch the relief fleet. His navy would crush the Italians in full view of the Greeks and prove in no uncertain terms that it was impossible to reinforce the city. This victory was exactly what he needed to relieve the pressure from Halil and ensure the extension of the siege.

At midafternoon, the fleets finally met. A single cannon shot quickly turned into dozens. The din of cannon fire and the screaming of men floated across the sea and could be heard clearly. Mehmet strained his eyes to see what was going on, but it was difficult to make out the individual ships as they smashed together. He expected shouts of victory any moment.

As time passed, however, he could make out the Genoese flags and see that these ships continued to sail toward the Horn, seemingly cutting through his fleet. The wind whipped in his face, it was blowing favorably for the Italians and Greeks, allowing the Genoese ships and the imperial transport to use their sails while the Ottomans had to rely on oar power. The ships kept coming, their speed under wind power allowing them to press through the Ottomans and the choppy water preventing Mehmet's ships from closing quickly enough to board them.

Mehmet was furious. How could this be? All of the odds were in his favor. He had to crush these ships. If they were able to somehow get through, it would be a disaster for him personally, and for the morale of his men. What was this idiot Admiral getting at?

Then a miracle occurred. Mehmet could feel the wind slacken and then the air became entirely still. He could see the sails of the Frankish fleet falter, and the ships slowed to a halt. They were quickly surrounded by Ottoman ships on all sides. Now his men could pull up close and throw hooks, ropes, and ladders aboard the enemy ships.

The screaming and shouting increased. Mehmet could see the battle more closely now as the ships floated slowly toward the Horn. The Genoese ships sat higher up, with tall decks. This appeared to give the Italians an advantage as they battled with the Ottomans. Mehmet's men were forced to climb upward into a forest of shields and spears. Crossbowmen hung from ropes and masts above, firing bolts into the Turks as they struggled to gain control of the ships. Cannon shot rained against the ships but seemed to have no effect.

Still, there could be no doubt of the final decision. Without the wind, the fresh ships were surrounded. There were multiple Ottoman ships pressed against each ship of the enemy. Mehmet could see Turks battling with grappling hooks and with ladders, and there was fighting aboard at least two of the Italian ships. It would only be a matter of time before they were all captured. Capturing them was even better than sinking them. He would parade the provisions in front of the city and perhaps even impale another round of prisoners to reinforce his earlier point.

The ships battled for hours, floating ever closer to the Horn and to Mehmet. Baltaoglu's ship, which was now connected, along with a number of other Ottoman vessels, to the imperial transport, had floated into earshot.

Mehmet spurred his horse down the hill and into the waters of the Bosporus. He wished he could ride out and take control of the battle. What was this fool of an admiral doing? He screamed commands at the flagship, ordering the admiral to take the ships now, threatening, encouraging. He felt a mixture of helplessness, anger, and excitement. If he could only be on one of the ships. Why did he not board one this morning when he had had a chance? If he were on the Admiral's ship, he would have already destroyed these Italians. His commander clearly did not know how to motivate his men. Mehmet was being failed again.

Still, it appeared his men would eventually succeed. Each Italian ship was now completely surrounded and connected to multiple Ottoman ships. No enemy ship had fallen yet, but would soon. The Greeks and Italians were fighting courageously, but they were taking casualties. The Ottomans were losing men too, however they had an almost endless supply of reinforcements and could rotate their ships out of the line and replace them with fresh warriors. Mehmet watched anxiously, his sword drawn, shouting his commands and straining to see which ship would surrender or fall first. Victory would be his.

As the sun was setting, the wind began again. He could feel it in the water, beginning gently and picking up. Surely it was too late for the Italians to escape? He watched frantic activity on the enemy ships. Even as they continued to fight off the Ottomans, they also reset their sails, which were soon filled with wind. The ships began to pick up speed, slowly at first and then more quickly. The Italians concentrated on cutting the grappling ropes, and soon they were breaking free from the tight mass of Ottoman ships. Mehmet screamed in anger, shouting at his men to stop the ships. There was nothing he could do; the Italians were gradually pulling away, turning into the Horn toward the sea chain. Greek fire ships stood off the chain, ready to assist the fleet. Mehmet could hear the cheers rising from across the Golden Horn. The Greeks of Constantinople were celebrating. The Ottomans had failed.

Mehmet leaped off his horse and fell to his knees in the freezing surf, beating his fists against the sand and screaming. How could this happen! One hundred ships to four. Thousands of men against a few hundred! How could Allah allow this? What curse was on him? What curse on his fleet? He had built this fleet so carefully. He had studied why his ancestors and others had failed to take the city. Sea power was one of the key factors. He had addressed it by building this great fleet to stop any relief force and to attack the sea walls.

But the fleet had proved an utter failure. First they had been denied access to the Horn by the sea chain. Now, and even more disastrous, a tiny force had outfought and outmaneuvered his ships, and given the Greeks an unforeseen victory. If four ships could defy him, what could twenty do? Perhaps destroy his fleet entirely!

These four ships could not turn the tide, but certainly a larger fleet could. If he could not stop Constantinople from being relieved, then his army would fail. He *had* failed. How could he continue the siege now? Halil had already exerted pressure this morning. Now the conditions were even worse. What should he do? Should he save his position and accept the peace terms? Then he would be even more under Halil's thumb. He probably would have to dismiss Zaganos and the rest of his faction of ministers. He would become a puppet. But he would be alive. If he defied Halil now and continued the siege, he might be dead in a few days, perhaps even tonight.

This was Baltaoglu's fault. He would kill that Bulgarian bastard with his own hands.

Mehmet looked out over the Golden Horn and watched the Greeks. They were cheering and clapping, even dancing in joy. He could see the happiness in every expression. His own people, by contrast, watched silently.

And now the failure of two days ago became even greater. His victories at the castles seemed shallow. He had been able to do nothing against the great city.

Instead, Constantine had defeated him at every turn. He did not have time for this! His father could afford months and nobody would complain. Nobody would have dared complain. But he was not given that luxury. His advisors circled him like vultures, ready to swoop down and destroy him the moment he was weak. And he was weak now. Weak because of this fool of an admiral.

He was so angry he could barely see. He mounted his horse and galloped along the Bosporus shore toward the fleet. He arrived far ahead of the retreating ships and dismounted, pacing back and forth like a caged tiger while he awaited the return of his failed fleet. The ships seemed to take an eternity. The sultan seethed; all he could think of was punishing this idiot for ruining all of his plans.

The ships moved closer, including the admiral's flagship. Mehmet could see Baltaoglu on the deck; he was carefully watching the sultan. He must know what was coming.

The flagship finally docked and the admiral jumped down and immediately fell to his knees with his head facing down and his arms out, touching the ground in abject prostration.

Mehmet rushed forward screaming and delivered a kick to his head. The Bulgarian fell over hard, crashing against the ground and rocking back and forth in pain. Mehmet turned to one of his guards. "Impale this dog!" he commanded. "He failed me and embarrassed us before the Greeks! Let everyone see the price of failure!"

"My Lord, surely you will not kill him." Mehmet was surprised to hear the voice of Halil. When had the grand vizier arrived? "I would ask that you spare his life at least."

Mehmet glared at Halil and thoughts raced through him. He wanted to kill Baltaoglu with his own hands. Could he kill both of them before anyone attempted to intervene? He raised his weapon to strike, but Halil stepped quickly in between with his hands raised. "No, Sultan. Please. I ask you to spare his life."

What should he do? He started to calm down, forcing himself to think. He was not sure why the grand vizier would care one way or another about Baltaoglu, but was there an opportunity here. If he spared the admiral, then Halil would be in his debt. Perhaps that would give him a few more days. He needed time. He needed it more than he needed the head of this fool. He hesitated a moment longer and then decided.

"For you, my Grand Vizier, I will spare his life. But do not forget this favor." He turned to Baltaoglu. "You are hereby stripped of all titles, lands, and money. You will be lashed one hundred times here and now. Then you will be assigned as a slave to one of your own ships."

Mehmet kicked the admiral again, then stepped away. His guards rushed forward and seized Baltaoglu. They dragged him screaming to a wooden pylon that had been driven into the ground near the beach to temporarily anchor ships. The guards lashed his hands to the pole and then ripped off his shirt, exposing his bare back.

A particularly strong Janissary came forward at Mehmet's beckoning, holding a menacing horsewhip. He pulled the whip backward and then quickly forward, lashing Baltaoglu's back. The former admiral screamed, his entire body going rigid. A red mark appeared across his back and quickly filled with blood. Another lash. A second mark formed and Baltaoglu writhed in agony. A third lash and the Bulgarian passed out, his knees buckling to the ground. Mehmet stood still with Halil beside him, and watched all one hundred lashes administered. Mehmet did not enjoy the blood, or the wretched tatters of skin that were all that remained of the admiral's back. But this served its purpose. Halil was visibly sickened and upset. Their ride back to the city walls was quiet. Mehmet hoped he had made his point.

Halil and Mehmet arrived at the sultan's tent in time for the planned council meeting. Zaganos joined them, along with Mehmet's other field commanders and a number of the members of the old guard, who sat with Halil. The council ate a late dinner and chatted about trivial matters. After dinner was cleared away, they turned to the business at hand.

Not surprisingly, Halil immediately raised the peace overture. He briefed the council and completed his remarks by recommending that the sultan counter with a huge annual tribute requirement of seventy thousand ducats per year. If this was accepted, it would cripple the feeble economy of Constantinople and the city would probably fall within a year or two just from economic collapse. There were murmurs of agreement from a number of the ministers. Mehmet watched the expressions carefully. He was alarmed to see that several of the younger members of the council, members whom he had hand selected, now appeared to side with Halil.

Zaganos spoke next. He argued against accepting a peace. "I agree with Halil that the fleet has proved a disappointment. We had counted on using it to stop any aid from coming into the city. We now know that that is not going to work. If a big relief fleet does appear, we will do everything we can to block it, but we must calculate that such a fleet would reach Constantinople safely."

"All the more reason to lift the siege," retorted Halil.

"I was not finished! I agree this is a greater risk, but we are very close to taking the city. We almost broke through. It is only a matter of time before we get in. We should proceed. There will never be a better opportunity. The Hungarians could attack us at any moment. So far they have not. The Italians are split and indecisive. This religious Union is recent, and the pope has not yet reacted. If we wait, we may face a united attack, led by Constantine and John Hunyadi. We cannot secure our rear while Constantinople remains behind in enemy hands. Let us end this now!"

There were murmurs of agreement from some of the council, but clearly Zaganos now represented the minority position. Mehmet was running out of time.

Halil hesitated. "I disagree with Zaganos, but as always, this is your choice, my Lord."

Mehmet stood and looked around slowly, meeting the eyes of each of the council members. He paused as if considering what to do. "I appreciate everyone's advice. I think we should follow a compromise position. Let us continue the siege for now, but let us send a counteroffer to Constantine. If he leaves the city, he can have all of the Peloponnesus as his kingdom, *and* we will grant him a peace treaty and a yearly stipend for the rest of his lifetime. We will also agree to a mutual defense treaty against any attack by any power on his territory. He may take all wealth and all people with him that he is capable of transporting. This would give him security for his lifetime."

"Those are generous terms, Sultan," said Halil. "Perhaps some would say the terms were too generous. But he will not accept it. He will never leave the city."

"So be it. We will make this generous offer, and if he accepts it or not, it is Allah's will. I am not going to worry about fleets and armies that have not arrived. The Hungarians and the Italians may be coming, but they are not here now. We are here. We have our men in place. We will attack until we breach the walls. If we fail, it will be my failure. I will face the consequences, whatever Allah wills. The siege continues."

The council members bowed, acquiescing at least for now to the will of the young sultan.

"Let us hope we can prevent further reinforcement from the sea, my Lord." This was Halil's parting shot, and he was clearly emphasizing the sultan's failure.

"Yes, indeed, let us hope and pray." Mehmet would do more than pray. He would act.

CHAPTER ELEVEN

FRIDAY APRIL 20, 1453

Constantine sat mounted near the Acropolis and watched silently with great tension as the naval battle unfolded. He had been torn by so many conflicting emotions. First the excitement of a relief fleet, followed by disappointment that it was only four ships. Then horror at the massive Turkish fleet attempting to block the Italians, and finally elation when the wind picked up and the ships escaped toward the Golden Horn. Surely this was a miracle from God. How could four ships evade one hundred, particularly when they were surrounded for hours with no wind?

Now, as the tiny fleet made its way through the sea chain that was opened for them, he felt peace and happiness. He acknowledged the cheers and waves of his people as they shared this great moment of victory. He bowed his head and prayed, thanking God for delivering this precious fleet to the city.

He was joined by Sphrantzes, and the two of them rode down along the sea wall to the harbor, where they would anxiously await the docking of the fleet. The harbor was crowded with Greeks and Italians, smiling and celebrating. Constantine looked around. In the crowd he spotted Zophia. She was looking at him. He waved and smiled. She smiled back, knowing how much this small gesture meant to him. He did not try to approach her. He knew she would not speak to him, but he was happy she was here, sharing this great victory with him, even if it was from afar.

He had been given another respite, a gift that only God could have granted. Indeed, only the divine hand of God could have led the meager flotilla of ships past the massive Turkish fleet and safely into the harbor. Now, not only had they enjoyed another victory at the hands of their Ottoman foes, but they were going to be reinforced with at least some provisions and men. Constantine had the greatest hope that the men arriving would have news of additional reinforcements, and some sense of when they would arrive.

The Italian ships and the imperial transport floated into the docks. Constantine saw that they were all badly damaged by cannon fire and the decks were slick with blood. Wounded men lay in various places, some of them screaming in pain. The passage had been hard fought and the damage was more extensive up close, but they had made it through.

A middle-aged man with gray hair, dressed in black, jumped down from the nearest ship and called for wine. He was clearly a captain. Constantine dismounted and walked over to him.

"I am Emperor Constantine. Who are you?"

The man appraised the emperor and then bowed. "I'm Francesco Lecanella."

"Are you the captain of this ship?"

"I am the captain of this fleet."

"Where are the rest of your ships, Captain?"

"There are no others, my Lord. I was hired by the pope to outfit three ships to reinforce the city. I have over two hundred fighting men, and also weapons, powder, and some coin. I came across your imperial grain ship in the Aegean near the entrance of the Dardanelles. I invited your captain to travel with me up the straits. We passed the strait without incident and made our way into the Sea of Marmara. We had good weather and fair winds and passed through to the city. I was surprised to find the Turkish fleet here. I did not know they had anything that large. I thought we were doomed. Thank God these infidels cannot sail or fight at sea to save their lives. Four against hundreds. What a tale that will make for the generations to hear!"

Constantine was disappointed that there were not more ships, but he did not let it show. He clapped Lecanella on the back. "Do you bring news of additional fleets?" asked the emperor hopefully.

"Alas, none that I know of, Emperor. I would imagine additional ships *will* be coming any time. I do not have hard information, but as I was outfitting my fleet, I certainly heard rumor of additional reinforcements."

This statement pleased Constantine greatly and he smiled in appreciation. "Thank you for your brave assistance. I have never seen such expert sailing and fighting. Constantinople welcomes you with open arms. I'm afraid you might be stuck with us for a while, unless you care to brave the Turks again."

"Thank you, my Lord. I'm happy to have made the trip. I knew it was likely I would have to stay in the city for at least a while after I arrived, although I must admit I had no idea the Turks had such a massive fleet. Had I known that, I would not have come here in the first place. Thank God they are as hapless at sailing as my Venetian brothers or I might not be here to tell the tale."

"Do you have any other news?"

"Yes. When I left Rome, the pope had just sent a messenger to the Venetians to request additional aid. He also sent a message to John Hunyadi. It can only be a matter of time before a very large force arrives by either land or sea to assist the city. You must simply hold out for a month or two."

"I think we can do so, my friend. My main concern was not the land walls, although we have been surprised by their cannon, which have done some considerable damage to our walls. My greatest concern has been their fleet. Thankfully we were able to keep the Golden Horn clear with our sea chain, and now we also know that a relief fleet of any size should be able to fight off the Turks at sea and reinforce the city. A fleet large enough might even allow us to go on the attack and wipe out the Ottoman ships."

"Surely we could do so with fifty or so ships. If we can put together a decent sized fleet, I would be happy to lead an attack."

Constantine was excited. This was truly the greatest news he had received in months. Huge relief forces were apparently on their way. If he could just hold out, he should be able to drive the Turks from the walls, and potentially even go on the attack. The next relief fleet, assuming it was large enough, would give him the fifty ships he needed to destroy the Turkish fleet. Without a navy, Mehmet would likely retreat, and if not . . . well, the Hungarians would soon be here as well.

He could not help falling into a bit of fantasy. What would he do if he ever caught Mehmet? Would he kill him? Would he hold the knife himself and slit the throat of this brash bastard? He had respected Mehmet's father. He had been a terrible force but also civilized. A man of his word. A man of culture and honor. Constantine's feelings for Murad were complex and deep.

He held Mehmet in much less regard, although he feared him greatly—even more than Murad, he realized. Mehmet could not be bargained with or reasoned with, at least not without giving up the one thing that defined Constantine, the city. Yes, he would kill the sultan if he ever fell into his hands. He would relish it. He prayed the sultan never captured him—he was sure of what would await him.

Constantine considered additional opportunities. The incompetence of the Turkish fleet not only meant possible relief from Italy, it also meant there could be aid from the Black Sea. This meant a Georgian relief fleet was a possibility. He had struggled with whether to drop the marriage proposal, at least publicly in the city. He desperately missed Zophia. To have lost the true love of his life at the moment he needed her most tortured him constantly. But he could not bring himself to do it. While the city had hope, he would sacrifice his happiness, his honor, his soul if need be, to protect his people. For now he was forgetting himself, and leaving his guest waiting.

"Welcome again, Francesco. I will assure you that you and your men will be cared for, along with your ships. I have to attend to some other matters, but please come to the palace tomorrow and let us talk further. I know my fleet commander Loukas Notaras will also want to discuss the entire battle with you in detail, so we understand Turkish tactics and how you held them off for so long."

The Italian bowed. Constantine remounted and beckoned to a few guards to come with him. He rode casually through the streets accompanied by cheers from his people. He smiled and waved encouragingly.

He arrived back at Blachernae well past nightfall to learn that a message had arrived from the sultan.

Constantine received the written message and reviewed it before dinner. He then had some wine and nibbled at his plate without much appetite, considering the offer from the sultan. He had offered much. Much more than he had ever offered before. If Constantine would only leave the city he could take everyone with him. He would be given all of the Peloponnesus as his own. This grant had been offered before, but he was also given a guaranteed protection for life, and protection from any Italian or other force that might try to attack the Greeks. He would be like Moses. He would lead his people to safety.

So what was more important, his people or the city? Why was he constantly left with these decisions? If the sultan would just go away, or offer nothing, he would have simple decisions. Instead he had to decide what to do with this offer. If the city fell, he would have sacrificed his people and left them to murder, rape, and slavery. Could he justify that? For what? For his ego? Or because he did not know anything in life except protecting Constantinople? What was Constantinople except a collection of stones on defensible ground? Certainly it had been the first great Christian city, but other Christian cities had fallen and still the world moved on. Did he owe his commitment to the city itself, or to his people?

The city would not suffer if it was taken. Constantine had to be honest with himself; the result would be the opposite. Constantinople had been a dim shadow of its former self since the Latins sacked it in the thirteenth century. The city could house millions and stood astride two continents and two great waterways. The Ottomans were young and vibrant. They would populate the city and make it great again, rebuild it as a true capital. Constantine could do little more than strip the churches to repair the land walls. There were no people to come here, no money to improve Constantinople. If he left, he could protect his people without harming the city he loved.

On the other hand, there was this small chance. Not a small chance of holding the city, as he was hopeful he could do that. A small chance he could have it all, that he could drive the Turks from Europe forever and restore the Greeks to a great empire again. He would not be the first emperor to have done so. Justinian had rebuilt the empire from a steady decline, and so had Basil II. Time and again the empire had seemed on the edge of ruin and had been resurrected by the right man at the right time. Was Constantine such a man? Was now such a moment? Should he risk the people on the small chance he could restore the greatness of the Greeks?

What about his responsibility to God? This was God's city. It was not a Latin city, or an Eastern city: It was a Christian city, the very first city built specifically to Jesus and to God. The Virgin Mother was their sacred protector. Could he abandon the city at this greatest moment of need? Was not the bible full of desperate situations that in the end were saved by a faithful servant's trust in God's power? Surely if God did not wish the Turks to enter the city, they would not.

He extinguished the candles at his table and knelt on the cold marble floor in the darkness. He prayed fervently for God to give him the right answer, to tell him, please, what to do. This was all too much for him. He prayed all night in the darkness, an agonizing, lonely, freezing evening. His knees throbbed in pain; his back ached. He was exhausted.

As morning light peeked through, he arose, stretching out his sore muscles, and threw warm robes on to eliminate the chill. He had not received any message, any sign, as he had hoped. He knew it was not his place to demand one. Without a sign, he felt he must carry on as best he could. He would do all he ever knew to do. He would defend the city.

Constantine breakfasted with Notaras and Sphrantzes. He reviewed the offer of peace with them, and his intended response. Notaras agreed entirely. Sphrantzes was surprisingly vocal in opposition.

"I think you should consider this offer, my Lord. The city is going to fall. It might not be now, but it will be sometime. If you take the people with you, you will be a hero. Who could blame you for the city falling? The West? Who cares! What have they done for us? Even when we give them everything they want, they have not come. And I don't consider that paltry fleet that arrived yesterday aid. That was a token, nothing more."

"Again, Sphrantzes, he cannot abandon the city. This is God's city," responded Notaras.

Sphrantzes scoffed. "You were quick to suggest that Constantine should leave the city and go get aid. Better for him to leave with everyone."

"You misunderstand me, as always. If Constantine left alone, he could gather additional aid to defend us. And even if the city fell then, he could bring forces to drive the Ottomans out. It is never and will never be my belief that we can abandon Constantinople to the Turks. This is the first city of the Christian world. We have a duty before God to defend it."

"God already has abandoned this city, you idiot! If it is not clear to you, it is clear to just about everyone else. We should save the Greek people. I cannot believe we have received an offer like this. Years of protection from the Turks. Protection from everyone else. Money and safety for everyone. We should take it. I implore you to consider it, my Lord."

Constantine was surprised to hear his own internal arguments repeated so accurately in the positions of his two friends. He was about to respond when they were interrupted by Giovanni Longo, who rushed into the room out of breath. He bowed quickly.

"My Lord. Important news. We have observed significant activity near Galata. Troops are pulling up and moving. Thousands of them."

"What do you think is going on?"

"It could be a number of things, my Lord. This could be a simple reshuffling of forces. On the other hand, it could be the beginning of a withdrawal."

"A withdrawal? Is that possible?"

"I do not want to speculate about the reasons they might leave. But if I was pulling back, I certainly would start with forces that are the farthest away from the walls. That way you can delay for the longest possible time the enemy's knowledge and any potential counterattacks."

"I want to see it myself," said Constantine.

"What? We cannot risk that, my Lord. What if you were captured?"

Notaras and Sphrantzes murmured their agreement.

"I am going. If they are leaving, I want to see it. I am tired of sitting here doing nothing. Notaras, make the arrangements."

Constantine left and returned to his private rooms. He changed into innocuous clothing, including a hooded robe, and returned to the council room. He knew he was being reckless, but he was tired of inaction. Even on the day of the breach, he had been too far away to actually fight the Turks. With Giovanni in command, he was removed from making direct orders related to the defense of the city. He suddenly felt the deep desire to take some action, take some risk. He wanted to share the danger of his people directly.

"I'm ready. Giovanni, I want you to come with me. Notaras, you will deal with things until I return."

Constantine left with Giovanni. They rode quickly from the palace to the harbor, where they were met by a Greek captain who was charged with bringing the emperor across the Horn to Galata. He quickly boarded the ship and the two men stood at the rail looking out across the Horn as the ship slowly left the dock and headed to the Genoese colony. Constantine was not sending word ahead, and did not intend to. He did not want his presence in Galata announced.

He was silent during the short journey across the Horn. The distance from the harbor to Galata was measured in hundreds of yards. When the ship docked at Galata's quay, Giovanni and Constantine quickly disembarked and disappeared into the small city, heading to the north where he could observe the Greek forces. So far no one had challenged them, or recognized the emperor.

Eventually they reached the landward walls and were able to climb up without interference to look out over the Ottoman forces below. Constantine saw immediately that the Turks were not retreating. They had pulled away from the walls and concentrated a mile or so off to the north. But the Turks were not leaving. They were constructing something. Even from this distance he could see frantic activity. Large groups of men were dragging hewn logs into place and laying them down in flat lines together. Other men appeared to be lashing the logs together. The Ottomans were clearly fashioning some sort of road. This log road extended away from the Bosporus and up a gradual hill. It appeared to be a supply road, although Constantine could not imagine why it was needed. What was clear was that the Ottomans were not going to lift the siege.

He was disappointed. He would not have to make any decisions if the Turks were leaving. He watched for a few more minutes and then beckoned Giovanni to leave.

Soon they were back aboard the ship and sailing toward Constantinople. Constantine watched his city as they slowly approached it. This was the first time he had been out of Constantinople since the siege began. If he took Mehmet's offer, he would soon sail out of the Golden Horn for good. If he did not, he might never leave the city again.

He soaked up the view, enjoying a moment of peace as he watched his beloved city. As he drew closer he felt clarity. He realized he could not abandon Constantinople. Not now, anyway. He loved it too much. His people and the city were the same. Eking out a living in the Peloponnesus might be appealing, but really all Constantine would be doing was saving his people for a few years. Even if Mehmet kept his word, which he might or might not, Constantine was only receiving an offer for his lifetime. Once he was dead, the Turks would be free to storm in and occupy the Peloponnesus, and the Greek dream would die. The only way he could preserve his people, his empire, was to hold the city and then try to drive the Turks out of Europe.

The ship docked again at the city's harbor. Constantine and Giovanni made their way back to the palace. They met again shortly with Sphrantzes and Notaras and told them what they had seen. Notaras went pale. He asked Constantine to describe in great detail everything he had observed.

"What's wrong, Notaras?" asked the Emperor.

"I'm sure I know what's going on, my Lord."

"What?"

"He's not building a supply road. I know what he's doing. I'm just shocked that he is trying it. Our crafty young sultan surprises me again and again."

"What are you talking about, Notaras?" asked Constantine impatiently.

"Come to the council chamber and I'll tell you. I'm afraid it is the worst possible news, and I do not think we can stop him."

CHAPTER TWELVE

SATURDAY, APRIL 21, 1453

Mehmet sat in his tent early in the morning going over some documents he had brought along with him from Edirne. He had ordered treatises pulled from the archives and brought along on a variety of topics from military tactics to sewage problems. He had searched these treatises for several hours until he had found the one he was looking for.

The document was only one page long and did not give him the level of detail he had hoped for. Still, he had remembered seeing it in the past, and he was happy now to have found it among the papers he had brought. He spent several hours reviewing the details and thinking over the questions in his mind. He then summoned Zaganos to his tent.

The pasha arrived an hour later, looking tired, as if he had been shaken awake. He eyed Mehmet carefully, obviously determining whether he was in any danger. Mehmet smiled to himself, always enjoying a little the fear he was able to cause even in those closest to him.

"Thank you for coming tonight. I have something I want to discuss with you."

"What is it, Sultan?"

"As you know, the fleet has been an utter disaster for us. I feel at this point it has caused almost more damage than benefit. I had hoped it would be the deciding factor, and would break into the Horn and wipe out the Greek fleet on the first day. We could then have attacked the vulnerable harbors and perhaps captured the city right away."

"I know this was your plan, and I was as disappointed as you that it did not work out. We did not anticipate the sea chain."

"Yes, the sea chain and the incompetence of that fool Baltaoglu and the entire fleet! A commander with more courage would have battled through that hole in the boom regardless of the losses. He would have found a way! That embarrassment yesterday was beyond measure! Not only have we gained nothing at sea, we have hurt the morale of our overall forces in the bargain."

"But surely you have remedied that by replacing Baltaoglu? The new commander will do better."

"I am not sure. The miserable failure was not all Baltaoglu's fault. He cannot lead each and every ship. The rest of the fleet could not stop the Italians any more than he could, fool that he is. I fear the problems are much greater. We do not possess the skills or the proper vessels for this job. We have to face facts, Zaganos, or we cannot solve the problem."

"I think you show great wisdom by admitting the truth, Sultan. But what can we do about it? We can't fix these problems overnight."

"No. Of course you are right. We must make do with what we have. But it occurs to me that we can take defeat in this case and make it victory by doing something bold. And it must be the fleet that does it."

"What do you have in mind?"

"We must get the ships into the Horn."

"Another attack on the chain? I agree it would be a great victory if we could do so. But how will you ensure we are not defeated again? If we lose the fleet at the sea chain, we will have to lift the siege. We cannot afford another significant defeat."

"I cannot ensure we can get through the chain. We must go around it."

"What?" Mehmet saw that Zaganos was completely confused by this suggestion. Again Mehmet smiled to himself. Zaganos was a brilliant land commander, but like almost all Ottomans, he had little use for the sea.

"We will port the ships."

"What do you mean, *port* them?"

"We will move them over land, on the land side of Galata, and into the Horn."

Zaganos looked doubtful. "Can such a thing be done? I am ignorant, Sultan, forgive me. But are not ships built for the water? How can they sail over land?"

"Yes, it can and will be done. Take a look at this document. I had read it before but did not remember all of the details. This paper describes the process itself. We should be able to do this. It is more manpower than wit, and I have an abundance of the former, though apparently not enough of the latter."

Zaganos read the treatise with great interest, his eyes widening as they scanned each detail. "I have never heard of such a thing. I didn't know it was possible."

"It is possible, and we are going to do it. We are going to shock the Greeks yet again, and our own men as well. We will strike a tremendous blow to their morale."

"I hope so, Sultan. We have not had much success with this navy so far, regardless of your brilliance in creating it. We do not need to win at sea to win this siege. Is it worth the risk?"

"I have considered that. It is a risk, but I think it is one we can control. If we pull it off, we will startle them." Mehmet smiled. "Besides, the ships will be on land. We know what we are doing there."

Zaganos laughed. "True enough. When will we begin?"

"Immediately. Tonight. Now."

"All right. I'll start gathering men near the fleet docking. We are also going to need a force to cut down trees, and we'll have to secure a large amount of grease and rope to pull the ships. Do you want me to take care of these details?"

"Yes. I will be there later."

Zaganos bowed and left the tent. Mehmet conducted his prayers and then sat for a long time in the darkness, going over the details of his plan in his mind. Zaganos was right, he was taking a tremendous risk. If he failed, he would have to lift the siege. If he lifted the siege, he would probably be deposed. He might make it back to Edirne, but once Halil gathered the council and discussed the failure, Mehmet was sure his life would be forfeit. Death or a puppet.

Was the portage too much of a risk? What were his alternatives? He could try another attack on the walls, but his cannon had not scored another breach. He also could attack the sea chain again, but as Zaganos had said, he trusted his ships on land at this point more than at sea. On land he could control the process. He could stand nearby and put his hands on things. If there was a problem, his orders would be immediately followed. It might be foolish to believe so, but he felt he could not fail if was directly in charge.

He reread the description of porting a few more times by flickering candlelight and fell asleep early. He would need his rest for the long day ahead.

Later in the morning the sultan set out from his tent. The cannon continued to fire at the walls as soon as each could be reloaded. Mehmet checked the damage, mentally measuring the progress since yesterday. There had been no significant new breaches, but the cannonade continued and served to keep the defenders awake and on edge. He left orders that if there was a significant breach, then fast riders were to gallop to his position at Galata and inform him immediately. There was to be no attack until he was informed and had returned. After ensuring his orders were in place, Mehmet mounted his horse and departed.

Mehmet and a retinue of his guards traveled around the end of the Golden Horn, on to the Galata peninsula, and then across to the Bosporus, where the fleet lay at anchor. As he approached the harbor, he noted that

Zaganos had not been idle. Huge piles of logs were already stacked, along with vats of animal fat that would serve as grease. At least five thousand men were working on the road that would port the ships. Mehmet was impressed with the work his friend had completed in just one night. As always, Zaganos was a force to be reckoned with, and Mehmet reminded himself that he must be both praised and controlled.

The job of porting the ships would be herculean. Unfortunately, just like Constantinople, the land between the Bosporus and the Horn rose gradually to a ridge and then back down again. Zaganos had put the men to digging out a portage road and smoothing it as much as possible. There was not sufficient time to dig an actual channel through the ridge, but the men were doing their best to minimize the tremendous work of manhandling the ships over land.

Mehmet found Zaganos near the harbor. Here more workers were constructing a cradle that angled down into the water. Turks worked furiously with shirts off, lashing the logs together and then greasing them with animal fat until they were so slippery that one could no longer even hold onto them.

More logs were being placed on the dug-out road onward up the hill. These logs were positioned seven or eight astride with a small channel in the middle for the keel of the ship. The first ship had already been connected with huge lines and pulled up to the beginning of the cradle.

Mehmet greeted Zaganos, congratulating him. "As always, I find my commands to you fulfilled to the limit of my expectations. Would that others could follow them as do you."

"Thank you, Sultan. I have but obeyed your orders."

"Yes, but you have also exceeded my expectations."

"And also mine, Sultan."

Mehmet recognized the voice and turned to see Halil, who had apparently just arrived. The grand vizier was like a snake in the grass, always appearing, unexpected and unwanted. The sultan nodded his head.

"Another brilliant execution," noted Halil. "How did you come across such knowledge?"

Mehmet was pleased. He was sure Halil had not expected this. He had surprised his grand vizier again. The more he could keep Halil off balance, the longer he could hope to carry on the siege without interference.

"I had no knowledge of moving ships by land. It simply occurred to me that the sea chain was a bigger obstacle than this hill. Perhaps Allah has blessed me with this knowledge."

"Allah blesses us with many things, such as the knowledge of when to go forward and when to *step back*. Hopefully you will succeed, my Sultan. A failure here will be very damaging. I am not sure the men could take another failure after the defeat at sea."

Mehmet held his tongue. The anger was, as always, mixed with an almost overwhelming fear and loathing he could never shake when Halil challenged him. What did he want from Halil? Approval? Friendship? True service? He was not sure, but he was ashamed of himself for having such strong emotions and feeling so helpless around him. Halil was not the sultan. Mehmet was. Yet the vizier held power over Mehmet even now. Mehmet feared Halil. It was something deeper than a threat of future failures. He did not understand it, and he hated it.

For the thousandth time he wanted to draw his sword and remove Halil's head, but instead he merely nodded grimly. "Yes indeed, we shall have to ensure success, my friend, for our empire and for Allah."

"That is all *we* wait and hope for."

Mehmet did not miss the use of the word "we," a clear allusion to the senior council members. "I shall have to guarantee I do not disappoint, then."

Halil bowed and turned his horse, riding away. He was clearly off to report his findings to the rest of the old guard. Mehmet watched him depart, seething with anger.

He was tormented by doubts again and again. Why could he not discipline his mind the way he had disciplined his body? He had trained himself to hide emotion. He could go days without food and could march in cold or heat until other men fell before him. He could not do the same with his mind. Try as he might, he was tormented by his father's disapproval, by Halil's betrayal, and by the lack of respect he received from his own people. If only he could conquer these feelings and finally have internal peace.

Mehmet shook his head hard, physically trying to shake out the dread he always felt around Halil. He knew one cure for his mind: activity. If he kept himself busy, the doubts would recede. He turned to Zaganos. "Let us get the first ship out of the water."

Zaganos shouted to several men standing in attendance; they turned and ran down to preappointed positions. More orders were shouted, and men came running from several directions and were soon positioning themselves along the lengths of the huge lines. When hundreds of men were in place on each of the lines, Zaganos raised his hand and shouted the order to pull. The men strained forward as one, struggling with great groans. The ship glided up until it hit the wooden cradle and then stuck, refusing to move farther forward.

Zaganos screamed encouragement. The men pulled harder, veins popping on their foreheads and sweat running down their faces. The ship creaked and shuddered. Mehmet feared the lines would snap or the ship would crush the cradle. Finally the ship moved slowly forward and angled upward, the bow rising slightly as it began pulling out of the water. Once the ship was caught by the cradle it moved smoothly, but very slowly.

Mehmet was astounded by the sight of the giant ship slowly emerging. He noticed similar expressions on his men as they watched the ship's bow, then midship, and finally stern arising from the Bosporus and glide along the greased wooden road.

Zaganos took a break from directing the movement and came over to Mehmet to congratulate him. The two stood along the side of the ship as it passed slowly by.

"My Sultan, you conceive of a dream and it becomes reality. May your dream of Constantinople come to pass as well."

Mehmet was pleased, both by the progress and by Zaganos's words.

"Congratulations go to you as well, my friend. You have worked wonders arranging all of these details so quickly. I have no more faithful councilor, general, and friend. Truly I am blessed."

"Thank you, Sultan. I am your servant." He paused. "I will be honest. I was not sure this would really work. I am still not sure it will work to conclusion, although I did not believe the ship would even make it out of the water."

"I had no doubt we could do this; it is Allah's will that we—"

The sound of a terrible cracking interrupted Mehmet, and he looked up in surprise to see the ship tilting dangerously toward him. Zaganos reached out and grabbed the sultan by the arm, almost dislocating his shoulder with the force as he pulled him away from the falling ship. They ran several steps in stride and then dove. They just cleared the edge of the ship as it crashed against the ground. The mast barely missed the two men, and broken timbers flew through the air.

Mehmet felt burning pain tear through his leg. He stumbled to the ground. He looked down and saw a spur of wood the size of a small dagger sticking completely through his thigh. Blood was pouring out of the wound. Dizziness caused his head to spin. He gritted his teeth to avoid crying out. Only a coward would scream.

Through the pain he felt his anger rising. Again at the edge of victory he had failed. He turned and looked at the wreckage of the ship. He could imagine Halil riding back as soon as he heard the news and staring smugly at the fallen vessel. He would comment sympathetically about the unfortunate incident while inside, the grand vizier would be celebrating another failure. Mehmet would not allow it. These ships would be moved if they had to be disassembled and then rebuilt.

"Are you all right, Sultan?" asked Zaganos.

"I'm fine. I need someone to pull this out and then bind it. Are you hurt?"

"I appear unhurt."

"Good. I want you to get back to work on this project immediately. Find out what the problem is and then fix it. Obviously we need some lines on both sides of the ship, and perhaps the channel between the wood needs to be wider. Whatever the problem is, I want the first ship in the Golden Horn in two days. If we have to work every Ottoman in our army to death to make it happen, we will make it happen."

"I will get to work on it immediately. I will get the ships in the Horn or die trying. Now you need to get some attention for your leg."

Mehmet was carried on a flat board by a number of guards to a nearby doctor. The doctor immediately examined the wound and went to work removing the shard. Mehmet grimaced against the pain when the huge wooden sliver was pulled from his leg. He felt consciousness fading, but he gritted his teeth to ensure he would not call out. The sultan heard screaming and wondered where it was coming from. He realized it was his own voice. Mehmet fought against the pain and the darkness, but soon he felt them overwhelming him, and he lost consciousness.

Mehmet dreamed. He saw his boyhood rooms in the palace, but he remained a man. He walked through the hallways and was greeted by guards, but not as sultan. He made his way to the throne room and found a man sitting in his place. He realized it was his father. He approached his father nervously. Mehmet had always felt Murad did not really approve of him. That he was disappointed. He had always sought his father's approval but never received it. He still remembered the sharp chastisement he had received when Murad had returned to take the throne at Halil's request. According to Halil, the empire was on the verge of revolution because of Mehmet's childish decisions and rash behavior.

What had Mehmet done wrong? How could he have possibly been expected to do better? He had not even been trained as a sultan when he was a young man.

Then his father had given up the throne without ever really directing or advising Mehmet on how to rule himself. So the young sultan had done what he could. He received advice from every direction, advice that often conflicted. Nobody seemed to care what he wanted, and even though he was supposed to be all-powerful, no one listened to his commands or followed them. In a short time they took it all away, and his father returned to criticize him for failing to learn the lessons Murad had never taught him. Now here he was before him, his father, sitting again on his throne.

"Father," Mehmet humbly addressed him, bowing low to the sultan.

"Son. You have disappointed me again. You were told by Halil not to attack Constantinople, but you ignored him. Did I not myself advise you to wait until you were ready? Instead you attack almost immediately and rashly."

"I did not act rashly, Father. I prepared. I built a navy. I built cannon. I secured the peace with the West."

"Hah! You trust the West? They will attack you when they are ready, and they will not worry about honoring agreements. Did not Hunyadi attack me after we swore a peace? He had the agreement declared invalid because I was not a Christian. Your navy? A failure at every turn. The cannon? Have they gotten you into the city? I spent my lifetime trying to capture Constantinople. You think you can do what I could not? You were not even able to rule."

Mehmet felt the pain again. The pain he always associated with his father and with Halil. Disappointment and failure. His father had never given him a chance.

"I have prepared well. The cannon are breaching the walls. The fleet is out of my control. I will admit I expected more out of them, but what am I to do? The peace agreements should hold the West long enough to complete the siege. What more could I have done to prepare?"

"You could have waited. Always, you are in a rush. That's why you lost your throne in the first place. The one thing you have failed to gain is the confidence of your people, of your advisors. Some doubted you before this siege even began. The doubt is growing. If you had won some victories in the field first, and allowed some time to go by, you would have the full confidence of your people. Without this confidence, you cannot maintain a long siege. You have gambled everything on one throw of the dice. That is not the Ottoman way. If you fail, at best you will be dethroned and perhaps killed, at worst the Ottomans will be driven out of Europe. You could erase more than a hundred years of history."

Another voice could be heard. "I have tried to tell him, Sultan. I have tried to lead him, but he is the same as always, he will not listen." Mehmet looked over. Halil had stepped out of the shadows, an arrogant smirk on his face.

"Ah, my Grand Vizier. You have done everything you can with this boy. You know what you must do."

"Yes, my Sultan."

Mehmet grew angry and terrified. "I am the Sultan, not you! You are dead!" He turned to Halil. "You will serve me! You will call me Sultan."

Halil turned to him. "For now."

Mehmet woke with a start in bed. He felt weak and his clothes were soaked. He recognized his personal physician. "Sultan, you have had a bad fever from your wound. The fever has broken. You must stay in bed for a few days, though."

Mehmet thought about that. He started to rise, although he was dizzy. "How long have I been asleep?"

"About twenty hours."

Bad, but not as bad as it could have been. He rose farther and pulled his legs out over the edge. He had to get back to the siege. "Bring me my boots, mail, and sword."

"Sultan, you cannot go now. You need to stay and rest."

Mehmet stood shakily. "Bring my things, I do not have time."

His belongings were brought and he dressed as quickly as he could, assisted by the physician and a few guards. He then limped slowly out of the tent. His leg was wrapped in clean bandages that were stained red in the front. The pain was almost unbearable. He thought of returning to his bed, but dismissed the idea. He had no time.

Mehmet left the tent and looked around. He realized he was still near the walls of Galata. They must have shifted his physician's tent over to assist the sultan near where he was wounded. His horse was waiting with guards, who were already mounted.

He slowly and painfully pulled himself up into the saddle. When he was mounted he turned his horse and rode off at a slow trot. He needed to see what progress was being made. Zaganos had better not have failed him.

He rode slowly up the center ridge of Galata and crested the hill. He smiled then. Before him, a long line of wooden ships was slowly moving along the land, as if by magic. He peered out to his left at the Horn. A few Ottoman ships were already in the harbor and another was about to slide in. He looked farther out into the Horn to see if the Greeks were forming to attack. So far they were not. He wondered if they would brave it. Mehmet had ordered that a number of cannon be brought over from the main assault and placed on the shores of the Horn. If the Greeks threatened his fleet, they would face a significant bombardment from land. Perhaps that was what was holding them back now. He soared with pride. Pride for himself, pride for Zaganos, and pride for his people. His fleet was in the Horn. The Greeks would be hard pressed to stop them now if they mounted a significant attack on the chain. They might even be able to fight their way into the harbors and take the city the way the Italians had more than two hundred years ago.

He thought of Halil and his father. He thought of his people. Perhaps they did all think him rash and a fool. Perhaps they thought he gambled too much. He didn't care. He would make this gamble. He would never listen to Halil, unless he had no options left. He would prove to them all that he was a great man. If it was Allah's will, he would give the city to his people, to his faith. Or he would die trying. He would take the city, he knew it. If only he had time.

CHAPTER THIRTEEN

SATURDAY, APRIL 28, 1453

Constantine, Notaras, and Sphrantzes stared grimly out over the Golden Horn at the Turkish fleet. They had watched Mehmet for days slowly porting the ships over the wooden road he had constructed until there were seventy Turkish ships in the Horn. Constantine was thoughtful. Again, as with the cannon and the fleet, he had to grudgingly admire the sultan. He had badly underestimated his abilities. While many people had been relieved when Murad had died, Constantine had known he was facing an aggressive, even rash opponent. He was not surprised that Mehmet attacked the city so early in his reign. What had come as a shock was that he would do so in such an organized and innovative way.

Constantine had received no information about Mehmet that would have led him to believe he was capable of such organization or brilliance. When he had come to power, many Italian leaders congratulated Constantine, sure that they would have years of peace. The emperor had known better, and had worked as hard as he could with the limited resources available to him to prepare for a siege he knew would come sooner rather than later.

He had planned for the attack of a rash youth. He was not ready to face such a sophisticated and well-prepared leader. Mehmet had come to Constantinople with more men than his father had. He had brought a navy. He had brought cannon. All this, and he showed tremendous ability to adapt to changes in fortune. Constantine had hoped that the series of defeats Mehmet had undergone since the siege began would erode the leader's resolve and he would give up and leave. Instead, with each defeat, the sultan just adapted and tried new tactics. Constantine knew he would be very lucky indeed if Mehmet did not find some way to conquer the city.

Now the emperor had to overcome a further challenge. He had believed after the recent reinforcement of the city that the Turkish fleet was not a factor. Constantinople was safe behind the sea wall and apparently able to receive relief fleets that could ram their way through the inferior and inexperienced Turkish fleet. Now the situation had drastically changed. Now the Turks would have ships directly in the inner harbor of the city.

With ships within the Golden Horn, there were three additional problems. First, the sea chain was effectively neutralized. While the chain kept the two halves of the Turkish fleet from uniting, it did nothing now to protect the Golden Horn. Second, the Turkish fleet presented a threat to the mixed Italian and Greek fleet within the Horn. This fleet had served as a buffer in case the sea chain fell, and also had already proved effective at protecting the chain and shepherding the relief fleet to the city. Third, a large chunk of additional sea wall was now open to a potential attack by the Turks. This meant that Constantine and Giovanni would have to pull reserves out of their razor-thin defenses to defend the sea wall along the Horn from the possibility of a sudden attack.

Did God hate him? Must each victory be met with an immediate defeat? He had been so excited when the fleet came through. And then the news that perhaps Mehmet had decided to evacuate the city. This apparent miracle turned into horror when Constantine realized what was really happening. Instead of fleeing, Mehmet was once again adapting and overcoming a weakness. Constantine forced himself to be calm.

His life was essentially defined by constant disappointment. He could deal with this turn of events, but it was time to figure out how.

"Loukas, my friend," said the Emperor. "You were exactly correct. The road was for porting these cursed ships into our backyard. How do we deal with the problem?"

"My Lord, we need to attack this fleet and destroy it as quickly as possible. If we do not, they will probably destroy the sea chain or attack the city."

"I understand the problem," responded Constantine, a bit irritably. "I need solutions, not a recitation of the obvious."

Notaras bowed and Constantine realized he was letting his strain show through. He smiled and put a hand on his friend's shoulder. "I am sorry. I didn't mean to upset you. Of course your advice and thoughts are important to me."

Notaras smiled in return. "It's no matter, my liege. I would suggest we attack the Turkish fleet at night with our fire ships, and destroy it."

"When would you suggest we make the attempt?"

"We have to do it right away, my Lord. We do not really have the men to guard the sea walls, and if we let the Turks get settled they might launch a surprise attack on *our* fleet."

"Do you think them capable?"

"They certainly performed poorly last time, but that does not mean they will continue to do so. We cannot risk the loss of our fleet. If we were defeated in the Golden Horn, I don't know how the city could survive. Our sea walls are thin and feeble compared to the land walls. If there are substantial troops ferried over, we would not be able to hold them back, not with the forces we have available to us."

"Sphrantzes, what do you think?"

"Does it matter what he thinks? What does he know of the navy?"

Constantine saw Sphrantzes stiffen. "Notaras, I'm tired of your—"

"Enough!" interrupted Constantine, weary of the two men's constant infighting. "I want to hear from Sphrantzes."

"I agree with Notaras, so long as he is successful. A failure with substantial losses would be worse than doing nothing."

Constantine considered the issue. Sphrantzes was right: If they lost a portion of the fleet on an attack, they would be even worse off than they were right now. Still, he could not allow the Turks free reign in the Horn. "Notaras, mount the attack."

"Yes, my Lord." Notaras bowed and quickly departed.

Sphrantzes also soon departed to review the status of the land walls and check in with Giovanni. Constantine stayed through the afternoon and early evening, watching the preparations at the harbor. Notaras was doing his best to keep them secret, ordering that only one ship be made ready at a time so that the Turks were not alerted that a general naval attack was being organized. Sphrantzes reported later in the evening that he was unable to locate Giovanni. Perhaps the Italian leader was out inspecting forces in another part of the city.

Evening fell into darkness. The preparations were gradually completed and Notaras was ready to go. He was personally leading the attack. Constantine positioned himself on a rooftop near the harbor with a commanding view of the Golden Horn. Sphrantzes and Giovanni, who had returned from a review of the walls, joined him to watch the attack.

Slowly and almost imperceptibly in the darkness, they could make out their ships slipping off the dock and into the Horn. Ten shadows. There was very little sound and no light. Constantine wondered how Notaras would keep the ships from colliding with each other in the darkness. He hoped everything would go well. Soon the ships were fading into the black night and they had to simply wait.

Constantine chatted nervously with his advisors as time ticked by. Finally he made out a dim light across the Horn. The first ship must have made contact with the Turkish fleet. Another light flickered, and then another and another until there were a dozen, and then dozens. Something was wrong. The lights were spread out and far too numerous to represent the ten-ship fleet of the Greeks. These lights were coming from the Turkish fleet and from the shore nearby. The lights had come on almost simultaneously, not the reaction to a surprise attack. Rather . . .

"They were warned," whispered the emperor.

"How can that be, my Lord?" asked Sphrantzes.

"I do not know, but they were not surprised. Look at them. They were already on the ships with lights ready. They knew the attack was coming."

How had they known? Were they just well prepared for any attack? Constantine could not see how they could have been *that* prepared. It would be one thing to be vigilant, but having fire ready for each ship and having the watch fires almost simultaneously appear on what seemed to be every ship was very unlikely.

Someone had informed the Turks of what was going on. But who? None of his close advisors would tell the Turks anything. How could it benefit them? They must have had someone watching at the harbor. Had any small boats left ahead of the fleet? Perhaps someone snuck through the land walls? That seemed highly improbable. There must have been a spy in the harbor, or perhaps in the Horn on a small boat keeping a lookout. Whatever the reason, surprise had not been achieved, and surprise was essential.

Cannon fire and flashes of light could now be seen and were followed by the delayed reports over the water. They watched silently, helplessly, as the battle lit up the opposite shore. Eventually the flashes began to fade away, and then all was silent. They waited for what seemed an endless time in the darkness for their ships to reappear. Finally Constantine could make out first one, then two shadows reemerging from the darkness. Two ships total.

They rushed down to the docks as the vessels pulled in. They were battered and pitted from cannon fire. Constantine saw with relief that Notaras's ship was one of the two. His admiral soon jumped down onto the dock.

"They were waiting for us. I do not know how, but they were ready for us. We crossed the Horn completely quiet and in the dark. There is no way they could have known we were coming. They were packed with Turkish soldiers, armed to the teeth, cannon primed. We were betrayed."

"Betrayed, or was this a simple failure?" asked Sphrantzes. "With no disrespect, Notaras, you should have anticipated that they might be prepared. Why did you not retreat immediately when you saw they were ready for you? Now we are down eight ships. We cannot afford such losses. You should have done your job, or brought your ships home. You have done neither, and now we are in a critically weak position. How can we defend against an attack now? You should be replaced! You have cost us the city!"

Notaras turned red and lunged at Sphrantzes, striking him hard in the cheek and sending him flying to the ground. "You bastard, Sphrantzes! Is it not enough I have lost so many ships and men? Must I endure your foul accusations? What do you know of battle, you spineless worm? You whisper your poison to the emperor, but you do nothing to save the city!"

"Hah! At least I do not hand it over to the Turks! You have as much as done so with your foolish assault. You attacked with far more ships than our Italian friends had when they entered the city, and you have lost eight when they lost none. Perhaps we need an Italian leader for the fleet. They know the worth of their ships and do not give them up so easily," spat Sphrantzes.

"You are truly an idiot. How was I to turn my ships at the last moment? We were already prepared for battle. I was ready for the possibility that they would see us coming and have time to organize some quick defenses. I was not prepared for an ambush. No one could have saved those ships. Certainly not a court lackey like you!"

"Notaras! Sphrantzes!" shouted Constantine. "I've had enough. This loss is terrible, worse than anything I could have expected. Let us not make it worse with accusations that will only harm our cause. Notaras, my friend, get some rest and we will evaluate things in the morning. Set a close watch on the Horn though, to ensure they do not counterattack in the night.

"Sphrantzes, come with me; you have done enough harm here."

They rode off into the darkness, picking their way through the city along the sea walls as they traveled back toward the palace.

"My Lord, I'm sorry I lost my temper. There is just so much at risk."

"I am not angry. Perhaps those things even needed to be said. I agree with you that Notaras should not have depended so much on surprise. There are traitors and spies in the city. He must know that. He should have been ready for anything."

"Thank you, my Lord, but it gives me no pleasure to be right in this. What can we do now?"

Constantine hesitated. It was a good question. Now things were even worse. They had lost an important part of the fleet, and in losing these ships they had also given the Turks confidence in the Ottoman fighting ability at sea. This would likely encourage them to launch more attacks and even potentially to attack the sea wall. What could he do? Did he think this was going to be simple, that the Turks would do whatever he wanted them to? He must adapt, as always.

"We will take a small reserve from elsewhere in the city and station them near the Horn sea walls in case of an attack. It seems we can spare a few men from the sea walls on the Marmara side, since there have been no attacks there yet. I am not going to replace Notaras, but I will order him to have our fleet at a constant state of readiness in case we are attacked again."

"All sensible ideas, although I think you should replace—"

"I'm not doing it, Sphrantzes. Enough."

Sphrantzes bowed. "As you wish, my Lord."

"I am going to do one other thing, and I want you to coordinate this. I want you to take a small ship and disguise it with men dressed as Turks. Find a bold captain. I want you to order this ship to sail on the morning tide. I want the ship to head out all the way past the Dardanelles if need be. I need to know when the relief fleets are going to get here. Have them find out as much as possible, then turn around and report in. I need to know how long I need to hold the city before help will arrive."

"An excellent idea, my Lord. I will do so immediately. One other question. Do you think the Turks were tipped off we were coming?"

"I do not know. I would like to know."

"I'll see if I can poke around and find out, my Lord."

"Thank you, Sphrantzes. You are a good friend, even if you're a little opinionated at times."

Sphrantzes smiled. "Nobody is perfect, my Lord." He whipped his horse around and headed back to the harbor.

Constantine was left in the darkness with his suspicions. A spy? Of course. It only made sense. How else could the Turks have been so perfectly prepared? But who might it be? So very few people had known of the plan to attack. Perhaps a guard? A cook? Who had been around when they went over the preparations? *Another problem to worry about.* He needed someone to talk to, someone he could trust.

Only when his friend was long out of sight did the emperor turn his horse away from the palace and ride slowly to Zophia's house. He knew she would be displeased to see him. He knew she would likely turn him away. He had to try. He was falling apart without her. He prayed a silent prayer to God, asking for mercy for his city, and mercy for himself.

Constantine dismounted before Zophia's house and knocked softly on her door. There was no answer. He knocked again and eventually she opened the door. She was surprised to see him. He searched her eyes to see what emotions were playing over them. He saw excitement and happiness, which quickly turned to a stern glare.

"I asked you not to come here, Constantine. I do not know how clear I have to be."

"It's the end of the world, my dear, isn't it? Can I not at least talk to you?" Where did that come from? *The end of the world?* Finally he had said it. He had for so long refused to acknowledge the situation of the city and certainly tried to keep it from others. Did he really feel it was the end? It was possible, he realized. Saying it out loud for some reason made him feel calmer. He wished he could just be done with it. Even if he fell in battle, at least it would be the end of this weary lifetime of disappointment.

"You do not really mean that, Constantine. You will not give up. You do not have it in you."

Of course she was right, as she always was. "May I please come in, just for a few minutes?"

She paused and he could see the pain in her eyes. "No. I cannot let you. I told you."

"Please, I'm begging you. I need you. Just for a few minutes. I promise I won't touch you."

She sighed. "For a few minutes, then. And just for tea."

She turned around and walked into the kitchen. Constantine followed her. He looked around fondly, feeling so happy to be here. He was overwhelmed with memories. Her scent filled the room. They had spent so much time here. A refuge from all of his troubles. He looked at the roaring fire and the furs laid out before it. He remembered making love to her so many times here. So many different evenings together. Not just being together but talking, laughing, crying together.

"So how goes the siege? I have not seen any Turks breaking down my door yet, so I assume we still hold the city?" She teased him a little, like she used to, and it made Constantine yearn for her even more.

"Oh, you know, everything is excellent. Really no obstacles at all."

"Oh, stop it, Constantine," she laughed. "Truly, how is the situation?"

"Truthfully, terrible, but not without hope. The reinforcements and food we received from the Genoese helped. I think our food supplies will last a few more months, by which time the Turks should have left, or we should have received additional reinforcements. The Turks keep battering the walls by day and Giovanni rebuilds them by night. They have not breached the walls again since the first time, and we are managing to hold our own. Although we have lost the Golden Horn. Well, Notaras did."

"That sounds like Sphrantzes talking."

"What if Sphrantzes is right? What if Notaras is a poor commander?"

"What of it? How many ships do you have left? And I do not believe it for a minute anyway. Notaras is the one who came up with the idea to rebuild the sea chain, right? And did he not defeat the Turkish fleet when they attacked the chain? It seems he has done pretty well. Do not let petty rivalries cloud your judgment."

"I suppose you are right, my love. I do grow tired of their constant bickering. That is the last thing I need in the middle of this nightmare. It is almost as bad as not being able to see you."

She stiffened. "That was not my choice. How is your princess, by the way? I have not seen any Georgian fleets ravaging the Turks."

"Please, my darling. Let us not talk about that." He moved closer to her, putting his hand on her shoulder. She started to pull back, but he held her. "I have missed you so terribly, Zophia. I need you. I cannot go on without you. Can you not please put this foolishness aside?"

She drew close to him, putting her arms around him, and pulled him to her. She held him tightly. He could feel her shaking, sobbing. She held him for long moments. Then she drew away, wiping her tears.

"I love you, Constantine. I always will love you. Nothing has changed. But I have to remain true to who I am. You have made your choices. I will be here, but I cannot be with you."

"Can we please just spend time together? I need someone to talk to, someone to trust and to listen to me. Someone to share with. I cannot do this without you." He moved forward to hold her again, but she stepped back and put up her hands.

"I am sorry, Constantine. I cannot do it. I cannot spend time with you without falling apart. I need and want you, too. If I spend any time with you, I will weaken and take you to my bed again. I want to do so right now."

"Then do it. Please!"

"I cannot. Please, I do not have the strength to say no. I need you to leave. I need you to leave now. I'm sorry, my love. I love you so much. You know I do. But I cannot be with you. I cannot spend time with you. I have to be true to myself."

"You know why I had to do what I did."

"As I have told you, I understand why you feel you had to do what you did, but whether you feel it is necessary or not, I will not be your mistress. I am either yours alone or I am not yours at all."

Constantine fell to his knees, clinging to her legs, weeping. "Please, Zophia. Please, I need you. I cannot do this anymore."

She held his head, held him close, weeping with him. "Be strong, my dear. I have never known anyone stronger than you. I will always be with you in my spirit, in my soul, you know that. But I cannot be physically together with you, so long as you are seeking out another. Now, my love, I have to ask you to leave me."

He embraced her again, holding her tight. He felt something, something he had never felt before. He knew her so well, every part of her. He moved his hand down to her stomach. He felt a fullness he didn't remember. She grabbed his wrist and pulled his hand away. He looked into her eyes, and he knew in a moment his suspicion was true.

"Zophia . . . my dearest. A baby? Why didn't you tell me?"

Tears ran down her face. "My Lord, my love. I could never reveal this to you after you told me of the betrothal. I needed you to make your choice without knowing about this child. If you had chosen me because of a baby, I would never have known if it was me you wanted, or if you felt forced to choose. How could I deny you aid for the city? I cannot be with you, but could I let the city fall for my own selfish reasons? I don't know if you are right or I am, but you are our leader. You have made your choices."

Constantine felt bewildered. "You had no right to keep this from me."

"I had every right. You made your decision. A baby changes nothing."

"This baby changes everything. Now you must let me see you."

"No, my dearest. Everything remains the same. I would never have told you. You still must decide what to do. I know the world is on your shoulders. Please do not let this change anything. Please do what you must. Now, my love, you must go. I cannot stay here with you any longer. I am crumbling."

He held on for a few more minutes, enjoying her smell and the feeling of her soft hands running through his hair. He reached down and caressed her stomach again, felt his child inside her. His future. He soaked up these few moments, knowing they would have to serve to comfort him in the many days to come.

CHAPTER FOURTEEN

MONDAY, MAY 7, 1453

Mehmet sat astride his horse, watching a terrible bombardment of the walls. He had ordered his cannon to fire continuously since yesterday morning. He had concentrated all of the fire on a small portion of the central land wall, and had amassed his men, most particularly the Janissaries, to rush forward as soon as a sufficient breach was blown through.

The great victory in the Golden Horn had bolstered his position and given him respite from Halil's constant calls to lift the siege. But he knew he could not wait forever. Each day brought the fear of a relief fleet from the Italians, or could bring an invading Hungarian army. He must break the walls as quickly as he could, particularly now that the Greeks were spread even thinner by the threat of sea invasion in the Golden Horn.

He was tense and exhausted. The weeks of worry were starting to take their toll, even on his young body. He had few cards left to play. The movement of the fleet into the Horn had been brilliant, he knew, and had taken the Greeks and his senior advisors by surprise, but in reality it had done only a little to improve the tactical situation. So long as any Greek fleet remained in the Horn, he really could not risk an attack on the sea walls, not after the pathetic performance against the tiny Genoese relief fleet.

Certainly it was true that his fleet had beaten back the surprise attack by the Greek fleet, but he had been forewarned with plenty of time to prepare. Otherwise he might have lost his entire fleet. Thank Allah he had a spy among his enemies willing to give him these secrets. He would surely have had to withdraw if he had lost the fleet, and that was probably the same as losing his life.

That was why he was pressing this attack now. He had to do something to get into the city. A long siege continued to be too risky, and he could already sense that Halil and the other old guard advisors were beginning to grumble again. He did have a final card to play. He had secretly ordered the digging of a number of tunnels that, when completed, could be used to blow huge holes in the walls. However, these tunnels would not be done for some days. In the meantime, if he could breach the walls with his cannon again, he hoped he could force his way into the city.

Zaganos joined him after nightfall as the cannon continued to pound the walls.

"Good evening, my Lord."

"Ah, good evening, my friend. What news can you bring me?"

"Not too much is going on in my area, my Lord. There have been a few cannon attacks on our ships by the Greeks. They sank a couple small ships, but we quickly shifted to compensate. I do not see it as any kind of long-term threat. How are things here?"

"We have pounded this small section of the wall for two days now. As you can see, the wall has cracked in several areas, and there are some small holes near the ground, but nothing significant enough to allow an attack. I will not repeat the mistake of attacking a small breach."

"Very wise. We gave them a cheap victory last time. I agree we must wait for a significant breach before we attempt the walls again. Perhaps we should—"

Zaganos was cut off by an enormous explosion against the land walls. They watched a huge chunk of wall shatter and tumble down to the ground. A cloud of smoke and dust billowed up, illuminated by the fire and the flashes of cannon. For some time they could not make out the extent of the damage. When the smoke began to clear, they were shocked: A forty-foot segment of the outer wall had tumbled completely down. Greeks screamed and scrambled in every direction.

Mehmet shouted to his men, "Attack! Attack now! Take the city!"

An enormous roar erupted from the Ottomans. Mehmet felt his blood boiling red hot. This was the moment! The city was his! He drew his own sword, charging in with his men as they screamed and ran toward the city. A hand grabbed his reins and pulled him back. It was Zaganos. "No, my Lord. You must stay back and stay safe. If you are killed, all will be lost."

Mehmet stared wildly at Zaganos. He considered cutting the general's hand off at the wrist and continuing forward. Who was he to tell him no? But he realized his friend was correct. He should not put himself in danger of a stray bullet or arrow. He had plenty of time to enter the city after his men secured the breach. Victory was only minutes away, hours at the most.

He shouted at his men, encouraging them as they marched forward over the filled-in Foss and streamed toward the massive breach in the outer wall.

Mehmet stayed back with Zaganos, a bare hundred yards away from the wall, where they could watch firsthand the taking of the city. His Janissaries were soon jammed in with what appeared to be hundreds of Greeks, armored and armed, and battling for the life of the city. The din of swords crashing against other swords, of cannon, and the screams of the wounded thundered through the night air. Flashes of light and fire illuminated the struggle. Mehmet shouted encouragements mixed with curses. He promised a thousand gold pieces to the first Ottoman to plant a banner on the city walls. His men shouted back to him in excitement and joy as they surged forward, pressing ever more tightly into the breach.

Arrows and musket fire poured into the Ottomans from the walls above. Mehmet's men were taking huge casualties, primarily from this missile fire. But he had tens of thousands of men crammed into a very small area, and the losses did nothing more than slow down the attack. As the minutes turned to an hour, he observed the Greek lines beginning to thin. His men had pushed forward slightly into the huge breach, forming a crescent. He rode forward even farther, ducking an occasional arrow from the wall, so he could further encourage his men. He was enjoying himself immensely. This was the moment he had waited for, planned, and prayed for. He would take the city and achieve the dream of his father, and his father's father. The dream of almost a thousand years, to take the great Christian city for Allah and make it the center of the world for a new Islamic empire.

Midnight passed, and the fighting continued. Mehmet had expected the city to fall long since, but the bravery and persistence of the Greeks was surprising. He could not fail to be impressed with them. These Greeks with no hope, with everything against them, continued to battle for their city when clearly it must fall, and it must fall now.

As the hours passed, Mehmet's enthusiasm turned to a growing frustration. He was not sure, but it appeared the Greeks were actually pushing back the crescent toward the wall. How could hundreds defeat his tens of thousands? His men, so enthusiastic at first, were tiring. They had stopped shouting and some were beginning to slink away from the walls in the darkness, seeking safety and their tents. The first wanderings of dawn across the sky showed the city still miraculously holding.

Zaganos placed a gentle hand on Mehmet's shoulder. "We should pull back for now, my Lord. We have made great progress today. Let us give the men some rest, and surely we shall take the city today or tonight."

"No! We will take the city now. I will not allow them to pull back. Better to kill them as they try to flee. Let them fear me more than they fear these wretched Greeks." Mehmet felt his rage rising. How could the city have survived the night? His men were worthless; they would be punished. They must be punished.

"My Lord, they have fought all night. They are exhausted. We need to pull back and regroup. There are so many dead and wounded near the breach now that we cannot press the attack any longer. Let us pull back and then hit them with fresh resources tonight. Give the men a few hours of rest and time to eat and recover."

Mehmet could have torn his hair out in frustration. But he knew Zaganos was a great General and that his advice was sound. The Greeks could not repair this hole in one day. It was impossible.

"I will take your advice, Zaganos, but I want the city taken tonight. Order the men back and give them a few hours of rest."

Mehmet rode back to his tent and dismounted. He ordered food and drink, tearing a goblet from his servant and throwing it to the ground. He raised a mailed fist and nearly struck the frightened man, but thought better of it and simply ordered the cowering servant out of his tent. He lay down, exhausted, his head spinning. He tried to close his eyes and sleep for a short time, but he was too frustrated. How could his men have failed him? Should he impale some or behead them to set an example? Would that action help or hurt things? Why were these infidel Greeks so impossible to defeat? He had crushed them before. His father had crushed them so many times it was difficult to count. They often fought bravely, but never like this.

What was it about this damned city? Was it impossible to capture? Was his father correct in giving up and finally leaving the city alone? Doubts spun through his head for another hour or so before he finally drifted off into a fitful sleep.

Mehmet awoke in the early afternoon. He left the tent to review the walls and was stunned. The Greeks were furiously constructing a wooden structure in the midst of the breach. Again he had to grudgingly admire the Greek initiative. Instead of attempting to rebuild the walls with stone, which was probably impossible with such short time and such a huge hole, they instead were crafting a makeshift wooden fortress to plug the hole. He had not thought such a thing was possible with a hole this size.

The wood already covered the entire breach and was being steadily built up. He realized that it was already too late to storm the wall again. He would have to batter this area with cannon as well, or choose another section of wall to attack. The moment of initiative had been lost. Why had Zaganos urged him to pull the men back? Was he in league with Halil? Mehmet dismissed this thought. He knew his friend certainly was not. There was no way he could have known that the Greeks would react so quickly. Even if he had continued to press the attack, it was likely the Greeks could have held. They even could have built the walls during the attack if need be. No, Zaganos had recommended the right decision. He would regroup and wait. He called off the attack for the evening and asked for Zaganos to join him for dinner.

Zaganos showed up for dinner promptly. He appeared nervous, and Mehmet realized his friend was afraid of what might happen to him because of his failure at the wall. The sultan smiled to himself. He enjoyed power; if only he could have it without the current restraints. Restraints imposed because of the foolishness of his youth.

Why must he still pay? He knew he had worked hard every moment since his terrible childhood failure to ensure he would never make the same mistakes again. How could he be sure, though, that it wasn't some internal failing on his part? Perhaps he simply lacked some essential skill to rule? He certainly did not possess his father's ability to inspire love. His father had not been simply tolerated; he was the beloved leader of his people. Mehmet had never been able to accomplish the same. His people might grow to respect him, but they would never love him.

So be it. He did not need their love. But without the forgiveness of love, he had to inspire both respect and fear. He already possessed the latter, but only accomplishments as a leader would give him the former. Thus this great gamble.

Was it going to pay off? He had been sure when he began that he could not fail. He was more prepared than perhaps anyone who had ever brought a force to the gates of Constantinople. Moreover, the city was more vulnerable than it had ever been. This was not a capital bursting with population, riches, and power. This was a mere shadow of its former self, a last gasp for the Greeks before the inevitable wave of the Ottomans washed forever over them. Did they not understand that? Why could they not simply surrender? He would honor his offer to them! He needed a period to build Constantinople back into a great city, his great city. The center of his new empire. He would give peace to all the West, at least for a time, and then he would turn and wash over them. Soon the world would be one empire, one religion, for the glory of the Ottomans and Allah.

He must stop thinking. Keep going. He was committed and could not back out now. He had been so close last night. So close. But now he had to move on.

"Tell me about the mining progress, my friend. How are they doing?"

Zaganos looked relieved. "I can certainly do so, my Lord. I did want to speak about last night's failure. I—"

"Do not worry about that, Zaganos. The decision was mine, and I appreciated your advice. The decision was the correct one. I had hoped we would win through, but the Greeks showed more resistance than I thought they were capable of. What we need are multiple breaches at the same time. I believe they are using a reserve force to rush to the walls. If they have to deal with multiple breaches, they will be overwhelmed. A series of mining explosions should accomplish just that."

"I appreciate your wisdom, my Lord. Concerning the mining, as you ordered, I have implemented a number of different steps. We have engineers digging tunnels at seven different locations. They have made significant progress in each tunnel, although at different speeds, depending on the type of soil, rock composition, and so on that they have encountered. I believe they will be ready to explode simultaneously within just a few days. If we are successful with even half of them, we should have three or four breaches at the same time. If we strike quickly, we will overwhelm the walls and take the city."

"Excellent. Excellent job. I do not want this to be our only plan, though, so keep up the attacks on the wooden palisade too. If we can blow through that again, I still think we may be able to get into the city. I would like to inspect a tunnel after dark."

"I am not sure that is wise, my Lord. These tunnels are fragile and at times collapse."

"If so, it would be Allah's will. I want to see a tunnel."

"Very well, my Lord. We can go after dinner."

When they had eaten a light dinner of cold lamb and rice and discussed some additional details about the siege, Zaganos beckoned the sultan out of the tent. They did not bother to bring horses because one of the tunnels was relatively close. They made their way as quietly as possible through the camp and eventually arrived at the entrance to the tunnel, which was within one of the tents to disguise the process. Zaganos climbed down first, along with one of the engineers as a guide, and Mehmet followed.

The tunnel was narrow, barely two men wide, and only a few feet tall, so that the men could not stand but rather had to bend over to walk. The air was hot, dusty, and bitter. The tunnel was lit with torches nailed periodically to the walls. Mehmet saw that every few feet or so the tunnel was reinforced with wooden beams. He found the tunnel unpleasant. He could not imagine laboring for days at a time under the ground like this. He listened to the engineer's description of their efforts for some time, then thanked him for the tour and crawled back out of the hole. He ordered Zaganos to double the rations for the tunnelers, and to promise them a double share in the spoils if the city was taken by the planned explosions. He thanked Zaganos for the evening and the tour and made his way back with his personal guards to his tent. When he arrived, he learned that the spy had returned and was waiting.

He immediately entered and found the man sitting down, waiting in the darkness. The spy knelt before him, hands out in full prostration.

"What do you have for me?" asked Mehmet.

"Many new things, my Lord."

"And what do you want in return?" So far the man had asked for nothing for his information, but Mehmet knew this was a game with but one ending. He would be asked a price in exchange for these secrets.

"I ask only to be of service."

"You have been of service, and you will have my gratitude and much more." The information about the fleet and the size of the defense force had already been invaluable. What new information would he have? "Tell me everything."

"First, we have no knowledge of a definite relief fleet coming from the Italians, or anyone else for that matter."

"That's good to know. What about the Hungarians?"

"We received back a short message that Hunyadi was interested in the situation, but no commitment. I don't think he intends to assist us. There was another request sent, but we should have had an answer by now."

Mehmet was relieved by both pieces of news, although he was not sure he could trust this man. Still, it would help him to plan, particularly since the information so far had been so reliable.

"Tell me about the breach. How were you able to withstand it?"

"We were barely able to, my Lord. We thought we had lost the city. We have a reserve force set up to rush to any breach. If they had not arrived in time, the city would have fallen. As it was, half of the reserve force was wiped out in the fighting at the breach. If you had not withdrawn, I think you would have taken Constantinopole."

So it was a mistake to pull back? He knew it! Why had he listened to Zaganos? He needed to trust his own instincts in these things. The opportunity to take the city had been there, and he let it slip through his hands. Next time he would not let his men pull back.

If they complained, he would kill a few. They would push until they were through without respite.

"Anything else you can tell me?"

"Not at this time, my Lord."

"I thank you for telling me these things. As I said before, if your words are true, you will be rewarded when the city falls. If they are false, you shall suffer like nobody else shall suffer. Do you understand?"

The spy bowed. "Yes, my Lord."

"Now leave me."

The man departed and Mehmet sat down, ordering drink and food to be brought to him while he pondered this new information. So the Greeks had no definite help? Interesting. His greatest fear was a relief fleet, or perhaps even more menacing, an overwhelming attack from the Hungarians. John Hunyadi had been stopped before, but only barely. He was the greatest field commander Mehmet's father had ever faced. Mehmet knew that if the foolish infidels ever rallied around him and Hunyadi was provided with a substantial army, the Hungarian would threaten the Ottoman presence in Europe.

These foolish Christians. So petty and divided. Fighting city to city, and even within kingdoms, for money and power. It had been so easy for Mehmet's father to pit one against the other. His father had been trapped in Anatolia when a large army invaded his European territories with Hunyadi in the lead. Europe was lost if Murad could not return. What happened? He bought his passage across from the Genoese. These Christians sold out their fellow infidels, ultimately resulting in thousands of dead and the loss of the greatest opportunity to remove the Turks forever from Europe. All for a little gold and favorable trading rights.

Now the same thing was happening again. Mehmet was vulnerable while his forces were concentrated against Constantinople. If the Italians and Hungarians would only work together for a small period of time they could catch him against the walls of the city both by sea and by land. They might destroy his army, even kill him, and drive the Ottomans from Europe.

Instead they had signed treaties with Mehmet. Treaties that they were apparently honoring. If this spy's words were true, then no help was coming to the city. He would not trust completely, but it gave him confidence that he would be able to take the city before any real help arrived.

Take the city! It had almost been his. Why had he listened to Zaganos? The fool, he was getting too conservative in his middle years. A younger general would have pushed harder. He would have been pressing Mehmet to continue the attack, rather than advising him to retreat. The city would already have fallen. Had Zaganos betrayed him? The thought wandered through his mind again. He could not believe it was true. A betrayal could only be to the benefit of Halil. How would that help Zaganos? If Mehmet fell, surely his "new friends," his Christian converts, would fall with him. Zaganos could not be motivated by assisting Halil, and if he was not helping the grand vizier, then he must have been sincere in his belief that the city could not be taken at that juncture.

Should Mehmet remove Zaganos from command? He could not see the profit in such a decision. Perhaps he should tie him closer to the battle itself. He had kept Zaganos away from the land walls except for consultations, instead stationing him across the Golden Horn near the walls of Galata. What if he placed him directly in charge of the forces in the center? Initially he had not done so because he wanted to assure Zaganos was not given too much credit for victory. But what if things did not go well?

No matter. If the city could not be taken and Zaganos was in charge of the main attack, then Mehmet would place the blame on his general. This would give Halil a way out. Halil wouldn't have to condemn Mehmet if he didn't want to, instead he could condemn Zaganos. Wasn't Halil's real objection to Mehmet that he would not take his advice, that he had raised upstart converts to the highest positions in the land? He would place Zaganos at the forefront of the fighting. If he triumphed, excellent; if he failed, he would punish him.

Interesting. The benefits of the decision seemed to outweigh the risk of any additional glory Zaganos might garner if the city was taken. Mehmet would get most of the glory in such a case anyway. He liked the thought. He would move Zaganos to the center of the action and let him take over. But if the walls were breached again, they would attack until the sultan said to stop. There would be no measured retreat again.

Mehmet hastily wrote a note and then called for his guards to locate a courier. He handed the courier the message and asked him to deliver it to Zaganos, the new general of the center.

CHAPTER FIFTEEN

TUESDAY, MAY 8, 1453

Constantine stood with Giovanni and watched Greek and Italian workmen desperately hammering together the makeshift wooden palisade to fill the enormous gap in the outer wall. Again Constantine thanked God and the Virgin for bringing him Giovanni. When the wall had exploded, he had been sure the city was going to fall. The quick action of the Italian brought the reserves to the breach rapidly. Courageous fighting and the superior armor and weapons of the Greeks had prevented the fall of the city, but Constantine knew they would have been doomed without the wooden structure that was even now being frantically completed.

Miraculously, the Ottomans had pulled back from their furious attack when all seemed lost. This allowed the Greeks to work quickly in the early morning to construct a new and far more extensive wooden barricade. In only a few hours, the full hole was stopped up with the solid wood barrier. This new barrier was showing the same remarkable ability to withstand cannon shot, and Giovanni assured Constantine it would hold so long as materials and men were ready to repair it as necessary.

The attack had been very costly to the defenders. Almost two hundred Greeks and Italians had been killed or wounded. Constantine was now forced to pull even more men off the walls in other portions of the city to rebuild the reserve force. The quality of the fighters was also less than the original force, as Giovanni had culled the best armored, most experienced men in the first place to create the fast response reserve. Would these lesser men hold up to a ferocious attack like the one that had occurred last night? It was just another worry for Constantine, among all the worries.

Still, Constantinople held. Another day, another miraculous day. Surely it was God's will that the Greeks had held the wall against such odds for so long last night. Would this success be enough to drive the Ottomans away? At some point, they must give up and leave. Or the city would be relieved by an Italian fleet, or a Hungarian army. Something had to happen to save the city. The city was always saved. Constantine would not allow it to fall when he was emperor. He could not allow it.

He walked down near the walls and began chatting encouragingly with the soldiers and the builders, patting shoulders and shaking hands. The men were exhausted, but when they saw their emperor they smiled. Constantine was exhausted too. Exhausted and depressed. He did not show it. He smiled and spoke about the end of the siege and the eventual defeat of the Ottomans. He thanked the men for their service and sacrifice for the city.

Giovanni called him back after a time, and Constantine left to cheers from the men. He was ready to return to the palace for some much-needed sleep. "What is it, my friend?" he asked the Italian commander.

"Grave news, my Lord."

Constantine chuckled. "More grave news. Can there really be any more? Let me guess, the Italians and Hungarians are joining forces with the Ottomans and are going to attack the city as well? Or maybe there is a plague that has killed all our soldiers? Or an army of demons is attacking the city from hell?"

"The last thing is nearer the mark than you might guess."

"What do you mean?"

"I have had reports from multiple sources. There is a muffled sound of hammering below the ground."

"What are you talking about?"

"I am afraid the Ottomans are tunneling, my Lord."

Constantine felt icy cold inside. "What do you mean, tunneling?"

"I am afraid they may be digging underneath, presumably to blow holes in the walls. I am hearing reports from multiple locations, so if it is true, then there may be a number of tunnel excavations at the same time. That would make sense, my Lord, if they are attempting to overwhelm our defenses with multiple breaches."

"They hardly need multiple breaches, as the last one nearly finished us off."

"Yes, my Lord, but of course there is no way they can know that for sure. They have failed now with several single-breach attacks. The sultan may be losing confidence in the ability of his men to battle their way through one breach. By the same token, one could have nothing to do with the other. These tunnels take some time to develop. This strategy may be an unrelated effort to create a breach."

Constantine thought about that. "I guess it does not really matter the reason. The point is that there are likely tunnels being built under the city. What can we do about it?"

"I may have an answer to that, My Lord. I have someone I would like to introduce you to."

"I will."

Giovanni left and returned a few minutes later, trailed by a shorter man. He was heavily armored, with reddish-brown hair, freckles, and pale skin. "My Lord, this is John Grant. He came to the city with my company. He is from a faraway land. I apologize that he does not speak any Greek."

"Where is he from?"

"He's from Scotland originally, my Lord, and later he served in the military in Germany. He has extensive experience dealing with tunneling operations."

Constantine looked the man over and then greeted him in Italian. "Well met, John Grant. Giovanni tells me you have experience with tunneling. What can you tell me?"

"Thank you, my Lord," said Grant, bowing low before continuing. "It is true I have experience in dealing with tunneling from my time in Germany."

"How does that help us now specifically?"

"What do you know about tunneling?"

"Frankly, very little."

"The key to dealing with tunneling is to find out where the tunnels are likely being dug, and dig counter tunnels."

"What is a counter tunnel?"

"That is a good question, my Lord. A counter tunnel is basically a tunnel that we construct under the ground leading right into their tunnel. Then we attack the people below, kill them, and cave in their tunnel."

"Is that difficult to do?"

"It is, my Lord, particularly when there are many tunnels to address. But it is critical. If we do not stop them, they will certainly blow holes in your walls. Based on what I saw yesterday, I imagine the city will not be able to handle multiple attacks at the same time."

"What do you need?"

"I need men, wooden beams, shovels, and a small fighting force."

"How many men?"

"I require several hundred, my Lord, and I need them now. We should start digging at all points where sounds have been detected. If we do not do this, and if we do not do it immediately, it will be too late. I do not want to alarm you, but it might already be too late."

"What do you mean, too late?"

"If they are too far along it will not matter. We will need some time to locate the tunnels. It is possible they are already in position, and capable of blowing up the walls right now. All I can do is try to stop them. I cannot promise anything."

"Do it. You'll have everything you need." Constantine could not believe it. Was it possible to actually have more things to worry about? As if the breach, and the ships, and the siege, and no reinforcements, or food, or money, and Italian bickering were not enough problems. How would he find more men for Grant to utilize? Could he really afford to further thin the ranks? He would have to find the men, whatever the cost. It made no difference whether the sea walls were well defended if the land walls fell. He would have to pray that the Ottomans failed to realize his weakness. He would have to remove more men and leave the walls facing the sea practically defenseless.

He turned to Giovanni to give the order, switching back to Greek. Giovanni agreed with his assessment and immediately relayed the orders to remove some of the defenders from the sea walls. If Constantinople was attacked by the Ottoman fleet now, there would be little chance to defend the walls before men would be over them and into the city. So be it. The end result of the siege was God's will.

He thought of Zophia again, of his child. He wanted to go to her, to see her. He knew she would not see him again until he had made up his mind. He had tried to consider what to do, but he was so exhausted and he was attacked by a thousand details a day. He needed time to decide.

SATURDAY, MAY 12, 1453

God was still with Constantinople. There was no immediate series of explosions from below the ground. Over the next several days, Grant, working around the clock, had been able to successfully dig into several tunnels and collapse them. He came back describing terrible and bloody underground battles, the stuff of nightmares. But he was producing results. There were still more tunnels out there and the Turks were moving closer to the walls with some of them. The threat was not gone, but an immediate crisis certainly had been averted.

Unfortunately, another crisis was brewing that might tear apart the city. Constantine had requested that the Venetians allow several ships in the harbor to be unloaded of men and arms. The Venetian Bailey had agreed, and made the order.

The sailors had rebelled and refused to come ashore or remove their arms and cannon. They were unwilling to do so apparently because they felt the city was doomed, and that they would be abandoning their only chance to escape if they acquiesced to the order.

Constantine needed the men and supplies, but this was not the most significant problem. The rebellion of these sailors had acted like a match to a powder keg. Other Italians, particularly the Genoese, were quick to accuse the Venetians of betrayal and cowardice. The Venetians, in response, were threatening to load up their people and leave the city. If Constantine lost the remaining Venetians, he would lose fully a tenth of his men. Additionally, any relief fleet would likely be partially if not heavily made up of Venetians. He could not afford to lose them.

He called for a small council of representatives to meet at St. Sophia that evening. He hoped to iron out the differences and keep the peace. His only fear in gathering all the Italian leaders together in one place was that one of them might insult another and only make things worse. Still, he had to do something before he woke up and the Venetians were simply gone.

He rode back from the walls to his palace and sat down with Loukas Notaras for a private lunch. He had not had very much time to spend with his friend in the past few days, as Notaras was busy with the fleet and Constantine had been at the land wall and dealing with the tunnels.

He arrived and shortly thereafter sat down with Notaras to eat. "Well met, my friend. How are things in the Horn?"

"Still tricky, my Lord. We have not lost any more ships, but they certainly have kept us busy. They fire periodic cannon shots at us, and they also send a few ships here and there at the walls. We send ships out after them, but they always turn around and head back to shore. They have also tested the booms with their outer fleet, but again, once we set out after them they quickly turn away."

"So no serious threats?"

"Not so far. I think they are just testing our responses. Frankly, if you want my assessment, I believe the incident with the Genoese relief fleet really shook the Turks' confidence. I think they are worried about pushing too hard at sea."

"That does not make sense to me. What about their victory in our surprise attack?"

"That was not really a victory at sea, my Lord, as their land cannon did most of the damage in that attack. And obviously they had been tipped off, because they were so clearly expecting us. I do not think that has changed their concerns about attacking us at sea."

Constantine wondered if Loukas was being entirely truthful with him. Again Sphrantzes's concerns had clouded his mind. Was it true they were afraid to attack, or was Notaras making an excuse to minimize his defeat? The emperor had not known his friend to shy from responsibility in the past, but never had there been more at stake. What if Notaras was wrong and the Ottomans did mount a huge, sudden attack? Would the Greek navy be prepared for it? If he suffered another defeat, would it leave the sea walls completely vulnerable and cause the city to fall? He had never doubted Notaras before. He realized there was nothing he could do about it. If he replaced him now, it would take the new commander days to learn the entire strategic situation. That could be more dangerous than leaving Notaras in place. Constantine would simply have to absorb this worry along with all the other worries and uncertainties he constantly faced. He smiled to himself. What was one more problem?

"Did you ever respond to Mehmet's offer about peace terms?" asked Notaras.

"No, I did not. I thought about simply saying no, but there did not seem to be any advantage in doing so. If he thinks we are still pondering it, then perhaps that will cloud his thinking."

"What about your thinking, my Lord? Respectfully, I hope you are not leaving this surrender proposal open as a possibility."

"Of course not," responded Constantine, irritably. But was he? It was true that he had held back. Was there a part of him that was considering taking the offer, some dark part of his mind? He had caught himself thinking about it, particularly late at night, dreaming of peace, of comfort, of leading his people to safety. He could see himself in a small home, having turned the cares of the world over to someone else, Zophia next to him looking out over the Aegean Sea, their child playing nearby. Was the offer still open? Should he stop being stubborn and consider it? Sphrantzes thought he should. Notaras could not conceive of it. What would Zophia think? He had not discussed it with her, and now he was not sure he would. Did it matter? Could he ever bring himself to do anything more than consider the idea? He doubted he could, at least until it was too late.

"Well, Loukas, I'm glad we had a chance for your reports and discussion, as always. I am sure you need to get back to the fleet. I have a meeting to try to sort out this dreadful Italian crisis."

Notaras laughed. "I am sure you will do fine with that, my Lord. The Italians would not be Italians if they were not at each other's throats. They bluster far more than they act."

"Yes, but they do act at times, and when they do, it is not always in our interest. Take care, my friend; I will see you soon."

At dusk, Constantine mounted his horse and left the palace with an escort of his personal guards. He was now traveling with more armed men, both for personal security and to assist as an extra reserve force. In the past, he had frequently traveled alone, or with one or two guards. Recently he had found he felt less secure; the city seemed more dangerous. This was not only because of the battle but also because he feared betrayal. He now typically had twenty-five armed men with him whenever he set out.

He made his way slowly through the city, the cannon booming in the background periodically, an almost constant noise since the siege began. He nodded to greetings from citizens and kept an eye on the condition of the city as he made his way to St. Sophia.

At the entrance of the great cathedral, he was greeted by Giovanni, representing the Genoese faction in the city, and by Girolamo Minotto, the Venetian Bailey. The Bailey was a tall, fair-skinned Italian in his late thirties. He had a graying beard and wore black robes with a heavy circular medallion containing the symbol of St. Mark. There were also several representatives from other Italian cities, including Naples, and the Catalan Company. The Italians wore cloaks of different colors, and the Catalan Company was bedecked in bright velvet hats of yellow and red, vividly contrasting with the somber browns and blacks of the Greeks.

The assembled men bowed when Constantine entered. He then asked the Bailey to explain Venice's position.

"Thank you, my Lord. I must lodge a complaint in the strongest form. We have suffered enough insults at the hands of these Genoese, and the rest. I certainly understand that some Venetian sailors disobeyed orders—"

"Disobeyed so they could run if the city falls!" interrupted Giovanni.

The Bailey spat on the ground. "That is what I speak of!"

"Venetians have already fled the city. What have the Genoese done? I came to the city. We have sent the only reinforcements the city has received. All you Venetians do is whine about your contributions, while you are probably negotiating with the sultan to quit the city. Is that why you will not leave your ships?"

"How dare you! We have fought hard and true. We have not betrayed Constantinople. But we will not stay and fight where our help is not wanted!" The Bailey turned to walk away.

"Enough!" shouted Constantine. "I have never accused you of cowardice or duplicity."

"Your commander does!"

"He does not speak for me in this."

"Then why did you appoint a Genoan in the first place?"

"Come now. This situation has nothing to do with favoritism. Giovanni's reputation preceded him. I have a Scot defending us from a tunnel attack right now. Do I favor Scotland? I'd never met a Scot before I was introduced to him, but I resolved to trust him because he has experience we need. We have all managed for years to get along well enough, even with all of your rivalries and infighting that I have never been able to understand. I do not need Genoan more than Venetian, nor vice versa. Do I even have to tell you all this? I desperately need you all. We do not have enough men by far to defend this city. We all know this. Can we afford to strip the walls further? And for what, for petty squabbling? Come now, let us shake hands and be friends again."

The Bailey stared hard at Giovanni. "I will not be the first to do it; I did not cause this."

"Nor I."

Constantine sighed. He grabbed the hands of both men and pulled them together. They shook hands, hesitantly at first, and then firmly.

"There we have it. Now we can return to our present problems, which are desperate enough indeed. Gentlemen, I must be frank with you about our situation. Our men have been thinned out by the fighting to the point that I do not know if we can repel another attack. Fortunately, it appears that the Ottomans are waiting until they can breach multiple locations at the same time. Several times now in the last few days they have blown a single hole in the wall, but they have not attacked us. As you know, most of these attacks have focused on the Charisius Gate and the Gate of St. Romanus, which they apparently believe are the weak points in our defenses. What I do not know how to counter is if they do break through at several points, if they—"

"My Lord!"

Constantine looked up. A messenger had arrived, sweaty and red faced. "My Lord, the Ottomans are attacking!"

"Attacking where? Have they broken through?"

"Near the palace, Sire, near the Blachernae Gate."

"They blew a hole in the wall near the palace?" The Ottomans had not concentrated any fire on that portion of the wall. Constantine did not even understand how they could have moved their cannon into place quickly enough to mount an attack without his knowledge.

"No, my Lord. They have stormed the wall with ladders. There are thousands of them against the wall! We are fighting as hard as we can, but I do not know what happened. I was sent to find you and Giovanni as quickly as possible."

Constantine looked at Giovanni for a moment, then he yelled at his men to follow and sprinted out with Giovanni close behind. He mounted quickly and took off at a gallop toward the land walls, not even bothering to make sure his men were following. He thundered through the dark streets. The din of battle, which started as a whisper, grew into a thunderous roar.

He arrived to a nightmare. He was stunned. There were Turks everywhere, hundreds of them, battling in the streets of Constantinople. Greeks were screaming and running in every direction, including some soldiers who were dropping their weapons and fleeing the scene. He could hear screams that the city was lost.

Was all lost? Should he turn his horse and flee? No! His internal voice screamed to him. He must stay and fight. He turned and quickly found Giovanni, who was ashen faced and motionless, as if he did not know what to do.

"Giovanni!" he shouted. "Rally your men, battle to the left; I will take care of the right!" He screamed at his guards to join them.

They charged on horseback into a line of Ottomans. Constantine raised his sword and swung down hard, hacking off the hand of a

Janissary who was reaching up to grab his reins. A spear flew past his head, only inches away. He swung his sword left and right, cutting off the arm of one and slashing the face of another.

He was probably only moments from death. He knew it, but it did not cause him fear. All of the loss and fear and disappointment was leaving him. He felt a strange peace. He called to his guards who were battling with him. They drove the first line of Turks back, but so many more were coming.

On and on he battled in the darkness. He was cut on his arm and face, superficial cuts, or at least he hoped so. He felt so much power rushing through him. Time had slowed down. There was no more Constantinople, no more empire, just now, this moment. His horse was felled beneath him and he crashed to the ground, but he killed his attacker and found his feet, and continued to battle.

Hours passed, or maybe days, he could not tell. The rush of excitement was fading away. He felt more and more exhausted. Still the Turks rushed forward, and still he fought them back. He waited for a sword or a musket to end his life, but so far it had not come. He did not fear death, he was merely curious that he was still alive.

He realized it was beginning to grow lighter. He had fought all night. He glanced around and saw that there were still a few guards with him, battling the Turks. He did not know whether the rest lived or died. The Ottomans were not rushing in anymore. He observed that the tempo of the fight had slowed gradually. He dispatched another Turk and nobody appeared in front of him. He attacked a soldier who was pressing one of his guards and stabbed him in the back. The soldier dropped to the ground, screaming, and the imperial guard stabbed him in the heart. Constantine looked up. There were no more Ottomans near him. The din of battle had faded away. The streets were filled with the bodies of the dead and the groans and screams of the wounded. Blood ran in scarlet rivulets through the street.

Constantine walked wearily toward the wall. He could not believe it. Somehow the Turks had gone. How could that be the case? There had been hundreds over the wall, maybe more than a thousand. They had caught the Greeks totally by surprise, attacking with ladders instead of waiting for a breach, and attacking a portion of the wall that they had previously ignored.

Constantine fell to his knees and gave thanks to God. If ever he had doubted the existence of God, this miracle had convinced him. Constantinople had been saved somehow. Surely this would be enough for Mehmet. Surely he would leave the city now, when even this gamble had failed. Constantine felt a hand on his back. He looked up and saw Giovanni, bruised, cut, exhausted, but still alive. The Genoan grasped his hand and pulled him to his feet. They looked at each other for long moments and then embraced, clasping each other on the back, sharing this miraculous victory.

As they laughed and recounted stories of the battle, John Grant arrived. "I have news, my Lord. We have captured one of the enemy engineers. Under torture he has revealed the location of the remaining tunnels. We can destroy them now."

More good news. Surely from God also. Constantine thanked Grant and walked slowly with Giovanni up the stairs of one of the towers on the inner wall. After the steep climb, he looked out over the city. A huge area near the palace was covered in smoke and the waste of battle. There were bodies everywhere, mostly Turks. Constantine turned and looked out past the walls. The Ottomans had pulled back to their tents. It was quiet. Even the cannon had stopped. He could almost feel the dejection of his enemies. *Let them despair. Thank you, God, my Father. Let them leave.*

CHAPTER SIXTEEN

SUNDAY, MAY 20, 1453

Mehmet knelt praying alone in his tent. Allah had abandoned him. He would be the fool again, a pygmy among the giants of his forefathers. Surely Halil was already gathering his support. He would be there at his tent, perhaps even with armed guards, demanding he surrender his title. But this time Murad would not be there to protect him. His father could not come back and rule again. He was gone. Halil would be forced to kill the sultan. He had no other choice if he wanted to take power. Mehmet felt for his dagger. He would not surrender lightly. He would take lives. If Halil was foolish enough to come within his range, he would kill his grand vizier first, and at least have the satisfaction of watching him die before he himself was beheaded or strangled. He relished the thought of plunging his dagger deep into Halil's chest.

He heard a stirring at the door of his tent. He pulled his dagger out halfway and turned quickly. Halil did not stand at his door. It was Zaganos.

Zaganos greeted him, bowing. Was it to be his friend striking the first blow after all? Had he made a deal with Halil to somehow save his own life? Mehmet could not believe that was the case. Zaganos would back his leader to the death. He would never side with Halil, unless of course he planned to become sultan himself? Was such a thing possible? Certainly Zaganos was a popular soldier, but he would be even more objectionable to Halil and the old guard than Mehmet. He could still trust his friend, as much as he could ever trust anyone. He looked up and smiled grimly, although he did not remove his hand from his dagger.

"Well, my friend, have you come for my head?" he joked. His whole body was tense, ready to spring if necessary.

"What? Don't be absurd, my Lord. You may have cause to fear Halil, and given the circumstances, those fears are not to be treated lightly, but you do not have and never will have anything to fear from me."

"I jest with you. But joking aside, what shall we do? Build more tunnels to be buried? More ships to be sunk? Or perhaps another failure at the wall? This city curses me as it cursed my father and all our people. Why can we not take it? Perhaps we are made to suffer by Allah for all of our stupidity, our arrogance? Is this possible?"

"I do not see why we would be punished."

"Do you not? We have split our faith. Our rulers have squabbled over territory and power, and we fight among ourselves instead of conquering the infidels. Maybe that is why we fail?"

"And the Christians are better? They cannot unite even to save themselves, let alone to conquer. They are fading, dying. Constantinople is but an example of the sickness in all of them. Do not worry, my Lord, the city will eventually fall, and eventually all of Christianity with it."

Mehmet caught Zaganos's emphasis on "eventually." He did not believe in the attack anymore either. The sultan felt suddenly tired, and terribly alone. He had had enough. Now he just wanted to end this all and be safe.

"Halil is right. We should never have come here. Not now, perhaps not ever. This venture has used up half of my father's treasury, thousands of men, and for what? We cannot take the city. I cannot bear this anymore, Zaganos. Help me. I do not want to be killed. Is it too late to leave the city and keep my throne? I just want it all to end."

Zaganos was clearly taken aback. Mehmet knew he had revealed himself in a way he had never done before. It had been years since he told anyone his true feelings. He did not care anymore. It was already too late, and at the end, he felt only fear and pity for himself. He had come so close, but he had failed.

Zaganos sat for long minutes without responding. Finally he spoke.

"I believe, my Lord, there is one more great assault in the men. They are tired and dejected, but they are not ready to leave yet. I think we can maneuver one more attack."

Mehmet had not expected this. He had expected Zaganos to tell him how to leave the city with honor, or to tell him it was too late. He felt a ray of hope with his older friend's support.

"What is your advice?"

"Let the men rest for a week or so. They are fatigued from the constant attacks. In the meantime, keep up the bombardments and also use the fleet to keep the Greeks occupied. This will exhaust them while we rebuild our strength. Avoid Halil during this time, and then, call a council with him. At the council, listen to his advice. He will advise that you lift the siege and make the best possible deal with Constantine for tribute. Instead, I advise that you suggest one more massive attack. If it fails, we will leave. He will not expect you to agree with him. Your offer of one more attack will seem reasonable to his allies; they will be forced to accept it. If the attack fails, you will have agreed to do what Halil wants, and likely he will be unable to do anything to you. We will also use this time to prepare your internal defenses, extra guards, weapons, et cetera. We should be able to fight off any sudden attack on you."

"And if the attack succeeds—or do you no longer think it possible?"

"If the attack succeeds, we do not need a plan, my Lord."

Mehmet felt the warmth inside him grow. He had chosen this man well. Zaganos was loyal after all. Not only loyal, but he did believe there was still a chance the city could be taken. Whether they succeeded or not, if Mehmet survived, Zaganos would be richly rewarded.

Mehmet embraced Zaganos, something he had never done before. He found himself sobbing, holding on tight, feeling the support of another person. He had held back so long, held himself in control. He eventually composed himself. "Thank you for your support. Whatever happens, I will not forget."

Zaganos bowed. "You may always depend on me, my Lord. What would I do? Betray you for Halil? Hah! My head would join yours the moment it was convenient. My star is tied to yours. I am your servant.

"And there is more. I believe in you, my Lord. You have almost brought this city to its knees. You have done more than your father ever did against Constantinople. More than almost anyone. If the city falls or does not at this point, that is Allah's will. But if we do fail, we will not go down without a fight. Halil may find it less than easy to depose you."

Mehmet bowed back, his old self again. He would not surrender, either the siege or to Halil. He would fight.

The spy came again to Mehmet's summons in the middle of the night. He bowed low and rose at Mehmet's command. "What can you tell me?" the sultan demanded.

"Your attack on Blachernae Palace was almost successful, Sultan. The attack caught us completely by surprise. The only reason it failed was again the timely reinforcement by reserve forces. Also, Constantine arrived rather unexpectedly with a large force of his guards. It is a miracle that the city held."

A miracle for the Greeks. What did it mean to Mehmet? Was this another sign that Allah did not favor his victory? He had come so close so many times in this siege.

"What of the tunneling? Why did we fail? How were we discovered?"

"Apparently the tunnelers made too much noise and alerted the defenders. There is an expert in tunnel warfare in the city. He made his services available to Constantine, and that is why your plan failed."

An expert on tunneling magically appearing in the city? Again, was Allah against him? Was he for some reason favoring the Christians? The history of Constantinople was the history of miraculous good luck for the inhabitants. The city should have fallen a dozen times but somehow again and again had been saved. Was this another example of the same?

"What is the situation now of the defenders?"

"It has changed some. Your ships in the harbor have required a repositioning of forces. There are now more men stationed along the sea walls near the Horn. Also, the defenders as a whole have thinned out some because of battle wounds and illness."

"Thinned out how much?"

"By hundreds, Sultan, not by thousands. Most of the defenders are very well armored, and of course they have the walls to defend them. I can tell you that everyone is suffering from fatigue and most of the defenders near the main points of attack have suffered at least minor wounds in the fighting."

Only hundreds of casualties? Mehmet had lost more than ten thousand men in the fighting so far. Was this man lying to him? He did know the Greeks were well armed, and of course the walls would assist them in reducing casualties.

However, Mehmet refused to believe that only a few hundred Greeks had been killed so far. He must watch for other lies. He again wondered what the purpose of this spy's betrayal was. Was he even truly a traitor, or was he here at Constantine's command to beguile Mehmet with half-truths and outright misinformation? Should he torture the man or kill him?

"Would another attack on the palace succeed?"

"Of course, there is no way for me to predict that, but I do not think so. I know there are now more defenders in that area, and I'm sure they are on guard. I think an attack on that portion of the wall would result in a quick defeat."

"That is what I would have expected to hear, but I wanted your opinion. Where should we attack?"

The spy hesitated. Was this more than he was willing to answer?

"Sultan, return to the attack before the Romanus and Charisius portions of the wall. You have nearly succeeded there multiple times. Blast a hole and battle through. That is the only way."

So the best plan this man had was the same plan Mehmet had already followed over and over? All of the failed sieges of Constantinople, with the exception of the Latin attack by sea, had come down to an inability to break through the walls. Mehmet had advanced one level. He could get through the walls but only on a limited front. On that limited front his men were fighting on equal terms with the Greeks, because only a relatively few Ottomans could get through at one time. He knew he was running out of time. He had hoped the spy would give him some new insight, but he had not. It all still came down to not only breaking through the wall, but breaking through the Greek defenders. He could do this only, if at all, through a sustained attack. If he had months, he could keep wearing the Greeks down, but he did not have months. He had weeks, maybe only days.

"Anything else you can tell me?"

"Not at this time, Sultan."

"Leave me, then."

The spy bowed and backed up to the tent entrance before turning to leave.

He had not really learned anything new except how frustratingly close he had come to taking the city through either the tunnels or the attack at the palace. Could he have no luck? Must everything play into Halil's hands? Again the fear returned to him that Allah would let him fail, that he would suffer humiliation and execution. Every Sultan since the founding of his people had advanced the empire gloriously. Everything they had done was met with success. Was he to be the first to end in failure? He would not allow it! He would lose every man in the coming attack; he would bring the empire down with him at the walls of Constantinople if he must. The city would be his. He would prove them all wrong. He would prove Murad and Halil wrong. Allah willing.

SATURDAY, MAY 26, 1453

A week passed. The grand council of the sultan met again to debate the siege. Halil and many of the elder councilors arrived together, and late. Mehmet watched his grand vizier carefully. He appeared supremely confident. Clearly Halil felt this was his moment, and that Mehmet was already finished. Mehmet had nearly given up, but that moment had passed. Whatever would happen in the next few days, the sultan was prepared to fight. For now it was time to implement Zaganos's plan.

Mehmet began by giving an update of the past ten days. He explained that no substantial breaches had occurred on the walls, and so he had used the time to rest the men while keeping the Greeks busy in the Golden Horn with several minor attacks on the sea chain and on the fleet itself. None of the attacks had been intended as full assaults, but rather simply to keep the Greeks on their guard constantly.

Halil rose to respond, bowing before the sultan. Mehmet noticed his bow was shallow and quick. Mehmet's anger flashed, tempting him to quick, cathartic violence. But he held his temper.

Halil spoke. "My Lord, we all appreciate your hard work and this aggressive attempt on the city. However, I think we must admit that it has failed. Two months have now passed without success. We are no nearer to taking the city than when we started, or when your father started, for that matter. Each month that goes by, we are vulnerable to attack by the Hungarians, the Italians, or even our enemies in Anatolia or Persia. We have been lucky so far; no enemies have used our position to their advantage. This cannot last.

"Your father knew when to leave the city. You are *certainly* as wise as he was. As you know, I counseled against this attack from the beginning for all of the reasons we now face. The city will fall at the right time, my Lord. Let us force the Greeks to pay as much as can be negotiated, and leave them to rot. We can then offer favorable terms to the Venetians and Genoese. They will choose to trade with us instead of the Greeks. We can strangle the city slowly. It will fall as ripe fruit into our hands."

There was a general murmur of agreement from the senior councilors. The Grand Mufti stood and added his own words in agreement with Halil.

Mehmet rose to respond. It was time to corner his grand vizier. "Thank you, Halil, for your wise words. I agree with you."

There was shock in the room. Surprise came across Halil's eyes, then quickly fled as he regained his composure. Mehmet smiled. Surely the grand vizier had not expected this. He had expected Mehmet to argue that he would never lift the siege, to throw a fit, to scream. Halil would then hatch his plot to remove him, or perhaps the plot was already well laid and an attack was prepared for this very night. Whatever the plan, he clearly had not prepared for this.

"Well, my Lord, this is most welcome news. When can we expect to pull back our forces? I would suggest we leave a covering force and slowly remove our men at night. Or do you wish to negotiate the best tribute from Constantine before we withdraw? That might be the most prudent course of action, as we would likely receive the best terms. I know this is a difficult time, my Lord, but I think you are showing great wisdom. You are *starting* to grow up. Your father would be proud of you."

Mehmet seethed. How dare he make such a statement? Particularly in public. Zaganos had been correct. They had discussed this night in detail. His general had predicted that after Halil recovered from the initial shock, he might try to goad Mehmet into doing something extreme. If he could get Mehmet to attack him, he might be able to depose the sultan on the spot. He was thankful Zaganos had warned him ahead of time, as it took every ounce of his control not to order Halil's head on a plate.

He waited a few moments and then responded. "I appreciate your sentiments, Halil, even if they are difficult to hear. But you did not let me finish my thoughts. I agree with your advice, *but* I would like to find out how the men are feeling. If they are willing, I would suggest one more massive assault on the city. If they are ready and able, we would attack in three days. If they are not, then we will leave in a few days. In the meantime, I am going to offer Constantine the most generous terms I have ever made him, but I am still requesting he leave the city. Perhaps we can still have Constantinople at no further cost."

Halil looked around, gauging the level of support. He had been outmaneuvered, and he clearly knew it. His eyes rested on Zaganos for a long moment, burning with hatred. Finally he turned to Mehmet and bowed. "All excellent ideas, my Lord. I would be happy to assess the feelings of the men—"

"Thank you, Halil, but I need my grand vizier here for advice. I am going to send Zaganos."

"Excellent. I am sure the men will prove willing to mount another attack. If that is unsuccessful, hopefully we will not be too weakened to meet any other attacks that have been prepared by our enemies while we have focused on the city. With my Lord's permission I will begin preparing the orders to evacuate the siege."

"That is fine, Halil. Just don't prepare them too quickly. There is still one attack to mount." Mehmet turned to the council as a whole. "Let us pray the attack is successful. If it is Allah's will, the city will be ours. Allah willing, we attack in three days."

CHAPTER SEVENTEEN

FRIDAY, MAY 25, 1453

Constantine sat at his work table in his bedchamber in the early morning hours, reading reports by candlelight while he reviewed updates about the city's defenses and estimates of the Ottoman forces and distribution.

The emperor was exhausted. He found sleep difficult, and the constant and rapid changes of fortune during the siege had frayed his nerves almost to the breaking point. Constantine had hoped Mehmet would lift the siege after the failure of his tunneling operation and the lost battle near Blachernae Palace. Unfortunately, the sultan had not done so. Days had gone by and with each, Constantine felt more depressed, with a creeping sense of doom. He could feel this sinking melancholy mirrored in the city and in his soldiers as they slowly lost hope that the siege would ever end. Instead, they endured day after day of bombardment and almost constant naval attacks. His men could handle only so much. Constantine knew this. He hoped Mehmet and his Ottomans would break first.

He thought of Zophia. He had not seen her in weeks now. Still he could not decide what to do. She had told him not to change his mind because of the baby. That the baby didn't change anything. How could she claim that? He knew what he wanted to do, but he still held out hope that the Georgians would come with a relief fleet and save the city. He needed this now more than ever.

He reopened the secret report from the Venetian vessel he had disguised and sent out looking for the relief fleets. He had not shared this news with anyone since he had received it two days before, although he was sure rumors would have spread in the city. The ship had returned after traveling out of the Dardanelles and through the Greek islands in mid-May. It had searched but found no evidence or rumor of a relief fleet. Any help that might be coming from the West would be weeks, if not months, away. Unless the Hungarians were coming by land, or the Georgians could battle through from the Black Sea, it appeared the city was on its own.

Constantine was still stunned by the news. He had done everything he could to protect the city. His greatest sacrifice, forcing the Union of the Churches on his people, had been nothing short of sacrificing the people themselves for the survival of the city. He had been sure this would bring a swift and substantial relief force from the pope, yet nothing had appeared. Was this sacrifice to be for nothing? Further, he had sacrificed his love, his own happiness, when he sent betrothal requests to Georgia. Where was the assistance from that kingdom? Had his ship even made it to the king with the proposal?

He rose and wearily pulled on clothing, dressing himself rather than allowing others to do so, in marked contrast to previous emperors. Of course, the limited resources of the tiny empire, even before the siege, had forced Constantine to be frugal. Would he have employed the hundreds or even thousands of slaves and servants his predecessors had if he had the vast resources of the old empire available to him?

He laughed ruefully to himself, thinking of all his maneuvers and manipulations. What had they gained him? That question came again to his mind as he finished dressing and went to a morning briefing with Giovanni, Notaras, and Sphrantzes. As he entered the dining hall, his laughter stayed with him. Somehow the irony of it all had improved his mood.

"Good morning, what news do you bring to cheer me today?"

"Some interesting developments, my Lord, although others may not think so," said Sphrantzes.

"Tell me."

"We have received a stunning offer of peace from Mehmet."

"I thought the last offer was generous, but still impossible to accept. What could he add? Is he offering to lift the siege?"

"Unfortunately not, my Lord, but I do think you should carefully consider this offer. Mehmet offers again to let you leave the city with all of your people who wish to leave with you. He also offers to allow you to take the royal treasury with you, and everything else that may be carried."

"Hah! The royal treasury! I can certainly carry that in my pocket. What else?"

"He offers to give you not only the Peloponnesus but also Attica and Macedonia as your kingdom, with a fifty-year guarantee of peace."

Constantine was impressed. Mehmet was offering to give Constantine the ancient mainland of the Greeks. Constantine could rule in Athens, still a great city, rich in history with an excellent nearby seaport. The sultan was offering not only peace during Constantine's lifetime, but peace for fifty years. This plan would give any successor peace also, at least for many years to come. He could save his people. More than that, he could marry Zophia and raise their child in safety. They would have a future. A real future instead of this nightmare.

"What say you all?"

"I think you should carefully consider this, my Lord," said Sphrantzes. "What use is Constantinople to us? We live with ninety thousand people in a city built for a million. Even if we hold the city, our trade is cut off from the east by the Turkish forts, and most of the trade from the West goes to Galata in any event. I think we lose nothing."

"Nothing but honor and God's blessing," retorted Notaras. "This is God's city, the first great city built to God. We cannot abandon it. The city has never fallen except to other Christians, and then it was recovered.

If you abandon the city, you will be damned, my Lord, and everyone with you. If the city falls, it is God's will, but you cannot choose to abandon it."

"As usual, my friend acts with enthusiasm and faith not borne out by reality," responded Sphrantzes. "The city will fall, Notaras. And you will suffer for it, I assure you. Do not condemn our emperor to your foolishness."

Notaras rose red-faced, his hands balled into fists. "You dare to call me a fool?"

"Quiet!" shouted Constantine. "Can you two not discuss anything as men? Sit down and be peaceful, at least!" He turned to Giovanni. "What say you?"

"My Lord, I believe we can hold the city. I do not think we could hold it forever, but we must also consider the Turks' position. They must be exhausted from their efforts. They have been repulsed in every attempt to take the city. I believe this newest offer of peace reflects exactly how desperate their position has become. If we hold out but a few more days, we may wake and find them gone."

Constantine considered the views of all of his councilors for long minutes before responding with a question. "Are there any updates from outside? Any news from Hungary, or the West, or the East?"

"My Lord, we have heard nothing from anyone. We must assume we are on our own," said Notaras. "I do not think any help can assist us at this point in time, at least for any immediate attacks."

So it truly had come to this. They were alone. Strangely, Constantine felt peace with this. He had always had to rely on himself, and on the pitiful resources available to him. Outside help had failed him again and again, especially against the Turks. So be it.

What about this peace offer? It gave everything. But nothing. The last offer was more than generous: a kingdom and a lifetime of security. But all of Mehmet's proposals required that he give up his city. His life had been devoted to the protection of Constantinople. He could not give it up. If he had one more victory at the walls, the sultan and his people would leave. When they left, he would slowly rebuild the power of the Greeks from the remaining possessions. He would never again rely on the West; the Hungarians perhaps, but never the pope and these selfish Italian city-states.

What about Zophia and his child? If the city fell, they would die or worse. Still, could he rob his child of their legacy? If Zophia had a son, that son would be emperor one day. If they could just win this war, Constantine should have years to reconstruct the city, to strengthen the armies and rebuild commerce. His son might rule over a renewed empire—might even take back their lands and free the Greeks living under the Turkish yoke. He knew what he had to do.

"My friends, I believe we must reject this offer. I agree with Giovanni. If the city can hold out a few more days, perhaps one more assault, then we will survive. I cannot and will not give up the city to the Turks. I owe it to our people to protect our city, for their sake, for their children's sake, for our future. But we need something to raise the spirits of the people after so much weariness. I am going to lead a parade along the land walls this afternoon. I want our Greek priests to accompany me. We will parade our holiest relic, our blessed icon of the Virgin, the Hodegetria."

Constantine looked at Notaras, his loyal and deeply religious friend. "Please make the arrangements. I would like us to gather before the palace at midafternoon and we will parade on foot along the entire length of the land walls. Please also invite Zophia to attend, and to walk with me."

Constantine could see the happiness in Notaras's eyes at this honor. He bowed. "Thank you, my Lord."

After the noon hour, Constantine dressed in formal clothing with a purple robe. He placed a gold wreath crown on his head and took out a long walking stick made of olive wood shod with a beaten-silver end. He summoned a few guards and made his way out through the gates of the palace. He was surprised at the throng waiting outside for him.

There must be several thousand people, dressed in their best clothing and waiting for their emperor.

A huge cheer rose up when they caught sight of him. He basked in their warm glow, surprised again at their love for him despite everything they had been through. He spotted Zophia near the front and walked over to greet her. She embraced him briefly, her fragrance driving him wild. She smiled at him and put her arm through his. He was surprised by her generosity; she was giving public approval to their relationship, even if he knew privately she would not do so. He smiled gratefully to her and whispered that he loved her. She smiled in return but did not respond.

A delegation of priests came to the front of the crowd, carrying on a litter platform the precious icon of the Hodegetria, a large painted talisman of the Holy Virgin. The Hodegetria had been carried before the walls throughout the history of the city, including during terrible sieges like those of the Avars in 626 and the Arabs in 718. Another cheer rose from the crowd as they saw their most precious relic and the symbol of the Virgin's protection of the city.

The delegation moved slowly away, carrying the icon from the walls of Blachernae Palace and along the land walls themselves. Constantine and Zophia followed immediately behind, along with Notaras and assorted nobles. Following behind this delegation was the crowd itself, singing ancient songs and uttering prayers for the deliverance of the city.

Constantine could feel the people responding. As the delegation passed the gates and towers of the inner wall, soldiers cheered. Civilians laughed and shouted from houses and shops. The city was coming together under this great symbol of God's love and protection.

For more than an hour the procession wound through the streets near the wall, bringing hope and joy to the people. Constantine was filled with peace and happiness, enjoying Zophia beside him and the admiration of his people. He turned to talk to Zophia, telling her again that he loved her.

"Constantine, no."

He was hurt by her response, but realized quickly that she was not responding to him but still looking forward. He turned his head and his heart sank. The precious Hodegetria had fallen from the platform that held it and was facedown at an angle, sunk deeply in the mud. Priests scurried forward and were attempting to pick it up, but seemed unable to lift it again.

Constantine heard a collective groan from the crowd, including the men on the walls. To the deeply religious and deeply suspicious people of his city, omens were carefully viewed and discussed for every possible meaning. This event would be interpreted as a calamity, as an omen of terrible doom. The emperor ran forward and ordered the priests out of the way. He placed his hands on the heavy frame of the icon and lifted. He could not budge the icon. He heard more murmuring from the crowd. He ordered several priests to assist him, and with their help he pulled with all of his strength. Slowly the icon moved, inch by inch until it pulled free of the sticky mud. The relic was covered with sludge. He assisted the priests in pulling it back into place, and rope was found to lash the icon back onto the platform. But the damage had already been done.

Constantine turned and spoke to the people, offering thanks for the parade and encouraging everyone to continue the struggle. He watched the faces carefully. He caught Zophia's eyes, tears streaming down her face. He knew nothing he could say would change things. Rumor would pass like wildfire through the city. The icon had fallen. The Virgin had fallen. The city would fall.

SATURDAY, MAY 26, 1453

The next morning dawned ominously. A thick, heavy fog sat over the city, chilling Constantine to the bone, even indoors. The fog crept through doors, reaching with misty fingers for the inhabitants within. The emperor climbed the tallest tower of his palace to try to get a view of the city. When he reached the top and looked out he was stunned. A bright orange light, almost like flame, hung over the top of St. Sophia. The light danced above the sea of fog right over the dome, making the great cathedral appear to burn.

Constantine was shaken. What did this portend? Taken with the catastrophe from yesterday, how could he interpret anything but doom? He felt ill, tired, beaten. He made his way slowly down and returned to his bed. He found the chill could not be held back, no matter how many blankets he piled on or how much he stoked the fires in his bed-chamber. He spent the day feverish, chilled, sleeping intermittently only to be woken by terrifying nightmares. He was too weak to rise back out of bed that day, and he finally slept fitfully as darkness fell.

He awoke the next day, Sunday, feeling exhausted. The fever, however, had passed. He spent the day meeting with various delegations from the city and reviewing reports of the conditions of the defenses. The problems were typical. The Italians were bickering among themselves for this or that perceived slight. Food reserves were beginning to be a worry, although the city could hold out well into the summer. Water was not an issue. Constantine did confirm that the cistern entrances had been sealed up and otherwise disguised. In the event the city fell, the Ottomans might not become aware of these water reserves, and this might be a factor in any future Christian attempts to retake the city.

In the early evening, at twilight, Constantine felt well enough to ride out with his guard to the city walls. He was looking for Giovanni. He dismounted and passed through the tall inner wall at one of the locked gates and out to the space between the walls. He made his way to the wooden palisade that Giovanni had constructed miraculously overnight, so many nights ago. The palisade had held, against all hope, against the constant cannonades and attacks of the Turks.

Constantine found Giovanni, who was overseeing the rebuilding of a damaged portion of the wooden wall. He waved Constantine over and bowed.

"How are our defenses, Giovanni?"

"They hold, my Lord. By some miracle they hold. I have never had to reconstruct a barricade so many times, but then again I have never faced this many cannon. Still, we have held all these days; we can hold still further as needed."

"We need miracles, after everything we have faced. I know you have heard of the terrible omens the past two days. The people are terrified. They believe it is the end."

"There will be no end while I have life to breathe—"

As Giovanni said this he stiffened and grimaced in pain. Hot liquid splashed over Constantine. He quickly wiped it away and realized with horror that it was blood. A ragged hole the size of a large coin had appeared in Giovanni's armor just above his upper right chest, an obvious gunshot wound. Blood spurted out in waves. Constantine shouted for help, and several guards ran forward and quickly pulled Giovanni to the ground. A cloth was pressed against the wound and a doctor called for.

Constantine assisted in carrying the Genoan out of the palisade and through the wall. They placed him on a cart, which quickly rumbled off to the hospital. Constantine mounted and followed the cart, calling words of encouragement to the Italian leader. They were soon at the hospital. Giovanni was carried quickly in and placed on a bed where several doctors went to work on his wound. Constantine stayed nearby, holding Giovanni's hand. The Italian groaned and writhed in agony, but remained unconscious. Finally, when they had done everything they could, Constantine pulled the lead doctor aside.

"Tell me the situation, and please be blunt with me."

"My Lord, there are many factors, I'm not sure what to say . . ."

"I've asked for the truth. Give it to me."

"He will likely not last the night, my Lord. He has lost so much blood. He was hit near his heart. We have taken out several pieces of metal, but that caused more bleeding. If there is any more shrapnel we have missed, he will surely take ill and die. He may also die from the bleeding. All we can do now is wait and pray. I will know more tomorrow."

Constantine wanted to stay longer, but he realized the defenses were critical. He rode back to the palisade and found that one of Giovanni's commanders had taken over. The Genoese men had many questions about their commander. Constantine gave them what encouragement he could, then seeing the situation was stable at the wall, he promised to return in the morning with further news of Giovanni.

Constantine rode away from the walls and only then was able to finally consider this turn of events. He was distraught, almost without hope, perhaps more so than he had ever been in his life. The terrible omens of the past few days and his illness had sapped his strength. Now he had lost Giovanni. He realized how much the Genoan's leadership, knowledge, and even personality had maintained the morale of the men at the wall. Constantine felt confident that his men knew enough after all these weeks to patch up the palisade as it was damaged, but if there was a major attack, would the men stay and fight without their commander?

His despair began to simmer and turn to hot anger. He had done everything and given up all in defense of the city. Just when it appeared that Mehmet would retreat, the situation was falling apart. He only needed a few more days, at least he hoped so. Why was everything and everyone failing him now? He needed a miracle, something to turn the spirit of the city around.

When he arrived back at the palace he ordered Cardinal Isidore to be summoned immediately. Constantine changed out of his blood-splattered clothing, ate dinner alone, and waited. It was near midnight when Isidore appeared. Constantine met the cardinal in the great hall, sitting regally on his throne. Isidore entered wearing his formal robes and hat, shimmering in scarlet. His face was visibly shaken and he was clearly wondering about this ominous summons. Isidore bowed deeply. "My Lord, thank you for asking me here. How may I serve you?"

"Where are my ships?"

"Excuse me, my Lord, can you be more specific?"

"Yes, where are my Goddamned promised ships?"

Isidore's face lost all of its color. "These things take time. I'm sure they will be here any day now."

"No, they will not."

"How can you know that?"

"I sent a ship out secretly to search. There are no ships gathering, even out into the islands past the straits. You promised aid, your pope promised aid. I gave you everything, you have given me nothing!"

"My Lord, you have to realize the distances involved. If only you have more patience."

"More patience! Your relief fleet, if such a thing ever existed, will do nothing more than bring food and arms to the Turks! I have trusted you, and you have failed me. Get out of my sight! Get out of my cathedral. I will be conducting the Greek mass there tomorrow. You are to vacate St. Sophia tonight."

"My Lord, you cannot mean that. Such an action would be an incredible betrayal of your word. You have promised union; you cannot go back on your word."

"You are wrong, Isidore. I am emperor, and I will do as I wish. I might only rule this city, but here my word is law. Get out tonight. If you are there tomorrow, I will turn you loose outside the walls with all your priests. You can try a union with the Turks if you wish."

Isidore bowed again and quickly left. Constantine sat back on his throne and laughed out loud. Suddenly he felt a great weight lifting off him. He was true to his people again. They might be alone, and they might all die alone, but they would have their faith, they would have their church. They would pray together, and celebrate God's sacred and true mass again. He would be Constantine again, and they would be his people. He would have his whole world back—all of it.

MONDAY, MAY 28, 1453

Constantine woke feeling refreshed. He had slept through the night with no nightmares and no interruptions. The emperor felt better than he had since before the siege began. He dressed quickly and ordered his horse brought round. Constantine left early with his guard and rode to the hospital to check on Giovanni.

Miraculously, his friend was not there. Not only had Giovanni survived the night, but to the amazement of his caretakers, he had insisted on getting up this morning and returning to the walls. This news was beyond all Constantine's hopes. He rode out to the walls and found Giovanni. The Genoan was still badly hurt, and was directing activities at the wall from a chair he had had brought up to the tower. But he smiled upon seeing Constantine.

"I am not in hell yet."

"I am sure when it is your time, you will be in paradise, my friend," responded Constantine. He was so happy to see Giovanni alive and at the wall. The chances of the city surviving another attack were so much greater with him here leading the defenses. "What are the Turks up to today?"

"Good question. They are up to something, that is for sure. Apparently there were all kinds of movements last night, various groups getting into position. They have kept up a very heavy cannonade all day today. I think there is another assault coming. However, they are not massing their men this morning. I would predict the attack will come tomorrow at dawn. We will be ready in any event, but I do not think anything will happen until sunrise tomorrow."

"Thank you for your thoughts. I will be away from the walls today and tonight but will send word where you can find me if anything happens. I will be back at the walls in the morning before first light."

Constantine left Giovanni at noon and rode out into the city. He inspected his men all along the wall, shaking their hands and inquiring about the health and supplies of the forces. He also spoke with Greek merchants and citizens as he encountered them near the walls, inviting them to come to St. Sophia that evening. Many had already heard and thanked Constantine for giving them back their cathedral. All enthusiastically promised to attend.

Constantine returned to the palace near evening. He put on his best royal cloak and his finest golden crown of leaves. He left the palace at twilight and traveled with his guards through the streets of Constantinople. He was greeted by enthusiastic cheers. The morale of the city had changed drastically as news spread that Constantine had rescinded the Union. He had forged his own miracle.

He arrived at the porch of St. Sophia before a huge waiting crowd. The roar of greeting was deafening. He waved and smiled, the happiness of the people filling him with even greater peace. He looked around everywhere for Zophia, but did not find her among the crowd.

He dismounted and walked slowly through the crowd, shaking hands. His subjects reached out to touch him, to feel his robes. They blessed him and uttered prayers for him and the city. He made his way into the cathedral and up to the second level to his royal seat overlooking the sanctuary below.

After the huge crowd had jammed into St. Sophia and taken their places, the Greek priests entered to tremendous cheering. They quickly called for silence and the mass began.

Constantine could feel the tangible joy of the people as they worshiped together in their great cathedral for the first time in so many months. This, and the great danger facing the populace, made each moment of ceremony contain greater, deeper meaning. Even Constantine, who was practical about his religion, was deeply moved by the ceremony. He felt great peace and calm coming over him as he looked down on his people. They were no longer the beggars of the West, giving themselves up to whichever master promised assistance. They were standing alone as Greeks, even if just for this moment in time. Constantine felt complete, ready for whatever would come. But he had one more thing to do, or rather undo.

He left the cathedral after the mass, again carried through the enthusiastic crowd. He mounted his horse and sent his guard away, all save one. He rode quietly through the dark streets, enjoying the peace and calm. Finally he arrived at Zophia's house. He dismounted and knocked on the door. Gently at first and then with greater urgency. She answered, showing no surprise that he was there.

"I expected you at St. Sophia's tonight."

She smiled. "Interesting, I expected you here."

"I have undone the Union."

"I know."

"You must know the rest then."

"I know it, but you must say it."

He smiled in return. "I renounce any betrothal inquiries. I will look no more to any foreigner for a marriage of advantage. I want you. I need you. You are all I have ever needed. I want us to marry and have our child. We will be together, no matter how much time we have." He began to cry, falling to his knees before her, holding her legs tightly to him, his head against her stomach, against their child. He felt her hands on his head, gently caressing his hair.

"I am yours, then, my Lord. I have always been yours. We are yours."

Constantine composed himself and ordered his remaining guard to inform Giovanni where he would be in case of an emergency. He was just finished when Zophia dragged him inside, kissing him passionately and whispering gentle words of love.

CHAPTER EIGHTEEN

Monday, May 28, 1453

Mehmet sat astride his horse with Zaganos near the walls of Galata. They had spent the morning inspecting Zaganos's original command across the Golden Horn from the main force. Mehmet had ordered a day of prayer and quiet rest before the massive assault, which was scheduled for shortly after midnight. They would attack in the dark. He had instructed the commanders to attack in waves, starting with the most expendable men and with each wave moving toward his most elite forces. The waves would replace each other to give the earlier waves an opportunity to rest. He had ordered that they would continue this attack over and over until the city fell. The men would employ ladders to broaden the scope of the onslaught and assure that at least some of the defenders could not rush to any breaches. There would be no stopping.

Of course, he realized that there was a limit. At some point, within a few hours, his men would grow too exhausted to continue the fight. He had perhaps eight hours from the beginning of the attack to win the city. If he failed, he would have to quit the siege. If that happened and he was lucky, he would merely be under Halil's thumb. If he was unlucky, Halil would have him assassinated. Everything depended on this attack.

The cannon boomed across the Golden Horn. He could see smoke rising from the city walls where the bombardment was striking the city.

He knew all of the activity the past few days must have exhausted the defenders. By ordering an attack at night, rather than in the morning, he hoped to further surprise the Greeks.

He rode up near the walls of Galata, smiling at the nervous reaction of the few guards above. He knew despite the messages of neutrality he had received that in reality most of the men had crossed the Horn to defend Constantinople. He observed the walls of the Genoan city for some time, and the tall Tower of Christ. They would be his in time. Without Constantinople, Galata could never survive.

After a time, he turned his horse and rode out with Zaganos around the end of the Horn and over to the main Ottoman camp before the land walls of Constantinople. The atmosphere was quiet as he passed the tents of common soldiers. He watched his men carefully as he went by, trying to gauge their emotions. Were they afraid? Angry? Hopeful? Determined?

They were determined, he realized. It was as if they shared this great moment with him, as if they realized that if they failed he would fail. He felt closer to his people than he ever had, and he realized for the first time in his life they were one with him. Perhaps it was not love, but it was shared commitment and a respect for him as their leader. He struggled to contain his emotions. He felt his eyes tearing up. He would never let his men see him weep. He could never allow it. He must be strong; he must never lose control.

He reached his tent, dismounted, and entered alone. He knelt and prayed to Allah, thanking him for this great fortune, this sign of blessing. In a moment of clarity he realized that perhaps even more than the city, the respect of his people meant everything to him. Mehmet bowed his head into the cushions and sobbed. He cried again, something he had so rarely done these past years, allowing himself release. He wept silently into the cushions, muffling his emotions. He cried out in silence to his father. His body shook. He was so scared, he realized. What if he failed? Death seemed so near suddenly. He did not want to die. He had killed so frequently, but he had always felt protected. He was the sultan, after all.

"Sultan, may I speak with you?"

Mehmet bolted upright. He was shocked to hear a voice disturb his peace, especially when he realized whose voice it was. Thankfully he was facing away from the entrance and could not be seen immediately. He simply appeared to be praying. He wiped his eyes against the cushions in a fluid motion as he pulled himself up. He then turned to face his grand vizier. "Halil, what may I do for you?"

"Sultan, I have come to plead with you in private to reconsider."

Mehmet's full guard was up. Why was Halil here? Did he come with others? Was he making his move even before the last attack? He must be careful. His life depended on it.

"Reconsider what?"

"This next attack, Sultan. You may break the spirit of your army and lose the last faith of your council. If that happens I cannot guarantee your safety."

"What do you suggest?"

"Let us pull back now. We still have most of our forces. The men have lost morale, but you cannot be blamed for that. We will assign blame to the brashness of youth. Yes, you went against my advice, but you are young. Who can blame you? We will go north and ransack a few Serbian towns. A victory or two and the people will forget."

"That would satisfy you?"

"Of course, my Sultan, I live only to advise you. If you let me guide you in these things, I will give you the greatness you desire. I helped your father rule the world. I can do the same for you. But you have always treated me as an enemy. I am your greatest friend! Or more like an uncle, perhaps. A disappointed uncle at times, yes, but a loving one. I have watched you make your mistakes, and you have fought me when I have tried to give you advice."

Mehmet seethed. But a part of him wanted Halil's approval. A part of him wanted to give in. "What else?"

Halil seemed encouraged by this. "Please, Sultan, I beg you. Let me guide you. Take my advice. It is not too late. We can be a great partnership. I have a master plan for the next ten years. The next twenty. If you let me guide you, I promise you will achieve everything your heart desires. But you must stop fighting me! If you continue to challenge me in all things, I cannot protect you. We are at the brink. The attack tomorrow is doomed. How can we succeed now when we have failed again and again?

"You have done brilliantly, Mehmet. You have exceeded my expectations in so many ways in this siege. But still we fail. And we will fail. We have wasted so many resources against these walls. We are not yet in danger, but how much longer can we wait before Hunyadi pounces on us? Even if we get away from the walls, we will lose that many more men in a fruitless attack tomorrow. We need to retreat and regroup. Let me save the army! Let me save you!"

"I will consider what you have said. Thank you for coming." Mehmet bowed to Halil, and his grand vizier bowed in return and left the tent.

A part of Mehmet had listened. Even after steeling his heart against Halil and deciding he would take this gamble, a part of him wanted to listen. A part of him yearned to surrender. He had carried all the worries of the world for so long, and done so not only with no trustworthy direction but most of the time in direct conflict with his grand vizier. He was exhausted from the conflict. Exhausted and unsure of himself. He had forged his own destiny and had done so carefully, but all of his plans had failed.

Halil was right. There was nothing special about the coming attack. In fact, he had to admit to himself, he had already mounted attacks under more favorable conditions than the one that was planned. He had already tried slamming troops at a breach for hours at a time. He simply could not get enough men into enough space, and this left the Greeks able to defend themselves and thwart his attacks. What was different about this next attack? He realized the only difference was desperation. He desperately needed the last attack to work, or he would lose everything.

Was Halil really his enemy? Certainly he had contacted Mehmet's father and replaced Mehmet when the sultan was first placed on the throne. But Mehmet had to admit to himself that the grand vizier probably had had to do so. Mehmet had been so young, so rash. If Halil had not taken action, Mehmet might have been killed then.

What should he do? He had felt such single-minded purpose for so long, he did not know how to react to this crisis. And the clarity that Halil might have been justified in some of his earlier decisions only made the present that much more confusing.

What if he did follow Halil's recommendation? Certainly it was likely the grand vizier would leave him in power if he backed off on the attack now. But what would the other ramifications be? He would probably have to remove his hand-picked council members. He might even have to execute a few of them, including Zaganos. Would that bother him? He cared for Zaganos, but if it came down to it, he could not sacrifice his own life for his friend's.

And that would not be the end. With the council entirely behind Halil and with a public acknowledgment that the siege had been a mistake, Mehmet would be forced to follow all of Halil's recommendations going forward. Would the grand vizier truly raise him to greatness? If he did assist him, would it be worth it? Would it be better to achieve greatness no matter what, or to be his own man or die trying?

Mehmet thought of his father. Murad had been a great man. Halil had been his advisor, but never dominated him. Halil would not have dared. Thinking of his father filled Mehmet with anger and bitterness. Why had he left him with this mess? Why had he not trained him properly and mentored him? Murad had ignored him and then had thrust him into the forefront far too soon.

James D. Shipman

His father had done nothing for him. He would be damned if his father would remain above him. He had not shaped Mehmet. Mehmet would shape himself, as he had always done. If he died at the gates of Constantinople, so be it. He would die attempting what his father was never capable of achieving.

Mehmet began scrawling a note to Halil, a letter of explanation. After a few lines he stopped and tore up the letter. He owed Halil no explanation. He owed Halil nothing.

In the gathering dusk he severed the last ties to his father, and the last ties to his grand vizier. In a few hours all would be decided. It would be him or Halil. He felt a calm peace. If he died, he would die a martyr at the walls of Constantinople. Or he would live a hero. So let it be.

Mehmet left his tent and called loudly for his horse and armor. He was soon dressed and mounted. He rode out into his camp alone, calling his men to battle for the glory of Allah. He was cheered by his men, who were gathering for the coming attack. He was ready. Ready for the great chance. To conquer or perish.

By the thousands, the men moved into position near the sultan in the darkness. The cannon kept up a constant barrage against the walls, masking the sound of the men in the night as they assembled for battle.

Zaganos joined Mehmet shortly after midnight. He grasped the arm of the sultan and held it tightly for a moment. "Glory to you on this night of fortune, Sultan."

Mehmet smiled. Zaganos was his warrior. He had always been. The sultan had held him at arms' length out of fear, fear bred from the experiences of his youth. No more. If he conquered, he would raise his friend to the greatest position in the land. He would trust this one man. He had earned it.

"Yes, Pasha, tonight is our night. We must conquer, my friend, or I fear we shall not last the night."

Zaganos smiled. "I have no doubt you are right. I am not interested in handing my head to Halil."

Not for the first time, Mehmet imagined exacting revenge on Halil. How sweet it would be. He realized his vengeance might be only hours away. The thought gave him even more strength. Again he felt the confidence, the strange peace. Such peace could only come from Allah. He was blessed. He would succeed. He must succeed. He clasped Zaganos on the back and drew his sword. "Constantinople is ours!" he shouted. "Allah wills it!"

The darkness erupted with shouting. The moment of destiny was here.

CHAPTER NINETEEN

John Hunyadi rode ahead of his marching army down the narrow mountain trail. They had passed out of the territory of Walachia several days before, and were well within the area controlled by the Ottomans. The pass opened up before him into a flat grassy valley with periodic copses of trees and scattered farms and villages.

An Ottoman force awaited them in the center of the valley on the top of a hill. Hunyadi could not accurately make out the size of the force but estimated five hundred. There were horses nearby, but the Ottomans were on foot and apparently dug in at the rise of a small ridge.

Hunyadi immediately turned to one of his men and ordered that the main force be brought up as quickly as possible. It was before noon and the Hungarian leader believed an attack could be mounted well before dark.

His field commanders were soon assembled, and Hunyadi quickly laid out an attack plan. He dismissed his commanders and then turned to give additional instructions to his personal guard. The Hungarian was excited: He had not experienced combat in a long while now, particularly against the Turks.

He led his cavalry, five hundred heavily armored knights, down the sloping trail, into the flat land of the valley and then across to the base of the central hill. The knights lined up quickly to his right and left, facing up the sloping hill to the Ottomans above. The hill was unobstructed except for a few trees and rocks near the top. The Turks had dug defensive positions behind the rocks, and stacked wood and dirt before them to shield their position. Hunyadi eyed the defenses and then sent messengers to his commanders, making slight modifications to his plans.

As his knights remained in position facing the hill, his men-at-arms moved into position on each side of the cavalry, passing until they occupied forward positions to his left and right, facing uphill. The Turks were now surrounded on three sides. The men-at-arms were on foot, and armed with long swords and shields.

Hunyadi expected the Ottomans to break and run, but they held their position even as his forces moved into place. He was impressed with the courage of the Turkish commander and his small force, who must surely realize their hopeless position.

Hunyadi drew his sword and gave a command. His men-at-arms began advancing up the hill on both sides. The knights remained motionless as the advance commenced. The Ottomans began firing arrows at the advancing forces, but there were few archers and the casualties were insignificant. Hunyadi called out again and the advancing forces broke into a double march, charging up the hill. The Hungarian raised his sword and yelled, his voice booming in the valley. Hunyadi and his knights spurred their horses, galloping up the hill at full speed, weapons drawn, hooves thundering.

A scattered volley of arrows flew down the hill at Hunyadi. A few struck knights and bounced harmlessly off their heavy armor. The distance to the Turks closed quickly and in moments they would be on them.

Hunyadi shouted again, even louder this time, and drew his horse up sharply. His knights did the same, as did his men at arms, drawing a tight circle around the fortifications, less than fifty yards away. Simultaneously a dark cloud appeared in the sky behind the Ottomans.

Thousands of arrows arced through the air and crashed in among the Turks. Hundreds were wounded or dead in an instant. The Turks, distracted by the approaching forces on three sides, had not seen Hunyadi's archers moving quietly into place at their unprotected rear.

The screams of the wounded echoed down the hill as volley after volley of arrows landed among the Turks. Half of the defenders were killed in less than a minute. A few Ottomans attempted to climb over the fortifications and escape down the hill, but they were quickly cut down by the Hungarian foot soldiers.

The battle was over in minutes. Hunyadi had lost sixteen men. He ordered that the remaining Ottomans be disarmed but not harmed. He looked to the local villagers to take care of them. His men quickly buried their own dead and then formed up ranks and moved on. The entire attack, from the moment he spotted the Turks to the moment he departed, had lasted less than fifteen minutes. There was still plenty of daylight, and Hunyadi ordered the men to move on, as they would stop long after nightfall. Now that he had passed into Ottoman territory, he wanted to arrive at Constantinople as quickly as possible, to minimize the risk of attack and to ensure the element of surprise. He was still two hundred miles away, and it would take a week of hard marching.

He had hoped to meet Gregory again on the trail. The Greek should have reported long ago, and it made sense that Constantine would send him back as quickly as possible to continue the communication. He hoped word had at least reached Constantine that he was on his way. It was possible that information would lead Mehmet to lift the siege. That would be a blessing for the city, although it would complicate things for Hunyadi, particularly if Constantine broke his word and did not sally out from the city to aid in the decisive battle. The Hungarian hoped he had measured Constantine correctly. If not, he would be badly outnumbered again against an Ottoman force in Ottoman territory. No matter; he had no idiot king in tow this time to ruin his plans.

Captain Uberti anchored at Chios. He was at his fourth Greek harbor in as many weeks, slowly making his way toward the Dardanelles as he had been ordered to do. He was busy overseeing the loading of livestock into the hull of his ship.

He had delayed enough that he hoped to satisfy his Venetian overlords. He was tired of the slow progress. His men were anxious and beginning to question his commands. Many of the men on his ship had sailed with him for years, and they knew him well. He had never taken this long to complete a mission, particularly when they were supposed to be rushing men and supplies as quickly as possible to Constantinople.

He was having trouble sleeping. He kept dreaming of the Turks ravaging Constantinople. In his dream they ran through the streets of the city, cutting down women and children while screaming in bloodlust. The warriors raped and murdered the citizens while Uberti looked on helplessly. For some reason he was on land and impotent to help them. He had no true skills as a warrior; his ship was his weapon. The dreams robbed him of sleep, and he felt a growing guilt.

His first mate interrupted his thoughts. "The ship is nearly loaded. I do not think there is another place to stuff a single provision in this whole fleet. Pardon me, sir, but was all this really necessary? Is it not more important to get to the city with something than to ensure we supply every last crumb and arrow?"

Uberti could see the look on the first mate's face. He suspected something, no doubt. This was the first time Uberti had ever had his men second-guess him. He grew angry. This complication was more than he had bargained for or was willing to put up with. It was one thing to play the game of politics for profit, particularly under duress. It was another to risk his reputation and the respect of his men.

He had had enough. He turned to the mate. "Sound the alarm. I want every man and every ship ready to sail in the next two hours. We are going to Constantinople without further delay, and the devil take the Turks if they try to stop me!"

The first mate grinned. "That is what I have been expecting to hear for weeks now, sir. I will get our men moving. To hell with the Turks, whatever stands in our way!"

The first mate quickly left and the Captain stood by, watching the men on his ship and in the fleet ready the ships for immediate sailing. He felt better than he had in weeks. He had delayed enough to save face regardless of what happened now. What he intended to do was sail immediately to the great city, battle his way in if necessary, and land his reinforcements. He would then set sail and wreak havoc upon any ships the Ottomans cared to send his way. His blood was up, and he enjoyed it immensely. Let the bastards come!

In exactly two hours the fleet set sail, and it was soon heading north under a favorable wind. He was assured that all was right and he gave orders for the evening watch. He supped with his men and noticed that all were lighthearted and content. He smiled to himself in satisfaction, and after a final inspection of his ship and men, he returned to his quarters and fell into a contented and dreamless sleep.

CHAPTER TWENTY

TUESDAY, MAY 29, 1453, 1:30 A.M.

Constantine lay in Zophia's arms, holding her tight. They were both still awake, naked, and holding on to each other. He was gently stroking her hair, with his head slightly above hers so he could nestle his nose against her head. He breathed in her scent. Her smell was overwhelming to him after so long.

"I am so happy right now," she whispered, pulling even closer to him.

Constantine smiled to himself. "I love you so much, my love. Thank you for being here for me now."

"I have always been here for you. But I could not be if you were seeking someone else's love."

"I am done with that, Zophia, and I am done with trusting the West and begging for their help. They promise much, demand much, but deliver little. With virtually no help, we have held our city. If God sees fit to deliver us, we will depend on Greeks only from now on."

"That is all the people ever wanted—all I ever wanted. These Italians fight among themselves. They will betray you at any time for profit or just to satisfy vengeance against one another. They cannot be trusted."

"That is true of the cities, but not of individuals. Look at Giovanni, and all these Italians here, fighting for what they think is right. Many of them have ties to the city, or to Galata, but some do not even have that. Some are here simply fighting for God's city. Certainly we must be thankful for them."

"What will we do if the siege is lifted?" she asked.

"What do you mean?"

"I mean . . . what will you and I do?"

He laughed. "Why, we will marry, my dear. I will hold you up to the world and I will keep you by my side. I will never let you go! We will raise our child together."

"Our boy, you mean?"

"What?"

"I have a son growing inside me. I can feel him. I know it."

A son. He would have a son. An heir to the throne. He felt his eyes welling up. He reached his hand down to touch her stomach again. "I love you so much, my dearest."

"I love you too."

There was a loud banging at the door. Constantine sighed and reluctantly left the warm bed, putting on a dressing robe and opening the door. One of his guards was there, flushed and apparently in a panic. "My Lord, we need you immediately at the walls!"

"What is going on?"

"They are attacking, my Lord. Huge numbers. Giovanni sent me to find you."

Zophia came to the door. "What is it?"

"They are storming the walls. I have to go."

She moved closer, putting her arms around him. "Do not go; I'm afraid." She kissed his neck.

"I have to go." He kissed her back on the lips, smiling and running his hands through her hair. "I will tend to things and be back before breakfast. I want to spend all day with you today. We will plan our future together."

She smiled back, pulling him close again and embracing him tightly.

He stepped reluctantly away and dressed quickly while she silently watched him. He then drew her to him, holding her close. "I love you, my dear. You are my life."

"And you are mine." He looked in her eyes a moment longer, and then walked quickly out the door.

Constantine made his way from Zophia's home and found a large contingent of his personal guard mounted and waiting. He mounted his horse and took off at a gallop toward the city wall. He arrived within minutes. At first he could hear only the din of the cannons, but as he came closer to the wall, he could hear the screams of battle and the clang of metal against metal, stone, and wood.

He dismounted along with his men and used his key to open one of the gates of the tall inner walls, allowing him out into the area between the inner and outer walls near the palisade. As he approached the wooden keep, he was shocked to see the press of Turks against the outer wall. Before him there seemed to be thousands of Ottomans, all pushing relentlessly toward the walls of the palisade. The roar of battle became deafening as he came closer.

The emperor finally reached the wooden walls and found Giovanni. The Italian was directing the battle from a chair, still apparently unable to stand. He had one hand holding a cloth over his wound. He recognized Constantine in the dim light and waved him over, grimacing from the effort.

"You look unwell, my friend."

"I feel unwell, my Lord," he joked. "Alas, what is to be done? These Turks seem unwilling to give me time to recover. I suppose I will have to follow their schedule, rather than mine."

"Are things holding up?"

"Yes, my Lord. Perfectly so far. The attack started about an hour ago. It seems very coordinated and primarily focused right here. I have had reports of attacks at other points on the walls, and even at sea, but they seem to be largely feints."

"Do you know the quality of the forces we are facing?"

"They do not seem to be their best, at least not yet. They are poorly armed for the most part, and undisciplined. But there are many of them, and they keep coming."

"How are our men holding up?"

"Good so far, but again, they can only fight for so long. We must hope that the Turks give up in a few hours. Otherwise I can make no guarantees."

The Turks pressed on, pushing hard against the walls. Constantine drew his own sword and motioned his guards to press forward into the battle as well.

Soon he was lost in the excitement of the fighting, and everything simplified to the moment, all the worries of the city melting away as he directed men forward to points on the walls where Ottomans were forcing their way over a few at a time.

Hours passed. Constantine was alert and focused. He always felt so alive in the middle of a battle. Everything slowed down. He experienced calm, almost peace, as if he were detached from this reality.

A well-armored Turk broke over the wall and rushed through several Greeks, charging forward toward Constantine. The emperor parried a heavy but awkward blow from the Ottoman warrior, ducked a second stroke, and drove his sword up through the man's throat. Hot blood splashed out, splattering Constantine. He choked in disgust and pulled his blade quickly out, kicking the Turk over into the dirt. He drew a cloth out and wiped his face clean. The palisade was drenched in blood and the bodies of wounded and dead men. Most of the defenders were still alive, but many were wounded, and Constantine could tell they were beginning to tire.

There was a short lull in the fighting. Constantine left the immediate battle area and found Giovanni still sitting and obviously in great pain. "I see you still live," the Italian observed upon spotting the emperor.

"So far," said Constantine, smiling. "These Turks seem to mean their business today."

"That they do. If I did not know better, I would speculate they intend to fight on until they take our fair city."

Constantine felt a chill of fear. "Do not even joke about such things!"

"I am sorry, my Lord. Just trying to make light of a terrible situation. I would say we have done well, and so have you. You fought for nearly three hours without any respite. The Turks certainly are giving it their everything. But they are pulling back now. I am hoping that is the end of it."

Even as Giovanni made this remark they heard a new flurry of shouting. A fresh wave of men was charging the walls. Constantine turned and rushed back into the fight.

New ladders were thrust against the walls of the Palisade. The Greeks and Italians pushed them back almost as quickly, but exposed themselves to musket and arrow fire when they did. Despite their best efforts, some of the ladders remained in place, and Turks streamed over the walls and jumped in among the defenders. Constantine noted these Ottomans were better armed, and he recognized the regalia and the distinctive white caps of the Janissaries. These men were fanatical and skilled warriors with the best armor and weapons. They wore chain mail with steel breastplates and helmets.

The Janissaries attacked with relentless, almost suicidal ferocity. Moreover they were fresh, and there were thousands of them. Constantine realized with growing panic that more and more of them were scaling the wooden walls alive, and moving into position to combat the defenders. Constantine's men were slowly being pushed away from the walls themselves and toward the middle of the palisade. The emperor could hear Giovanni screaming encouragement mixed with threats at the men as the press of Turks became more and more overwhelming.

Another hour passed. Constantine was exhausted and his arms bled from a dozen superficial wounds. The fighting was the most intense he had ever experienced. The Janissaries were fierce. Thankfully the tight fighting area allowed the Greeks and Italians to concentrate their force and limit the number of Turks that could press the attack at any given time. The emperor could barely lift his sword but kept forcing himself to fight. He felt dizzy, and wondered if he would pass out standing in the hard press of men.

He felt a hand on his shoulder, and he ripped it off, turning with sword raised. He checked his stroke when he realized that Giovanni had joined him near the front of the attack. The Italian looked pale. His armor was blood streaked and he appeared even more exhausted than Constantine felt.

"You should be sitting down!" shouted Constantine over the roar of the battle.

"I am needed here now. There is no time for resting or nursing wounds! We have got to drive our men forward to the walls. The Turks are coming over now unchallenged. Soon there will be too many. We have to drive them back now or we are going to lose the palisade!"

Constantine assessed the battle and agreed with Giovanni. Janissaries had driven Constantine's men back well beyond the wall. In the short time the emperor could focus on the wall, several Turks had climbed to the top of scaling ladders and jumped down inside the palisade. If his men did not press the Turks back quickly, there would be too many inside and they would no longer be able to hold them back.

"Let us pull my guard together near me and we will drive the men forward!"

Giovanni did not answer. Constantine turned back and realized with horror his friend was on the ground, twisting back and forth and holding his leg. Constantine knelt over the Genoan and saw that there was a new and terrible wound. Giovanni had been shot in the upper thigh. Blood gushed out of the gaping hole in red spurts. He was screaming in pain, and an almost animal-like terror. He grabbed hold of Constantine's arm. "Get me out of here, I need a doctor! I'm going to die! The battle is lost! The city is lost!"

Constantine had never seen the Genoan like this. His eyes were crazed and he coughed and sputtered. He seemed to have lost himself in pain and fear. The emperor had to act quickly. Constantine struck Giovanni across the face. "Quiet! This is no time to lose faith! You must stay here and rally. We need you now, at this moment!"

Giovanni looked up wild-eyed at the emperor. "I am sorry, I cannot. This is too much. It is over. I am in too much pain." The Italian turned to several of his men. "Carry me away, I need aid."

The battle swirled on around Constantine. He had only moments to decide. He could try to keep Giovanni here, but it would cost the Italian his life. Not only that, but he was in a panic and might create even more panic around him. Constantine waved the men forward. He grabbed Giovanni's shoulder and pressed it slightly. "Farewell, my friend. Fare thee well."

Giovanni smiled through the pain, recognizing Constantine's gesture. He was lifted up between the men who carried him as gently as possible away from the palisade. Constantine watched him for a moment and then turned back to the battle, which was becoming more desperate by the moment.

He heard shouts from the men. "Giovanni is lost. The city is lost!" He shouted the men down, ordering them to remain calm and focus on the battle. He stepped back into the heaving fight and lost himself in the effort to rally the men. He was shocked again by the intensity of the fighting. He had never been in combat so savage. He hacked away with his sword, killing several Turks quickly and screaming for his guards and the men to rally with him and drive the Ottomans from the wall. He could see the banners of the Turks waving on the palisade now, and more and more Janissaries streaming over. He had minutes, maybe only seconds to stem the gap.

He turned and was alarmed to see that men were beginning to stream away from the battle. Giovanni's departure had apparently caused a more generalized retreat. He screamed at the men to stay at their posts, to rally around him. A number looked his way, but none returned. He was losing them. He was losing his city.

He turned back to the battle. There were only a few defenders now, all Greek, battling hopelessly against a surging tide of Janissaries. Constantine smiled. He felt a strange calm. The city was falling. He could do nothing more to stop it. He had done so much. He had done all he could do. What about Zophia and his son? He was losing his future, losing everything he loved. He felt sadness, but he knew this was God's will. He prayed quickly for them and for all his people.

Constantine reached back and ripped off his purple cape and the imperial eagles from his shoulders. He tossed them out over the advancing Turks. He was just another Greek now. A Greek fighting for his city. He charged in screaming. He slashed at one Turk and then another, driving them back with his fury.

A flash of bright light erupted in his mind. He felt himself spinning and heard a terrible ringing in his ears. He could not see or feel anything except the roar of the ringing. Something had happened. He was not sure, could not think, could not concentrate. He felt his body hit the ground. He struggled to rise, but he could not feel his legs. His ears continued to ring, and he could see only blurry shapes and bright flashes. He felt a sharp pain in his chest and ribs. The pain exploded. He coughed up blood and felt himself gasping for air. Another tearing pain burned through his right leg. He was fighting to stay awake, trying to process the pain and where it was coming from. He felt waves of darkness pouring over him and the pain and light slip away.

He could see his city, his beloved Constantinople. All of it before him, below him. How could he be above it? The pain had fled, and he felt more alive than ever. He sprang up from the walls and out over the city. The sky was beautiful. St. Sophia glimmered like gold below a shimmering sun. He floated above, gently wandering through the streets. The people below were busy with their daily labors. His people.

He spotted a beautiful woman wearing a pure white gown, bathed in light. She held a baby in her arms. He glided gently to her. He realized it was Zophia. She smiled and lifted her hand, guiding him home. He was home. The worries were fading. He had his city and his love. He was at peace.

CHAPTER TWENTY-ONE

TUESDAY, MAY 29, 1453 6:00 A.M.

Zophia paced in the darkness, fraught with worry. She felt something must be wrong. She had prayed and prayed that Constantine would be safe, that the city would be safe, but she could not feel any comfort. She had faced all fifty-three days of the siege with anxiety and fear, but never like this morning. Somehow when Constantine had left her she was convinced she would never see him again.

At least they had been together. A few glorious hours making love and holding each other. He had finally given himself to her for the future, no matter what that future held or how long it would last. They had loved with an intensity neither had ever known. She had felt a deep unspeakable fear she had not wanted to face.

Had she been correct in withholding herself from him during his time of need? For keeping the baby from him? This thought had tormented her throughout the siege. She had felt terrible denying Constantine, keeping him at arms' length. But she could not be true to herself otherwise. She was never happy as just his lover, but it was acceptable when it was exclusive. Once he had decided to find someone new, she could not be with him any longer, even with all the reasons he gave her. She understood why he had felt he had to make those decisions, but she could not give in to his compromise. For her, there was no compromise. One faith, one heart.

She had been so happy when he had finally let go of all this false hope. Faith in false religion. Expectations of help from the West. False faith that a new bride would give him aid from Georgia that would lift the siege. She had known all along that they could only depend on each other. Depend on the city. Depend on their God.

Was she right? Was the city falling even as she considered these thoughts? In her mind it did not matter. If they compromised everything for a few more years, just for a little safety, they gained nothing. She didn't want to raise their child in exile.

But would God not give her a little more time with her love? A little more time with their beautiful city? With their future family? She hoped so, but why this terrible feeling?

She finished dressing and left her home. Her servants had saddled her horse at her request. She rode out in the crisp predawn light, heading north toward the walls. She could see smoke rising from the walls, but then smoke had risen practically every day since the siege first began. That did not mean anything.

However, she now noticed a tense thickness about the air. Almost as if it sought to strangle her, or to hold her back. Maybe it was just her uneasy feeling. She rode north and soon neared the land walls. Now the light was breaking into the sky. She would approach the walls and hail some of the guards. They would be able to tell her where Constantine was, and hopefully pass him a message. Perhaps she could even climb one of the towers and wait for him there.

As she came closer, she realized something was wrong. As she came in sight of the walls, she could see people running toward her. They were clutching clothes and possessions, terror in their eyes. Some were screaming. A woman less than a hundred yards from Zophia made eye contact with her. She had tears streaming down her face. She was reaching out to Zophia as if to plead with her. As Zophia watched, the woman tripped. Behind her she was horrified to see an Ottoman running, almost as if directly at her. But the Turk stopped and knelt down quickly, sword in hand. He grabbed the woman by the hair, yanking her half to her feet. He pulled her head around roughly and began dragging her away from the street toward a home. She screamed and tried to fight him, but he was too strong for her. He kicked open a door and pulled her inside.

Zophia was frozen with the terror of the scene. Greeks and Italians ran past her. All she could think of was Constantine. If the Turks were in the city, where was he? He must be at the walls. Could she not reach him? She needed him, needed to make sure he was alive. She started her horse forward a few steps but was not able to force herself any farther toward the walls. She knew in her heart it was already too late.

Another group of Ottomans was running down the street toward her, closing by the moment. A few men broke off from the group in different directions, kicking in doors or wrestling people to the ground. She watched a Turk behead an elderly Greek woman who had paused in the street to try to catch her breath. The head rolled down the street, teeth chattering. The body stood for several seconds and then fell, almost gracefully, to the paved stone.

The Turks were closing quickly. She had to do something. She fought with herself for a few more moments, considering charging through the Ottomans to try to get to the walls. She realized she would never make it. There were at least thirty men coming toward her now. Several had seen her and were shouting and pointing, obviously taking her for a prize.

She reversed her horse quickly and kicked her heels, driving the horse forward at a gallop. She could not breathe. She was stunned, crying, barely able to see, but she knew she had to get away as quickly as possible. She did not know where to go, but she had to flee from the walls, flee from these terrible men. Where was her Constantine?

She wielded her horse off the main roads and into a vacant field. She galloped across the field and into a forested area near some crumbling buildings. She turned at the edge of the woods to make sure she was not being pursued. She could not see any Turks in the fields or near the buildings where she had just come from. She let her horse rest for a few minutes and caught her own breath.

Was it possible the Turks had only broken through in a small section? She wanted to believe desperately that the city could still hold, and more important, that Constantine might still be alive. Should she ride back to the walls from another direction? She wanted to, but she realized that would be a reckless decision. Even if there were only a few Turks in the city, she would be placing herself in harm's way. Whether the breakthrough was limited or widespread, she could not return toward the land walls.

Why were there no soldiers running to defend the city? Zophia knew there were men stationed along the sea walls. They should be coming up the main roads to mount a secondary defense. Did that mean the attack had not really broken through? Or did it mean the city was completely lost and the defenders were abandoning their posts?

Again she realized that the answers to her questions did not matter. She could not assist in the defense of the city, and might even present a valuable hostage to the Turks if she was captured. She needed to get away from the land walls. Perhaps the defenders on the sea walls did not even know about the breakthrough? Should she try to warn them? She could not imagine that the defenses had broken down so significantly that nobody had sent a warning back to the city, but it was possible. She had to do something.

Zophia paused for a few more minutes and thought things through. She decided she must try to warn the other defenders in case they did not know. She turned her horse and set off again, riding through the thin tree line and back out to the streets. She rode past terrified citizens who were trying to get a few possessions gathered while running out of their homes, attempting to keep their families together. Everyone was stumbling around in stunned disbelief.

Zophia quickly realized that the news had spread far beyond her already. She also realized from the actions of the people around her that they had given up hope. The city had fallen. How had their blessed Constantinople fallen? Was there any way to save the city?

As she rode farther away from the walls, the dome of St. Sophia began to rise up. Amid her tears and anguish she focused on the dome. She felt a moment of peace. She knew she had to go there. She wanted to be in her church. She hoped if Constantine had survived, he might have made his way there. He would not go back to the palace, as it was connected to the walls and might have already fallen. If there was still any hope the city could be defended, she could use the church as a base camp to gather and send out information. She thought of stopping first to try to send a message back to the walls. She looked around for any soldiers or even a willing citizen, but there was no one. The only people in the streets were running away in a panic as quickly as possible. She would not be able to do anything until she was farther away from the land walls.

She started out toward St. Sophia but then decided she would first ride over to the harbor of the Golden Horn to see what was happening. She was able to reach the Horn in only a few minutes. The scene was chaos. Huge crowds had formed near the docks. The people were primarily Italians but also many Greeks, clutching a few possessions. They were pressed forward, trying to climb aboard the Genoese and Venetian galleys. The sailors stood on the decks of the ships, weapons out, preventing most of the people from embarking. The crowd was screaming, pleading for help, to be allowed to board and escape from the city.

Zophia looked out over the Horn and could see the Turkish fleet closing in on the city both from across the Horn and from the Bosporus. The sea chain was no longer defended and some of the Ottoman ships were already astride it. Sailors were hacking at the wooden booms that connected the links. The chain would be broken in a matter of minutes, and the full fleet would be in the Horn. She also noticed that some of the Italian ships had already departed from the harbor, and some were sailing toward Galata, perhaps hoping for protection from the independent Genoese city.

With some luck, a few people were going to be able to escape by ship. Should she try to do so? She almost laughed in her despair. She would never leave her city, her emperor. God would protect her and the city, and if God did not, then it was his will that the city would fall and his will that the people would suffer. She accepted this, but like Jesus in the garden, she feared what was to come. She turned her horse slowly away and continued on to St. Sophia.

As she approached the great cathedral, she saw others making their way to the church, some individuals and many families, all streaming to St. Sophia. She remembered the ancient legend that the church would never fall, that even if the city's walls were breached, God would intervene and save the city before St. Sophia fell.

She entered the nave of the church under the great doors and made her way to the sanctuary. Normally the women worshiped upstairs in the gallery, but today men and women were huddled together on the main floor below the great dome. Fathers and mothers knelt in prayer, holding their children tightly. Tears streamed down many faces.

Many recognized Zophia and came forward to kiss her and touch her robes. They asked about Constantine: Had she seen him? Did she know what was happening in the city? She did not. But she gave them what comfort she could. She led small prayers with clusters of people. She brought blankets to children and held them for a few minutes, feeling them shiver beneath her. She looked up at the great archangels above, and prayed to Jesus and the Virgin to protect them, to deliver them, to save the city.

A Greek soldier entered the back of the cathedral and shouted that the Turks were getting closer. He had lost his weapon and was wounded in the head, blood trickling down his face. A great bellow of dread rose out of the crowd. Zophia saw the terror. She tried to avoid the eyes of the children. Acolytes ran to the great doors, closing and locking them.

The priests at the altar called the people together for prayer. The crowd moved closer to the altar, holding hands, keeping their children close, praying for deliverance, begging the Holy Father to keep the cathedral safe, to keep the city safe.

Zophia prayed with the rest of them. She prayed for the city. Her glorious Constantinople. The city had stood for eleven hundred years, a beacon of light amid the darkness. Certainly there had been much evil done within Constantinople, as in all human cities, but amid the dark terrors of the centuries, the city had kept the people safe and happy.

She prayed for the people of Constantinople. They were hardly a tithe of the former population but they were still the people of this city. They belonged to it, and it belonged to them. Everything was about to change forever. They were losing their city. And they were losing their freedom, their honor, their lives. Nothing would ever be the same for any of them again.

She prayed for Constantine, her only and great love on this earth. She was so thankful for every moment they had had together. She smiled as she thought of their time talking, enjoying the city, holding each other, making love. She could have asked for nobody and nothing better. She hoped to join him soon. Join him in heaven. She felt in her heart he was already gone. She whispered to him, "I will see you soon, my dear. Please help me through what is to come."

As she prayed, she could hear the banging begin behind her. Loud and deep banging on the doors. They were here. The lamenting of the crowd grew. She could hear crying, the whimpering of the children. There was a chopping sound; the Turks were beating on the doors with axes. She heard a crash. She kept her eyes closed, praying for them all. The Turks were through.

Zophia whispered a final few words of prayer and turned to see. The great doors were ripped open and dozens of Ottomans were pouring in, well armored and with swords drawn. A priest ran up to demand that they not defile the great church. A Turk stepped forward and cut his head from his body with one stroke. Zophia felt a tug on her arm. A little girl, no more than eight, was standing near her with her parents. They were all trembling in fear. Zophia smiled down at her as best she could. The child wanted to hold Zophia's hand as well as her mother's. Zophia took the tiny hand and held it, trying to let some courage and comfort flow through.

More Turks were streaming through the doors by the moment. They were spreading out. Soon they reached the families. They began by killing all of the elderly and the very young children. Zophia was horrified when one Ottoman ripped a baby out of the arms of its mother and dashed it against the wall. They were sorting the families for slaves, and it was clear the young, strong, and particularly the beautiful women were the most desirable.

The Turks were ripping the families apart, taking the people they wanted as possessions. Beautiful young women were dragged toward the entrance or thrown down to the marble floor right in the middle of the church to be raped.

An Ottoman reached Zophia and the family. She could feel the little girl hanging on as tightly as she could. The Turk was angry and wild-eyed. Zophia asked him to spare the family. She spoke Turkish, which surprised him and caused him to stop for a moment. He looked at her and then raised his sword and lashed out at the father, wounding him horribly in the chest and arm. The father fell backward on the marble, slipping on his own blood, which pumped out of his chest from the gaping wound. The little girl and her mother screamed in terror. The Turk stepped forward and stabbed the father again in the chest, driving his sword deep inside him. The body shivered and then was still.

The Turk ripped his sword out of the father and turned to the rest of them. He grabbed a silk sash he had tucked into his belt and tied the mother and daughter together by the hands and then pushed them down to the floor. Zophia felt another hand grab hers. A second Turk had grabbed hold of her and was attempting to pull her away. The first Ottoman turned and screamed at the second one, raising his sword threateningly. The second Turk let go and moved away, seeking his own prizes.

The Ottoman stepped forward and roughly grabbed Zophia by the hair. He knocked her back onto the bloody marble, falling on top of her. He was strong and Zophia could smell his foul, alcohol-laced breath. She tried to fight him off, but he was far too strong. He pulled up her robes and fiddled with his pants. She felt a sharp pain as he brutally shoved himself inside her, holding her neck with a gloved hand and choking her as he raped her.

She was helpless, angry, and humiliated. There was nothing she could do. Even screaming was impossible. He pressed on her, grunting and thrusting inside her. She opened her eyes and looked into the eyes of the Archangel Michael staring down at her from above. She thought of Constantine, trying to drive this horror from her mind. She hoped he had not suffered too much, that his death had been just a moment. She hoped this Turk would kill her after and she could join Constantine in heaven. She prayed this to Michael and to God.

With a final loud grunt the Turk finished and pushed himself roughly off. He grabbed Zophia again by the hair and dragged her to the mother and her young girl. He tied Zophia to the mother, and once they were secure, he left in search of other prizes.

The mother was staring at Zophia in shock, holding her young daughter, who was cowering against her. Zophia tried to compose herself as best she could and pulled the mother and child closer to her, trying to provide what comfort she could despite the trauma she had just endured. She felt a sharp cramping in her stomach. She looked down. There was bleeding. She felt her heart breaking. Her world was dying before her.

In a daze, she looked around her to see what was happening. The Turks were continuing to collect and tie people together, and were mercilessly killing those too young or too old to have any worth. They were also pillaging everything of value in reach, grabbing gold and silver chalices and icons, and hacking away at gilded frames on the walls. A group of priests were standing near the altar, trying to hold on to a few precious relics. They were surrounded by armed Ottomans with swords raised, threatening them loudly and lunging at the priests. The standoff could not last long. Those who had been torn away from their family members were calling out to each other in the sanctuary, trying to keep in contact as long as possible. These desperate cries were intermixed with the screams of women being raped and the moans of the wounded and dying.

Perhaps half an hour passed, and *their* Ottoman returned, leading a string of seven additional slaves. He tied these to the mother, and then to Zophia's horror he returned to her. He was smiling now and slurring words to her. He did not even bother untying her from the little girl but simply pressed Zophia back to the cold and bloody marble and began raping her again, less brutally this time but just as terribly. She closed her eyes, praying, thinking of her fallen city, and thinking of Constantine.

CHAPTER TWENTY-TWO

TUESDAY, MAY 29, 1453, EARLY MORNING

Mehmet sat astride his horse in the early morning. He had watched the Ottoman irregulars, his most expendable troops, attacking the palisade for several hours. He could see the press of men against the wooden walls with each flash of cannon. The attacking men were exhausted and would not continue their assault much longer, but that was fine by the sultan. They had served their purpose, keeping a constant assault against the defenders that would have served to tire and weaken them and to inflict at least some casualties.

Zaganos was next to him, sharing this moment with his sultan. They both knew their lives were probably at stake, Zaganos's more than Mehmet's, for even if Halil felt unable to remove the sultan, he surely would demand the death of this upstart Christian convert for any bargain.

Zaganos spoke to an aide who sent messages quickly through the ranks, calling back the auxiliary forces. Within a few minutes they were all away from the wall, but there was no pause. With a new order, the Anatolian contingent of regular Ottoman soldiers streamed forward, attacking the same small portion of the wooden palisade, keeping up the pressure, looking for weaknesses. Throughout, the cannons roared, sending a constant barrage at the walls. Some of the shots landed short of the walls, wounding and killing scores of Turks. It did not matter. The sultan had men to spare, and whether this assault failed or succeeded, the casualties would matter little.

"How are we doing?" he asked Zaganos.

"So far, well, my Lord."

"What does that mean?"

Zaganos laughed. "Perhaps it means nothing. There have been no disasters, but then none were expected. We are keeping up pressure, and they must be getting tired inside. Everything is going according to plan so far. However, it all will depend on whether we get into the city."

"What more can we do?"

"Nothing, my Lord. It is in Allah's hands."

Several more hours passed. The Anatolian troops battled hard, relentlessly pushing forward. They seemed to be making some progress, but from where Mehmet stood, it did not seem they could get consistent forces over the walls. They would throw up a few ladders; the Greeks would push them back. A few Turks would make it over the wall, but never enough. And already they, too, were tiring from the battle.

Mehmet turned again to Zaganos. "Call the Janissaries forward; I will address them."

The moment had come for Mehmet. The most important moment of his life. He had gambled everything on this siege, against the advice of all the senior advisors, against his father's advice when he was still alive. He was thought rash and impetuous by Halil and all of the senior councilors of the empire. Were they correct? He had been so sure of himself. He had planned so carefully. Was he not Allah's shadow on the earth? Had he not known since he was a young boy that it was his destiny to take this city? Had he not suffered embarrassment and doubt for years?

Now it was down to this one moment. He had one more attack to make. He had only his Janissaries left. He had depended on Christian converts as his top advisors, and now he would rely on Christian converts to capture the city. If they failed, he would fail with them.

Soon they were gathered near his tent and ready for Mehmet to address them. They numbered approximately five thousand. They cheered Mehmet with his approach.

"My elite warriors of Allah. You see the Greeks still standing before us? They are infidels. They hold your city back from you. They hold back your treasure, your gold and silver and slaves. Will you let them?"

"No!" roared the men.

"Inside this city there is wealth immeasurable. More than a thousand years' of treasure. When you breach these walls, you will have three days to take everything you want. That is the will and promise of Allah. All of this is given to you if you will take it. Will you take it?"

The men shouted the affirmative this time, beating swords and spears on their shields.

"We cannot stay here forever. The infidels have friends, the Italians and the Hungarians. We must take the city now. I have weakened these Greeks with the attacks of lesser men, but I have left the victory for you. You go forth now to glory. You must take the city or you must not come back! Will you take it?"

The men screamed their approval, even louder now. They were wild-eyed and stirred with passion. Mehmet had ordered the Anatolians back a few minutes before. The timing was perfect. He rode back toward the city at a trot, his Janissaries running alongside him, chanting and cheering him. He stopped for a moment, drew his sword, and then spurred his horse forward in a gallop. A huge roar erupted from the Janissaries, who charged the walls in a sprint. Mehmet stopped his horse about a hundred yards from the walls. The Janissaries crashed into the palisade like a wave crashing on the rocks. They were shouting, screaming, throwing up ladders, and streaming over, swinging their swords savagely as they went.

Mehmet watched the attack, his heart in his throat. They must succeed and they must do it now, or everything was lost. Within just a few minutes he thought he was beginning to notice a change. Before, the ladders would hit the wall but stay up only for a few moments. Now, there were a dozen or more ladders in place, and they seemed to be staying there. Janissaries were ascending in a steady stream and climbing or falling over the walls. He felt a surge of exhilaration. Was it possible they were succeeding? Were they going to take the city? He was delighted to see an Ottoman banner waving over the stockade. Would it last?

He was surrounded by men on both sides. Long lines had formed in each direction as far as the eye could see. The men of the previous assaults had come to watch the final one. They were exhausted, some wounded. They had come without command to witness this assault, as if they knew the fate of the city depended on this last desperate attempt.

Minutes passed. The ladders remained. Mehmet held his breath. Were they advancing? Was it possible the city was his at last? He noticed the eastern sky beginning to brighten slightly. Dawn was not far off. Perhaps the start of a new world for him.

Another flash. He saw not one banner but several. They waved wildly over the palisade. He thought he saw cheering and excitement from the Janissaries still below the wall. He turned to Zaganos.

"Ride forward and see what is happening."

The Pasha spurred his horse forward into the darkness. Mehmet waited without patience. Each moment seemed to last an hour. Finally he made out Zaganos's form returning to him.

"We are through, my Lord! We are through! The city is ours! The city is ours!"

Mehmet looked up and saw the city through another flash of light. Now there were banners waving not just at the palisade but also on the great walls themselves. His banners. He had done it. With Allah's blessing, he had done it. The city was his. Constantinople was his.

He must press the advantage while he could. It was not too late to lose the city. He shouted to the men standing with him. "Attack! Everyone attack! The city is ours! The city is ours! Do not lose it now! Go forward for Allah! Claim what is yours!"

The men let forth a tremendous roar of excitement and charged forward, massing behind the Janissaries who were still climbing over the walls of the palisade. Mehmet felt a hand on his shoulder. He turned to see Zaganos smiling at him. His general bowed in his saddle.

"You have done it, my Lord. You are the conqueror of the world now. Nobody will ever doubt you again!"

Mehmet bowed in return. He closed his eyes and then looked out again. The light from the east was bright enough to illuminate the walls of the city. His city. His men had now broken through the wooden walls and were pouring into Constantinople. He closed his eyes again and prayed to Allah, thanking him for delivering the city to him. He thought of his father, and spoke to him silently in his mind. "I have done it, Father. I have fulfilled your dream and the destiny of our people. I have brought you your capitol."

Mehmet sat for hours on his horse with Zaganos, watching his men pass through the walls of Constantinople. He received messengers from within the city describing the final hours of the Christian city.

He learned with surprise that there was almost no resistance once the initial fight at the palisade was finished. Apparently the commander of the Greeks had been wounded and carried out by some of his Genoese retainers. In their rush to leave, his men had left open one of the small doors leading through the great inner walls of the city, and other men had begun fleeing the palisade. A few deserters had triggered a panicked retreat and the Janissaries had quickly battled through the great wall and into the city itself.

After securing this entrance they had spread out into the city cautiously, expecting additional fighting but encountering almost none. Greeks were everywhere fleeing, but mostly women, children, and old men with their possessions. The Janissaries encountered small bands of Greek soldiers who still were fighting, but only a very small number. They eventually found one of the great gates and opened it, allowing huge numbers of Ottomans to storm in at one time.

Traveling away from the walls, they had spread out and begun moving east. The Janissaries remained together in organized groups, but the regular Ottoman soldiers and the auxiliary troops had quickly dissipated into mobs of looters, breaking into homes in search of treasure and slaves.

The Janissary reported that the looters had become organized, flagging each house that was already pillaged so that those who came behind them could move on to the next house or neighborhood. The troops were killing many of the older men and women and the very young children. This tactic was to be expected because they would offer little value as slaves. Mehmet gave an order that the young children were to be spared. Children could serve him very well in the future; the old could not. He also reiterated his order that the main holy churches and palaces could be looted, but the structures themselves should not be damaged. The punishment would be death.

The sultan received a separate report from one of his personal guards and commanders who had been directed to review conditions in the Golden Horn. Mehmet was not pleased with what he learned. The Turkish fleet had broken through the sea chain and both the Horn fleet and the Bosporus fleet had made their way to the city harbors and docked. However, instead of containing or destroying the Italian and Greek ships in the harbor, they had abandoned their ships to join in the looting of the city. This action was entirely against his orders.

Mehmet seethed with anger. The fleet, a tremendous innovation, had nonetheless failed him at every level during the siege. He must capture as many Italian mariners as possible, as well as their ships, and utilize them to build a more efficient and effective fleet in the future. He gave orders that sailors were to be rounded up and forced back onto their ships immediately, to form a line of defense near the broken sea chain. They were to capture or stop as many fleeing ships as possible, and also to identify all captured Italian and Greek sailors.

Mehmet also learned that a number of Italian ships had docked at

Galata, and then fled from there to the Golden Horn. Mehmet knew that while Galata had claimed official neutrality, it had hardly acted the part. He was sure he would receive a delegation within the next few days requesting that he honor all previous trade agreements and the independence of the city. They were sadly mistaken if they believed this would occur. He would require them to tear down their walls and submit to his authority. He might leave the city's population intact, as a show of good faith with the West, but Galata would be incorporated into the Ottoman Empire along with Constantinople.

Zaganos returned in the early afternoon. He greeted Mehmet enthusiastically. "The city is ours, my Lord. The reports are true. There was very little resistance in the city after we breached the walls. There has been considerable panic and quite a bit of killing. One other surprise, the city is in a very destitute state and there does not appear to be nearly the treasure we might have expected. They must have been in a very pitiful situation for the past few years. I am shocked they held out as long as they did."

"It was the will of Constantine. He was a great leader and a worthy opponent." Mehmet was surprised at his own words. He felt a strange warmth for the Greek emperor. Both had risked everything. Only one of them could prevail. Mehmet had proved victorious, but only with the last desperate push. "Have we found Constantine?"

"We have not, my Lord, but I can confirm a number of reports among the Greeks that he is dead. According to multiple witnesses he was with the defenders in the palisade and fell when they were overwhelmed by the Janissaries."

"I want his body found and brought to me. Arrange for it."

"I will, my Lord."

"When can I enter the city?"

"Now, if you want. I would suggest you bring a reasonable number of your personal guard, just to deter any individual Greek from trying to attack you. But there is no organized resistance left."

Mehmet smiled. "Let us arrange it and go, then."

Another hour passed while the necessary details were arranged. Thirty of the sultan's personal guards were gathered. The sultan's full council had by now made their way to Mehmet's tent and cheered him as he returned from the walls. Grand Vizier Halil was at the forefront, enthusiastically clapping. Mehmet thought he looked nervous.

"My Lord, my Lord, truly Allah has blessed us with you in our lifetime! You have exceeded all expectations and the accomplishments of all of your ancestors, including your illustrious father. You are the supreme Sultan!" Halil turned to the others. "Let us praise him!" There were renewed cheers.

Mehmet was delighted but not surprised. Halil had responded exactly as he would have expected, the same way the leader of Galata would act when he came begging for his city—like a guilty child caught red-handed in an act of disobedience. He bowed in return to Halil. This was not yet the time to deal with Halil. Soon he would.

The council members mounted up, and so did Mehmet's guards. The procession to the city would be made up of Mehmet and his guards in the lead, followed by the council members, and then a contingent of Janissaries and representatives of the other forces involved in the siege.

Mehmet rode slowly to the front of the procession, which had formed near the entrance to the sultan's tent. Although many of his men were within the city, thousands still remained in the camp. They were lined up now, waiting patiently to catch a glimpse of their sultan, their conquering leader. As he passed they cheered him, praising him and Allah for this great victory. Mehmet was filled with a peace and excitement he had never known. He had never been loved or revered by his people. At times they had hated him, always they feared him, but at this precious moment they loved him. He had given them what they all desired but had been denied all these years. The first Islamic army hammered against the walls of Constantinople in 674. They had come back over and over but never taken the city. Now they had won it. They had their great capital.

He led the procession slowly to the Edirne road outside the Charisius Gate. The great gate, which had closed against the siege but now stood open, was one of the main entrances into the city during peacetime. It stood at the highest point of the land walls, forty feet above sea level, a tall arch built within the walls. Mehmet walked his horse slowly forward, the walls rising with each step. The entrance to the gate was vacant, but just past it huge crowds of Ottomans waited. He walked slowly toward them, toward his destiny. For fifty-three days he had stood outside the walls. He had dreamed his entire life of setting foot inside the city. Now he would do so. Finally he passed the gate, looking up to admire the great thickness of the walls. He was met with a thunderous roar from the crowd. The city was his. All his dreams had come true. And the dreams of his people.

TUESDAY, MAY 29, 1453, 2:30 P.M.

Mehmet passed the land walls at the Charisius Gate and progressed slowly along the three miles to the main part of the city on the Mese road. He looked around with great curiosity. He was taken aback by the large areas of unused and decaying buildings and the open pastures and wooded areas of the city. Constantinople felt like an emaciated man near death still wearing his former clothes. Along the way, he passed the large Church of the Holy Apostles on his left. Just past this massive structure he saw the even more impressive Aqueduct of Valens, which brought water into the city. He passed then through the main square of Constantine, then the Amastrionon and the Forum Tauri, and finally the Forum of Constantine.

There were bodies everywhere, and blood flowed in the streets. He saw huddled groups of Greeks, tied together and being led to assembly areas that also contained piles of all types of treasure. Mehmet gave orders for a number of his guards to spread out in the city and inform the men that the looting would be ended at dark today, rather than after the traditional three days. He wanted to preserve some of the wealth of Constantinopole for himself, and he was surprised at just how poor and debilitated the city was. He ordered that all loot, including slaves, be inventoried so he could retain his traditional one-fifth share. All remaining loot would be apportioned in equal amounts to each soldier according to his station. He also ordered that they were to identify all nobles, priests, commanders, and other important persons and bring those names and locations to Mehmet. He then asked that all sailors be identified. The nobles and priests would be ransomed to the West at the maximum value and then released, unless Mehmet decided otherwise.

As Mehmet traveled leisurely on through the streets, the dome of St. Sophia began to rise steadily on the horizon. He was awed at its size.

Finally the sultan and his entourage reached St. Sophia itself. He dismounted and entered the huge narthex and then the sanctuary through the battered imperial gate. The cathedral was in chaos. He could hear the wailing within through the doors to the sanctuary, and he saw huge numbers of Greeks sitting huddled together, Ottomans walking among them with swords drawn. Occasionally a loud scream would echo above the general moaning.

Mehmet walked into the main cathedral, followed by a few guards and his council members. He was quickly recognized and soon the moaning faded away, replaced by hushed whispering. He looked around, gauging the situation. "Who is in charge here?" he demanded.

One of the Janissaries among the Greek prisoners stepped forward and bowed low. "I am not sure anyone is really in charge, my Lord. How may I be of service?"

"Tell me what's going on in here."

"We broke in a few hours ago. There was no resistance within. Since that time we have been gathering prisoners and also treasure."

Mehmet looked about the sanctuary, noting the blood and the damaged walls. "I gave strict instructions that the churches were not to be damaged in any way. Why was I not obeyed?"

"I am sorry, my Lord. I have not been involved in any of the looting. I have been collecting the prisoners."

Mehmet looked at the man for a moment. "Someone has to pay." He motioned for one of his guards, who came forward and struck the Janissary a blow to the head with a mace. The soldier crumpled under the blow, blood spurting all over the worn marble floor. The body convulsed for a few moments, and then was still.

The sanctuary was dead silent. All eyes were on Mehmet. He turned to the crowd. "I commanded that this church and all churches be left alone! This command was not followed! If I see any more damage here, I will kill everyone responsible! You will take your prisoners out to the courtyard and gather them to be sorted. If you are aware of anyone important, you are to bring that to the attention of a superior immediately. I congratulate you on taking the city. Allah be praised!"

Mehmet turned to speak to the council. "We have taken the city, my friends. We stand in the great cathedral of our enemies, the greatest church of the infidels. It is time for rewards. Halil, come forward!"

The grand vizier came forward, a bit nervously. This was the moment Mehmet had waited for, dreamed of, since he was a boy. "Halil, you are stripped of your titles and your wealth immediately. You have betrayed me and the people with your lack of faith, and you have sought bribes from the enemy."

"What?"

"You have been in contact with the enemy and you have sought bribes."

Halil was wild eyed, his nostrils flaring. "What do you speak of, my Lord? That is preposterous. Who says such things?"

"I do," came a voice from the shadows. Sphrantzes stepped out of the darkness, flanked by two of Mehmet's guards. He bowed to Mehmet and turned to the council members, speaking in Turkish. "I can attest that I have been working closely with Halil for several years now. I am the closest advisor of the Emperor Constantine. I have paid Halil bribes on a monthly basis for information about your government, the size of your forces, and the like. Halil has provided me with substantial information about this siege, including telling me that if we survived the attacks today, you would have to lift the siege."

There were gasps from the council. One of them shouted, "Traitor!"

Halil looked in shock at Sphrantzes. "Liar! I have never seen you before. He is lying! Mehmet has falsely incriminated me! Mehmet is lying to you!"

Mehmet laughed. "Always the guilty deny. Seize him!" Guards ran forward and restrained Halil. "You will be executed when I am ready. In the meantime, you may sit in prison and pray to Allah for your sins. Take him away!"

Mehmet watched the guards drag Halil away. He relished this moment more than any other, perhaps even more than entering the city itself. The ghosts of his father were fading away. When Halil was out of sight he turned and walked over to Sphrantzes, moving close enough that only Sphrantzes could hear him.

"You played your part well. Everything you told me was true. The information about the attacking fleet was particularly helpful."

"Thank you, my Lord. I hope you will give me the promised payment."

"Yes, you will be spared, and richly rewarded."

"And my freedom?"

"Ah, that I cannot grant. I am sorry, but I have had to reconsider that request."

"But, my Lord, we had an agreement."

"I must consider the needs of my people. I'm sorry." He smiled to himself. He found this traitor to his people distasteful and looked forward to disposing of him as soon as he could.

Sphrantzes was pale now. He looked around as if trying to find some support. "I have one more thing to offer, for my freedom."

Mehmet thought of cutting down this Greek right here and now, but his interest was piqued. "What more could you give me?"

"I can give you Constantine's lover."

"What?"

"I can give you Zophia. I know where she is. She was the closest person in the world to Constantine. She is young and beautiful."

Zophia. He had heard the name before and knew the rumors of Constantine's affections for her. He had also heard she was a great beauty, perhaps the greatest beauty of the empire. Could he find her without Sphrantzes? Even if Sphrantzes revealed her location, should he kill him anyway? Mehmet paused for a moment, considering. If he killed him in front of all of these Greeks, they would not trust him. He would need others for information and for his plans for the city. Also, if he killed him now, the other elders might become suspicious of his motives. He had gained great power and prestige by taking the city, but there was no reason to be reckless with his new power. What of the possibility that Sphrantzes would spread rumors about Mehmet to others in the West? Others would do so no matter what Sphrantzes said. And how could he tell his story without implicating himself as a traitor? Finally, he wanted to find this Zophia. Others might lead him to her, but then again, they might not. Soon the slaves would be divided and sent out. He might never find her.

"Show me to Zophia and I will let you go."

Sphrantzes breathed out heavily and smiled. "I will certainly do so, my Lord. She is here in the sanctuary now." Sphrantzes led Mehmet into the middle of the sanctuary. He was heavily surrounded by guards to assure no vengeful Greek would try to assassinate him. He led the sultan to a beautiful young woman with black hair. She had a pale, tear-streaked face and torn, bloodstained robes. She was tied to a young girl who clung to her, whimpering. "This is Zophia, my Lord."

The young woman's eyes widened through her obvious pain and she looked at Sphrantzes with anger. "How could you? How could you betray Constantine like this? What have you become?"

Sphrantzes bowed to her. "I have not become anything. You simply see me clearly now. Finally. I am a survivor. Without Constantine and the city I have no future, except to make my way as best I am able. You are unfortunately the price of my freedom. I do not do this out of any personal grudge." Sphrantzes turned to Mehmet and switched to Turkish. "As you can see, my Lord, this is in fact Zophia, Constantine's greatest treasure. He was with her in the morning when your attack came. I am sure he had her. She looks a little worse for wear now, but regardless, you can have her on the very same day."

Mehmet swung his arm and struck Sphrantzes across the face, knocking him to the hard marble floor. "You are a worm, and I see the best I can do for you is unleash you on the West to weasel your way into some other court to spread your rumors and lies. You will not further dishonor this woman, or I will cut out your tongue and feed it to you."

He turned to his guards. "Drag this scum out of this holy place. Find him an Italian ship and let him escape while he can. Give him thirty pieces of silver; I believe that is the proper Christian sum."

Sphrantzes was dragged away, his face bleeding and bruised. Mehmet bent down and placed his hand on Zophia's shoulder. "Are you well?"

"I am ill. Everything has been taken from me today."

Mehmet yelled for his guard to summon his physicians, then he gestured to the girl tied to Zophia. "Who is this girl?" he asked. "Do you know her?"

Zophia looked at Mehmet with eyes widening. She hesitated, then answered. "I do not know her, my Lord. She was tied to me. Her mother was torn from us about an hour ago. Her father is dead."

Mehmet turned to another guard. "Take this girl and try to find her mother. They are to be freed, returned to their home, given some gold, and protected. I want a guard at their door until all slaves have been removed from the city. Arrange for proper paperwork for them as well."

The guard removed a dagger and cut the cloth tying Zophia to the girl. Zophia spoke to her in Greek and explained what Mehmet had ordered. She hugged her tightly. The guard led her slowly away. "Thank you, my Lord. That was a great act of kindness."

"I but do honor to you. You are the love of my great foe. I wish he would have survived, but I fear that he has not. I wish he would have accepted my offers and left the city. I wanted his city, not his life."

"This city was his life. He sacrificed everything for it. He was not capable of leaving it behind. Now he can finally be at peace."

"I will honor him by protecting you. My personal physician will attend you until you recover. You will come into my household and will be given a monthly allowance and quarters. You may choose to marry someone of appropriate station in time. You may also consider converting to Islam. I will tell you everything I know about it. I will not force you. You will be protected and honored to the end of your days. I will want to talk to you from time to time about Constantine. I want to understand everything about him. I also want your advice about this city. I have dreamed of the city, but you have lived here. I intend to bring Ottomans and Greeks from throughout the empire to rebuild it and make it great again. I will restore Constantinople to its former glory, and eventually we will exceed it. This city will be the center of the world. Will you accept my proposal? I will force no choices on you."

"You are generous beyond words, my Lord. I am happy to share with you everything I know about the city and our people. I will, however, never give you information about free Greeks. I will not identify captured Greeks for you. I will not convert to Islam. If you intend these things, I ask that you take my life now."

Mehmet bowed. "I agree to your terms. As I said, nothing will be forced on you. Now I must thank Allah for this wondrous day."

His physician arrived and knelt down, gently moving Zophia to the marble floor. He immediately began attending to her.

Mehmet stood, taking a few more moments to ensure Zophia was properly cared for. He then motioned to his men, and gradually the other Greeks were led out of the sanctuary. Mehmet could not and would not free the others. He had made promises to his people that must be kept. When all of the slaves had been removed, he gathered the council near the great altar in the east wall of the cathedral.

"This is the moment we have dreamed of and waited for. The city is ours. This great cathedral is ours, the greatest building on earth. I rededicate this as Aya Sofia, our great mosque for the glory of Allah. Let us now pray together and give thanks."

The Grand Mufti came forward. He went to the altar and then turned slightly to the right, to face Mecca. He began his preparations. Mehmet and the council members ritually cleansed themselves and returned with the call to prayer. They began the first holy prayers, thanking and praising Allah. Mehmet smiled as he praised him. He was home.

CHAPTER TWENTY-THREE

WEDNESDAY, MAY 30, 1453

Captain Uberti stared out impatiently over the sunny and calm waters near the entrance to the Dardanelles. The wind simply would not cooperate.

He had stood off the straits for a day now, waiting for a favorable wind to push his fleet in and through. He had oars within the ship, but they could not carry his fleet quickly enough, and with the straits not much more than a mile wide in places and dominated by the Turks on both sides, he must wait for a strong wind to make the run into the Sea of Marmara.

He looked out at the remaining ships, watching sailors, soldiers, and captains pacing about just as he was. They were impatient to reach the city and assist in the destruction of the Turks.

A shout caught his attention, and he looked out quickly toward the straits. A single ship had appeared on the horizon. Uberti sounded the alarm, and the sailors sprang to, preparing cannon and setting their sails in case they had to fight this ship, or even a fleet that had not yet appeared. Uberti noted all of his ships were preparing for whatever this potential threat might be.

After the initial flurry of activity, there was little that could be done except watch the galley slowly approach. The captain kept a close look on the horizon and was relieved that no additional ships were appearing. If this was a threat, his fleet could certainly handle a single ship.

As the galley ranged closer he could make out the sails and flags. The vessel was Genoese. He ordered the news called through the fleet, and the men stood down from their defensive positions. His galley sailed forward in the light wind on a path to intercept the Genoese vessel.

Soon the ship was in hailing distance, and the Genoese sailors shouted that they had important news. The captain, after verifying in a few exchanges that the men were in fact Italians, ordered a long boat roped down into the water. He climbed down himself with two armed sailors and four rowers, and set out over the fifty yards of open water to the Genoese ship. He often took the risks himself, to assist his reputation with his crew.

They pulled up to the hull of the vessel and Uberti climbed up a rope net and aboard. He immediately noticed the fear and excitement among the crew. A captain gained an almost supernatural sense of his crew after years at sea, where fear or anger could lead to the loss of his ship. This crew was rattled, and it immediately heightened his sense of awareness, and of potential danger. Perhaps he should have allowed one of the mates to come after all.

"Who is in command here?" he demanded, a trifle more arrogantly than usual. He needed to assert his authority here.

A thin and short Italian stepped forward, bearing the same haunted look in his eyes as his men. "I am the captain, and this is my ship. I bear terrible news."

Captain Uberti relaxed a little. The men had suffered some sort of trauma, which meant they were probably not dangerous, only rattled. "What sort of news?"

"The great city has fallen."

Uberti had not expected that. They were on their way to save the city, and so were the Hungarians. "What do you mean? We are a relief force. Are you talking about Constantinople?"

"Yes. I was not part of the battle, but I was docked in Galata when the siege began. When the city fell, I took my ship over to the harbor and loaded some of the people fleeing, including the commander of the defenses. His name is Giovanni Longo. He is badly wounded but still alive."

"Where is he?"

"Below."

"I need to speak with him immediately."

"He comes in and out of consciousness. I do not know how much longer he will live. You are welcome to speak with him if he is awake."

Captain Uberti was led down into the hold of the ship. A small area in the hold had been cordoned off with blankets. He lifted the sheet and passed through. A wooden bed was nailed to the corner, and on the bed, covered by a blood-soaked sheet, was Longo. He was covered in sweat and twisted restlessly back and forth, moaning in pain. He was pale and appeared near death.

Uberti shook the Genoan gently. The commander appeared to be in such terrible condition that Uberti did not really expect him to be conscious, but the Genoan opened his eyes and stared with shock at the captain.

"I lost the city!" he shouted, eyes wide in fear. "I lost it. I fled like a coward. If I had stayed at the wall, the city would have survived. I am damned! I lost God's city to the infidels."

"What do you mean, *you* lost the city? What happened?"

"The Turks! The Turks are here!" Longo reached out and grabbed Uberti's shirt, pulling him down. "Run! You must run! The city has fallen. I lost the city!"

The captain tried several more times to speak to Longo, but he would not respond. He called out a last time, then his body was racked with a terrible cough, and he passed back out of consciousness.

Uberti stood over the Genoan for a while longer, and finally whispered a prayer. He turned and left the hold of the ship, climbing back to the deck.

"Were you able to get anything out of him?"

"No, he was too far gone. He blames himself for the loss of the city. Poor devil. What can you tell me?"

The Genoan captain described the siege of the city to Uberti: the multiple attacks, the Greek victories at sea, the portage of the Turkish fleet into the Horn, and the final battle and loss of the city. Particularly terrifying was the description of the desperate panic at the harbor, with thousands of Greeks trying to board the few available ships as the Turks closed in.

"What will you do now?" asked the Genoan finally.

Uberti was not sure. Should he continue to Constantinople and attack the Turks, or see if he could gather more refugees? He quickly dismissed that idea. If there were truly hundreds of Turkish ships, it would be suicide no matter how poorly the fleet was handled. He could turn his ships north and try to connect with Hunyadi to see if he could render assistance. Uberti realized the Hungarian would not likely proceed now that the distraction of the siege was over. Uberti did not have enough men or ships to operate independently. He made his decision.

"I will turn the fleet and travel to Rome to report what has happened here. You are welcome to join us as far as you wish to go."

The commander was obviously relieved and grateful. "I would appreciate some assistance. I have feared for my ship and my crew since the moment the city fell. I do need to stop and unload the wounded. I am going to stop at Chios."

"I will join you. We leave -within the hour."

Uberti quickly left and was rowed back to his ship. He told the story to his crew and ordered the message and the change of course passed to the rest of the ships. In less than an hour, the fleet was ready and began a slow rolling turn to port. Soon it was heading south with a light wind. Uberti stood long at the stern of his ship, staring at the entrance to the Dardanelles as it slowly faded away. He wondered if he would ever travel through them again, or sail through the Marmara to the great city of Constantinople.

SATURDAY, JUNE 9, 1453

John Hunyadi paced back and forth in front of his tent in the misty early morning. He was impatient to get started. His men were taking longer than he wished to pack up their supplies and line up for the next march.

He had camped his army up against a steep ridge. He was protected on two sides by the V-shaped hill, allowing a strong defensive position. His men were spread out in the valley in an assortment of tents. The army was only a few days away from Constantinople, and he wanted to press on as quickly as possible to relieve the city.

He knew his force was not nearly large enough to assure victory against the sultan in the open field. However, with the promised aid of the pope and the Venetians and the remaining Greeks in Constantinople, there was a rare, perhaps unique, opportunity to deal the young sultan a fatal blow. Hunyadi knew just how dangerous the Ottomans were to his nation and to all of Europe. If there was a chance they could be stopped, it was worth considerable risk. He would have liked to take more time and build a force at least twice this size. It was possible that even with aid from Constantinople and the Italians, he would still be defeated. But Hunyadi had always taken calculated risks, and they had nearly always paid off.

He read the letter from Pope Nicholas again. The letter absolved him for the second time from his agreement with Mehmet. The pope also promised a relief fleet of ships and at least ten thousand Venetians. With such a force and command of the sea, they could surprise the Ottomans against the walls of Constantinople and press them from all sides. The Turks' advantage in numbers would be useless if they were pressed tightly together, and they would hopefully panic and begin to surrender en masse.

In such an instance he would have no mercy. He would kill them all and their sultan with them, then swing around and take Edirne. He would run them out of Europe forever and set up a renewed Greek state as a buffer. The Greeks would not be his allies forever, but they would be weak and grateful, a combination that should keep them at arms' length at least for the rest of his life. His children would have to fight them, perhaps, but that was not for him to worry about.

All of the tents were now down, and his men were milling about, forming marching lines and mounting horses. When his own horse was brought around, he pulled himself up in his saddle, stretching his stiff bones. He smiled to himself. He was getting too old for this. When he was in his twenties, he could march all day and night and day again without rest. He did not feel the cold or heat, and hardly the wounds. Now, he felt everything. He was slowing down just a touch, and that could be fatal in battle. He must be extra wary. If he could win this next battle, he need never go to war again. He could retire in peace, a hero of his people, as long as the damned Germans left him alone.

A commotion at the edge of his sight stirred his attention. A lone messenger on horseback had entered the camp and was surrounded by his men. Hunyadi watched him motioning with hand movements and pointing frantically toward Hunyadi. News from the city or from the pope. He hoped the ships were ready and that Constantine had sufficient forces to assist in the attack and not just sit back behind his comfortable walls.

Hunyadi watched the messenger being led slowly to him. He pretended not to notice him, not wanting to appear anxious. He studied the valley again with mock interest, finally turning when the horseman was actually in his presence.

"What is it?" he asked with feigned indifference.

"It is I, my Lord: Gregory."

"Ah yes, Gregory. Then your message must be from Constantine. Is he begging for yet more from me? I already come with an army for him."

"He is dead."

"What?"

"The city has fallen, my Lord. Constantinople is no more. Constantine is dead."

The news shook Hunyadi to the core. Constantinople gone. This news was terrible. Hunyadi realized what prestige this victory would bring Mehmet in the Islamic world. Even among the Christians in the Balkans, there would be fear and admiration. The sultan would gather not only the treasures of the city, but tremendous wealth from the sale of slaves. Recruits seeking additional victory and spoils would swell his ranks. Worse yet, there was no longer a divided focus for the Ottoman forces. They would be coming for him. Coming for Hungary. Why had he not sent assistance earlier? Why had he not seen the terrible ramifications of the loss of this city?

He realized he had never believed it would fall. So many armies had beaten themselves to death on the walls of Constantinople. The city had survived as if by the hand of God. Somehow it had seemed Constantinople would always survive. Now it was gone. *The Roman Empire was gone.* The past had faded away before his eyes. The Ottomans had replaced it. Now they were the dominant force in Europe. The dominant force in the world. He must prepare his defenses. There would be no more distractions allowing him forays into Ottoman territory. He must save Hungary if he could.

Hunyadi invited Gregory to join him. The Greek gladly agreed. The Hungarian leader ordered his men to form ranks, but they marched north instead of south. North to Hungary and to safety. He would have time to prepare. He hoped when Mehmet came, it would be enough.

MONDAY, JULY 16, 1453

Pope Nicholas sat on his throne and held his afternoon audience. He was listening carefully to an updated report regarding the papal treasury. Hard work and austerity measures had begun to pay off, reducing debt and building a small reserve. He was slowly erasing the foolish mess with which his predecessor had left him.

Nicholas was in a good mood. The financial news had brightened an already sunny day. He thought perhaps he would go for a long walk after the audience to enjoy the gardens before dinner and evening prayers. He concluded the financial report and was rising to leave when the Venetian ambassador appeared at the door.

A shadow passed over Nicholas. He could tell something was wrong. Probably another complaint about the Genoese or the Neapolitans or any other squabbling Italian city. Why they could not simply work together was beyond him. Or better yet, why could they not unite under papal authority for the greater glory of Italy and God? If they could cooperate, they could dominate trade with the East. And with a new partnership with the Greeks after the Union of the Churches, much could be accomplished.

But whatever the issue was, he decided he had better hear it so he could get on with his walk. He put on his best smile and waved the Ambassador over.

"Ah, my friend, you have caught me just when I was ready to conclude my activities for the day. Perhaps this could wait until tomorrow?"

The ambassador bowed. "I am afraid it cannot, Your Holiness. I have terrible news."

"Let me guess. The Genoese have sunk one of your ships, and you want me to demand repayment?" Nicholas was half joking, his good mood still spilling over with a hope this news would not ruin it entirely.

"Constantinople has fallen."

Nicholas studied the ambassador's face, hoping the man was simply joking back with him. He saw immediately that he was not. Nicholas forgot his mood and his walk. "What do you mean? How do you know?"

"We received word by ship just a few days ago. The doge immediately ordered that the news be sent to you. Apparently Galata has also fallen. We have lost all access to the Black Sea. We have lost our trade routes to the East. We have lost our first defense against the Ottomans. Only God knows how long before they threaten Italy itself."

"Surely they will move against Hunyadi first. We must aid him. I shall call a crusade immediately."

"Of course Your Holiness is wise in all things. However, I might suggest that would be the worst thing you could do. We are divided and weak. We are strong only at sea. If we publicly attack the Ottomans before we are organized, they may move immediately against us. We could hardly stop them. It is best to let them swallow up the remaining Greek territories and then take on the Hungarians. We can keep them away from Italy by sea, and hopefully Hunyadi will stop them on land. I do not think we are prepared to fight them now."

The pope responded, "Of course, by doing this you are still in a position to trade with the Ottomans, and you are not required to unite with your fellow Italian cities. I know your games. You will do with the Hungarians what you did with the Greeks. You will give them half promises while behind their backs you will deal with the Turks and continue your wars with your sister cities. I grow tired of these machinations. I will consider what you advise. It may be the best course of action, but I want you to remember that one day you might find the Ottomans at your front door. What will you do then? Who will come to your aid when you have refused to come to theirs? God protect us all."

Nicholas concluded the audience, and then returned to his private chambers. He was scarcely able to walk. The great Christian city had fallen. In the ancient world, five great Christian cities had existed: Jerusalem, Alexandria, Antioch, Constantinople, and Rome. Now only the last survived, a crumbling ruin. Rome was in many ways the mirror of Constantinople. A faded memory of greatness long since passed. Would he find the Turks at Rome's walls one day? Tens of thousands of Ottoman warriors. What would he use to defend himself? A few hundred guards? Would the Venetians and Genoese even come to his aid? Had God abandoned them?

Constantine had done the right thing. He had embraced the true church. Nicholas had sent reinforcements and secured the assistance of Hunyadi. Most important, he had sent his special papal prayers to heaven. Did God not listen to his prayers? Did this Islamic Allah somehow have power over the Christian God? The Muslims claimed that God was one and the same. Preposterous heresy! Yet why did God not strike them down at the walls of Constantinople? Perhaps the Greeks needed their own Babylonian captivity. Certainly they had lived immoral, calculating lives and had broken from the true faith. Yet was he not living amid a den of thieves? These Venetians and Genoese and all the others could not be trusted for a moment. Any of them would destroy the others with hardly a thought, even in assistance of the terrible sultan if it profited them enough. Perhaps God was punishing them all.

All he could do was pray and work diligently. He must make his best decisions and hope that would be enough. He thought of the great cathedral of St. Sophia, surely now a defiled mosque. He thought of Constantine, faded away like his empire and his city.

Nicholas canceled his evening appearance. He extinguished the few candles in his room and fell to his knees on the hard stones. He spent the night awake in prayers for the Greeks and for his own people. May God protect them from the terror of the Turks.

AFTERWORD

The fall of Constantinople on Tuesday, May 29, 1453, sent shock waves throughout both the Christian and Islamic worlds. For the Christians, the fall of the city brought home the threat of an Ottoman domination of Europe. For the Islamic world, a long delayed dream, one of the dreams of the Prophet himself, was finally achieved. For both individuals and entire nations, the world would never be the same.

THE GREEKS AND ITALIANS

CONSTANTINOPLE

Constantinople flourished tremendously after its fall. The city had never really recovered from the Latin conquest in 1204. When the Greeks had reclaimed it in 1261 they had discovered a shell of a city, badly damaged and looted of most of its treasures and wealth.

After Mehmet captured Constantinople in 1453, he immediately began enormous efforts to revitalize the city. He imported thousands of Greeks and Turks from other parts of his empire to settle there, both for population purposes and so they could serve as artisans and skilled workers. Mehmet commenced a series of public works in the city, including building mosques and a palace. The city grew in population and importance and served once again as the center of a great empire.

Although the majority of the Greek population of the city was initially enslaved, Constantinople, now renamed Istanbul, became a multicultural city with a tolerance of different races and religions. A number of Orthodox churches were left in place, and Mehmet allowed a Greek monk named Gennadius, who had been a popular and outspoken critic of the Union, to serve as the Patriarch of Constantinople and thus the Patriarch of the Orthodox Church.

Istanbul today remains the largest city in Turkey, with a population of 14 million. The original confines of the city have been overgrown to include areas well beyond the original walls: the Galata peninsula and beyond, as well as large areas on the Asian side. St. Sophia, which became a mosque and is now a museum, remains one of the distinct landmarks in one of the most striking cityscapes in the world.

THE GREEK PEOPLE OF CONSTANTINOPLE

The Greek people of Constantinople numbered fewer than one hundred thousand at the time of the siege. The city had at one time contained more than five hundred thousand, but had declined substantially over the years, particularly after the Latin capture of Constantinople in 1204.

Historians estimate approximately four thousand Greeks were killed on May 29, 1453. The rest of the residents were, for the most, part placed in slavery. The wealthier and noble residents were often able to purchase their freedom through ransom either directly or through intermediaries. They were then able to travel to Italy, Hungary, or one of the remaining Greek territories.

The poorer classes were unable to purchase their freedom and were largely left to the whims of their new Turkish masters. They were spread throughout the Ottoman Empire and the Muslim world as a whole. Some of the residents were allowed to stay, and others may have been brought back to the city, particularly artisans and craftspeople.

There can be no doubt that the citizens suffered terribly. Families were killed or torn apart to be sold, never to see each other again. The lives of the vast majority of the citizens of Constantinople were forever and dramatically changed by the fall of the city.

IMPACT ON THE RENAISSANCE

Many historians since the fall of Constantinople have credited the loss of the city with spurring the beginning of the Italian Renaissance, or at least serving as a significant contributing factor. The reasoning is that Greek scholars, carrying precious manuscripts of the writings of Aristotle, Plato, and others, fled to Italy after the fall of the city, thereby bringing a reawakening of the ancient world to the Italian people, along with other sophisticated Greek reasoning from the Byzantine Empire.

More recently, this analysis has changed. The Renaissance had already begun well before the fall of Constantinople. Additionally, because of the poor conditions and limited means available to the Greek Empire (often referred to now as the Byzantine Empire, a term coined by British scholars in the nineteenth century), Greek intellectuals had been fleeing to Italy for years before the fall of the city itself.

However, the disaster of May 29, 1453 certainly brought a wealth of escaping Greeks and substantial documentation to Italy. The fall of Constantinople, and the decay of the empire beforehand, enhanced the Italian Renaissance, rather than creating it.

THE GREEK (ROMAN) EMPIRE

The Greek Empire, the last continuation of the Roman Empire, did not survive long after the fall of Constantinople. Although Constantine's brothers were still alive, there was no effort to crown another emperor.

The Morea, which was held by his brothers and consisted of the Greek Peloponnesus, held out against the Ottomans until 1460. Trebizond, an independent spin-off kingdom on the shores of the Black Sea, fell in 1461. A few islands with Greek speaking people were controlled by Italians or other non-Ottomans at times, but for the most part the Greek nation would be dominated by the Ottoman Empire for hundreds of years.

The Greeks waged a war of independence from 1821 to 1832, with assistance from Russia, the United Kingdom, and France. The nation ultimately gained its freedom, although huge areas of "greater Greece," including Thrace and the Anatolian Peninsula, have remained Turkish. After World War I, an effort to regain portions of this greater Greece met with disastrous results when the Turks rebelled in their own war of independence. Despite a desire on the part of some Greeks to regain Constantinople, the city has remained and will likely remain part of Turkey.

GIOVANNI LONGO DI GIUSTINIANI

Giovanni contributed immeasurably to the defense of Constantinople, but may have also contributed to the fall of the city. When he was wounded and carried off the battlefield on the morning of May 29, sources indicate his retreat led to a trickle and then a flood of retreat from the main point of battle. It is intriguing to speculate what might have happened if the Italian had not been wounded at this critical moment in the battle, or if he had stayed at his post. Certainly the Turks were tired and reportedly on the verge of lifting the siege. Perhaps they would have done so if this assault were unsuccessful. Of course, the ultimate fate of the city was likely already sealed. The Ottomans controlled all of the territory for hundreds of miles surrounding Constantinople. The chances that a grand crusade would have formed and driven the Turks from Europe is exceptionally remote, particularly given the substantial infighting and divided form of Europe at that time. More likely, the city would have been saved for another few years.

Giovanni escaped the city along with some of his men on an Italian vessel that successfully fled Constantinople in the chaotic aftermath of its fall. Giovanni, heartbroken and severely wounded, died in June 1453 and was buried at Chios.

LOUKAS NOTARAS

Grand Admiral Loukas Notaras met a tragic end soon after the city fell. He was captured along with his family. Initially he was released and promised a role in Mehmet's new city. However, the taciturn and unpredictable sultan soon changed his mind.

According to historical reports, Mehmet, under the influence of alcohol at a banquet, decided to call for Notaras's son to spend the night with him. Notaras objected. Mehmet then sent his guards to the grand duke's house to execute all of Notaras's sons. The guards returned with their heads, and then executed Notaras himself. It is likely that Mehmet had determined it was too dangerous to retain such a high-ranking Greek noble for fear of potential revolution.

GEORGE SPHRANTZES

George Sphrantzes, friend of Constantine, managed to escape from Constantinople after the fall of the city and made his way to the Peloponnesus, where Thomas, Constantine's brother, ruled. Eventually Sphrantzes entered a monastery.

In his later years, Sphrantzes wrote one of the most detailed histories of the fall of Constantinople. Historians for centuries have relied heavily on his work. More recently, it was discovered that some of the history may have been a forgery written a century later by an unreliable monk, and much of Sphrantzes's work has come into question.

Sphrantzes is portrayed in this novel as a traitor to the Greeks and an opportunist. There is no historical evidence he was involved in secret negotiations with Mehmet or Halil, although there is historical evidence that Halil was receiving bribes from the Greeks.

ZOPHIA

Zophia is the only fictional character in *Constantinopolis*. She is representative of the Greek people themselves and suffered the fate of the city.

Zophia, like the Greek people, was unwilling to accept the Union of the Churches. She was disappointed with Constantine for forcing the Union, but like the people, she understood why he had to do so.

Mehmet's treatment of Zophia is symbolic of his historically documented unpredictability. He provided safety and generosity to some Greeks while at the same time he was able to inflict a cruel ending, as he did with Loukas Notaras.

POPE NICHOLAS V

Pope Nicholas V was shocked when word reached him in July 1453 that Constantinople had fallen. He immediately preached a crusade against the Ottomans and made efforts to rally the West. Although the fall of Constantinople stunned Western leaders, they were too wrapped up in their own rivalries and internal struggles to take any concerted action. Nicholas died in 1455 after only eight years as pope.

JOHN HUNYADI

After the fall of Constantinople, it became apparent that Belgrade would soon be a target of the Ottomans. Belgrade was a fortress and a gateway to the invasion of Hungary. The Ottomans attacked in 1456, and Hunyadi again defeated the Turks, forcing Mehmet to retreat to Constantinople. However, Hunyadi caught an illness and died in August 1456.

Hunyadi was the greatest Christian military leader of the time, and as the result of his victories the Hungarians were not threatened again by the Ottomans for another seventy years.

CARDINAL ISIDORE

Cardinal Isidore survived the siege of Constantinople by dressing a dead body in his clothing. He was captured by the Turks but not recognized and was freed either by purchasing his freedom or by escaping.

He made his way back to Rome and was made the Bishop of Sabina. He subsequently returned to Moscow and was arrested again for attempting to force the Latin Rite on the Orthodox Christian Russians.

THE OTTOMANS

THE OTTOMAN EMPIRE

The Ottoman Empire, with Constantinople as its new capital, continued to expand under Mehmet and a series of capable sultans. The Ottoman Empire straddled the Eastern and Western worlds, and was arguably the most sophisticated and successful empire of the late Middle Ages and the early modern age.

The Ottomans conquered huge territories in North Africa, the Middle East, and Asia, and in Europe they expanded into the Balkans as far as Hungary. Ottoman armies laid siege to Vienna in 1529 and 1683.

The Ottomans were long one of the most powerful empires in the world and afforded the people under their rule relative peace and tranquility compared to other parts of the world, particularly Europe, which experienced dramatic war and conflict during the same period.

The Ottoman Empire began a slow decline in the late seventeenth century. Other European empires such as the Russian and Austro-Hungarian Empires rose to challenge the Ottomans. European technology and organization slowly caught up with and then surpassed the impressive Ottoman administrative system. Gradually territories fell to these other empires in a series of wars and local revolutions. By the nineteenth century, the Ottoman Empire was known as the "sick man of Europe," and was propped up often by the French and English, who feared the rise of Russian maritime power.

The Ottoman Empire allied itself with Germany during World War II. By this time, the Turks were badly outmatched and suffered eventual defeat to the Allies and a successful Arab revolt. After the war, the empire was divided but rose in revolution under the leadership of Mustafa Kemal Ataturk. The modern secular nation of Turkey was formed and included Constantinople (now Istanbul), a small part of Europe, and the Anatolian Peninsula. Turkey is largely Islamic but has remained a secular nation to this day; it is a significant power that bridges the European and Middle Eastern worlds.

ZAGANOS PASHA

After the siege of Constantinople, Zaganos Pasha was named Mehmet's grand vizier, replacing Halil. Zaganos immediately set out with galleys and surrounded Galata to halt any additional escape of Greeks and Italians.

Zaganos fell from favor after a failed attempt to capture Belgrade but returned to power in 1459, becoming the governor of Thessaly and Macedonia.

GRAND VIZIER HALIL

Grand Vizier Halil was executed by hanging in Edirne in August or September of 1453. He stood accused of receiving bribes from the Greeks and giving them secrets. There are historical references that Halil took bribes from the Greeks, although some sources debtate whether this was a charge trumped up by Mehmet as the primary or at least one of the reasons to execute the vizier.

Halil did represent the old guard of Ottoman advisors, who had largely served Mehmet's father and were in open conflict with Mehmet's new younger advisors, primarily Christian converts. Halil had summoned Murad back out of retirement when Mehmet first took the throne. Mehmet certainly must have had a complex relationship with Halil, depending on him but also fearing and distrusting him.

MEHMET II

After the capture of Constantinople, Mehmet immediately focused on rebuilding Constantinople and turning it into a magnificent capital for the Ottoman Empire. Mehmet was tolerant of the religious and ethnic differences in his empire, much more so than the contemporary Christian kingdoms at the time.

Over the next few years, he conquered the remaining portions of the Greek Empire, taking on the mantle of the Roman Empire and forging a new and dominant world empire that blended the West with the East.

He made further gains in Anatolia and also conquered nearly all of Serbia. He was stopped in 1456 at the city of Belgrade by Hungarian forces led by John Hunyadi.

Mehmet had a reputation for brutality, but he also could be generous and forgiving. He was a tremendous patron of the arts, and was well cultured. According to some historical sources, his brutality may be traceable to the traumatic events he suffered as a child when he was forced to take on so much responsibility at such an early age and then subsequently humiliated with the removal of that power. The sultan was certainly not unusually cruel for a leader of the time, nor for that matter were the Turks in general. The sack of Constantinople was a devastating event, but no more so than the sack of Jerusalem when Christian Crusaders captured it from the Muslims in 1099. Any city that failed to surrender to a besieging army in the Middle Ages would likely face brutal treatment if the city was ultimately taken.

Mehmet became famous for capturing Constantinople, particularly within the Islamic world. He is considered one of the greatest Ottoman sultans in the long history of the empire. With the capture of Constantinople, Mehmet found the acceptance and stature he had craved. He was feared, respected, and admired by his people.

THE MARBLE EMPEROR

CONSTANTINE XI PALAIOLOGOS

By all reliable accounts, the Emperor Constantine died at the siege of Constantinople on May 29, 1453, probably near the palisade after Giovanni was wounded. His body was never definitely identified, and some historical sources indicate he removed any imperial insignia and threw himself into the fighting. Mehmet was anxious to see Constantine's body. A head was ultimately delivered to him, but none of the prominent Greeks in Mehmet's control would positively identify the emperor.

Mehmet had the head preserved and sent around the major Islamic kingdoms along with a gift of four hundred Greek children as slaves for each major Islamic monarch.

Legend tells that Constantine was transformed into marble and removed from Constantinople by God. The Marble Emperor will arise one day and drive the Turks out of Constantinople.

ABOUT THE AUTHOR

 James D. Shipman is a northwestern author and attorney. He graduated from the University of Washington with a BA in history in 1995, and from Gonzaga University School of Law with a Juris Doctorate in 1998. Mr. Shipman is a lifelong student of history, particularly medieval history, the American Civil War, and World War II. He has published a number of short stories and poems, along with *Constantinopolis* and an upcoming civil war novel *Going Home.*

He resides north of Seattle with his three children. Mr. Shipman enjoys pottery, music, the outdoors, and spending time with his family. Connect with Mr. Shipman on his website, james-shipman.com.